KNIGHT'S ODYSSEY

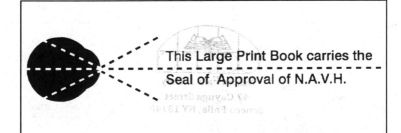

This Large Print Book carries the
Seal of Approval of N.A.V.H.

LEGENDS OF THE DESERT, BOOK 2

KNIGHT'S ODYSSEY

THE RETURN OF HENRY FOUNTAIN

W. MICHAEL FARMER

WHEELER PUBLISHING

A part of Gale, a Cengage Company

GALE
A Cengage Company

Farmington Hills, Mich • San Francisco • New York • Waterville, Maine
Meriden, Conn • Mason, Ohio • Chicago

Wheeler Publishing, a part of Gale, a Cengage Company.

Wheeler Publishing Large Print Western.
The text of this Large Print edition is unabridged.
Other aspects of the book may vary from the original edition.
Set in 16 pt. Plantin.

LIBRARY OF CONGRESS CIP DATA ON FILE.
CATALOGUING IN PUBLICATION FOR THIS BOOK
IS AVAILABLE FROM THE LIBRARY OF CONGRESS

ISBN-13: 978-1-4104-9857-1 (softcover)

Published in 2019 by arrangement with W. Michael Farmer

Printed in Mexico
1 2 3 4 5 6 7 23 22 21 20 19

To Corky,
My Wife and Best Friend

CONTENTS

ACKNOWLEDGMENTS

Melissa Starr's editing was a guiding light for this book. Her insightful comments kept the focus of the story where it needed to be and I owe her much for a job well done.

Lynda Sánchez's research in Mexico, deep understanding of Sierra Madre Apache history and culture, and her advice have been of great help in understanding the existing history of these little known times and people.

Building on the valuable and original research of Lynda Sánchez, her trips into the Sierra Madre, and scholars on both sides of the border (from 1980 to the present), Neil Goodwin's account, *The Apache Diaries,* finally revealed to the world the incredible work begun by his father, Grenville Goodwin, in 1927. This work has been an education and an inspiration, and I thank Neil for sharing the diary of his father in *The Apache Diaries.*

9

Bruce Kennedy's research, commentary, and knowledge of southwest history and geography have been invaluable contributions to this and other efforts. I gratefully acknowledge and thank him for his support.

When I return to New Mexico for further research on its land and history, Pat and Mike Alexander open their home to me and have been a constant source of support and encouragement, for which I am very grateful.

I want to express my sincere gratitude to all these friends and colleagues without whom this book would not have been possible.

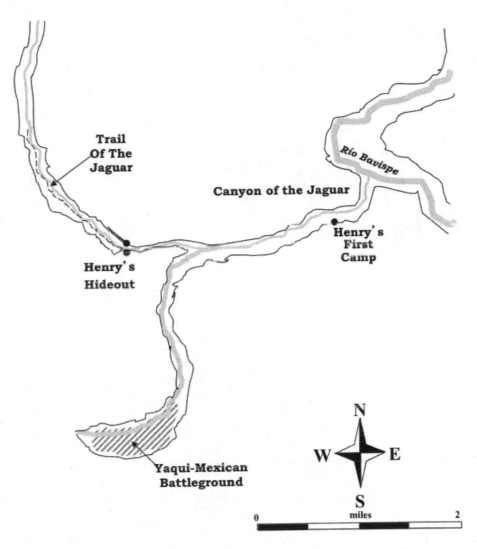

Trail
Of The
Jaguar

Río Bavispe

Canyon of the Jaguar

Henry's
First
Camp

Henry's
Hideout

Yaqui-Mexican
Battleground

N
W E
S

0   miles   2

Jaguar Canyon

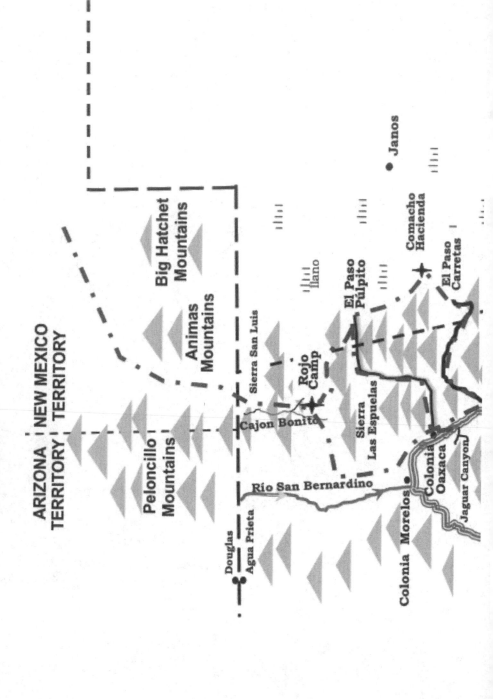

The Odyssey Trail

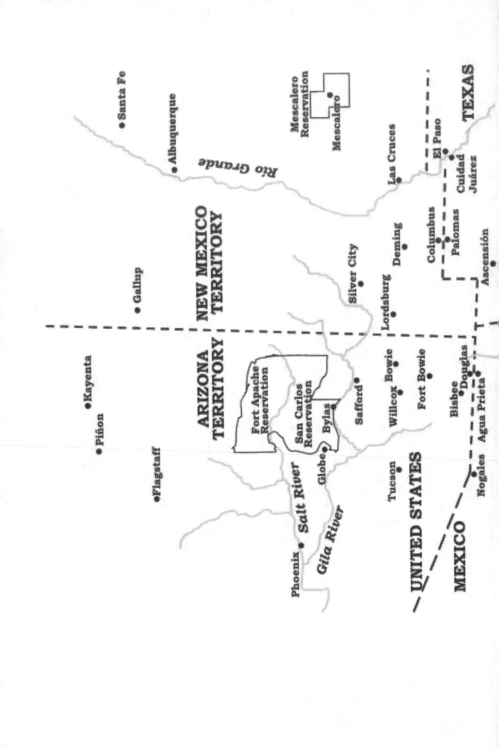

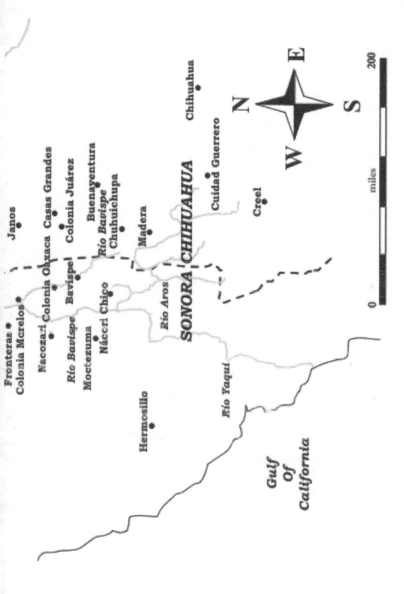

Land of the Knight's Odyssey

CHARACTERS

FICTIONAL CHARACTERS
Henry Fountain (as a young man)
Yellow Boy, Mescalero Apache
Sac Langeford
Lewis Clark Langeford
Pelo Rojo (Kitsizil Lichoo' in Apache)
Rafaela
Billy Creek
Moon on the Water, Mescalero Apache (Yellow Boy's second wife)
Comacho Family

HISTORICAL CHARACTERS
Apache Kid
Massai
Elias
Apache Juan
Doroteo Arango (Pancho Villa)
Oliver Lee Porfirio Díaz

SPANISH WORDS
AND PHRASES

A
Amigo — Friend
Años —Years
Aquí — Here

B
Buena suerte — Good luck
Buenas noches — Good evening

C
Caballos — Horses
Cabezas — Heads
Caliente — Hot
Camino — Road
Camisa roja — Red shirt
Cómo estás? — How are you?
Comprende? — Do you understand?
Comprendo — I understand.
Corazón — Heart
Cuidado! —Watch out!

19

D

Día — Day

Difícil — Difficult

Dónde están las mujeres? — Where are the women?

Dos — Two

E

El jefe — The chief

Ella — She

Ella es mi hija — She is my daughter.

Está bien — It is well.

Es verdad — It is true

Espíritu Negro — Black Spirit

Estas — These

Esta noche — Tonight

Esto es no nuevo — This is not new.

H

Hacendado — Wealthy land owner

Hasta — Until

Hasta luego — Until later

Hermana — Sister

Hermano — Brother

Hombre — Man

Hombrecito — Little Man

Hombrecito es mi hijo — Little Man is my son.

Hora — Time

Hoy no es su día a muerto — Today is not

20

your day to die.

L
Llano — Dry prairie

M
Mañana — Tomorrow
Mañana noche — Tomorrow night
Más — More
Mi hija — My daughter
Muchacho Amarillo — Yellow Boy
Mucho — Much or many
Muerte — Death, or die
Mujeres — Women
Muy — Very
Muy bien — Very well
Muy lindo — Very pretty
Muy mal — Very bad

N
Nada — Nothing
Negro — Black
Niños — Children
Noche — Night
No sé — I don't know.
No sé a ciencia cierta — I don't know for
certain.
Nuevo — New

O
Otro — Other
Ojos — Eyes

P
Padre — Father
Por — For
Por favor — Please
Por qué? — Why?
Pronto — Quick, quickly

Q
Que es — What is
Que paso? — What is happening?
Quién sabe? — Who knows?

R
Rebozo — Head scarf
Rojo — Red

S
Sierras — Mountains
Silencio! — Silence!
Sol — Sun
Son muy excitado — They are very excited.
Su — Your
Su hermano — Your brother

T
Tambien — Also
Tío — Uncle
Todo es bien — All is well.

U
Uno — One
Usted —You

V
Vamonos — Go.
Vaquero — Mexican cowboy
Venga — Come

Y
Y — And

PREFATORY NOTE

"The pursuit of truth, not facts, is the
business of fiction."
— Oakley Hall, Author of *Warlock*

Knight's Odyssey is a novel that includes
historical characters. Among them is Doroteo Arango, also known as Francisco Villa,
or Pancho Villa. Relatively little is known of
Arango's life as a young man. However, it is
known that he knew where the Sierra Madre Apache camps were, that he rode with a
bandido gang in the state of Chihuahua in
northern Mexico, that he was empathetic to
peons suffering under the Díaz government,
and that he was a skilled *pistolero*.

Several of the Apache characters in
Knight's Odyssey have historic bases. There
are many conflicting stories and legends of
what happened to Apache Kid and Massai,
who were once hunted by territorial law
officers and the U.S. Army. However, stories

collected from northern Mexico and from detailed research and interviews during the last seventy years suggest that they roamed freely across the southwestern United States and northern Mexico at the time of *Knight's Odyssey* and that they often lived with the Sierra Madre Apaches. Little is known of Apache Elias (also known as Natculbaye or José Maria Elias) or his son, Indio Juan (also known as Apache John), except through legends and stories told by a few elderly survivors living in the villages of northern Chihuahua and Sonora or through newspaper accounts, in which they were blamed for raids in Mexico and across the border after 1886.

Historical research continues on the Sierra Madre Apaches as a people. Between 1982 and 2001 Eve Ball and then Lynda Sánchez published valuable and original research based on Sánchez's trips to the Sierra Madre. As late as 1999, Neil Goodwin revealed in *The Apache Diaries,* based on the work of his father, Grenville Goodwin, that he found, in traces of the Apache camps, including in the stone wall remains of their lodges, evidence that numerous cattle had been processed nearby. It is an astonishing fact that Apaches continued to live within twenty miles of and probably crossed the

United States–Mexico border as late as 1930 to raid ranches. In 1930 there was an attempt to assemble an expedition of soldiers-of-fortune in Douglas, Arizona, to go into the Sierra Madre and wipe out the last of the Apaches. Fortunately, the United States Department of State and the Mexican federal government learned of the plan and stopped it. History does not yet know the final fate of these fierce shadows, who were often very close but never seen.

In these stories, a fictional Henry Fountain lived in three cultures: Apache, southwest American, and Mexican. Thus, he encountered a mixture of Athabascan dialects from the Apaches and colloquial English and Spanish from Mexicans and Americans. The dialect spoken by the Apaches in the Sierra Madre is uncertain. However, the Apaches were at war with the Mexicans for over two-hundred-fifty years and so naturally gravitated toward using Spanish as a second language. Simple words and phrases in Spanish have been used throughout *Knight's Odyssey* to give the reader an additional sense of character and place. For those readers who speak no or little Spanish, a brief glossary has been provided after the list of characters.

The mountains and plains of northern

Chihuahua and Sonora, just south of the border between the United States and Mexico, defined the land of the Sierra Madre Apaches. Even today, the Sierra Madre is a rugged and dangerous land relatively few have seen except from high vertical distances in airplanes. Maps have been provided to help the reader follow the odyssey of Henry Fountain during his years in Mexico, and to understand the historical range of the country he rode.

W. Michael Farmer
Smithfield, Virginia
March 2016

PROLOGUE

History records that my father, Albert Fountain, and I vanished one cold, dreary afternoon in the Tularosa Basin near White Sands, New Mexico Territory, the first of February in 1896. I am told experienced lawmen, Mescalero Apache trackers, and ranch hands who rode the Tularosa Basin range every day searched for weeks for some sign of us. They found nothing.

What history has not recorded is that even at the age of eight years, I swore to avenge my father after escaping his murderers. The two men, the Mescalero Apache Yellow Boy and old rancher Rufus Pike, who saved me from murder or death by hypothermia, were the same ones who helped me satisfy my oath of vengeance. To my great sorrow, Rufus Pike died in our bloody ambush of my father's killers; in his words, he was killed by a dead man. Yellow Boy helped me to understand that Rufus had been ready to die helping me because he was a man of justice, a man of honor, and that I must honor him by also living and thinking like a man of honor. With that lesson in mind, I disappeared with Yellow Boy into the Sierra Madre. We left New Mexico in case the law discovered our vengeance and came looking for us. After four years of living in a Sierra Madre Apache camp, Yellow Boy, his second wife, and son returned to their family on the Mescalero Reservation and I returned to settle accounts with the man I believed was behind the murder of my father and to tell my mother I still lived.

Now, at the urging of Yellow Boy, a man I call Grandfather, I make the "black tracks on the white skins" that will keep the record of my story. He says, "Others will want to know. Your story must not be lost. It will be told around the council fires for many harvests. All men, *Indah* (Anglos) or *Indeh* (Apaches), place a high value on courage and wisdom."

I have filled other journals telling the story of my early training by Rufus Pike to be a dead shot, by Yellow Boy to be Apache warrior, and how Yellow Boy, Rufus, and I ambushed and destroyed my father's murderers. This journal begins my story after that ambush. It is a tale of a long journey, an odyssey, I took to manhood among the Apaches in the Sierra Madre and how I finally found wisdom with Oliver Lee and returned to my mother. In the pages that follow my story continues.

Dr. Henry Fountain Grace,
Las Cruces, New Mexico,
June, 1951

1
THE ODYSSEY BEGINS

The day after we buried Rufus, Yellow Boy and I left the ranch in the stillness and long shadows of late afternoon and headed for Mexico. It was mid-September, 1902. Yellow Boy rode down the rutted trail out of Rufus's canyon and turned south, heading across a dark, shadowy sea of creosote bushes toward El Paso. We rode south and east of Tortugas Mountain, staying close to the Organs. After three or four miles, he turned west along a narrow trail winding through the creosotes toward the Rio Grande. The stars were out, and there was a half-moon. Still, the night felt like a huge, black maw swallowing us up.

At the river, frogs and cicadas were singing their harvest songs, and the fallen leaves of summer slowly drifted by on the water's smooth surface. Trailing south for another two or three miles, we followed a path through the dark shadows cast by trees and brush in the bosque. Then we crossed the river at a wide, shallow spot, often used by ranchers for a cattle crossing, where the water only came up to the mules' bellies. We stopped on the west side to let the animals drink and rest.

Climbing the gentle slope up off the river, we followed a series of switchbacks out of the valley up on to the western plateau. As certain as a compass needle, Yellow Boy set a steady canter slightly southwest out across the thinly scattered creosotes and cactus struggling to keep their hold on the rolling Chihuahuan Desert sweeping south. As if he were traveling by day, he knew exactly where the trail snaked through occasional mesquite thickets, and he found the best paths across deep arroyos. I guessed he had ridden this area many times and probably knew the way with his eyes closed. By the second time we stopped to rest the horses and mules, my curiosity was driving me crazy.

"Why are we heading west now? I thought you rode south, crossed the river near El Paso, and then went another day's ride south before you turned west into the sierras. At least, that's what Rufus told me."

He nodded. "*Sí*, in years of Geronimo, Apaches ride close to Janos or Casas

Grandes many times, then turn for sierras. Now many soldiers *y* Yaquis fight on *llano*. Many *ranchos grandes vaqueros en llano*. We use Janos trail, maybe they see us and chase. *No hombres aquí.* Trail *aquí es bueno.*"

We made our first day camp up on a little redoubt close by a small natural water tank north of the West Potrillo Mountains. The orange glow of the sun was just driving away the cold gray of dawn when we stopped. Crows roosting in the mesquites fussed at us for invading their water supply. Our camp had been a common stopping place in the Apachería for warriors in the days of Cochise and Geronimo, but only a few Anglos and Mexicans knew about it. There was a recess up in the rocks that diffused the smoke, so it was practically impossible to see if a fire had been made, even up close. Rock ledges provided cool cover from the sun during the day, making them a good place to nap under.

We unloaded the horses and mules, rubbed them down with handfuls of grass that grew between the rocks around the tank, and ate some jerky. When we finished it, Yellow Boy nodded toward a ledge for me to sleep under while he kept first watch. To be sure I wasn't about to share my bed with a rattlesnake or Gila monster, I found a yucca stalk and swept the ground under the ledge. I laid out my bedroll, and it didn't take more than a minute or two before I passed out.

When it was my turn to watch, Yellow Boy tapped me on the foot to awaken me. I climbed up on the boulders above us and found his shaded watching place under an ancient piñon that spread its gnarly roots in cracks between the boulders. From there, I had a clear view in nearly every direction. To the northwest, the Floridas stood out tall and proud. Farther to the west, I saw the Hatchet Mountains, and other mountains for which I had no names scattered to the north and south in the haze. If there was ever a place that could be called the Big Lonesome, our little camp was in the middle of it. There were no signs of humans anywhere.

It was hard to stay awake, but I didn't dare lose my concentration on what was going on around me. I didn't see anything else the rest of the day, not even a jackrabbit or a roadrunner.

As the sun fell into the vermilion haze in the west, a low background chorus of insect sounds and birds began in the cooling air. Yellow Boy yawned and stretched as he crawled out from under the ledge. He nodded to me and raised his brow. "*Que paso,* Hombrecito?"

"*Nada,* just an occasional buzzard. Do you want me to make a fire and cook some supper?"

In the falling light, Yellow Boy made a slow, full-circle scan of the land around us and shook his head. "No fire." That country was about as dangerous to cross as it had been fifteen years earlier when the Apaches were warring against the Anglos and Mexicans. There was a steady stream of smugglers, illegals, renegades, and *bandidos* passing through the country all along the border west from El Paso, and especially in the grassy valleys of New Mexico in and around what's called the bootheel.

I nodded. In the gathering dusk, we ate our cold rations, listening for anything that shouldn't be there. He stared for a long time toward the west, first at one spot, then another, cocking his head to his left side.

"What do you hear?"

He shook his head and held up his hand for me to be quiet. When the western sky was at last totally black, he turned to me and spoke in a low voice, "Look for dust from nightriders. *Mi* Power say *Cuidado!* Watch out! Be as coyote on this trail, Hombrecito. They wait!"

His concern about an ambush set my heart racing, and I was already anxious about traveling new ground. "What do you mean *they*? Who are *they*?"

He shrugged his shoulders and shook his head. "Maybe Yaquis, maybe *bandidos*, maybe soldiers, maybe the People. *Quien sabe?* Power say *cuidado!* Power speaks true. *Vamonos.*"

We saddled our horses, loaded the mules, let them drink their fill, mounted, and rode off into the still darkness. Yellow Boy stopped three times to rest the stock and to listen. It was still as a tomb. No breeze, no coyotes calling, no insects humming. It was as if all life, except us, had vanished.

We were north and east of the Cedar Mountains when the sun started to light the Floridas. We stopped in a long draw by a small spring. Since it was just at the end of the wet season, it was at its fullest, the only known water for miles. Yellow Boy scouted it carefully and found signs that five horses had been there a few hours earlier. Two of them were shod with iron horseshoes, but three were shod with rawhide, Apache style, so their tracks looked like they had been made by thumping the end of a fence post against the ground. Yellow Boy found some horse apples and could judge how long they'd been there by how dry they were.

He stared at the tracks for a while, and then out into the distance. "Horses trail south and west. *Bueno*. Rest *aquí*. Eat. *Vamonos* when *sol es no más*. *Usted* watch, Hombrecito. I sleep."

After unloading, taking care of the horses and mules, and eating, I crawled up the side of the draw to find a shady spot with a clear view, and Yellow Boy disappeared under some *piñons* for his nap.

As the sun chased the shadows from the draw, my brain burned with curiosity and speculation. I'd thought all night about the warning Yellow Boy's Power gave him. I had a sense of foreboding, and I couldn't shake it. Life with Rufus and Yellow Boy had taught me to trust my instincts. The unknown trail and Yellow Boy's vigilance made me even more sensitive to the importance of little, hard-to-see trail signs. Morning drifted into midday, but there were no signs of anything at all.

I was staring down the draw, trying to find the source of every nascent sound, when Yellow Boy's hand squeezed my shoulder. I jerked around, startled. I'd heard nothing as he approached, and I had not seen him leave his bed. He appeared like a ghost, materializing out of thin air.

"*Todo es bien,* Hombrecito?" Smiling, he squatted down beside me.

"*Sí, muy bien.*"

He pointed toward the *piñon* where he'd napped. "Sleep. We ride when *sol es no más.* Keep Shoots Today Kills Tomorrow by blanket. Trouble come, *usted* make sound of quail. Come *aquí pronto. Comprende?*"

"*Sí, comprendo.*"

I found his *piñon,* crawled under it, and stretched out with the big bore rifle Yellow Boy called Shoots Today Kills Tomorrow beside me. I had named it Little David because I had wanted to kill big men with it who had attacked my father and me. Like Yellow Boy's Henry rifle, the 1874 Sharps rifle I called Little David had become part of who I was.

As much as I wanted to, I couldn't sleep. My mind wrestled with the riders who left tracks the night before. Was the law already after us for killing Stone and Tally? Why was Yellow Boy's Power warning him to watch out? He always listened to his Power, and it had saved him many times. My eyes felt as if they were just closing when Yellow Boy tapped my foot with the barrel of his rifle. I snapped awake in twilight, cocking Little

David, my heart pounding.

Yellow Boy shook his head and made a sweeping motion parallel to the ground with his open palm. *"Es bien,* Hombrecito. Eat. *Vamonos."*

I crawled off the blanket and staggered to the spring, took long swallows of cool water, fed the animals, and let them drink their fill. Yellow Boy and I again had cold rations. The coming black of night pressed down on us. While we waited for the last dayglow to disappear, Yellow Boy lighted one of his Mexican cigars, the kind shaped like a black baseball bat and hard enough to drive nails. He smoked and, as he had the night before, carefully scanned the western horizon for far-off dust columns hanging in the still, cool air. He saw none, and we relaxed until we heard a coyote howl off in the distance to the west. A more distant one to the south answered it.

Yellow Boy frowned at the calls, motioned for me to grab Little David, and we saddled up. We refilled canteens, loaded the mules, rode quietly out of the draw, and loped west in the direction of the first coyote. After about five miles, we reached a big mesquite thicket and stopped. Rising in his saddle, Yellow Boy cocked his rifle and turned his head to listen. I heard nothing. I brought

41

Little David to full-cock.

At last, Yellow Boy let his rifle's hammer down to safety. I lowered the hammer on Little David, and we rode on. The ominous feeling in the black air was eerie. The animals sensed it, too, and were a little skittish. My palms were sweating, and my breathing, short and quick. I remembered what Rufus had told me about being *cold and cakilatin'* and calmed down. I told myself we were ready for whatever came.

After a few more miles, Yellow Boy stopped and pointed with his rifle into the blackness toward the Cedar Mountains. I didn't see anything at first. Then I caught a faint glimmer of light flickering close to the ground at least two miles away. It was probably a fire down in a depression reflected off rocks. Yellow Boy smiled and nodded in its direction. "Go and see. I stay *aquí.*"

I understood that to find the fire without being caught by those who made it was a test of my craft, so I nodded and slid off Midnight. I handed my reins and Little David up to Yellow Boy and stripped down to my breechcloth and high-top moccasin boots. Goose bumps puckered the skin on my back and legs. I held up my knife. He nodded and tossed Little David to me and said, "Go! Be as the night."

42

I started off at an easy trot. Even though the light in our line of sight was not more than a couple of miles away, I must have run three miles to reach it. I was lucky the moon was up. It was rough country with big mesquite thickets, stacks of boulders, and arroyos with steep, sand-covered sides I had to run through, making no more sound than the breeze swishing through the bushes.

I worked my way a little south of the light and then came back north toward it. A large mesquite thicket gave me cover for a clear view of the camp.

The light was from a small fire under a bubbling stewpot swung from an iron tripod. A middle-aged man, his shirt sleeves rolled up past those of his long johns, sat in the firelight, working on a piece of harness. His black, flat-brimmed hat was tipped back on his head. He laughed and joked with a little, curly-haired blond boy, who stood behind his shoulder watching him work.

"Boy, after I get this strap braided back on, you reckin old Maud'll wanna wear this horse collar to church? It's really in purdy good shape otherwise, ain't it?"

The child, not more than four or five years old, spoke with earnest seriousness. "Why, Daddy, I didn't know mules was of a mind

43

to go to church. You said yesterday them mules was makin' you lose your religion."

The man laughed, shaking his head, and the boy giggled. Seeing them nearly brought me to tears because they reminded me of the times I'd sat with Daddy on the porch at our house in Las Cruces while he made jokes about his political opponents.

On the other side of the fire, a young woman sat slicing potatoes on a board across her knees and tossing the pieces into the stewpot. Her deep auburn hair was piled loosely on top of her head, held in place with a carefree ribbon. She was attractive, but unassuming in the way she brushed stray hair away from her eyes and scratched her upper lip and nose with the wrist of the hand holding her potato-cutting knife. As she joined in their laughter, there was no doubt she viewed herself as queen of the realm.

"Those mules'd make the saints lose their religion, Lewis Clark. Daddy wants them mules to go to church so they'll learn not to be so mean. Maybe we ought to have you pull the wagon while Daddy takes 'em to church to get religion. I bet you'd have a good time pullin' it."

The child dropped his jaw, his eyes wide, and said, "I can't pull that wagon. It's too

44

big for me. Are you crazy?"

The girl laughed, and the man said, "Why, Lewis Clark, you eat some o' Sac's taters and cornbread, and you could pull this here wagon all the way to Colonia Morelos."

Lewis Clark crossed his arms and glared at his laughing sister. "I ain't gonna eat none of her taters. Them mules hasta pull our wagon. Daddy, don't make me pull that big wagon."

The man gave Lewis Clark's hair a tussle and said, "Naw, son, we're just teasin' you. You ain't gonna have to pull this wagon. Why, them mules wouldn't dream of lettin' you do that."

A large covered wagon sat on the far side of the fire from where I stood. I counted six mules and three horses hobbled near the edge of the fire's circle of light just beyond the wagon. Two bedrolls were laid out close by the fire. The wagon's open tailgate showed the end of a quilt and a mirror hanging from the back stave supporting the canvas cover.

I wondered why these travelers were camping in the middle of nowhere. The man had travel savvy. He had good, solid equipment, and his animals looked well fed. Unfortunately, he was trail foolish. His Winchester leaned against a boulder more than thirty feet away from his immediate reach, and his fire was visible for miles.

2
ATTACK

I was turning to leave when the man put the harness down, stood up and stretched his arms wide, and glanced in my direction. "Is there time for me an' Lewis Clark to oil the harness?"

She nodded. "Yes, sir, it's gonna be a little while before supper's ready. Go ahead with your work."

Still looking in my direction, he said, "Shore does smell mighty good, young lady. When we get to Mexico, you're gonna make some feller a mighty good wife."

I froze, my brain working fast, trying to decide what to do when he came after me. But he casually turned and walked toward a water barrel on the wagon, speaking over his shoulder as he picked up the dipper and reached in the barrel. "I'm about starved. Me 'n ol' Lewis Clark's gonna be fightin' over the last spoonful of that stew of yours."

The dipper's cup came out wet and sparkling in the firelight as he raised it to his lips. Three, soft, whistling thunks, like fists pounding a gloved hand, and a choking, gurgling sound suddenly filled the still, cold air. An arrow was stuck in the man's throat and two more were buried in his chest. The dipper fell from his hand. He slumped against the wagon wheel, slowly sliding to the ground, his right fist locked around the arrow in his throat.

Lewis Clark screamed, "Daddy! Daddy!"

The young woman jumped up, flipping the slicing board to one side, her eyes wide, her mouth forming an O of surprise and terror. At least she had the presence of mind to hold on to her knife as she ran to her father.

Five of them materialized out of the darkness. One, who was hiding in the mesquite less than ten feet in front of me, rushed toward the fallen man. Another grabbed Lewis Clark, and threw him over his shoulder.

Lewis Clark was still screaming, "Daddy, Daddy!" He pounded his little fists on the kidnapper's back and kicked as the man ran out of the circle of light and disappeared into the dark through the mesquites and creosotes.

Another went for the woman, but she kept

him at bay with her knife. She was a fighter. Baring her teeth, she faced him, swinging her knife back and forth in short, deadly sweeping arcs. He kept his distance, a laughing sneer on his face. I knew he was appreciating her courage and waiting until she made a mistake. The one hidden closest to me was already in the wagon, throwing out trunks and packing crates. Another, off in the dark, was tying the snorting, rearing horses and mules together on a lead line. An old man appeared at the edge of the fire's circle of light, his full lips curved in a smile of satisfied success. Like the others, he wore only a shirt, breechcloth, and button-toe moccasin boots that reached to his knees. It was eerie the way none of the attackers made a sound as he directed them with his rifle.

I was stunned by the surprise and speed of the attack, so it took a few seconds for my mind to engage. I knew I had to help these people. I brought the Sharps up and leaned into it, bracing it against my shoulder. The old man across the fire and the one trying to take the woman paused for a fraction of a second, trying to find the source of the hard, metallic click as I snapped the hammer back. The Sharps' hammer fell in a bright flash of angry thunder. The man chasing the woman staggered backwards with a big, bright, red hole in the center of his chest and fell on the fire, and the entire area went dark.

I ducked and moved two steps to the right, going down on my right knee as I reloaded. Flashes from two rifles, one near the animals and one from the old man, sent bullets swarming through the empty air where I had stood seconds before. I shot toward the rifle flash where the horses and mules were tied and heard a loud grunt of pain. Then the fire grew bright again as two others lifted the body off it. They disappeared as quickly as they'd come. There was only the sound of running feet and then nothing except muffled sobs as Sac knelt by her father.

Reloading, I ran up behind her, and she turned on me with a feral growl, her slashing knife missing my belly by less than an inch. I jumped back holding up my hand in peace. Shaking my head, all I could think to say was, "Friend, friend."

She clinched her fists and screamed, "Please help us! Where's my brother?"

I turned and ran in the direction taken by the man who had grabbed him. She was right behind me, sobbing. I knew her dress was being torn to shreds by the mesquite and prickly pear as we ran through the brush. She stumbled but quickly pushed herself up, and ran on, screaming for her brother.

Bent below most of the creosotes and mesquites, trying not to silhouette myself in the moonlight, I ran as fast as I could. The narrow, winding path angled down the side of a big arroyo. Once or twice in the far distance, I thought I heard Lewis Clark calling, "Daddy, Daddy!" His yells tore at my heart because I knew exactly how he felt.

I found where their horses had been tied a quarter of a mile south of the camp. The tracks showed three shod with rawhide and two with steel shoes trailing off southwest.

Gasping for breath, Sac ran up and grabbed my arm. "Did you . . . find my . . . little brother? Where's . . . he at? Who's . . . got him?"

I stammered, "I-I . . . don't know. They looked like Apaches. Maybe they were Yaquis from across the border."

"You're an Indian! Why don't you know who stole him?" She stamped her foot and spoke through clinched teeth, her jaw taking a hard, intractable set.

"Ma'am," I said, "I don't know. I'm not an Apache. I'm not even an Indian, but I'm proud to be called one. My friend will know who they are and what to do. I'm sure he heard the shots and came *pronto*. We'll help you get your little brother back and get both of you back to your people. Just calm down. Come on, let's go back."

She turned and ran back toward the camp. I jogged behind her, helping her up several times when she tripped and fell.

When we reached the firelight, her dress was in shreds and covered with sandburs, her face puffy and swollen from her tears. She stopped to scan the area, her eyes wild, filled with despair and fright. Yellow Boy was kneeling by her father, pulling the arrows from his body. When he heard us coming, he turned to face us, holding the bloody arrows in one hand and his cocked rifle in the other ready to fire, his face a thundercloud, dark and angry, ready for battle.

Sobbing and keening, Sac ran past him and knelt by her father. She rocked back and forth, holding his limp, bleeding body in her arms.

"*Que paso,* Hombrecito?" Yellow Boy's voice was soft, whispering with molten anger.

I told him how the attack came with no sound, except the child and woman crying out, and that I'd killed one of the attackers and probably wounded another. "I think we

52

crossed the attackers' trail last night because their horses were shoed the same way."

Yellow Boy's eyes narrowed as he slowly nodded. *"El jefe,* the leader, *usted* see *el jefe?"*

"He was an old man with long, gray hair tied back with a red bandana. He carried a lever gun and shot back when I killed the man trying to take the woman. He and another man pulled the one I killed off the fire and carried him away. I followed their tracks to an *arroyo* where they left their horses, but they were long gone by the time we got there. I don't think there was anyone else with them."

The dark cloud of anger on Yellow Boy's face grew blacker. *"Jefe es hombre Mexicanos* call Elias. Like Geronimo, wild, strong. His son *es* Juan. Sierra Madre Apaches. His stronghold *es* south of Rojo's camp. Juan *es* killer, raid in *norte muchos* times. *Muy mal hombres.* Juan, Elias raid, kill, torture. Think *es bueno.* Go *mucho* times *norte a* San Carlos Reservation. Steal women and horses. My Power says *vamonos pronto.* No stay here. Raid *muy mal.* No *bueno por* People. Raids bring *soldados en sierras. Soldados* kill People. People have no food, starve in winter. If *soldados* come, I kill Elias."

I vaguely took in what Yellow Boy was saying. My focus was still on the young woman and her situation. "So they'll keep the boy to raise?" I asked.

"*Sí. Muchacho* strong, he live. Weak, he die."

"Can we get him back? If we ride now, can't we catch 'em?"

"*Es* no good to hunt *muchacho* on Elias's trail. We follow, Elias *y* Juan maybe kill *muchacho,* ambush us, maybe kill us. We take *señorita* to Lordsburg. I know Elias camps in sierras. We find *muchacho,* take from Elias. Bring *muchacho* back to *señorita.*" He nodded toward the murdered man, and said, "Send *hombre* to grandfathers now. *Usted* tell *señorita.*"

I knelt by the young woman and put my hand on her shoulder. She looked at me with puffy eyes that yielded nothing and said, "I heard what your friend said, and I ain't goin' to Lordsburg. I'm responsible for my little brother now. I'm all he has left, and I won't sit by and pray and wait for somebody else to find him. Do you hear me, Indian Boy? I'm going with you to get Lewis Clark back. I don't care what I have to do, what I have to suffer, he's not livin' with

54

those godless, murderin' heathens as long as there's breath in my body."

I shook my head and said, "You don't understand. If you go with us, you'll have to live in Apache camps. You're not married, and you're strong and easy on the eyes. The men will want you for a wife, and you won't have anything to say about it, either, because with the Apaches, there's no room for unattached young women. If you're not part of the tribe, if you don't have family with them, you have to do anything a man who claims you wants. You'd be like a slave or a horse. You have to stay in Lordsburg where it's safe until we can find your brother."

She pushed my hand off her shoulder and said, "Indian Boy, I don't know you, and you don't know me, but you'd better believe me when I tell you you're not leaving me behind. If you do, I'll follow you. If you try to leave me in Lordsburg, I'll tell the law that Apaches killed my father and make so much stink they'll run the cavalry right into Mexico to wipe out your friend's people as well as the camp of the devil that killed my father."

Her spirit was unyielding, and I knew a strong-willed woman when I heard one. My mama had been the same way when she talked Daddy into taking me with him to

55

Lincoln. I also knew she meant it when she said she'd tell the law and the army about Apaches taking her brother. It was the last thing Yellow Boy's people needed while hiding in the Sierra Madre with winter coming. I didn't know what to do. I felt responsible for her and her little brother. I knew she believed she had to come, but I also knew she had no idea how hard life was in Apache camps. For that matter, I didn't either, except from the stories Yellow Boy and Rufus had told me. I looked toward Yellow Boy and found his face angry, his eyes glittering in the firelight. His nod was slight but certain.

"She comes, Hombrecito? Your woman, *usted* protect. *Usted hombre, no muchacho. Comprende?* Now, we send *padre* of woman to grandfathers. *Vamonos pronto.*"

Yellow Boy retrieved the cooking pot, sat down by the fire, and, using his knife, began spearing a few choice pieces of meat and potatoes. He hefted the pot toward me, raising his brows to ask if I wanted any. I shook my head. Food was the last thing on my mind. He shrugged his shoulders and kept gobbling it down.

I understood his intent when Yellow Boy said she was my woman. If she came with us, I was responsible for her. Being my

56

woman meant that other men wouldn't pay any attention to her. Being my woman meant she was part of Yellow Boy's family, since she had none of her own. Being my woman meant she'd have to treat me with respect, cook for me, appear to be subservient around me, and we'd share a blanket. I knew this might interfere with my sleep, but I certainly couldn't just take her by force if I expected her to care for me. I wouldn't anyway, and, of course, I'd never been with a woman before.

On top of that, a wife was the last thing I wanted, since I had a score to settle with Oliver Lee, the man who'd paid to have my daddy killed. I didn't want to be tied to a woman and children. When we got Lewis Clark back, we'd take them to their nearest relatives without delay.

I heard her whisper behind me, "I understand what he's sayin'. I know about Indian ways. It's all right. I'll stay with you. I'll do any chores that need doin'. I'll even sleep with you. You just understand that if you try to force me, I'll kill you, or I'll kill myself. Just help me find my little brother. He'll die if we don't find him soon." She found a handkerchief and blew her nose, then used the sleeve of her dress to wipe her eyes. Putting a hand on my shoulder, she asked,

"Will you help me bury my father?"

I gave her shoulder a squeeze of assurance and nodded. "Ma'am, I'll help you any way I can. I know what you're feeling. I lost my daddy to murderers a few years ago."

I found a depression in the rocks where we made a cairn. Yellow Boy and I carried her father to it after we helped her dress him in his Sunday suit. We wrapped him in a tarp, covered him with stones, and she read some Bible verses over him before saying a simple prayer.

We took everything out of the wagon we were able to pack on the mules and a couple of the horses. Yellow Boy wanted all the supplies we could carry for the People.

Before we left, the woman disappeared behind some bushes and changed her shredded dress for her daddy's clothes. They were much too big for her. She held up her canvas pants, at least ten inches bigger in the waist than she was, by suspenders cinched up to their limits. She kept the light cotton shirt fastened at the neck with a stud pin, and the sleeves buttoned at her wrists. The sleeves puffed out like balloons, and the shirt's collar was at least two inches too large. She put her hair up in one long braid and wound it up on the top of her head to stuff under her daddy's wide-brimmed hat.

At first glance, she'd pass for an Anglo boy in a man's clothes.

She sorted a few of her things into a pack bundle and tied it off tight. Yellow Boy wanted her to keep all the cloth she had and all the cooking utensils. She kept a knife on her belt, her father's Winchester, his old 1873 single-action army revolver, and a saddlebag filled with ammunition. These she carried on the saddle with her. She checked the loads in the revolver, spinning the cylinder, cocking the hammer back, and easing it down on the cylinder several times, and I could tell she knew what she was doing.

We gathered the mules and horses into two short pack trains. Yellow Boy ignored the raiders' trail heading south. The moon was nearly gone when he headed off into the creosotes out and around the Cedar Mountains, before gradually swinging toward the south. He took the lead rope for half the pack mules and the horses, and I took the other half. If we were attacked, at least they'd have to kill both of us to get it all. The woman rode between us as I used to do when I traveled with Yellow Boy and Rufus.

3
SAC LANGEFORD

When Yellow Boy stopped at a natural tank to water and rest the animals, Sac pitched in to help take care of the stock and shared our canteen when it was offered. Later, when she slumped down against a boulder, her voice came out of the darkness, sad and breaking, "Thank you for . . . for . . . helping me. You saved me . . . from slavery or being killed. I'm sorry I spoke to you the way I did. My name is Sac Langeford."

I didn't dare tell her my given name was Henry Fountain. She could tell too many people later on I was alive when we got her to civilization. I decided to give her the name Rufus gave me in his will. "Ma'am, I'm glad to know your name. I'm just sorry I had to meet you this way. I'm Henry . . . Grace, and my friend there is called Yellow Boy. He's a dead shot with that Yellow Boy Henry rifle, and he knows this country. We'll be safe."

"How did y'all become friends?" she asked.

"Yellow Boy saved me from my father's murderers when I was eight years old."

She came over, sat beside me and studied me for a minute, and said, "You look enough like him to be a blood relative. Are you half-Indian?"

"I'm half-Anglo and half-Mexican. We were on our way to visit his second wife in the Sierra Madre when we saw your campfire."

"His second wife?"

I nodded and explained, "She's the sister of his first wife, but she won't leave Mexico because of what the white men did to her family on the Mescalero Reservation back in the days of the Victorio war. Does it bother you that he has two wives?"

Sac shrugged and said, "No, not at all. My grandfather had four wives. We're Mormons. We were headed to Sonora a little south of Colonia Morelos to start a ranch close to my Uncle Jessie Langeford. He has three wives and moved to Mexico a few years ago when the government made the church stop sanctifyin' polygamy. My father had only my mother for a wife, and she died from a fever two years ago. We were going to Mexico to start over. Father thought the

61

Lord would provide him a good wife, or maybe two, down there."

I said, "I've never heard *Sac* used as a woman's name. What does it mean?"

"My father thought that Lewis and Clark were two of the greatest Americans who ever lived. He named me after the Indian woman, Sacagawea, who guided Lewis and Clark across the mountains while she carried her baby on her back. Daddy always called me Sac for short. I reckon you can figure out where Lewis Clark's name came from."

"Yes, ma'am."

She touched my hand gently and said, "Henry, I know you're just tryin' to be polite and kind, but don't call me ma'am anymore. I ain't more'n a couple of years older than you, and you're supposed to be responsible for me. Just call me Sac. Sac's fine for now."

I gave a quick nod and asked, "How old is your little brother?"

"Lewis Clark's five. If those Apaches don't outright kill him, I know they'll keep him because he's a tough little rascal. How long do you think it'll take to get him back?"

I turned toward Yellow Boy, who had listened to us without comment. He shook his head and shrugged his shoulders. "*Quien*

62

sabe? Elias moves camps many times, has three, maybe four camps *en* sierras close by Río Bavispe. He stays out of sight. Maybe we find Lewis Clark *en* ten suns, maybe two moons, maybe three. Maybe one season, maybe three. But we find. We steal *su hermano* back, *señorita*. Make fools of *Elias y Juan.* Ha."

I heard her desperation as she said, "Oh, please. We have to find him quick. He's just a little boy, and if their life is too hard with winter comin' in the mountains, he'll die."

Yellow Boy shook his head. "No die. Apache need new boys for coming time. Need for warriors. No worry. Maybe we find *pronto. Vamonos.*"

We tightened cinches and mounted. Yellow Boy kept turning south around the western end of the Cedar Mountains, but we rode only a couple more hours before light from the coming dawn found us. He led us to water in a jumble of boulders not far from where the Cedar Mountain foothills roll off into the Saltys. Sac was exhausted. Even so, she asked if she could cook us anything. I told her no fires until we were in the sierras. She found a ledge to crawl under so she could sleep out of the sun. Yellow Boy disappeared up in the rocks to take the first watch. I found a boulder to

63

sleep under and was nearly asleep before I closed my eyes.

Sac and Yellow Boy were up when the sun began to dim in the late afternoon haze. I waved to them and motioned that I'd come down from the lookout and help load the horses and mules, but Yellow Boy shook his head and waved me back. Apparently, he wanted to see what kind of white woman had insisted on following us into Mexico and find out if she was going to be of any use on the trail. The night shadows came quickly as the sun started falling behind the Peloncillo Mountains. Pyramid Peak, its outline a perfect triangle against the sun's fiery colors and soft shadows, sat just to the north and west of us.

It was a lot more work getting twelve horses and mules ready to travel than just the two horses and two mules Yellow Boy and I had used. Sac worked hard helping with packing and loading the animals, apparently without complaint. With Yellow Boy's old telescope, I could see that sweat ran down her face, making wet patches all over her shirt, and she strained to pick up some of the heavier bundles, but, by the time the last light faded in the west, the animals were ready to go. Yellow Boy waved me down from the lookout to join them in another cold meal.

We sat together, leaning against boulders, eating what was left of the stew and beans Sac had fixed for her family the night before. Yellow Boy finished eating and wiped the stew grease from his hands and knife on his legs and boots. He stared into the dark toward the south. We could just see the smooth outlines of the Animas Mountains and Animas Peak, even blacker than the deep twilight around us. A coyote yelped in the distance, drawing an answer from another farther away. Yellow Boy frowned for a moment, but relaxed as other yips came from a wide scatter of places down the valley in front of us.

Sac tipped back her hat and stared up at the stars marching slowly into view. "Henry, last night you said Yellow Boy saved you from your father's murderers. Did he raise you, too?"

I took a pull on my canteen and said, "Well, not exactly, but he helped a lot. When he found me hiding in a mesquite thicket, he knew that if he showed up at a ranch or in town with me, he'd be blamed and probably hung for killing my father rather than being given the reward he deserved, so he carried me to Rufus Pike, an old rancher he knew. Rufus owned a small ranch in the Organ Mountains outside of Las Cruces. Yellow Boy figured that Rufus could take me back home without being blamed for anything. The way things worked out, I wasn't able to go back home to my mother because I'd witnessed Daddy's murder. We knew those men would try to kill me if they found out I'd lived, so Rufus took care of me. Yellow Boy came by Rufus's shack two or three times a month to help with my training."

She leaned in closer to me. "Training?"

"Oh, you know . . . Indian skills, such as how to run all day in the heat, how to think tactically, how to use a knife and a bow, that kind of thing."

"Why isn't Rufus with you now? Too old to travel?"

I felt a big ball of fishhooks form in my throat as I stared at the ground, and I slowly shook my head. It was a minute or two before I could speak. I looked sideways at her and croaked, "No, he died a couple of weeks ago."

She put her hand to her lips and said, "Oh! I'm so sorry! You must still feel heartbroken like I do for my daddy. Was he ill a long time?"

"No, Jack Stone, one of the men who

killed my daddy, shot Rufus. Yellow Boy, Rufus, and I had ambushed Stone and four of his men in Dog Canyon over close to Alamogordo. One of them got away, so Yellow Boy chased him down and took care of him. Rufus and I stayed behind to pick up the bodies of the others and hide them. When Rufus saw Stone was still breathing, he told him who'd killed him. With the last of his strength, Stone lifted his revolver and shot Rufus in the liver. Rufus died two days later. I couldn't save him. Yellow Boy and I buried him near his home, and then we decided to slip into Mexico for a while."

When I saw the look on her face, I realized I'd said a lot more than I should have. I didn't understand why I'd felt compelled to tell her that story anyhow. Sac stared at me, her eyes wide, her brow raised. "You mean you, Rufus, and Yellow Boy murdered five men in an ambush? They didn't even have a trial? How could you do that? You seem like such a nice boy."

I got a little testy, hearing a young woman not much older than me call me a boy and a murderer to boot. I pointed at my chest and said, "I saw every one of those no good sons-of-bitches murder my father. I saw Red Tally put two rifle shots in my daddy's chest and the others stood around and smoked while they made jokes about it and watched him drown in his own blood. More than anything, I wanted justice, and I wanted my revenge. I wanted to kill them right then, and I was only eight years old.

"Rufus and Yellow Boy promised to help me get my revenge, but they also made me promise to wait until I was grown. I didn't wait. I couldn't wait. I broke my promise and got Rufus killed in the process. For that, I'm truly sorry. Still, I spent six years getting ready for my revenge, six years shooting this old Sharps nearly every day, six years carrying rocks the size of my head to build fences and a house, six years running miles and miles in the desert in the middle of the day, six years working and dreaming how it was going to be, and, by damn, we gave those bastards what they deserved!"

At that point, I realized I was nearly shouting, so I toned my voice down to my daddy's flat, confrontational monotone and said, "Call that ambush anything you want except murder. It was justice long overdue. You sure as hell didn't think it was murder when this *boy* put a hole in that Apache that was about to snatch you. You didn't complain when I ran off the others who shot your daddy with arrows, stole your little brother, and were about to make off with your horses, mules, and everything you owned."

I got up and walked over to stand near Yellow Boy. Sac buried her face in her hands, and her shoulders shook as she sobbed in the still, heavy night. I felt bad for not acting like a man who was confident enough in his manhood to ignore slights from ignorant people. Yellow Boy and Rufus had taught me better than that. I swallowed the disappointment in myself and was about to go and apologize to her when Yellow Boy stood up and said, "We go."

Sac grabbed her upper right sleeve in her left hand, wiped away the tears, and then turned to her horse without a word. Yellow Boy was already disappearing into the black, star-filled western horizon, headed for the north end of the Animas Mountains. Sac mounted her horse and hurried to fall in behind him. I grabbed the lead rope for my share of the stock and swung up into my saddle. The mare Rufus had bought me, Midnight, pranced around, tossing her head, fresh and ready to go. I was glad, because I knew Yellow Boy meant to cover a lot of ground that night.

Yellow Boy stayed up high and in the shadows of the ridges along the Animas Mountains. That made us very hard to see with the long strings of horses and mules we led. Nothing escaped his attention. He studied every bush and carefully scanned every possible hiding spot for someone who might jump us.

We stopped to rest after about ten miles. Sac slid off her horse and without a word disappeared behind some boulders. Although the pace was fast, the animals were holding up well. Yellow Boy and I moved a little downwind from them and sat cross-legged, back to back, watching the trail in both directions.

Yellow Boy rarely spoke unless spoken to, so I was surprised when he said, "*La señorita* works hard." To get a compliment like that from Yellow Boy was a high mark. I was glad he liked her.

"I think so too, but she angered me just before we left, and I was rude when I answered her. I guess I ought to tell her I'm sorry for the way I talked to her."

I felt him shrug his shoulders.

"Hmmph. I hear what you say. Did you speak true, Hombrecito?"

"Yes, I spoke the truth. You always taught me to do that. Why?"

"You speak true, you no talk backward. True words hard to speak, hard to hear. Sac understand. Sac a good woman."

"Maybe so, but I didn't speak like a strong man. I wish I had."

"Yes, you talk like young man full of fire. Now that you have woman with you, you learn plenty fast to talk like wise, strong man."

Sac returned from the rocks, took a long swallow from her canteen, and sat down by herself a few yards down the trail, wrapping her arms around her knees. I watched her for a couple of minutes before I said, "Sac, come on over here and sit back to back with us. It's warmer that way, and we can watch in all directions."

It was like another moon had come up. Her face brightened, and she scrambled over to sit with us, her back against our shoulders. We rested for maybe half an hour before Yellow Boy bounded up. *"Vamonos."*

I reached down to give her a hand up. She was slow at first to reach for it, but then, grasping my forearm firmly, she pulled herself up and whispered, "Thank you, Henry." It was nice to see her in good spirits again, and I knew she had forgiven me.

Even with less than a half-moon, there was plenty of light for traveling along the edges of the *playas,* and we made good time. We finally topped out of a slow, steady grade, and the water sparkling in the moonlight on the *playas* disappeared as we began a steeper descent that ended in the Animas Valley over in the bootheel of New Mexico.

Yellow Boy followed the valley due south. After three hours of steady riding, he stopped by a small stream trickling down from the mountains. We fed and watered the stock, loosened their cinches, ate what was left of the stew, and rested. Yellow Boy kept a close eye out for movement down in the valley, his rifle set to half-cock safety and ready for action, as always, resting butt first between his legs with the barrel against his shoulder.

Sac offered to keep watch, but Yellow Boy shook his head and said, "No, *señorita,* my eyes, more better for night . . . Tomorrow you watch, *sí?*" I knew he couldn't trust our safety to her in a country possibly filled with all kinds of hard-to-spot threats she didn't know or understand. She nodded and went off to find a good spot to sleep.

It must have been after midnight when we started again. The moon had passed overhead, and its light was making shadows on the other side of the valley and lighting up our side. Yellow Boy began a slow drift down into the valley, angling for the far side. He kept us in the valley's shadows and down in its low places as we crossed.

At dawn, Yellow Boy found us a place a little north of Animas Peak to camp for the day. It was in a draw that still had water standing in pools along a little wet-weather creek that ran down its center. After we took care of the horses and mules, we each found a pool of water, washed away the trail grime, and sat together eating pieces of beef jerky and canned peaches that were in the supplies brought from Rufus's ranch.

The peaches were candy sweet and slid down our throats in one or two bites. Even Sac had juice dripping off her chin when she finished. Yellow Boy and I belched in appreciation of that delicious meal, an inside joke we had learned in our days with Rufus Pike. Sac looked at us as if we had no manners at all, and then she smiled and tried a belch, too. Hers was a little puny, and we all laughed at it.

Yellow Boy found a place in the shade of the creek's bank to rest. Nodding toward Sac, he pointed his rifle straight up. "*Señorita,* you watch until sun is here. Then Hombrecito watch in afternoon. Tomorrow when sun come, we find my People in sierras."

Sac pulled her father's Winchester out of

her saddle scabbard and climbed up the draw to find a good lookout spot. I was relieved. When we went after Elias, we'd need to have reliable cover for our backs. Yellow Boy's instincts for knowing when to trust someone were far better than mine. If he thought she was dependable, then that was good enough for me. I found some shade down by a creek pool, but I was slow to doze off. It felt like I had been sleeping only a couple of minutes when I felt Sac tap the end of my boot with her rifle barrel. I staggered up, yawning.

"See anything?"

"Only the valley and that big mountain over yonder."

"Good. Why don't you use my spot here to sleep? It's going to be a long night's ride."

She dropped down on my spot, and, pulling off her old, floppy hat, shook free her thick, auburn braid. "Then can we find my little brother?"

"Whenever Yellow Boy is ready to start. You have to remember that he hasn't seen his wife and baby in a long time, but he knows where to look for Elias. Don't worry. I think we'll get Lewis Clark soon."

When the cool blanket of darkness started settling over the valley, Yellow Boy led off at a pace faster than normal, and I thought, *He's like a hard-ridden horse smelling the barn.* He skirted the edge of the Peloncillos in solid darkness before the coming of the moon. I would have gone much slower, but Yellow Boy knew the way and didn't waste time.

In a couple of hours, the moon began to glow to the north and east of the Animas Mountains, casting an eerie half-light on the black mountains in front of us. The valley started widening, and Yellow Boy began swinging east toward a dark knob in the distance called Buenavista. We had crossed into Mexico. In a couple of miles, we passed Buenavista and began riding toward a series of canyons opening before us like fingers on a hand. Yellow Boy took a large one that ran off to the west, and we rode down its middle right into Los Lobos Canyon. The trail continued to fall until we turned up another canyon that carried Agua Blanca Creek. We rode a long time without rest, fast and exposed, when the moon rose high to light our way.

When we reached another place filled with dark shadows, Yellow Boy called a halt and said we'd take a good rest and eat a little something. Agua Blanca Creek was in steady flow, and its water was good.

75

Before long, we began a long, steady climb upstream. I was certain Yellow Boy had been up this trail many times because he always knew where to turn, even in the dark. The walls of the canyon tracked west for a mile or so after we swung around a steep ridge and then passed a creek flowing into the Agua Blanca from the south. We turned into the southwest leg of the canyon and continued to climb. The stream flowing through the canyon was the Bonito River.

The higher we climbed, the steeper the canyon walls became, and we had to cross back and forth across the stream several times. It was hard to do because the water flow had picked up, and the horses had a hard time finding solid footing against the smooth stones lining the riverbed. Down around the river's edge, the roots of big trees and bushes impeded their footing.

In a couple of hours, Yellow Boy took a steep trail up the eastern side of the canyon. We topped out on a little plateau and began a slow climb up a ridge toward the southeast. The beginning of the day's sun glowed in iridescent orange fire to the east. Spread out in front of us was a rippling sea of ridges extending above a labyrinth of black streaks where the canyons lay.

We were past due for stopping for the day

when Yellow Boy paused and stared toward a high place on a plateau in front of us. He raised his rifle high and brought it low three times. A mournful coyote called us forward. He turned his head toward us and nodded before galloping toward the coyote howl up on the plateau.

4
ROJO'S CAMP

We rode on up the ridge. At the top, all I saw was a barely visible game trail vanishing into the bushes scattered among a few tall pine trees and a tall rock outcropping that looked like some gigantic finger pointing skyward, its base surrounded by large marbles. The sun was floating up over the horizon, a big, red ball squashed down at the top and bottom. I noticed a thin leather rope, almost a string, running from the top of the outcropping down into the brush and trees on the other side of the ridge. Yellow Boy stopped when we were directly under it. He spoke Apache in a low, but easy-to-hear voice. "Wake up, Laughing Woman. You miss our raid."

A smiling, middle-aged woman appeared at the top of the rocks. "I'm awake for this raid, Yellow Boy. Who rides with you?"

"They are my grandson and his woman, Hombrecito and Sac. Pass us."

"Go. We'll visit at the morning meal. Hurry. Moon's heart will soar in joy when she sees you."

"You guard the camp well, Laughing Woman."

He followed the rope off into the trees and bushes. Riding a few yards down from the top of the ridge, we came to a flat bench covered over in thick brush. When we passed through its edge, I was astonished.

A large corral held ten or fifteen horses and mules, and there were three smaller ones holding several cows and a few calves. The leather rope we followed was tied to the flapper of an old church bell hung between two notched posts. If the lookout pulled the rope, the bell would ring a warning to the camp.

A couple of boys, not more than ten or eleven, poked their heads out of the bushes and grinned. Yellow Boy saluted them, tipping his rifle to his hat. "The sun comes, little warriors. Stay watchful. I, Yellow Boy, or as the *Mexicanos* call me, Muchacho Amarillo, returns to his lodge."

They nodded, and Yellow Boy headed down the long, narrow trail toward the bottom of a canyon. I heard water burbling over rocks in a stream below. It took us about a quarter of an hour to navigate the bush-

and tree-lined trail. It was still dark and shadowy in the cool air at the bottom.

A wide, slow creek wound around and over big, smooth boulders. Yellow Boy crossed the creek and turned downstream. After a couple of hundred yards, we came to a shelf of trees and brush, maybe two hundred yards long, that reached across half the canyon from the eastern wall. The shelf was a few feet above the surface of the stream, which had widened out into a shallow, lazy mirror with barely a ripple on the surface. Trees and heavy brush lined the edge of the shelf, making it look impenetrable. Yellow Boy turned toward the eastern wall and rode up onto the shelf, using a small trail hidden by the brush.

We rode about a hundred feet into the surrounding bushes growing among sycamore, ash, walnut, and maple saplings and stopped. I heard Sac gasp. I stared in disbelief. We were on the edge of a camp. It was all but invisible from only a few yards away. Even smoke from the cooking fires couldn't be seen in the morning mists, and there were no village sounds — no dogs barking, no children yelling, no mules braying or horses snorting. We saw and heard nothing until we literally walked into the clearing.

Women, from young girls to grand-mothers, were preparing meals at nearly smokeless fires that were not much more than beds of hot coals. Several groups of men lounged about, speaking in soft voices to their friends. Children with black hair, scrubbed brown faces, and little outfits of sack-like dresses or shirts ran and played, but none made a sound. Babies strapped to cradleboards near their mothers' fires watched with large, black-marble eyes, taking in everything without the slightest complaint as they waited to be fed.

Ten brush wickiups, forming an outer perimeter closest to the creek, blended into the bushes perfectly. These surrounded five small cabins made with mud and stone clustered toward the back of a vertical canyon wall and near the center of the camp. Stones were stacked to form a wall five or six feet high that supported a roof of poles tied together to hold up a covering of canvas, cowhides, brush, or some combination of all three. Two of these were circular, the biggest about ten feet in diameter, the other maybe eight feet. The others were rectangular, about six feet wide by eight feet deep, where two or three adults might sleep. The lodges looked very solid, and it took me a while to figure out why the rectangular ones appeared odd: their walls had no sharp ninety-degree corners. Each wall literally curved into the other. I learned later the absence of sharp angles was by design. Sharp angles stand out in nature and suggest the presence of men. There was no fire in front of the rectangular lodge on the far end of the camp.

Every person in camp stopped what they were doing and stared at us. Time stood frozen for a few seconds until a smiling woman proudly walked up to us. She took the reins of Yellow Boy's paint pony and said something to him in Apache that I didn't understand, but I could tell it was a joyful greeting nonetheless.

Yellow Boy nodded and smiled down at her. He handed her his rifle, slid from the paint, and held both her arms while he looked in her eyes and replied to her in Apache. Then he reached down and scooped a baby boy up in his arms and addressed her in a mixture of English and Spanish so we could understand him. "I am at door of my lodge, Moon on the Water. We ride many miles this night to find you as sun comes. We and our animals need food and rest. My eyes fill with pleasure to see you and our son again."

He'd been gone nearly two months, but

he didn't hug or kiss her to show his delight at being with her. Sac watched them with a puzzled expression. I leaned over and whispered to her that, by Apache custom, public displays of affection between a man and his wife were bad manners. Regardless of custom, Moon on the Water's sparkling eyes and big smile showed her joy at the return of her husband.

I'd been around Apaches before, but I felt awkward and self-conscious. Sac stared straight ahead, a light sweat on her brow and upper lip, a barely noticeable tremor in her hands. From the way they studied us, she probably didn't know if these silent, alien people were ready to accept her or stone her, but I was certain our being with Yellow Boy was all we needed for acceptance.

Surveying the camp from my saddle, I saw several groups of two or three men rise from their sitting places and wander over to join the group around us. One man, in a group of three, was dressed in a three-piece business suit. It was similar to the ones I remembered my daddy wearing when he went to court. The suit was remarkably clean and in good shape. It seemed ludicrous for anyone to be formally dressed in a wilderness where nearly all the other men only wore shirts, breechcloths, and knee-length moccasins. The top of Suit's head was above most of the other men's. He wore a bright red bandana to hold back long, black hair from a narrow face that held beady, squinting eyes and a hard, unforgiving mouth. Under his coat, I saw a revolver set for a cross-draw in a fancy, double-loop Mexican holster hanging from a full cartridge belt riding high on his hip. A new Model 1892 Winchester rifle rested in the crook of his arm.

His eyes were locked on Sac, giving her a slow once-over that inspected every detail of her as if he were passing judgment on a prize horse. I felt my teeth clench, and I mentally marked him as an enemy.

A man to Suit's left wore an old cavalry hat and held a scraped and nicked, but well-oiled, ancient, Winchester '73 in the crook of his arm, and he wore a revolver in plain sight for everyone to see. His face, hard and unyielding, gave away none of his thoughts as he stared at us through narrowed eyes that missed nothing. He was someone I could see once and never forget. The man to Suit's right stood back a step, young and deferential, a page for a knight.

I was surprised to see three Mexican men standing on the other side of the main group and looking lean and hungry as wolves. Two of the Mexicans were armed with old, trapdoor rifles and two or three revolvers each. They wore bandoliers full of long cartridges across their chests. The third Mexican was taller than the other two. He wore a short jacket over an old-time, blue gambler's vest and tall, shiny, black cavalry boots. His only visible weapon was a long-barreled revolver in a plain, tan leather holster hanging from a full cartridge belt. Smiling, he showed every tooth under a big, black moustache, and his eyes sparkled with welcoming good humor as he pushed a shock of curly black hair out of his eyes.

A couple of Anglo cowboys were there, too. The taller one wore shotgun chaps and carried a Smith and Wesson Model 3 top-break revolver. Chewing on a straw, he stood resting his weight on one leg with his arms crossed over a fancy leather vest. Wearing a wide, gray Stetson, he pushed it back on his head to let his blond hair hang across his forehead, almost in his eyes. He had a slight, noncommittal grin as he, too, studied us carefully.

There was something odd about the second cowboy, whose clothes were much too big. Then I realized that the cowboy was a young woman: when she raised her head and pulled her hat off to get a better look at us, she revealed brilliant, green eyes and striking honey-blond hair pulled back into a bun. Her face was fine-featured, and her suntanned skin was clear and smooth. Her eyes were sad, as though she carried the weight of the world in her heart. I reckoned she was just a little older than Sac. She smiled and nodded a welcome toward us. I glanced at Sac, who was staring at her, too, and smiling back.

A man with long, red hair under an old, battered porkpie hat, but otherwise dressed in the classic Chiricahua Apache style, emerged from the blanket-covered door of the largest circular stone wall cabin. The crowd parted to make a path for him. Again, I was dumbfounded. He appeared to be the leader of the camp.

Speaking to his wife and the crowd in the Spanish they all used and understood, Yellow Boy lifted his arm toward me and said, "My grandson, Hombrecito, comes across the big river to the north. The men who killed his *padre* six harvests ago are no more. This debt of honor is settled. The woman is called Sac. We found her after her *padre* was killed and her brother of five harvests was taken by Elias in a raid on their camp. Now she is Hombrecito's woman.

Soon we take her brother back from Elias. Sac brings many presents. Tonight Rojo gives them to you. We ride hard all night to find you in the morning light. Now we rest."

The redhead listened with his arms crossed, hands grasping his elbows and, looking at the ground, slowly nodded. He was of average height for an Anglo, but tall for an Apache. His arms were big and heavily muscled, making his shirtsleeves ripple with tension when he crossed his arms. I knew he'd be a bad enemy or strong friend in a fight.

Yellow Boy turned to him. "*Hola, mi amigo,* Pelo Rojo. It's good to be in my lodge and with the People. Is there a lodge for Hombrecito and his woman, or will the women make a new one?"

Rojo replied, "Hombrecito and Sac, you are welcome at our fires. Sac has no mother? She learns the ways of our women from Moon on the Water. Hombrecito and Sac will stay close to your lodge, Muchacho Amarillo. Nogal and his family go to San Carlos. Stay no *más en* Mexico. Hombrecito and his woman take the lodge of Nogal. Come! Eat! Rest! Be at peace in the day with your family. We speak of Elias with the men tonight. We celebrate your return and give you thanks for your presents."

87

Men returned to their smokes and conversation. Children began new games, and women returned to their cooking fires, scooping up their babies as they went. Several of the women and boys helped Sac and me unload the horses and mules. A couple of boys led the horses and mules to a small corral farther down the canyon. Yellow Boy asked them to feed the horses and mules from the grain sacks left on the pack frames and to rub them down.

Nogal's lodge was the little rectangular stone cabin with no fire in front. Its roof was covered with canvas, and it was in excellent condition. Sac and I stuffed the things we'd saved from her father's wagon inside the lodge before joining Yellow Boy and Moon on the Water. Sac and Moon on the Water appeared to enjoy each other's company instantly. They spoke with signs and smiles and started playing "What's this?" in English and Apache. Moon gave Yellow Boy a bowl of meat stew she had bubbling over the fire, and handed her ladle and a bowl to Sac so she could serve me. Sac didn't hesitate to act her part and show respect for me. I have to admit, having a beautiful young woman serve me with a smile was quite a treat and an ego boost, even if it was just for appearances.

After eating our fill, Yellow Boy and I sat for a while, sipping a last cup of coffee and watching the camp. The morning breezes sweeping down the canyon were cool, and the sunlight filtering through the trees was warm and pleasant. Sac went to our lodge to arrange our gear so we had room to sleep. Moon straightened up around her fire before she took her young son downstream to get her day's supply of water and take their baths.

I broke the easy silence between Yellow Boy and me. "Is Rojo an Anglo?"

"Yes, and he's good leader. Rojo wise. Keeps warriors from going too soon to grandfathers. Elias is very bad leader, thinks every day is good day to die. Many of his warriors die too soon and gain nothing for People. Elias's son, Juan, no care when warriors die. Elias and Juan have many enemies. Yaquis hunt Elias for revenge; peons hunt for revenge; Mexicans hunt for revenge. All want heads of Elias and Juan."

I stared at the ground for a moment before asking the obvious question. "Then why do people follow him?"

Yellow Boy shrugged and said, "Many in Elias's camp give up. Go to San Carlos. Live in dust. Eat *Americano* bread. Say bread in San Carlos dust better than quick death with Elias. Some come here to Rojo. People who stay in Sierra Madre in Rojo's camp no go back to San Carlos."

"What about Nogal? He went back to San Carlos after living here."

"Yes, Nogal go back, but only because father of Nogal's woman live at San Carlos. Nogal's woman no smile *en* Rojo's camp. Nogal's woman no think, only cry. Nogal weak. No beat woman to make her quiet. No use own mind. Use woman's."

"Where'd Rojo come from?"

"Juh, great warrior chief, took Rojo in Geronimo's time. Raids near Pinos Altos — miner camp north of Sierra San Luis. Women care for Rojo when boy. His name in Apache is *Kitsizil Lichoo'*, His Red Hair. The women think *Kitsizil Lichoo'* very pretty. Juh teach him many things — war, hunt, strength from heart, giving to People. *Kitsizil Lichoo'* grows strong, wins many fights with Mexicans and Yaquis. Never goes north. Never fights own people."

We sat silent for a moment while Yellow Boy lighted a *cigarro.* Then I asked, "Well, who was the Mexican with the big black moustache and cavalry boots? What're the Mexicans doing here anyway? I thought Apaches and Mexicans hated each other."

"Cavalry Boots is Doroteo Arango, *ban-*

dido. Rides with leader called Pancho Villa. Villa gives meat to *peones.* No give *peones* cattle, only meat. *Hacendados* find *peones* with cattle, make slaves. Think *peones* steal cattle. *Peones* with only meat, *Hacendados* leave alone. *Peones* help Arango hide from army and *rurales.* Wolf gives little dogs food, now all fat.

"Apaches steal *hacendado* cattle with *bandidos.* Apache take meat to brothers at San Carlos. Trade meat for cloth, supplies, horses. Apache in Sierra Madre use cattle. Meat fills bellies, hides keep body warm, keeps rain off head. Arango helps Apache with cattle. Brings guns and bullets. Apache give Arango cattle, help drive to Texas. Arango sell cattle to *Americanos.* Apache hide Arango from *hacendado vaqueros* and *Mexicano* Army."

Yellow Boy offered me a puff from his *cigaro,* and I took it to be amicable. "Do you trust Arango?" I asked.

"Arango *es amigo.* Speaks true. He say if Apache rule sierras, they must stay and hide. No more cross border. He say *Americanos* don't understand Apaches in sierras. Rojo knows Arango speaks true. Elias no listen. Elias fool. No understand raids bring *Americano* or *Mexicano* Army. By time he learns, too late. Elias must stop raids north of Sierra San Luis now."

"I'm sorry I have so many questions, Grandfather, but why are the American cowboy and the golden-haired woman here?"

"Cowboy is Billy Creek. Has ranch in Texas. Ranch needs cattle. Like Arango, Billy Creek help Apache take *hacendado* cattle. Billy Creek bring Apache supplies and horses. Creek brings Apache good ponies. Apache give Billy Creek cattle, help drive to ranch, hide from *hacendado vaqueros* and *Mexicano* Army. Billy Creek Apache *amigo por* three, maybe four harvests.

"Woman with Billy Creek *es* Rafaela. She once a slave in Comacho *hacienda.* Comacho *es hombre muy mal,* very bad. Takes many slaves *y* has *mucho peones.* If *usted* look in *Comacho ojos, usted* no see life, only death. Geronimo takes Rafaela *en* raid on *Americanos.* Geronimo sells her to *peones.* Comacho takes her from *peones* many harvests ago. She run from *Comacho hacienda.* Billy Creek finds her *en* sierras. Comacho sends tracker for her. Billy Creek fix tracker."

At the inside joke, Yellow Boy grinned big enough to show his teeth, a real rarity for him.

"Billy Creek fix Comacho, too. Now Rafaela woman for Billy Creek. Rafaela like Sac."

"But Sac's not my woman. I'm just protecting her and keeping men like the one wearing the suit from taking her."

There was the barest trace of a smile as Yellow Boy spoke with a flat hand-wave parallel to the ground. "So you say, Hombrecito."

"Who's the one in the suit? I don't like him. He wants Sac, even I can tell that."

"Apache Kid, *bandido.* No good. Sometimes rides with Elias on *Americano* raids. Always want woman. No get many. Women no like him. They fight, hide. Kid speaks many times of lying with women. Mouth *grande. Mal.* No manners. You watch when he near Sac. Quick with *pistola.* No face enemy. Shoots *hombres* from ambush. You take no words from Apache Kid. He challenge, you fight. You beat him or he beat you. You fight, he make words no more and no use *pistola* from ambush. *Comprende?*"

"Sí."

"Tall warrior next to Kid carries death in his hands. Massai. One time rides with Geronimo. Leaves on big iron wagon to Florida with Geronimo. Massai come back; Geronimo no come back. Massai only one of Geronimo's warriors who comes back.

His woman and children taken east. They no come back. He steals another woman from Mescalero. They have more children. Lives wild. Lives free. Sometimes ride with Kid, sometimes Rojo, sometimes alone. Strong warrior, good fighter. Like Geronimo, Massai look in your eyes and kills you. Massai challenge? You no fight with Massai. *Comprende?*"

"*Sí. Comprendo.*"

"I fix so no man fight you."

"How will you do that?"

He grinned in good humor, looking like a wolf ready to pounce on a slow mouse. "Wait, Hombrecito. Maybe you see soon."

"One more question before we rest, Grandfather. How will we get Lewis Clark back?"

"I speak with Rojo. He knows Elias strongholds. Maybe a few warriors travel with us, maybe not, even so we go. Find Lewis Clark in Elias stronghold. Maybe take in the night. Maybe fight Elias. Maybe trade. Who knows? We take back. No more Elias keeps Lewis Clark."

"Will you let Sac come?"

"Yes, Sac is warrior. Lewis Clark is her blood. She come."

"Thank you, Grandfather. She is grateful to you for this. Now I rest."

"Bueno."

Tired and cramped, I wobbled a little as I stood up and moved slowly for the lodge Rojo provided us.

A blanket hung across the cabin's narrow doorway. I ducked inside and found Sac on her knees, arranging her bed. She had sorted my gear on one side of the cabin and hers on the other. My bedroll was laid out with my old McClellan saddle for a pillow. Little David's scabbard lay next to my bedroll, the Sharps on top, easy to reach and pointed at the door. All our gear was stacked just behind the saddles, and the things to be given away were already stacked outside by the door. She had her cooking gear and personal effects scattered out on her bedroll, getting it organized. The pistol and the rifle she carried on her saddle were hung on the wall within easy reach. Her hat hung on one of the pack frames; her boots were off, and her shirt was open, flashing a little cleavage.

She modestly grabbed the top of her shirt, shutting off the view, and said, "You should knock before you walk in on a lady."

"Sorry, blankets don't make much noise. Anyway, I thought we were supposed to be living like man and wife."

She bit her lip and shook her head.

95

"I'm sorry, Henry. I truly appreciate all you're doing for me. It's just that these have been the hardest days of my life. Just give me a little time to get used to our arrangement. Can you do that?"

"Sure. I'm not going to bother you." I helped her finish organizing the gear before we collapsed, weary, but content, on our bedrolls. She crossed her arms over her breasts, like a dead woman in a casket. After about three deep breaths, she was sound asleep. I rolled on my side and watched her sleep for a bit, but it wasn't long before I too was in a deep, dreamless sleep.

When I awakened, it was late afternoon. Women all over the camp were cooking over hot coals glowing red and orange in pits that made little smoke. Sac's bedroll was empty. I stuck my head outside and saw Yellow Boy sitting by his fire pit talking with a few men, Arango and Billy Creek among them.

I headed downstream to the corrals and found them cleverly built. Poles in the ground were connected by five or six strands of barbed wire. The shape of the corral followed the terrain, and the bushes growing along the wire were carefully woven into the fence. Unless someone happened to see the fence from above, it was unlikely he'd notice it unless he heard the animals on the other side. I looked inside the first small corral and saw our stock.

In the large corral next to them were the camp's horses and mules. They didn't look normal. Their ears flopped down in front rather than pointing up. Some of them had muzzles that didn't look quite right either. It took me a minute to realize that the mules' ears drooped because their ear tendons had been cut. They couldn't prick up their ears at a noise and be tempted to respond with a bray that gave them away. The nostrils of some of the burros, mules, and horses had been slit so they couldn't bray or neigh. Since it hadn't been done to all of them, I assumed the naturally quiet ones were left alone.

Midnight saw me, pricked up her ears, and came over to have her head scratched. I hadn't owned her for a long time as men count the passing of the seasons, but it felt like we'd been together a lifetime. I found the grain and fed all our stock.

Then I pulled off my shirt and moccasins and flopped in the stream. The cool water was a wonderful treat. I had a good scrub using the clean white sand caught in the clefts of the smooth rock bottom, and then pounded my shirt with a rock to wash it. By the time I walked back to our fire, the shadows were deepening into an inky black and a cool breeze tumbled down the canyon.

The smell of roasting steak dripping in fire coals made me hurry toward Moon's fire. Yellow Boy, with a piece of meat on the end of his knife, waved to me and said, "Eat, Hombrecito! Soon no more. We eat all."

I sat down by Yellow Boy, and Sac brought me a hunk of sizzling meat, roasted mescal, squawberries, and acorn bread on a pie tin. I was famished, but I ate slowly as I looked around the camp. It was a beautiful evening. Myriad frogs and cicadas along the stream lent a soothing chorus to the gentle splash of water gurgling in the creek. The low buzz of conversation peppered with occasional laughter drifted over from other groups by their cooking fires.

Yellow Boy finished his meal shortly after I began and wiped the grease from around his mouth to rub on his legs. He reached in a vest pocket, found one of his cigars, and lighted it with a splinter from the fire. He puffed contentedly for a few moments before he snatched up Redondo and put him on his knee. The child yelled in delight and Yellow Boy laughed aloud. It was a revelation to see a strong warrior enjoying his wife and child much like my father had enjoyed his family.

Sac sat with Moon on the Water, their faces a study in contrasts. Moon's face was filled with happiness and love for her husband and their child. Although Sac smiled often, her eyes were dark wells of heartbreak and longing for older, better times. I imagined she was trying to anticipate what the coming days might bring, and I saw dread filling her soul as the black night settled on the trees.

5

COUNCIL

Yellow Boy finished his cigar, stood, and gave Redondo a final swing in the air before returning him, giggling, to Moon. He picked up his rifle, nodded toward Rojo's cabin, and said, "Come, Hombrecito." I followed him, and, soon, Yellow Boy pulled back the blanket covering the entrance to Rojo's cabin, and we went inside. As soon as we entered, the collegial conversations we heard from outside the blanket ended, and all eyes turned to Yellow Boy and me. An oil lamp hung from a post, giving off a flickering yellow light, and a large pot glowing with coals sat near the middle to ward off the night chill. Rojo sat opposite the door and motioned us to sit in a space to his left. Fifteen or so men sat around the wall and across the floor. Apache Kid and Massai were there, and so were the Mexicans and Billy Creek.

Rojo nodded toward Yellow Boy, greeted

him in Apache, and asked about our travels. Yellow Boy replied in Apache, occasionally stopping to say a few words in Spanish to me to explain what he was telling them. He told of the war we made against the men who murdered Daddy, the end he made of Red Tally, and of the decision for me to come to the camp as his grandson in case the white man's law learned of the ambush and searched for us.

I received many admiring nods and smiles when he told how I'd killed Stone. Then Yellow Boy told of our trip and how Elias had killed Sac's father and took her little brother. He said it was only my courage and my shooting that saved her from being taken, too, and that now she was my woman.

I saw Kid frown, a slight smirk on his lips as he eyed me and gave his head a little shake. The Mexicans, except for Arango, stared at Yellow Boy with blank faces. Apparently, they hadn't understood a word he'd said. Arango, on the other hand, seemed to understand everything. He followed Yellow Boy's story with glittering eyes, occasionally smiling and nodding.

Yellow Boy, his voice becoming a hard monotone filled with anger, returned to the subject of Elias and the taking of Lewis Clark. "Since Geronimo rode the iron wagon toward the rising sun, the *Americanos* believe there are no more warriors to raid them. They believe all Apache warriors now squat in the dust on the reservations, waiting for food from the army. There are fewer soldiers in the forts and on the reservations every day. Their forts are soon empty. They fight Apaches no more and go away. Our women and children are safe. Our warriors will die old men.

"We live free here. It's a good life in Mexico. We can raid the *hacendados* for a few cattle. If we're not too greedy, they leave us alone. The Mexicans, all except Arango, who lives wild and free like the Apache, are afraid to come here after us. They can't find us, even if they have an army. If they come alone, they know they won't go home. But, if the *Americanos* don't keep believing Apache warriors are no more, their soldiers will come back. They'll come south and help the Mexicans find us. We'll be chased and hunted. To keep the soldiers away, we must not raid north of the Sierra San Luis. Elias and Juan, they know this. In many councils, they've agreed to only take reservation women, a few reservation range horses, and to spill no blood in raids to the north. Now they've killed a white man and stolen his little son. What they do, threatens us all. It must stop now."

A few murmurs of assent rose in Rojo's lodge. Yellow Boy paused, looked into the eyes of those around him, and said, "Tomorrow I leave to find Elias and Juan. I make sure they go north no more. Hombrecito and I will take back the child and give him to Hombrecito's woman. She's strong, a fighter, and will come with us. She brings Rojo's camp presents of cloth and other things our women value much. These we ask Rojo to give the camp. If there are warriors here who believe I'm right to stop Elias and Juan, then I ask them to come with us. I ask Rojo to tell me where Elias's last camp is so I can find him quickly and settle this. This is all I have to say."

There was no sound save for the low crackle of the coals burning in the pot near the center pole. Most of the men stared and frowned at us like we were crazy. Rojo said, "I've spoken to Elias and Juan of their raids north and warned them of the evil the *Americanos* can bring on us. I've told Elias and Juan they must stay away from here, that I'll kill them and their warriors if they come near this camp. A scout was here two suns ago and said they were in their camp, near the Bavispe River, three days' ride south. They have given an *Americano* boy to

103

their women. You might steal the boy back, but they have too many warriors for you to fight by yourself."

"You will ride with us?" asked Yellow Boy.

Rojo frowned and said, "The timing is bad. In two days, cattle on the Rancho Palomas to the northeast will be close enough for taking. We've waited many suns for them to come to a place where they're easy to steal and hide. Help us take them, and then we will help you take the boy back. We can help each other."

Yellow Boy, his face betraying no emotion except for the fire in his eyes, shook his head. "I'll leave tomorrow. Elias and Juan must stop the killing across the border *pronto* or the *Americano* army will come here with the Mexicans." He pointed the first two fingers of his right hand at his eyes. "They'll look in my eyes and know they'll die by my hand if the killings do not stop. They'll give me the boy as their proof they will kill there no more."

Kid shouted, "Ha! Yellow Boy, your power is in your rifle, but Elias and Juan, they'll kill you and the boy before you can lever the first bullet. You won't have time to draw a breath before their knives are on your throats. You're *loco*! Why do you think they'll do as you demand?"

Yellow Boy's eyes narrowed as he stared at Kid and said with a wolf's grin, "Hombrecito."

Kid's lips wrinkled into a dog's sneer. "Hombrecito? This boy you call Little Man? This boy hasn't ridden on even four raids to hold horses. He's called a warrior and takes a woman? He can do nothing! Elias and Juan will use Hombrecito to clean themselves after they make dirt. Rojo, I claim Hombrecito's woman after Elias cuts off their man parts and tears out their throats."

Yellow Boy's grin grew. I sat there feeling scared and a little angry. Elias and Juan could, as Kid said, slice my genitals off and cut my throat from ear to ear in the blink of an eye. What could Yellow Boy be thinking?

"Perhaps, Kid, you want to show Rojo and our brothers here how bad Hombrecito will be in a fight and how good you are? Perhaps there is a bet here?"

Kid frowned and sat up straight, crossing his arms. The sneer was gone. I was about to make my breechcloth dirty. I wasn't ready to go one-on-one with Kid. He'd kill me in an instant with his pistol or in a hand-to-hand knife fight.

Kid asked, "What are you saying?"

Yellow Boy shrugged his shoulders and

appeared to study the ground, his hand slowly, thoughtfully, caressing the barrel of his rifle. After a moment, he looked up. "I remember seeing you yesterday with a new Winchester rifle. Perhaps a shooting contest will speak for Hombrecito? Your new rifle against three of our mules?"

The frown disappeared, and the sneer returned.

"You're a fool, Yellow Boy. These men know I can shoot almost as good as you; this Little Man can't possibly shoot as good as us. Pick the contest, and I'll take your mules. When can I claim them?"

Yellow Boy pointed straight up and said, "Tomorrow."

"Good. I'll give one of the mules to the People for a feast before the sun falls tomorrow."

There was a general shifting of the men as they all turned back from eyeing the Kid to look at Yellow Boy, and then me, as if we were crazy. All, that is, except Arango, who smoked a small cigar clamped under his big, black moustache, and Rojo, whose face never changed expression.

Rojo stared at the ground for a moment and asked, "When will you leave for Elias's camp?"

"Tomorrow. After we eat a piece of Kid's

106

mule, we go."

There were soft chuckles around the room, but that didn't ease the tightness in my gut.

Rojo nodded and said, "Good. Now let us speak of the cattle raid." He took a stick and drew a map in the dirt of where the cattle were expected in two days. Showing the canyons where the camp's warriors planned to make the cattle disappear, he asked younger men to drive the herd, older ones to manage the corrals, and the entire camp to help with those slaughtered for meat. Arango and Billy Creek were to get help managing their share of the herd and changing brands. Stealing cattle was more complicated than I imagined. The camp slaughtered the cattle they lived on or sold the cattle they didn't need across the border and used the hides for nearly everything to wear when they couldn't get cloth. Arango and Billy Creek, for their share of the herd, provided cartridges, cloth, and other supplies the camp needed but couldn't make or rarely found to steal.

The moon was bright and high when the meeting broke up. The men stood around a short time, talking about the shooting contest, and then disappeared to the fires of their families. When we were alone, I contained myself no longer. "Yellow Boy, Kid must be very good with a rifle. If I lose the mules, I'll be made to look weak doing it."

He shook his head and snorted. "Study the wolf and learn to be a chief, Hombrecito. When a new wolf comes to the pack, he finds the leader and they fight. If the new wolf wins, he doesn't have to fight the other wolves because they know they'll lose, and the old leader stays out of his way. Kid, he watches Sac. He wants to run you off so he can take her. You must make your power with Shoots Today Kills Tomorrow known before he makes trouble. After you shoot tomorrow, his mouth will be shut, and he will never challenge you. He'll fear you. Sac will be safe. I make the challenge so he looks like a fool and cannot choose a way to make you look weak."

I saw the light behind his thinking and smiled. "What do you want me to shoot?"

"Massai's hat. Can you sit by the corral at the top of the ridge and hit it on a tree across the canyon?"

I thought about the distance. It had to be three or four hundred yards from the corral to the other side of the canyon. If the light was good, the hat, an old flat-brimmed officer's cavalry hat, could be found at that range in the pinhole on my vernier sight.

"Sure, I know I can hit it at that range."

Yellow Boy nodded. "Hombrecito better for long shots with Shoots Today Kills Tomorrow than Kid with Winchester. Maybe Kid shoots good for long bowshots. No good for three or four bowshots. You take his Winchester. We eat his mule."

"But he won't get our mules."

"*Sí*, but at council he vows to feed camp a mule tomorrow. He loses much standing if there is no mule." Yellow Boy laughed at his joke, and I did too, as we walked to our lodges through the cold night air.

Sac had lighted a candle and was sitting on her bedroll, her boots off and her arms around her knees, waiting for me. She stared up at me with wet, puffy eyes and asked, "When are we leavin' to take back Lewis Clark?"

"Tomorrow near sunset. A scout here two days ago said Elias and Juan were camped on the Bavispe River about three days' ride southwest of here. He said they had a new *Americano* boy and had turned him over to their women."

"Praise God! We'll be forever in your debt for savin' me and gettin' him back. Thank you, Henry. You're truly a blessing from God."

"No, Sac. If anybody gets him back, it'll

109

be Yellow Boy, with help from me and a few others. He's the one you need to thank. I'm just trying to do the right thing."

She grinned. "Well, I certainly will thank him. Keepin' our lives and stayin' together is all that counts, ain't it?"

I sat on my bedroll and leaned back on my elbows. "Yeah, it is. I learned that lesson a long time ago. I learned it the hard way, too, just like you did. By the way, Yellow Boy bet one of your mules that I can out-shoot the Apache Kid tomorrow."

"If Yellow Boy thinks we need to lose the mule, then it's all right, but who's the Apache Kid?"

"Kid's the warrior who wears the three-piece suit and eyes you all the time like he wants to take you to the bushes."

Sac grimaced and shook her head. "I'll kill him or kill myself first if he tries it. I have Daddy's knife in my boot, and I know how to use it. I thought Yellow Boy said if I slept in your blankets, the men would leave me alone."

A little wrinkle appeared between her eyes, and she asked, "Are you a better shot than Kid?"

"Yellow Boy thinks I can outshoot him at long range. Kid's a lone wolf. Yellow Boy figures that after our little shooting contest tomorrow, there won't be a man in camp who's interested in taking Hombrecito's woman, including Kid."

6
THE SHOOTING MATCH

I didn't sleep well that night. I knew I could beat Kid shooting at the range Yellow Boy had in mind, but what if I missed? We were out three mules, the men in the camp wouldn't respect me, and Kid would still be a real threat to Sac.

Her body, drawing deep, slumbering breaths on the other side of the pack frames, was limp and relaxed in peaceful sleep. It ground on me that I might let her down. I tossed and turned on my blankets trying to figure out what to do if I lost. My mind tried to fathom how it was that she, just being in the wrong place at the wrong time, made my life more complicated than I could ever have imagined even the week before.

The feeble, gray light was enough to jerk me awake. I sat up, confused, thinking for a moment I was back in Dog Canyon where I'd killed Stone. I looked around in the dim light, felt the cold, early morning air seeping through the blanket-covered door, and realized where I was. Sac was already up and gone. Feeling beat-up and weary, I straightened up my bedroll and stepped out into the morning chill.

Yellow Boy sat near Moon's low, hot fire watching the light come as he slurped coffee from a dented tin cup. Moon was making fry bread from some of our horse grain and grilling meat stuck on skewers hung over the fire. Sac was coming back up the path from the creek. A yoke across her shoulders helped her balance skins filled with water. She looked freshly scrubbed, her hairline still wet and her cheeks red from the creek's cold water. Redondo, occupied with a small leather ball, sat on the edge of some flat rocks Moon used for preparing meals.

I poured a cup of coffee from the pot sitting on the fire and sat down by Yellow Boy. Over on the other side of the camp, I didn't see any movement around Kid's fire. Rafaela, her long, honey-gold hair falling unbound over her shoulders, worked around her fire while Billy snored in his blankets. Arango's fire was still banked for the night, and no one stirred in the bedrolls around it.

The bushes rustled near the trail up from

113

the creek, and two riders popped into sight, heading straight for Rojo's fire. Their horses were lathered and had been ridden hard. The scouts slid off their horses and saluted Rojo, who stood to meet them. A couple of young boys, attentive and serious, ran to take their horses down to the corral. Yellow Boy watched the scouts and Rojo for a moment, his dark eyes taking in every detail, before he turned his attention back to his wife and child.

After our meal, Yellow Boy asked me for a box of .44 cartridges. I ran back to the lodge, dug a box of cartridges out of our supplies, and gave it to him. He took the cartridges and walked over to Kid's fire, where he sat down and began talking with Massai. Kid sat across from them watching Yellow Boy with a sneer of disdain.

I headed for the corral, fed the horses and mules, and decided to use Elmer as the pack mule for our journey. When I returned, Yellow Boy was just standing up at Kid's fire, and Massai was smiling and holding the box of cartridges. Kid, who sat across the fire, squinted at them, his face pinched in a hard frown.

Yellow Boy stopped by Rojo's fire while Sac and I assembled and packed the supplies in front of our lodge. I tried to watch

114

what was going on while we worked, but Yellow Boy and Rojo just sat quietly talking and smoking. By midmorning, slanting shafts of brilliant sunlight pierced the tall tree canopy around the edge of the camp. The supplies for the pack frame were ready to be loaded and covered. I saw Rojo motion for Billy Creek and Arango to join them, and Yellow Boy motioned for me to come, too.

Rojo said, "Night scouts say many Mexican Army soldiers and Comacho family *vaqueros* are chasing a band of Yaquis two days' ride south of here. The soldiers have big guns. The Yaquis hide in a canyon on the west side of the Bavispe River waiting to ambush the soldiers. There are women and children with the Yaquis. There'll be many dead after this fight. More soldiers are coming from Casas Grandes over El Paso Púlpito.

"Yellow Boy, your trail to the Elias camp needs to stay away from El Paso Púlpito and the army. It's best to travel west from here a day, and, then, swing south along the San Bernardino River until it runs into the Bavispe. Soldiers and maybe Yaqui are everywhere in the Bavispe Valley. To miss the fight, you need to stay on the east side going up the Bavispe River and travel only at night, at least until you're past Bavispe." Yellow Boy grunted and nodded. I just hoped we'd be able to avoid trouble.

Rojo said, "It's another half-day ride from Bavispe upriver to Elias's stronghold. We'll wait until the soldiers and *vaqueros* leave the Bavispe Valley and return toward Janos and Casas Grandes before we take cattle from the big ranchos north and east of us.

"We won't make any cattle raids and risk drawing the soldiers toward you as you ride to Elias's camp. Perhaps we'll have to wait ten suns, maybe more. I told Arango and Billy Creek we must do this, and they've agreed. Since they wait, they ask to join you, Hombrecito, and his woman to take back the child from Elias."

Arango nodded, looked at Yellow Boy, and said, "It's not right that Elias takes the child from Hombrecito's woman. We'll help take the child back. I know we'll learn much from a great warrior on this ride."

Yellow Boy studied Arango's face and then Billy's. He nodded. "Arango and Billy Creek are *amigos buenos.* When the sun falls behind the mountains, we ride. We'll take the trail as you say, Rojo. I travel only when the sun sleeps behind the western mountains. Only Elias knows if he lives or dies. I won't kill him unless it's his choice. We

116

return with the child in five, maybe six days. *Amigos,* come to the big corral above the canyon when the sun is high. Hombrecito takes Kid's new Winchester soon now."

I felt the screw take another turn in my gut when they all looked at me and smiled. Billy Creek said, "I betcha ol' Hombrecito here is gonna give this here camp as big a surprise as them Yaquis is gonna give them Mex soldiers. We're countin' on ya, old son."

The screw turned again as I nodded, my mouth too dry to speak. The meeting with Rojo broke up, and we returned to our fires. Sac raised her brow, but I just shrugged my shoulders and shook my head, feigning ignorance. I didn't want to talk with anyone until the match was over. I went to the cabin, retrieved Little David, and began my pre-shooting ritual of finding just the right trigger tension, checking the sights, and doing rapid dry-fires with empty cartridges. Across the camp, Kid cleaned his Winchester. He snapped off several rapid lever cycles and dry fires, all the while grinning as if to mock what I was doing.

Near the sun's zenith, I saw Massai leave Kid's fire and head up a narrow little trail on the eastern side of the canyon. While he climbed, everyone in camp sauntered up the trail with us to the corral on the canyon's western side.

Near the corral, Yellow Boy stopped on a grassy patch with a clear line of sight to Massai. Massai's hat looked mighty small going up the side of the canyon. Kid wandered over to stand beside us, the Winchester in the crook of his arm, and stared at Sac with a coyote grin that made me want to stick a blade in his guts. I sat down to wait, trying to appear calm and collected with Little David across my knees, but I was trembling inside. Yellow Boy stood with crossed arms watching Massai go up the trail on the other side. He nodded at Kid as Massai neared the top of the canyon.

I wanted to vomit, but I remembered the advice Rufus gave me after I missed my first shot trying to kill Jack Stone. *Henry, when nut-cuttin' time comes, ye gotta be cold and cakilatin'.* I took a deep breath, tried to focus my mind, and slowly let the air go. The trembling deep in my innards stopped. I stared at Kid, took his measure as he stared at me, and swore to myself I'd will my nerves and shooting eye to be better than his.

Massai reached the rim of the canyon and walked to an old cedar, ripped down the side by a lightning strike, growing within five yards of the canyon's edge. He wedged

118

the hat into the fork of a branch about the height of his head. The top of the hat was perpendicular to our line of sight; its sweat-soaked brown brim was about the only thing I could see against the dark green of the branches around it. If I hadn't known where to look, I might not have noticed it at all.

Massai raised his right arm when the hat was in place, and Yellow Boy raised his in return. Massai moved about fifty feet off to one side and sat down on a boulder to watch and wait. Kid watched the target set-up with apparent indifference.

Rojo and the rest of the camp gathered behind us. The only sounds came from the thousands of bush wrens in small flocks bursting from tree to tree down in the canyon and the snorts and stomps of horses and mules over in the corral.

Yellow Boy turned to Kid. "Massai's hat is the target. There will be four shots from here using any firing position you choose. Most hits closest to the center of the hat wins. Massai will mark each hit by Kid with a cross and each hit by Hombrecito with a circle. He will bring the hat back for all to see when the shooting is done. If you lose, I will claim your new Winchester. If Hombrecito loses, you have your pick of three of our mules. Do you agree?"

119

Kid shook his head. "No, one mule and the boy's rifle. One mule for the camp to feast my victory, and Hombrecito's rifle for me."

He put his hand over his heart, as though being magnanimous, and said, "I won't take half your mules because the boy can't shoot like a man. I'll show the boy how his weapon has power in a true warrior's hands."

Yellow Boy stared at Kid, the lines at the corners of his eyes tightening, his jaw muscles rippling. Rojo stepped from the edge of the crowd and held his arms out, palms up, in a gesture that said *stop*. He said in an angry voice, "Kid, you made your wager in my lodge last night. You won't dishonor me by changing what the men and I heard you wager. It's three mules from Yellow Boy against the new Winchester you hold."

There was a general hum of assent from the men in the crowd, but Yellow Boy shook his head and said, "No, Rojo. Kid wishes to change the bet. I accept, but it must be a rifle and a mule on each side. Do you accept the wager now, Kid?"

Kid grinned and said, "It's not an even wager since the boy's old gun has far less value than mine, but I accept. A mule and a rifle by each side. That is the bet."

Yellow Boy nodded. "*Bueno.* All have heard the terms of the wager. Do you want to shoot all in one round or one at a time, taking turns?"

Kid didn't hesitate. "All in one round. Since I'm the true warrior here, I'll shoot first. The boy will see and understand how well Kid shoots and not be ashamed he is beaten by a man."

Yellow Boy swept his hand parallel to the ground and waved for him to start. Kid stepped forward and spread out a blanket. He squatted, picked up a pinch of dust, and tossed it in the air, watching how fast the wind carried it off and in what direction. The hat was about three hundred yards from where he kneeled. He flipped up the rifle's ladder sight, stared for a few moments at the distant hat, and raised the ladder's notch about a third of the way up. Sitting down on the blanket, drawing his knees up to support his elbows, he sighted the Winchester and took long, careful aim.

I glanced over at Sac watching with Moon and Rafaela. She was holding Redondo over her shoulder, slowly rocking side to side to make him drowsy. When she saw me looking her way, she winked and gave a little fist shake. Rafaela looked my way too, stuck out her lower lip, and gave me a barely perceptible nod. I was ready to crow like a rooster.

Arango stood nearby. I kept my poker face, mentally sighting Little David on the hat, trying to imagine the sight picture, centering down.

Billy Creek slouched, resting his weight on his left leg, his right hand on his hip just above his revolver, his left thumb hooked in his cartridge belt, a cigarette dangling from the corner of his mouth. He stood just to the right of Arango and also studied every move Kid made. I knew that to many, with his drooping eyelids, he appeared nearly asleep, but he reminded me of a rattlesnake sizing up a jackrabbit for dinner.

The Winchester bucked against Kid's shoulder, sending a jarring, booming echo down the canyons. The end of a branch about two feet directly above the hat went flying. The men nodded approvingly. Only a few of them could get that close to such a distant target on first try. The little ones looked around the camp, wide-eyed and surprised at the sudden noise, but made no sounds of their own. I knew the Apaches rarely fired a weapon near their camp for fear of giving themselves away. However, on this day, I heard that Rojo had placed lookouts on distant ridges to warn of intruders who might notice our little contest.

Kid levered a new cartridge into the chamber and aimed again. The next shot came quicker and chips flew off the cedar's trunk just above the branch holding the hat. Again nods and grunts of approval in the crowd. Kid had taken two shots to get the range; the next two shots ought to hit the hat. It seemed he took an extra long time to sight the third shot. When it came, no branches or trunk chips went flying. He must have hit the hat, but I didn't see it move from the impact. The last shot was fired much quicker than the others. I thought I saw the hat wiggle a little, and knew Kid must have hit it at least once.

Yellow Boy stepped forward and raised his right arm. Massai walked over to mark the hat. He stood with his back to the crowd, and stayed awhile before trotting back to his boulder. My heart was pounding in my ears when he raised his arm. Yellow Boy turned toward me, gave the same signal to shoot he'd given Kid, and stepped out of the way.

I sat where I was and flipped up the vernier sight. I'd seen what the wind did to Kid's pinch of dust, so I set the vernier dials for wind and distance and dialed in the smallest pinhole I thought possible to use and still see the hat. There was barely enough light to use a pinhole that small, but I wanted the accuracy. I didn't want to just beat Kid, I wanted to humiliate him and make him and the rest of the men understand I was not just a boy: I was a warrior, a potential deadly enemy.

Holding three cartridges in the fingers of my left hand and dropping the breech, I loaded a fourth shiny two-and-a-half-inch brass cartridge slowly and deliberately. Resting my elbows on my knees, I sighted on the hat. The front sight crosshairs filled the hat. I pulled the set trigger and waited for the wavering crosshair point to settle on what I thought was the center of the hat. In half a breath, the old gun's roar shook the crowd and echoed down the canyons. A child whined and was hushed by its mother. Through the pinhole, I saw the hat give a little shake, but, to most of those watching, it must have looked like I'd missed.

A big grin covered Kid's face. He pointed toward the hat and said, *"El sombrero, Chico. El sombrero."*

I frowned and shook my head. He laughed aloud. Arango's toothy smile under his big moustache was getting bigger. Yellow Boy's thin lips were starting to turn upward in the barest hint of a grin. Billy smiled, hitched up his pants and cartridge belt using his wrists, and took a last puff on his cigarette before grinding it out with his boot.

As Rufus taught me through years of practice, I ejected the first big shell casing and loaded and fired the remaining three rounds in a smooth, steady rhythm. Barely pausing to aim, I took only seconds to sight the hat each time. The hat never seemed to move. With the final shot, Yellow Boy signaled Massai all clear. Massai left his boulder to mark the hat, and return with it.

Kid was ecstatic. He shook his rifle over his head and did little victory hops and circles as the crowd drifted back down the trail toward the main camp. When we reached camp, he walked over to me and said, "Give me your rifle now, boy. There's no need for you to be shamed in front of the whole camp when Massai returns. I can show you how to use that old thunder gun. Perhaps, if you do me a favor," he looked over at Sac, "I will return it to you, but not the mule. The mule is for the camp to celebrate my skill. Ha! Robbing all *Americanos* should be so easy."

I shook my head. "No. We wait for Massai to return. It's proper that the whole camp sees how much harder I must work to shoot as good as you."

He nodded. "Yellow Boy teaches you well,

Little . . . Man. Someday you might be a warrior. Remember what I said about getting it back."

I stared at him as though I didn't understand. He strutted over to stand by Rojo as we waited for Massai to come back down the canyon trail with the hat. Yellow Boy watched Kid and then stared at the ground to hide a growing grin. I winked at Sac. Her big smile made me want to crow again. Rafaela stood in a little group with Arango and Billy, all smiling, as Billy joked around.

Massai soon appeared at the end of the trail leading down from the top of the canyon. Kid raised his rifle again and saluted him, smiling. Massai was smiling, too. He handed the hat to Rojo, who stood between Yellow Boy and Kid.

Seeing Massai's marks on the hat, Kid's smile vanished. He turned his head toward me and stared, his eyes filled with fury. I smiled back. Without a word, he handed his new Winchester to Yellow Boy and walked away. Men and women looked at each other with frowns of confusion. Rojo raised the hat, holding it vertically by its brim, and turned slowly for all to see.

There was a crease on the brim's front edge, not even a hole, just a kind of burn mark that had a cross mark. In the center of the crown were four holes with circles around them, and they all fell within a three-inch diameter circle. The men stared at me in fear and admiration. Sac's smile didn't leave her face. Moon covered her mouth with her hand in disbelief.

With one arm over Billy Creek's shoulders and the other lifted high in victory, Arango whooped, *"Magnifico!"* Rafaela stood by Billy with her arms crossed, smiling. Yellow Boy raised the Winchester over his head for all to see and gave a big, *"Hey! Yah!"* He walked over and laid the new Winchester on my knees next to Little David.

Kid's Winchester was a beautiful weapon. I didn't doubt Kid had taken it after killing the original owner or stolen it from a mercantile store in some backwater village. I didn't feel quite right about keeping it. Yellow Boy had put Kid in his place and made the rest of the men have a very healthy respect for me. They now knew that if we had a blood feud, they might never hear the shot that killed them. I was a warrior to be respected and feared, even if I hadn't been on raids with them. After cleaning Little David, I put it away, picked up the Model '92, and walked over to Kid's fire.

As I approached, he was sitting cross-legged on his shooting blanket. He looked up from cleaning his old Remington revolver and glared at me. "So, Hombrecito, you come to gloat over winning my rifle? Stay away from my fire. You have humbled me enough this day."

"I don't come to have my fun with you, Kid. You shot well. Take your rifle back. It was given to me. I give it to you. Someday, I'll need a favor and will ask it of you. Let's be friends in the camp of Rojo."

Kid got to his feet slowly, his face solemn, his eyes narrowed, staring into mine. He placed his right hand on my shoulder and said, "You're wise beyond your years, Hombrecito. I accept your gift and give you my word. I'll honor whatever you ask of me as your friend. There'll be no more jokes from me. You're truly a man and a true warrior."

We sat by the fire and talked for a while as he finished cleaning his revolver. When he started cleaning the rifle, I told him I had more work to do before we traveled and bade him *adiós.*

7
BILLY CREEK

After I left Kid, I went down to the corral, caught Midnight and Sac's horse, and took them to the stream. I washed Midnight off, making her coat shine again like fresh tar. While I was rubbing her down, Billy Creek caught his horses and started washing them, too. We worked in silence for a little while before he spoke. "That there's a purdy little pony ya got, Hombrecito. Where'd ya git her?"

"My friend Rufus Pike gave her to me back in the summer. He bought her from Buck Greer over at the Van Patten Ranch. She won't win any races, but she's sure-footed as a mountain goat, and can trot and gallop all day and most of the night."

Billy grinned. "Why, I know ol' Buck. We used to run wild cattle up outta the bosque on the big *río* ten or fifteen year ago and get drunk fer a week at Juanita's over to El Paso. I ain't seen him in a purdy good while.

129

He was a tough ol' bird when I knowed him, though. Tell him I said howdy next time ya see him, would ya?"

I nodded, but I had to grin. The last time I'd seen Buck, I'd tracked him without his knowing I was there.

"Now don't take no offense at this, but where'd ya learn to shoot like ya did there at noontime? Ya kinda caught us all by surprise. I knowed ya had a lot of pressure on ya, so I wasn't 'spectin' ya to do too good, even if ya could shoot. But I ain't never seen nobody shoot like them there hat shots. It just warn't natural. Ya flat made a fool outta ol' Kid, not that he didn't deserve it. Did ol' Yeller Boy teach ya to shoot?"

"No, but me and Yellow Boy had the same teacher: Rufus Pike taught us both to shoot when we were kids. Yellow Boy can make shots with his rifle I'd never dream possible, but it's because his Power is in that old Henry. Me? I've just practiced until I can put that bullet where I see it going."

Billy wiped his forehead with a red bandana and said, "You any good with a *pistola*?"

"Naw," I said imitating Rufus. "I can load it and pull the trigger, that's about all. Rufus, he always said that a pistol was a

130

close-in weapon, and, since I was a distance shooter, I shouldn't be wasting my time on pistols."

"Yes, sir! He's right about it bein' a close-in weapon, but ya gonna need one in this here country, 'specially if ya get in some manly arguments. Ol' Arango's the best they is in this here camp. He thinks ye're somethin' special with that there long gun o' yorn, an' so do I. Maybe ya could trade him some *pistola* lessons fer some long-gun lessons."

"I think that's a right fine idea. I'll ask him."

I swapped sides on Midnight and said, "Mind if I ask you a personal question?"

"Why naw! I don't mind at all." He'd finished currying his horse, the makings for a cigarette ready in his hands.

"Well, I was just wondering where your woman came from. She sure seems devoted to you."

"Ain't nothin' special 'bout that. Yore woman dotes on you, too. My woman was stole by Apaches from a miner's family up around Pinos Altos over to New Mexico when she was three or four. Apaches traded her to a Mex family fer some bullets an' a burro. That family kept her 'bout ten year till ol' man Comacho run across 'em over

131

in Janos when the family was a-gittin' supplies. He had to have her, an' he took her. Her Mex family didn't much care 'cause he filled up their cart with supplies. Ol' Comacho was gonna use her round his *hacienda,* an' I mean use her. Know what I mean?" He lighted his cigarette, took a deep draw, and let it out slowly. He spat out a couple of loose strands of tobacco stuck on his lips.

"She's a virgin first time he took her. He knowed how to whup her so's the bruises didn't show. His wife, she thought Rafaela was a-eggin' him on to git extry privileges, so ol' lady Comacho give her a hard time, too."

As I started washing Sac's horse, I frowned and asked, "How'd she get away from them?"

"Rafaela run off to the mountains. She'd been up there 'bout three days an' was 'bout starved an' froze to death. She was runnin' from a tracker Comacho sent after her. I was on the way to Rojo's camp to git me some more cattle when I found her. She was skeered to death of me at first, but I was gentle with her and give her some beans and a blanket. She didn't want me to light no fire 'cause she knowed the tracker was around. So I took care of that there tracker first, an' then we had us a fire."

I smiled and couldn't resist asking, "What happened to the tracker?"

"Aw, I jest got the jump on him and dangled him head first from a tree. Jest left him swingin' there upside down a-yellin'. Figured Comacho's *vaqueros*'d come lookin' fer him if'n he was lucky. If'n they didn't, I knowed the Apaches'd take good care of him, an' if they didn't, a bear or big cat'd find him. Probably make a right tasty meal fer 'em, too.

"I got Rafaela rested up in a day or two and convinced her to come on with me to Rojo's camp. She was skeered to death o' these here Apaches, though. Didn't blame her none since Apaches'd kidnapped her an' all, and the Mesicans, they's purdy skeered of 'em, too. Ain't no tellin' the kind o' tales they tol' her, an' they's likely true. But ol' Rojo's people, they's real decent to her, an' she warmed up to 'em purdy fast. She stayed with me, but we was like you and Miss Sac."

I felt my face and ears turn hot and knew I must be redder than Kid's bandana, but Billy didn't seem to notice and just kept talking. "I ain't never forced no woman. My daddy teached me right 'bout women. It took her a long time to git friendly, but I didn't care. I reckin I knowed I had to have

133

her first time I seen them eyes. I wanted her to want me, know whut I mean? So it was easy to wait till she's a-wantin' me, too.

"I finally got her to tell me why she's a-runnin' away from that big, fancy Comacho *hacienda.* I ain't never been so mad as when she told me 'bout whut ol' man Comacho done to her, so me an' a couple o' Rojo's warriors had us a little ride over to th' *hacienda.* While they kept a eye out fer trouble, I sneaked in and caught the old bastard and the *señora* a-snorin' away. I cold cocked 'em both. I gagged his wife an' tied her up in a chair so she could watch what happened to the *señor.* I had him tied spread-eagle on his bed 'fore he woke up. You ain't never seen such fear in a man's eyes. He started running on about giving me money to let him go. I jest stood there a-starin' at him. My blood was purdy hot.

"I told him I was there fer Rafaela, that she was gonna have some justice fer th' sorry way he treated her. He calmed down then, an' said, like he's a dickerin' fer the price of a horse, 'How much?' That there jest made my blood hotter. I says, 'Not a *centavo.*' He had this puzzled look on his face like he was wonderin' why I was there.

"I whipped off my bandaner an' was on him like lightnin' an' gagged him up good.

Then they both got big eyes when I whipped out my skinnin' knife."

I gasped and said, "You . . . you didn't skin him alive, did you?"

He laughed and said, "Naw! I cut his nuts off an' took 'em back to Rafaela. He ain't gonna be rapin' none of them young women in his *hacienda* no more. That there's fer damn shore."

What he told me was awful, but I couldn't help grinning at the story and feeling satisfied that old Comacho got some unexpected justice. I finished washing and grooming Sac's horse while Billy sat under a tree and swapped stories with me. I liked Billy a lot.

After finishing with Sac's horse, I took a swim and cleaned up. Billy trudged back to camp with me before disappearing to find Rafaela and get their gear ready to go. I lay down in the little lodge for a nap and had just about dozed off when Sac threw back the door blanket and stepped inside. I squinted at her with one eye, saw her hair was still wet, and figured she must have been at the women's bathing spot about a quarter of a mile downstream.

She was running her fingers through her hair to get it dry. Seeing I was awake, she sat down, smiling, and said, "Henry, I couldn't believe your shooting today. I don't think Kid or any other man will bother me after seeing what you did to that hat." She looked down at her blanket and whispered, "I'm proud to be your woman."

My head must have swelled three sizes, but I said in a gentle voice, "You're not my woman. When we get Lewis Clark back, you'll want to leave. You want to get back to your relatives, don't you?"

"I'm not so sure I do anymore. These people here, they've treated me better than most whites treat the Mormons. You're not the young kid I thought you were. The more I watch the way you handle yourself, the more I think of you as a full-grown man. You're kind, and I know you're powerful enough to be respected by much older and more experienced men. Do you want me to stay?"

She looked me straight in the eye as her fingers continued their long, slow strokes through her dark auburn hair, her eyes filled with mischief and daring. "I'd even come across these packs right now to sleep on your side, if you wanted me to."

I felt like I'd been struck by lightning. A kaleidoscope of feelings and images exploded in my mind. My ego was inflating with every breath, and, if the truth be known, that wasn't the only thing growing. I was being offered a wide-open door to the great mystery, and then the image of Rufus came into my mind, saying, *Henry, ye gotta be cold and cakilatin' to survive in this here country.*

I'd been ready to become a married man at that instant until Rufus's ghost appeared in my mind with his advice. It was like bathing in a cold river. It gave me enough sense to say, "Sac, I want you to come over to my side of the bedrolls and this blanket mighty bad. But you stay where you are, and let's think on what this means and what we want, at least until we get Lewis Clark back. You never know. Maybe you'll have a change of heart by then."

She smiled. "That ain't going to happen, Henry, but I'll wait. Maybe we can talk some more about this while we're on the trail. I just feel in my heart that God wants me to be yours. I know you'll come to feel that way, too."

I nodded, smiling, but said no more as I lay back. It was going to be a long night.

8
ACROSS THE SIERRAS

We left Rojo's camp after our evening meal. There were six of us: Yellow Boy, me, Sac, Billy Creek, Rafaela, and Arango. We had Elmer loaded with more than enough provisions for six days. The whole camp turned out to see us off. Everyone was in a good mood because we'd feasted on Kid's mule as promised. As I rode by, Kid gave me a little salute, a light touch to his forehead with the barrel of his rifle.

We rode up the heavily shadowed trail through the bushes to the top of the ridge, waved to the lookout watching us from the top of the rocks, and then eased down the other side of the ridge to Cajón Bonito. We used the same trail we'd ridden to reach Rojo's camp. It was coming on dark when we got to the little stream rolling along the bottom of El Cajón Bonito.

Following the water tumbling down the canyon a short distance, Yellow Boy turned west down a narrow canyon with high cliff walls. We tracked through it at a steady trot as darkness covered us in cool air. The inky-black and little echoes off the walls in that canyon made me feel like we were rattling down a long, dark pipe. In many ways, it reminded me of Rufus's place when the moon wasn't up.

From there on, I didn't have any idea where we were. The moon came up as we wound through steep canyons, climbed high ridges, and rode along trails that went up steep cliff sides. Yellow Boy told us to stay close together in single file because the trails were narrow and falls off the edge of the canyon cliffs were long and deadly. He told me not to hesitate to let Elmer go if he slipped — better Elmer hitting the rocks three hundred feet below than me. Most men wouldn't have ridden those trails at high noon, much less on a shadow-filled, moonlit night, but Yellow Boy knew them well, never hesitating to choose which trail to follow.

We rested two or three times on high ridges. Yellow Boy studied the dark canyons below us, using his telescope to look for fires from camps we needed to avoid. Rafaela and Sac were soon sisters, sharing their secrets, kindred in Anglo blood if not in culture. Creek, Arango, and I relaxed, saying nothing as we listened for any extraordinary sounds mixed in with the night breezes pushing through the bushes and trees.

We stopped to lay up for the day below a ridge far down a long winding canyon pass dropping out of the west side of the *sierras* into the San Bernardino Valley. Yellow Boy pointed west across a wide valley. In the fast approaching light, I stared, looking for I knew not what, until I saw, off to the south, a faint glimmer of moonlight on water, the San Bernardino River.

Yellow Boy led us down the trail until we were a little below a mid-level ridgeline. He turned off the trail and, within a hundred yards, came to a large cave hidden by *piñons* and juniper bushes. It was more an enclosed overhang than a true hole in the ground. The back wall was rough-ridged sandstone with streaks of red and light, mud-colored browns. Shedding junipers and *piñons* provided a soft, cedar-scented floor that was more comfortable for walking or sleeping than a rug in any fancy house. It appeared the Apaches had used the cave often. Under the overhang, we found a fire pit layered with bits of charcoal and nearby a stack of wood someone had worked over with an ax. The top of the overhang had accumulated a black, sooty veneer from years, maybe centuries, of use. There was a small spring leaking water from a wall on one side to form a good-size pool of ice-cold drinking water inside the cave entrance.

Whistling under her breath, Sac rolled her bedroll out beside mine and joined Rafaela in starting a small fire to make coffee and a pot of beans to go with grilled mule meat. After taking care of the animals, Arango, Creek, and I relaxed, lounging with Yellow Boy while the women worked.

Arango asked Yellow Boy what he planned to do at Elias's camp. Yellow Boy took his knife and scratched a simple map in the dirt. He spoke using a combination of Spanish and English so even Sac could understand him.

"Here Río San Bernardino, here Colonia Morelos. Río San Bernardino runs to Río Bavispe. Tonight follow San Bernardino *y* Bavispe ríos south. Go around Colonia Morelos. In two days, we find Elias camp. Watch camp, find women with Lewis Clark. Take Lewis Clark. Ride for Rojo's camp. Hombrecito covers trail, uses Shoots Today Kills Tomorrow. He makes Elias's *hombres* stay in camp." He nodded, looking at each of us in turn to be sure we understood. We all nodded back.

After we ate, Arango took the first watch. The rest of us collapsed on our bedrolls. Sac tossed and turned on her bedroll, apparently excited at the prospect of getting Lewis Clark back. Billy woke me in late midafternoon for my turn at watch. I found it hard to wake up because it had been quiet all day, and it was cool and comfortable in the cave.

As I kept watch, I studied the valley, seeing again the San Bernardino glinting through the trees along its banks. Through the distant haze far to the south, I thought I saw an occasional glimmer off the Bavispe. As the light began to fail, the other men stirred and began loading and saddling the animals.

Yellow Boy rode down to reconnoiter the San Bernardino when it was my turn to watch. When he came back, he held up a *vaquero*'s damp *sombrero.* A bullet hole was dead center in the front, but there was no blood on it, and we hadn't heard any shots. It must have floated downstream for several miles. He said, "This night, *mis amigos,* we are as coyote, *muy* careful."

It took a couple of hours to reach the San Bernardino. Following the river trails, we covered ground much faster than the night before. We kept a sharp eye out for signs of light from campfires or other riders, and we weren't long traveling down the San Bernardino before we saw scattered lights clustered in one location, Colonia Morelos. Yellow Boy swung east off the river back toward the *sierras* and gave Colonia Morelos a wide berth.

We rode across several dirt roads that led toward the mountains on our left, but we saw no signs of life in that valley of moon shadows. The countryside reminded me of the Tularosa Basin except everything was bigger, thicker, and sharper — the rocks, mesquite, creosotes, barrel cactus, and prickly pear patches. There wasn't a smooth edge on anything, anywhere.

It must have been close to midnight. We were following nearly a straight line down the Bavispe Valley, occasionally hitting the Bavispe River Trail winding in and out of the trees along the riverbank. The moon hung suspended, bright, almost unmoving in a patch of stars off to the west. The tall shadows of the Sierra El Tigre mountains, on the west side, reached almost halfway across the valley.

We stopped to rest and water the animals in the Bavispe across from the wide, black mouth of a canyon disappearing into the

Sierra El Tigre. I was just reaching for a canteen when Midnight and Elmer started jerking around, wild-eyed and scared. Then all the horses started prancing around and snorting. It was all we could do to keep them from running away. The frogs and insects grew quiet.

From across the river I heard a deep, throaty animal cough. It wasn't exactly a roar; it was more a set of coughs. Uh, Uh, Uh, and then lower, uh, uh, uh. I felt every hair on the back of my neck stand out straight and goose bumps race down my arms. I heard Yellow Boy cock his Henry, so I cocked Little David. Billy and Arango pulled and cocked their pistols. Sac had out her father's old pistol, so heavy she could hardly lift it with one hand while she struggled to hold her horse with the other. Rafaela had the good sense to slide off her roan and stand, calm and composed, her Winchester in the crook of her left arm while she kept a firm hold on her horse's reins up close to the bit. Yellow Boy held up his hand and waved us back into the shadows, away from the edge of the stream, pointing the Henry toward the far side.

A huge, whiskey-orange colored cat, covered with big, black rosette spots, paused in the shadows dappled with white moonlight. Its white underside showed black stripes and occasional solid black spots as it stepped out of the long sycamore and cottonwood tree shadows into the bright moonlight to drink at the river. It was much larger than any mountain lion I had ever seen, but only a little taller with a massive chest, a big square face, and muscles that rippled up and down its legs.

It stood there a few moments sizing us up, its long tail a metronome keeping a slow, thoughtful beat. The cat drank from the dark, fast-flowing river, while watching us with eyes that caught the moonlight, making them stand out red in the dark as if it were some apparition from the afterworld come to take us. When it finished, it looked us over again, and in a blink was gone in the shadows up the canyon. My mouth was suddenly very dry.

We all stood there, frozen in place, trying to absorb what we had just seen. As the thudding in my chest slowed down, Sac turned to me, her eyes big and questioning. I watched Billy put his arm around Rafaela as the hammers on all the guns came down slow and easy.

I looked at Arango. He was smiling. "*Magnifico, eh? Es el tigre,* the jaguar."

Yellow Boy nodded. He waved us toward

the mountains in shadowy outline against the star-filled sky on the other side of the river, "Sierra El Tigre."

"Will he come after us?" I asked, hoping my voice didn't reveal my fear.

"No," Yellow Boy said. "Belly full."

"How do you know that?"

Yellow Boy tilted his nose up and pulled in a deep draught of the cool air. I did the same thing, imitating him. There was a faint but unmistakable odor of death floating on the breeze out of the canyon. He put his hand up to his ear as though listening. I did the same thing, straining to hear what he heard. There were faint sounds of dogs fighting. Wolves? Coyotes? Maybe both. I frowned and nodded toward the canyon, not saying anything.

Before Yellow Boy could reply, Arango said, "Yaquis *y Mexicano* Army, they meet *en cañón. Mucho muerte y muerte* (death and dying), *mis amigos, muy mal. Vamonos, Señor Muchacho Amarillo?*"

Grabbing his saddle horn, Yellow Boy swung up on his paint in a smooth fluid motion. *"Sí, vamonos."*

I worried about that jaguar as we rode upriver, in and out of willows, around huge sycamores and cottonwoods, and then cross country, when the river's course started winding like a snake on hot sand. I recalled some scary tales Rufus told me about how once in a long while, mountain lions discovered how easy it was to kill humans and then started attacking lone riders or dragging off children playing too far from their ranch house or village. He said that when it happened, some tribes believed the animal was a witch and left the country to get away from it. Those who stayed, white or Indian, often needed a long time to track the big cat down and might lose several men before they did. I knew that if the jaguar had developed a taste for human flesh, it would be very dangerous, so we had to keep a close eye out for it as well as for men. Most men, much less a woman or child, wouldn't have a chance if it deliberately hunted them and attacked.

9
THE CAMP OF ELIAS

We weren't over three or four miles away from where we'd seen the jaguar when Yellow Boy suddenly motioned for us to ride into the tree shadows off the river trail. We dismounted and stood, hardly breathing, while he, unmoving just off the edge of the trail, stared upriver. It was blacker than the inside of a coal mine under those trees, and the thought of that jaguar being near made me nervous. I stepped over by Yellow Boy and whispered, "What is it?"

"*Caballos. Silencio!*"

Soon I heard splashes in the river and stones rattling on the trail. Horses, like wispy vapor, appeared out of the moonlight shadows. Five Apaches were strung out single file. The moonlight and shadows shifting across their faces gave them an eerie, ominous look as they disappeared past us. Sac edged closer to me, her breath coming in short, desperate pants. I put my arm around her shoulders and felt her trembling. I whispered, "It's all right. They'll never see or hear us."

Yellow Boy looked around at me, frowning, shaking his head for me to be quiet. I knew better than to make any sound and felt like a fool. But Sac seemed to calm a little as she buried her face on my shoulder. The noise from the Apache horses trailed off downriver. Then she whispered into my shoulder, "I'm sorry, Henry. That cat and those Indians have made me witless."

I patted her back and pulled her closer to me, smelling her scent, like crushed flowers. "It's okay. They're long gone. We'll be back on the trail soon."

Motioning to us, Yellow Boy nodded down the trail. "I ride upriver, scout for more riders. Arango, *usted* know this trail, *sí?*"

Arango nodded.

"*Usted* lead, others follow. Stay *tres caballos* apart. Stay this side of river, close by *sierras,* pass San Miguel *y* trail to El Paso Carretas, pass Bavispe, and stop at first *agua en* second canyon upriver from Bavispe. I find before *sol* above *sierras. Adiós.*" He mounted and disappeared into the shadows.

Arango soon followed. Paralleling the river, he set a beeline across the rough country. The two women followed behind

149

Arango. Billy rode behind the women, and I rode in the back, leading Elmer and keeping a close eye out for anything following us.

We rode across rough, barren country for two or three hours without incident. The moon was starting to fall behind Sierra El Tigre when we saw the brilliant, white San Miguel church tower catching its last moonlight before the dawn. We crossed a trail toward a crack in the smooth, steep cliffs and the dark shadows outlining the canyon that began El Paso Carretas. Arango led us around San Miguel's whitewashed *adobe* houses and then set a fast trot down the road to Bavispe.

In the black early dawn, we saw a light that must have come from Bavispe, and tacked toward the east, staying across the river from Bavispe, screened by the willows and sycamore trees along the river's edge. It was so peaceful; I didn't even hear a dog bark in Bavispe.

The light was making the country easy to see when we finally rode up the second canyon south of Bavispe and found the water Yellow Boy said to camp by. The women wanted to make a fire and cook. We were all hungry, but Arango said to wait until Yellow Boy told us it was clear.

Yellow Boy soon rode up and told us to rest for the day but not to make a fire. It was at least another half-night's ride down the river before we reached the canyon leading to Elias's camp. We ate some jerky, had some acorn cakes, drank our fill of cold spring water, and rested, taking short watches because the women watched, too.

That night, leaving when it was full dark, we passed two small villages, ten or twelve miles apart upstream of Bavispe, and then cut across country because the river bent back almost due east. We found the river again and followed it the rest of the night. Well before dawn, we rode past a large canyon that snaked its way east up into the mountains. In a couple of more miles, we came to a second canyon and rode up a small draw on the other side of the river opposite it. It was too dark to tell much about where we were. Yellow Boy told us to find the spring and not to light a fire while he scouted the far canyon for Elias's camp. Billy kept watch while the rest of us spread out our bedrolls. We were soon asleep under the big trees that were a dead giveaway for the spring.

It was late morning. All of us except Arango, who took the first watch, were dozing in the shade of some Humphrey oaks and sycamores. Yellow Boy appeared across the river just after I'd got up for some water. It was a relief to see him ford the river because he had been gone much longer than I'd expected. He looked weary as he gulped water out of the pool there under the trees.

He plopped down beside Sac and me, took a deep breath, and puffed it out. Arango, Billy Creek, and Rafaela gathered around us, and Yellow Boy said, "Elias's camp is high up canyon. I hide. Wait *por sol.* Watch. No see warriors. Camp has women, children, Elias, *y* old *hombres.* No Lewis Clark!"

Sac's eyes filled with tears. She spoke in a sorrowful, wavering voice. "Where . . . where is he?"

Yellow Boy shrugged his shoulders and shook his head. *"No lo sé.* We know *mañana."*

Sac asked, "What do you want to do?"

Yellow Boy grinned. "I palaver. Hombrecito shoot."

The women frowned in confusion. I wasn't sure what to think. Arango and

152

Creek were grinning.

Yellow Boy took his knife and began scratching in the dirt. "Elias *aquí.* Hombrecito *aquí,* above canyon on ridge. When Hombrecito leaves, goes down other side of ridge, Elias no see, no can follow." He made a squiggle in the dirt to show the first canyon. "*Es* long shot *por hombre con* Winchester. Easy shot *por* Hombrecito *con* Shoots Today Kills Tomorrow. Arango, Billy, *y mujeres con caballos aquí* below ridge."

He held two fingers up to his eyes. "I watch Hombrecito. When he is ready to shoot, I speak to Elias. Ask for Lewis Clark. If he no tell, Hombrecito shoot warning shot. Still no tell, shoot closer. Elias feel *mucho* danger. Thinks maybe he die." Yellow Boy nodded his head in certainty. "He tells *mi* of Lewis Clark. We find."

Arango and Creek, grinning, nodded. Now we understood what Yellow Boy had meant when he told the men in Rojo's council I was all he needed to get Lewis Clark back. We spent a while making plans and trying to figure out what to do for every Elias countermove, or what to do if the sound of gunfire echoing in the hills brought men we didn't expect.

Yellow Boy was convinced the group we saw riding downriver was part of Elias's

153

band, and that there were probably others besides them riding to the canyon where we'd seen the jaguar. It was just too good an opportunity to pick up supplies from the dead or wounded in the big battle not to scout it. He thought we had at least a day, maybe two, to tease an answer out of Elias about Lewis Clark's whereabouts before disappearing to avoid the returning warriors. Even then, it was going to be a cat-and-mouse chase back to Rojo's camp.

We rested and then crossed the river to the first canyon. We made camp about a half-mile up from the river. A stream trickled through the canyon, and Yellow Boy found a recess under a rock overhang fronted by trees where the women could make a fire without the smoke or light being seen. He asked Arango and Billy to scout the stream where we camped to find where Elias kept his horses and cattle. He told me to get Little David, and we'd look over the path up to Elias's camp and learn the camp's layout.

It took over an hour of hard climbing up the south side of the ridge forming Elias's canyon to reach the spot Yellow Boy had in mind. We had to be careful not to show ourselves to Elias's lookouts on the other side. If they saw us, the whole camp might come after us or else just disappear, fearful that we were part of a bigger band attacking them. We worked our way out of the trees and into the rocks where Yellow Boy wanted me. He chose an excellent spot from which to put the fear of God into Elias.

We were about sixty feet higher than Elias's camp, which was less than two hundred yards away, and my back was toward the east, so his people would have to look into the morning sun to see from where the shots were fired. I saw women scraping fresh hides and children playing with carved wooden dolls as they did in Rojo's camp. A couple of old men sat smoking cigarettes in the shade of a big pine tree, but I didn't see more than one or two other men in the camp. Yellow Boy pulled out his telescope and scrutinized the scene across the canyon. He finally grunted in satisfaction and handed it to me. He pointed toward a large fire pit near the center of camp. A few yards off to one side were five large, open-mouth clay jars. The older children hiked to the stream of water down in the canyon to fill large bladders with water and haul them back to keep the jars full.

Off to one side of the fire was the place where the old men were lounging as they watched the women work. The camp had two little stone cabins similar to the ones in Rojo's camp, but there were many more wickiups than at Rojo's.

Pointing to one spot and then another in the camp, Yellow Boy told me what he needed me to do. I nodded, hoping I was as good a shot as he believed I was.

Dusk came just as we left, making it easier for us to find our way off the top of the canyon's ridge without being seen. When we were a little below the ridge, there was no sign people were camped on the other side or any evidence of their fires. Just as in Rojo's camp, there were no human noises, no animal sounds, nothing.

Sac and Rafaela made a great stew that night. We might have eaten it all for dinner except we wanted to save some for the morning meal. I wanted to leave before dawn to have plenty of time to get in place before Yellow Boy headed up the north slope of the canyon.

Again, we talked through the possibilities of what might happen to plan for contingencies. Arango was to go up the canyon, where he and Creek had found the horse corral and cattle pens, and stop and silence anyone who came for a horse. While Yellow Boy was in Elias's camp, Arango was going to open

156

up the pens and drive the stock toward the Bavispe and provide covering fire if it were needed. We figured the need to retrieve his cattle and horses before they were scattered up and down the river ought to put a little extra pressure on Elias to speak up quickly about Lewis Clark. The women were to hold our horses ready to ride at the first canyon in the willows by the river. Billy was to block the entrance to the second canyon in case the warriors came back before we expected.

Sac was a mess. Though it just didn't make sense that the Apaches would go to the trouble of stealing him and then kill him, I could tell that the more she thought about it, the tighter her nerves wound. I watched her, feeling helpless to do or say anything that might make her feel better, but Rafaela was a godsend. She knew what to say. They talked for a long time in low voices by the feeble light from our little fire. At last, Rafaela's soft-spoken words gave Sac the support and strength she needed to face the next day and Elias's revelation, whatever it might be.

Yellow Boy sat with his back to a big cottonwood tree, blowing cigar smoke into the still, cool air. Billy and Arango cleaned their Winchesters and made aimless conversation about how they were going to get rich from all the cattle they stole. Cobwebs started filling my brain, so I put the Sharps in its case and crawled off to my bedroll. I was just at the doorway to the land of dreams when I felt Sac lie down beside me. She didn't say a word, just smoothed my hair for a while, and, holding my hand, snuggled up close as I relaxed into a deep sleep.

It was pitch-black when I felt Yellow Boy tapping me on my foot with his rifle. I eased Sac's head off my shoulder and sat up. Yellow Boy handed me a cup of hot coffee left from the pot that had sat over the coals all night. It was bitter and strong, jolting me awake with the first sip. I ate some of the stew left from supper and was ready to go.

Yellow Boy handed me the Sharps case, a full canteen, and some jerky. He walked with me to the pine marking the beginning of the path up the side of the canyon. His hand was strong on my shoulder, and he gave me a little squeeze of reassurance. "Climb easy, Hombrecito. Long time before you shoot. I no move until *usted* ready. Remember," he said, grinning and tapping his head with his forefinger, *"cold and cakilatin'."* He stuck his chin out defiantly, gave a quick nod, turned, and was gone.

It was still darker than pitch when I began my climb up the ridge. I doubt I could have done it if I hadn't memorized the path and its landmarks when Yellow Boy and I had climbed it the day before. The climb was the trickiest part of Yellow Boy's plan. One misstep on my part could make enough noise to spring Elias's camp into action. It might take weeks before we found them again if they ran. I was lucky the path we'd followed the day before passed numerous trees because I was able to hold on to them as I pulled myself up the path. Each time I put a foot down, I tested first to be sure the ground under it supported me. The air was cold, but I was sweating like a field hand in July.

As the light became stronger, it became evident I was going slower than I had expected. The urge to hurry was almost overpowering, but with the years Yellow Boy spent teaching me self-discipline, I managed to stay steady without a slip.

My hands were raw, and I had scratches on my face from being switched by unseen branches when I crawled into the rocks where Yellow Boy wanted me. The sun was coming and the dawn was creeping off the ridges. In the rapidly growing light on the other side of the canyon, I saw dark figures, nearly all women and small children, doing their morning chores or tottering about in the cold air. I pulled a small mirror from my pocket and waited for the sun to get high enough so I could signal Arango I was ready. At last, the sun floated up over the mountains, and I flashed that I was ready. Arango immediately flashed back an acknowledgment and relayed the signal to Yellow Boy, who waited partway up the other side of the canyon.

I pulled the Sharps out of its case, flipped up the vernier sight, and sighted through a pinhole to where Elias often sat in council, the spot on the other side where Yellow Boy wanted me to shoot. It was in dark shadows. The rising sun would make it easier to see. I pointed the Sharps at different places in Elias's camp and determined the different sight pictures I might have to use.

Soon I saw Elias come out of one of the little stone cabins, go down the ridge, water a bush, and return to his woman's fire. She pulled a piece of meat off a stick, wrapped it in bread that looked like a big tortilla, and handed it to him. I watched him through Rufus's old field glasses. Elias was an old man, but he carried the weight of his years easily. He was straight and proud, the lines in his face hard and unyielding. I remembered his face well from the attack on Sac's family. I had no fear or hate for him. He was a force of nature, just something for me to deal with that day.

As I waited, the early hours of the day drifted by slowly and easily like the high, puffball clouds overhead. I used the glasses to find and follow Yellow Boy, a shadow fading from tree to tree, bush to bush, as he crept up the ridgeline toward Elias's camp. He moved within a hundred yards of the camp's edge, found a place to stretch out under some *piñons,* and waited.

It would be hard for most people to believe how well Yellow Boy melted into the background unless they had seen him do it. I knew exactly where to look and still had to stare at the spot to find him. One time that morning, I looked away from him to study the camp and almost panicked when I looked back and missed seeing him. I thought that maybe he was already moving toward the camp. But after some frantic searching up and down the path he took to the camp, I swung the glasses back to the *piñons* and managed to find him, a shapeless boulder in the shadows faded into the long, blond grass under the trees.

The sun arched higher, bringing the middle of the morning. The edge of its light swept up the mountains, shifting ever eastward in a steady march back toward the chunk of log where Elias sat carving a piece of wood into a faceless doll for a child standing at his elbow. He talked and smoked with the old men as he worked. The edge of the advancing light was ten or fifteen feet away from Elias when Yellow Boy rose up and dusted the leaves and grass off his pants, breechcloth, and cavalry jacket, straightened his hat, and put his Henry in the crook of his arm. With the gravitas of a general reviewing his troops, he began a steady march toward Elias.

When I saw Elias stand, I knew it was time for business. I fumbled around opening my box of cartridges and pulled out five. I laid them in a bowl-shaped indentation in a rock by my elbow. Then I dropped the breech on the Sharps, loaded it, and held three shells in my right hand for quick reloads. I had already sighted the Sharps on Elias sitting in the shadows, using a large pinhole in the vernier sight. He was a gray blur in the shadows with the smaller, more accurate pinhole I wanted to use. The sun rose still higher, driving the shadows back. The edge of its light was nearly at Elias's feet. At last there was enough light for a smaller pinhole. I rotated it into place and had a clear sight picture. All I had to do was pull Little David's trigger and old Elias was on his way to the land of the grandfathers.

The morning air was very still except for an occasional light breeze down the canyon, so there was no need to adjust the sights for lateral wind drift. I estimated the distance again and made a very slight vernier adjustment upward. Staring through the pinhole to check the line of sight and sight picture again, I was ready.

Yellow Boy was within sixty yards of Elias when a small child saw him. He whined to his mother and pointed. For an instant, she stared in disbelief, then reached out and grabbed the child up in her arms. She yelled something at Elias as she and the other women with small children ran to the opposite side of the camp. Four of the women who had no children stood their ground. Two grabbed old cap-and-ball rifles they kept nearby, and another laid an arrow on a bow. They stood ready to fight and die at the first sign from Elias.

Elias and one of the old men grabbed their Winchesters and levered rounds into the chambers. The second old man threw an old, used and abused High Wall breechloader to his shoulder, supporting it near the trigger guard by bracing his forearm against his body. They all pointed their weapons at Yellow Boy and waited for Elias's command to shoot. I sighted on Elias's chest. If he made the slightest move to signal anyone to fire, he was a dead man.

Yellow Boy's rifle never left the crook of his arm. He held up his right hand, palm out, and, pushing it forward two or three times, paused for an instant as if to say, "Hold." He continued, fearless, in a steady walk toward them. The edge of the advancing sun's light was on Elias's legs. Elias and his people were frozen in place. They each looked like a person coming upon a coiled snake ready to strike. I was so far away I couldn't understand anything being said. Yellow Boy told me later about his words with Elias.

He said that, at twenty yards, Elias began to relax and said, "I know you. You're of Rojo's camp above the Cajón Bonito. Why do you enter the camp of Elias uninvited like a proud wolf?"

Yellow Boy told him, "I come to speak with Elias. I mean no harm to anyone in this camp. Let's sit and smoke in the clear light of day."

As the sun was just starting to strike Elias's face, I saw him lower his rifle and point Yellow Boy to a chunk of log across from his. The rest of the camp relaxed, the old men sitting with Elias holding their weapons ready as they sat staring at the audacious invader.

Yellow Boy, sitting across from Elias with his side to me, planted the Henry's stock between his feet, resting the barrel against his leg. Elias laid his rifle across his knees, the sunlight, golden and bright, fully in his face. I knew he was virtually blind in my direction. He pulled a cigar out of his vest pocket, and, using a splinter aflame from the little fire pit at his back, lit it, and passed the splinter to Yellow Boy, who pulled one of his cigars from inside his cavalry coat, lighted it, and smoked to the four directions. Now Elias knew this was serious business.

Elias smoked to the four directions while he eyed Yellow Boy. Even though he knew Yellow Boy and his capability with his Henry rifle, Yellow Boy told me later that Elias showed him no respect, refusing to address him by his name. Instead, he said, "So, Proud Wolf, why do you stalk my camp? I usually hunt and kill wolves, not speak with them."

Yellow Boy said he took a couple of deliberate puffs, rolling his cigar between his fingers for two or three beats before he

165

looked straight in Elias's eyes, which is itself a challenge and a sign of disrespect in Apache society, and said, "I come for the *Americano* boy you stole on your last raid north." This is what I saw with the field glasses, combined with the way Yellow Boy later described the rest of their exchange:

Elias frowned, cocking his head to one side in feigned puzzlement. "Is he yours? You did not take him. If I have such a child, why should I give him to you?"

Yellow Boy smiled, slowly shook his head, and said, "He's the boy whose father your men killed with an arrow in his throat and two in his chest. He is the boy whose sister with red-fire hair you nearly took before my grandson killed your man and ran you and the others off to hide in the mesquite. My grandson is a great warrior, is he not?"

Elias nodded, his lips pulled back over his teeth in a snarling grin. "So your grandson killed Jingo? His woman carries his child in her belly. Perhaps I will let her stick you with an arrow and avenge her husband. That will make it even between us until I kill your grandson."

Yellow Boy stared into Elias's eyes and again rolled his cigar between his fingers before answering, "That's bad, stupid thinking."

Elias asked, "Why is that, Proud Wolf? You think I won't do it? My warriors demand revenge."

At this point, Yellow Boy pointed at the chunk of log between Elias's legs where he sat, giving the signal I'd been waiting for. Elias glanced down at the log, his face questioning what Yellow Boy meant.

The Sharps thundered an answer echoing up and down the canyon like a rolling wave. A shower of splinters flew from the log and stuck like tiny arrows in Elias's long-legged moccasins and bare inner thighs. The bullet passed all the way through the old log and scalped a thin streak of bark off a tree directly behind them.

I saw Elias jerked back in a reflexive flinch. Then he started for his rifle. Then, apparently thinking better of his chances when he stared up the ridge into the sun, he put his hand back to his knee. By the time he drew back his hand, I'd replaced my spent cartridge. I had him in my sights again, waiting.

Yellow Boy said Elias's teeth flashed in a twisted snarl of outrage, and then his face became a mask showing no emotion. He said, "This is not the end of this, Yellow Boy. I'm no fool. Neither are you fool enough to believe I'll let you shame me in front of women and old men. I'll bathe my hands in your blood for this, and your attack gives you nothing. The boy is gone."

Yellow Boy asked, "Where is he?"

Elias waved in irritation toward the women on the far side of the camp with the small children. "He didn't stop whining and crying for his sister and *padre.* He made too much noise, so we traded him. The *niño* is in the *hacienda* of Señor Comacho, a fortress guarded all the time by many *vaqueros.* Ha! You'll never get him back. Yellow Boy, you're a fool. If Comacho doesn't kill you, I will."

Faint sounds of cattle bawling and running at the bottom of the canyon drifted up to me and the camp. Looking down through the trees into the canyon, I could see them moving toward the Bavispe, along with some horses. Arango had opened the cattle pens and horse corral. Yellow Boy cocked his head and listened. Elias, frowning, listened, too. Then Yellow Boy said, "Hear me, Elias. The *Americanos* believe there are no more free Apaches since Geronimo. Your raids across the border will change their minds. Then all who live the old ways in these mountains will be attacked. The *Americanos* will try to wipe out the last Apaches here. They will send manhunters and big armies into the south as they did when they chased Geronimo. We will disappear like the grandfathers no longer before our eyes. Only our shadows will roam these lands. Elias and Juan must stop raids to the north."

Elias shook his head, smiling. "If I do not?"

Yellow Boy looked him square in the eyes. "One day you'll sit and not know death approaches you. It will come like this."

He pointed at Elias's log seat again. I put another bullet into the log. It hit within two inches of the first and thunked in the tree I'd grazed with the first shot. Elias flinched again as the splinters flew into his thighs and moccasins.

The booming thunder from the Sharps was still echoing down the canyon when Yellow Boy spoke. "I say to you, Elias, come after me, and you'll die. Forget this insult and live. I only want the child. You're a great warrior. You have no need to prove yourself. Send men after me, and women will wail death songs in your camp. I leave now. Stay where you sit until the sun is there, or you'll die." He pointed straight up. Noon was at least a couple of hours away.

Then Yellow Boy pointed once more to the stump, and I put another round in it next to the others, sending more splinters flying. Elias flinched again, stared at Yellow Boy with hatred-filled eyes, and slowly nodded.

Yellow Boy hefted the Henry into the crook of his arm, stood, and, turning his back on the camp, walked back toward his path through the pines and oaks. I waited in my shooting spot. He disappeared into the trees down the side of the canyon. I continued to wait. Ten minutes passed, then fifteen. Elias, his hand held low, slowly waved the old man with the high wall rifle to stand up. As he stood on wobbly feet, the Sharps thundered again, placing a fourth round in the three-inch diameter circle between Elias's legs. He shook his head and squinted toward the eastern sky. The old man sat back down like a hungry cowhand at Sunday dinner. I left a cartridge in the chamber, put a spare cartridge in my breechcloth belt, and swept clean the place where I sat.

10
THE GETAWAY

I eased out of the rocks, made the short climb up over the ridge above me, and worked my way down into the first canyon. Whipped and scratched by the oaks, cedars, and brush, I half-slid, half-walked to the bottom trail. I found Yellow Boy waiting with his paint and Midnight, ready to ride. By the time we reached the river, it was past midday. We were unbelievably lucky. We hadn't even been shot at or come close to having our throats cut, and we knew where Lewis Clark was. We had to hurry if we were to avoid the men returning from the battleground between the Yaquis and the Mexicans.

We found Arango, Creek, Sac, and Rafaela waiting in the willows on the banks of the Bavispe. Sac ran up to Midnight and grabbed the bridle, her face grim. "Is he . . . is he . . ." she stammered, tears already leaking out of her eyes.

Yellow Boy rode up to her and spoke in a low, reassuring voice. *"Muchacho* lives. Elias trades to Comacho *vaqueros.* Lewis Clark slave *en* Comacho *hacienda.* We take back from Comacho. *Vamonos.* Elias *y hombres* come *pronto."*

We took off downriver, staying on the east side. It was risky riding in the daylight, but even more dangerous to wait around for Elias's men to return to camp and start their chase right on our heels. We stopped several times to rest the horses and to eat a little food. The gentle glow of lights in Bavispe showed in the distance a little after sunset. Yellow Boy led the way and swung wide of the little village.

A few miles downriver past Bavispe, we passed San Miguel and then struck the well-traveled trail up through El Paso Carretas. When we stopped and camped off the main trail in a hidden overhang smaller than the first one we had used two nights earlier, I said, "Grandfather, tell us how we will take Lewis Clark back."

Yellow Boy leaned back on an elbow, took a deep draw from his cigar, and blew the smoke out. *"Hombre* with Elias traded him to *vaquero jefe* who thinks *Señor* Comacho laugh if an *Americano* is his slave."

Sac stared at him, her hand over her mouth, her eyes filled with horror. Rafaela sat down and put her arm around Sac's trembling shoulders, speaking softly to comfort her. Billy Creek was red in the face and gritted his teeth as he made a cigarette. Arango had pulled his revolver. The mechanical clicks it made as he slowly rotated the cylinder with the hammer on half-cock seemed like they came from a ticking bomb. He didn't look at Yellow Boy at all; he just kept an ear cocked in his direction. I said nothing. I knew Yellow Boy had been thinking about what to do since his visit with Elias.

Almost in tears, Sac asked, "How in God's name will we ever get Lewis Clark back? Rafaela told me what Comacho did to her. What will he do to a little boy?"

She broke down sobbing, burying her face in her arms. Yellow Boy stared at her. When he spoke again, his voice was calm and demanding. "Woman, be strong! *Sol viene mañana. Vamonos a* Comacho *rancho.* Hide. Watch. Find *muchacho.* Take. Return *a* Rojo's camp."

Billy Creek, nodding, struck a sulfur match with his right thumbnail to light his cigarette. The flash of light on his face showed his eyes narrowed. He took a deep

173

draw and blew the smoke out through a wicked grin, a wolf ready for the hunt. Arango smiled, let the hammer down easy on his old revolver, and twirled it before sliding it back into its holster.

Yellow Boy looked in my direction. I nodded. He asked Sac, *"Comprende?"*

She rubbed her red eyes and nodded with a long snuffling sigh.

Yellow Boy, Billy, and Arango finished their smokes but said no more. I straightened out my bedroll and lay down. A wave of exhaustion swept over me. I was fighting sleep as I put Little David within easy reach. I felt Sac lie down next to me and draw a blanket up over us as she snuffled once more and wrapped her arm over my side. I was too tired to speak.

The others let me sleep all night without taking a turn at watch. I awoke to a new fire gathering strength in the fire pit. Arango and Billy were not in their bedrolls, Yellow Boy was gone, and Sac and Rafaela were off in the back of the cave whispering as they made bread. I crawled from my blankets to find a bush.

Coming back down the path from washing at a spring, I found a ledge with a spectacular view of the pass and the *llano* beyond off to the east. I sat down and dangled my feet off into free space. El Paso Carretas was wide enough, and we were far enough through it that from my vantage point I saw pieces of the pass trail for several miles down the eastern side and a mile or two back down the west side toward San Miguel and Bavispe.

High cirrus clouds, tinted light pink, fast fading to brilliant white, streaked the western sky. Crows, flying out of roosts in big sycamore trees down by the river, streamed through the pass headed east. I drew the cool air deep in my lungs and waited to exhale. It was good to be alive.

Sac's hand landed on my shoulder, a light touch that became heavy as she supported herself to sit down. She dangled her legs off the ledge, folded her hands in her lap, and sighed. Her body drove the chill from my skin, and her musky odor of sleep and the smoke from the fire warmed my soul.

She said, "I was so scared yesterday. The waiting was awful. I think I'd rather be shot at than sit and wait while something awful might be happening."

Instead of hugging Sac, I discreetly leaned into her in an armless hug that displayed little but said everything, and she leaned back into me. I felt stirrings of desire for her, but I only said, "Patience was the hardest thing I had to learn from Rufus and Yellow Boy. Learning patience and to trust my compadres took a long time. Old Rufus used to tell me I had to be 'cold and cakilatin' to survive. He meant that I couldn't let emotion cloud my understanding in deciding how to fight an enemy. You've got to learn that, too. Things are gonna be okay. You'll see. We'll get Lewis Clark back, and he'll be fine."

She sniffed, nodding. "I know. If the Lord's willing and it's humanly possible, we'll get him back. You and these people with us . . . I'll never be able to repay you for all you've done for us, never."

We stood up and headed for the fire and something to eat. Arango told us Yellow Boy had left before dawn saying he was going to look for a path across the pass that wouldn't expose us to travelers on the main trail. If he found one, we'd travel during the day and not wait until dark. That way we might reach the Comacho *hacienda* by nightfall.

Rafaela and Sac served us up beans, tortillas, and coffee, a king's table in that high, cool air. At midmorning, Yellow Boy returned after finding the path we needed. We saddled and loaded the horses and Elmer and began a hard climb up the canyon away from the overhang. The climb was so steep, we had to walk and lead the animals up to a path that looked like a thin piece of yellow twine winding up the ridge through the trees and across canyons and draws. It occasionally disappeared in the dappled sunlight and shadows, a hidden highway for animals and stealthy travelers. Far below, we could see the trail winding through El Paso Carretas shadowed by the cant of the sun as it tracked across the eastern side of the mountains.

11
THE COMACHO *HACIENDA*

By midafternoon, the broad expanse of the dry plains spread out before us and disappeared into the blue haze. When we were close to the *llano,* Yellow Boy called a stop to rest the animals. We stared at the great plain dotted with large herds of cattle that raised little plumes of dust as they wandered through the sparsely scattered mesquite and creosotes to find stretches of weeds and brown and golden grass. I'd seen similar scenes many times in the Tularosa Basin country.

"When *sol es aquí,*" Yellow Boy said and pointed more than three-quarters of the way down the sun's arc to the western horizon, "we reach Comacho *hacienda. Es* fortress, *muy* strong. Walls maybe five or six rifles high and one or two wide. Sits against high cliffs, faces west. Trail runs up cliffs from *hacienda. Vaqueros* use to light signal fire on top of cliffs for help when Apache come.

No Apache ever take *hacienda.* Try many times.

"We camp on ridge at end of cliff and watch *hacienda por* Lewis Clark. Comacho keep him close to *hacienda.* Teach work. Break spirit. Billy Creek *y* Rafaela know *hacienda.*" He glanced toward them and asked, "Where do slaves sleep?"

Billy said, "Oh, they's all over the *hacienda.* They's kept purdy close to the masters so's they ken come quick when they's called. I 'spec' ol' Lewis Clark, he's too little fer anything 'cept work with the kitchen women. That there's where he's at."

He glanced at Rafaela who nodded grimly and said, "Kitchen's in the back along the wall closest to the cliff. It ain't far from the little creek that runs between the cliffs and the *hacienda.*"

Yellow Boy stared in the direction of the *hacienda,* and the only sign that he had understood what Billy had told him was his eyes narrowing in a squint of concentration. Soon he nodded and said, *"Bueno. Vamonos."*

We rode down out of the mountains, staying on the path that paralleled the pass trail. The entire day, we saw no one on the main trail. The canyon through which we rode gradually opened up onto the *llano.* We

179

swung due east tracking around big mesquites and creosotes for cover on the thin, grass-covered plains and headed for a low range of mountains. Whenever he could, Yellow Boy kept us in low draws and *arroyos,* so our outline was not on the horizon.

Near dark, we came up out of a wide wash and began following a trail on a steep rise. When we reached the top of the rise, the ground fell away in a long, winding cliff running almost due north. A couple of hundred feet below us, a small stream lined with willows and a few cottonwoods and sycamores ran along the bottom of the cliffs. Large groups of cattle were scattered from just beyond the cliffs all the way to the eastern slopes of the mountains hiding in the shadows of the last dying glow from the sun. A couple of miles from where we stopped, lights flickered around several large white buildings, one of which had high, white adobe walls — the Comacho *hacienda.*

Yellow Boy dropped down off the edge of the rise and rode out of sight below the ridge edge. We followed him past where I thought the *hacienda* was sitting below us and rode on for another half-mile before we came to a ridge that lay east and west, intersecting the cliffs. We rode a little while longer just below this ridge and then up over the ridgeline to a crevice in the cliffs facing the northern side of the *hacienda,* and we stopped. Yellow Boy had us wait while he rode the steep trail from the crevice down toward the bottom.

The moon was just above the eastern horizon when he reappeared and signaled us to follow him. About halfway down the cliff, the trail crossed a bench about fifty feet wide before making a sharp turn and heading over the bench edge for the creek. Yellow Boy turned toward a thicket of ocotillo at the far end of the bench.

I knew about ocotillo, for it covered the entrance to a little canyon Yellow Boy, Rufus, and I used in the Jarilla Mountains in the Tularosa Basin. Yellow Boy had a carefully concealed path through it in the Jarillas, and it worked very well keeping cattle or curious ranch hands away. Here, I knew he hadn't had time to scout through it or to determine what was behind it. Its stems were longer and bigger than the ocotillo in the Jarillas, and its thorns looked longer and sharper. I gritted my teeth to endure the suffering the thorns would inflict when we rode near them but just as we got to the edge of the thicket Yellow Boy turned his paint toward a huge boulder on the left side and disappeared around it.

A narrow path wound past several boulders and into a small canyon formed by a crack in the ridge just off the bench. The trail through the little canyon wound on for two or three hundred yards and stopped at a small natural water tank. About fifty feet up the cliff side of the canyon, a large shelf projected over the top of us so we couldn't see the top of the ridge we'd ridden across earlier. Riding through that little canyon was like riding down a tunnel with about a third of the top right side cut away. At the end of the canyon, there were deep recesses under the overhanging shelves where we could lay our bedrolls out, stay out of the sun, and have a little privacy when we wanted.

Yellow Boy told us to make no fire that night because its glow might be seen flickering off the cliff walls. The next day we could make a fire and let it burn down to coals for cooking in the evening. After we took care of the animals, we ran some long stems of ocotillo through the recesses to be sure we weren't going to have rattlesnakes for bedmates, and laid out our bedrolls. Yellow Boy told Arango and Billy not to smoke, since the flash of light from their matches might be seen. He signaled me to follow him, and we climbed up to the top edge of the canyon to see where we were relative to the *hacienda.*

The climb to the top of the canyon was not hard, but it was slow since we had to be careful not to dislodge rocks that might give us away, and the light wasn't steady, with occasional clouds drifting across the moon. We crawled up on a flat ledge and looked down. The *hacienda* was about a hundred feet below us and perhaps two hundred yards distant. We could see everything from there. I saw shadows moving along the courtyard's far wall as people, unseen, passed in and out of light from a couple of fires. I was stunned. It never occurred to me that we were so close.

I studied every inch of the *hacienda,* committing details to memory as Yellow Boy had taught me to do during all those years he trained me. Every five feet or so, the *hacienda* had slits in the walls for guns, and in some places the gun slits were two rows high. The walls were at least twenty feet high. The ground around the *hacienda* was smooth. There were no *arroyos* or bushes in which to hide that could get an attacker close to the walls except near the back, which was protected by the big cliffs. There were three windmills, one of which was in the *hacienda* courtyard. Stables and bunkhouses were outside the main walls of the *hacienda*. A series of paths protected by *adobe* and rock fences ran between them. Cattle grazing nearby were kept at least a quarter of a mile away by a barbed wire fence stretching all the way to the cliffs encircling the *hacienda*.

I thought the *hacienda* was an excellent fortress, except for building it too close to a cliff where an enemy could hide and shoot down on the inside. Yellow Boy studied the *hacienda* and the cliff face behind it for a long time. He finally grunted, sat up, and motioned me to follow him back down to camp.

We crabbed back down into our hiding place and heard guns being cocked as we came up to our little camp. I was relieved when I saw Arango's white teeth in a smile. He whispered to the others and eased the hammer down on his revolver. "*Es Señores* Muchacho Amarillo *y* Hombrecito."

Billy sat under a blanket with his arm around Rafaela's shoulders. Sac sat with her blanket wrapped around her, and Arango sat on a big rock. Yellow Boy sat down by a small boulder. Sac smiled when I joined her, threw the edge of her blanket over my shoulders, and slid up close to me. Billy spoke first. "How's it look over there, fellers?"

I waited for Yellow Boy to speak.

"*Hacienda* close. Easy shot *por* Shoots Today Kills Tomorrow. *Hacienda es muy* strong. Walls *grande*. Many places *por* rifles. Wind wheel inside, always good water. *Muchos vaqueros* behind walls."

Billy nodded. "I sneaked in there before. Ol' man Comacho'll vouch fer that. What about that cliff above it? Why can't a body jest git up there an' keep 'em pinned down fer as long as need be?"

I saw Arango nod the same question. Yellow Boy said, "Cliff smooth. No hiding. Rope ladder stop halfway up cliff."

Arango frowned. "Why?"

Yellow Boy shrugged his shoulders and grinned, a wolf who understood the rabbit hole. "*No soy por certainamente. Es* same as Rufus trick, Hombrecito?"

I had not seen the rope ladder, and it took me a little while to understand his hint. It hit me with startling clarity. I smiled and said, "The ladder goes to a ledge where armed men can cover the *hacienda.* It was the same idea Rufus used for us to cover his shack or hide from attackers. There was a ledge on one of the cliffs by his shack. We didn't need a rope ladder to get to it. We'd

185

just used handholds in the cliff side. The Comacho men must have food, water, and cartridges, and maybe even rifles, stored up there. If the *hacienda* comes under attack, then men can climb that ladder up to the place on the cliff and provide covering fire so the men inside don't get shot to pieces."

Billy laughed and slapped his knee. "That there is purdy smart, ain't it, boys? But what about fellers shootin' down from top o' the cliff?"

Using his hands, Yellow Boy showed how shooters on top of the cliff couldn't see the men on the ledge. "*Hombres* on ledge can climb to cliff top from both ends of shelf. Catch shooters on top in crossfire. No place for hiding *por* shooters on top. Die *pronto en* crossfire."

Yellow Boy stifled a yawn and said, "*Mañana* we find Lewis Clark. Then, soon, we take him. Sleep now. When *sol* come, *mujeres* make fire *pero* no smoke. Hombrecito, *usted* watch first, then Arango *y* Billy Creek. Before *sol,* I go to cliff ledge, watch *hacienda. Te intendiendo todo,* you understand everything?"

We all nodded. I found a canteen and started back down the path to the top of the canyon. I heard Sac call to me in a loud whisper, "Henry, wait. I'll come with you."

I looked over at Yellow Boy to see if it was all right for her to watch, too. He sat back and grinned, so I whispered back, "Sure, come on. But it's cold up there."

I led off up the path to the top with her right behind me. We sat down where the view of the *hacienda* was best. Sac sat next to me and drew part of her blanket over my shoulders, letting her arm rest there. The fires in the courtyard had burned down to coals and put out little light. I saw the dark outline of a guard wander around the outside wall, stop and light a smoke, and continue on his stroll. Off in the distance, toward the mountains, a coyote howled.

We sat in silence watching the *hacienda* as the moon swung across its arc. The air was cold enough to turn our breath into little clouds that quickly vanished in the soft light, but Sac's body next to mine was warm and comforting.

She leaned close and whispered, "Henry, please kiss me."

I felt goose bumps spring to life down the back of my neck. I shivered a little inside. I hesitated for a moment, staring straight ahead at the *hacienda,* then turned and kissed her ever so lightly on the cheek, just enough to feel the light peach fuzz and my breath bounce back to me. She leaned back

187

on one hand, her face in shadow, staring at me with the hint of a smile on her lips and mischief sparkling in her eyes. I stared back, afraid to blink, afraid she'd vanish. My heart paused, waiting for her to make it beat.

Her hand brushed my cheek, slid under the hair on my neck, and pulled my head to hers. Soft and warm, her lips drew me to her like magic, and the doors of my heart swung open to release delight, confusion, and an overpowering desire for the knowledge of the great mystery, a genie I knew I'd never get back in its bottle.

We must have kissed for a minute or more. I was oblivious to the rest of the world, in a state of ecstasy and wonder at the unfolding mystery. I felt heat stirring in my breechcloth, and my heart pumping like I'd run miles. I pushed my lips harder against hers. Then there was her hand on my shoulder gently pushing me back. She looked in my eyes, her breath mixing with mine in long, pulling draughts as if she'd been running, too.

She bowed her head, looking sideways into my eyes, and said, "You've taken my heart. Promise you'll never give it back."

"I promise. I promise for as long as I live I'll treasure your heart."

"I want to make love with you Henry, as a

wife with her husband, but not in this place, not when death is coming, not when there are others so close by. I want to make love with you when it's just you and me."

"I feel that way too. I can wait until we're alone."

She nodded. "Can I stay here with you until your watch is over?"

I drew her warm body next to mine. We wrapped the blanket over our shoulders warming each other, watching the *hacienda* in silence. Coyotes yipped lonesome calls and faded away.

12
FINDING LEWIS CLARK

That first morning in the little canyon above the Comacho *hacienda,* I was up at first light. Yellow Boy was gone, but his paint was still in the rope corral with the other horses and Elmer. Sac and Rafaela had slipped down through the junipers to the little creek drifting behind the *hacienda* where they gathered wood and cow chips for a fire. When they got back to camp, they made coffee, grilled a little bacon, and boiled some beans. We were all hungry.

When the early soft golden light fell against its walls, we started surveying the *hacienda* using Billy's old pair of cavalry glasses. Yellow Boy had taken his telescope with him. I figured he planned to study the *hacienda* from the spot on the cliff where the rope ladder ended.

We watched the *hacienda* from sunrise until dark, never seeing Lewis Clark. That wasn't too surprising because we couldn't see anyone unless they were near the south wall. Occasionally, I swung the glasses over to the brown-, red-, and black-streaked cliff where I thought Yellow Boy was roosting. I never saw any evidence he was there, which didn't surprise me either.

As the day wore on, Sac worried more and more about Lewis Clark. She didn't say much, but it was obvious her nerves were winding tighter than a tenor guitar string. She'd sit down for a moment, and then get up, pacing around, nervously smoothing her hair back from her face.

With the sun finally setting over the mountains, we sat around the fire's coals and finished off the coffee before Rafaela made another pot. Sac insisted on sitting at the spot where we'd watched the house, hoping she might catch a glimpse of Lewis Clark against the firelight in the *hacienda* courtyard. Rafaela kept her company.

I poured a second cup of coffee. Blowing the steam off the top, I heard, *"Buenas noches, amigos."* I jumped as if someone had jabbed me in the rear with a mesquite thorn and spilled hot coffee on my fingers.

Out of the corner of my eye, I saw Billy and Arango's coffee cups go flying. Their revolvers, faster than my eye could follow, cleared their holsters, making quick clicks as the hammers came back. Yellow Boy stepped into the circle of light carrying a good-sized haunch of beef on his shoulder. Billy and Arango blew out a little air and relaxed, slowly holstering their big revolvers. Arango smiled, but I heard him mutter something in Spanish about sneaky Apaches.

The women came running as soon as they heard the commotion. They stopped and stared as soon as they saw Yellow Boy standing there. He patted his belly. "All day, no eat!"

Rafaela took the meat, smiled, and sat down by the fire pit to slice off pieces to skewer on a stick over the coals.

"Did you see Lewis Clark? Is he in the *hacienda*?" I asked.

"*Sí,* Lewis Clark *es en hacienda.* Big Eye find." He patted his leather possibles bag to indicate his telescope. "Eat, then talk."

Before long, the meat was sizzling over the fire and its juices were making little flashes of light as they dripped on the coals to make smoke with a smell that made us drool. Soon, we lay back full and with contented sighs.

Sac sat down next to Rafaela, resting her elbow on a knee, her head on her hand. At last, Yellow Boy lit a *cigarro,* smoked to the four directions, and said, "Before *sol* come, take path by water. *Mucho* trees, easy hide. Find rope up cliff. Climb. No *hombres* on cliff lookout. Water, meat, guns, *y* muchos bullets there. Many *hombres* there *muchos* times. See all *hacienda. Sol* comes. Watch. See Lewis Clark kept by cook-pot women."

He made a grand sweep with his arm, and said, "Carry *agua* when *sol* comes until *sol* go. *Agua* from wind wheel to cook pots. *Agua* to *vaqueros y caballos.* Spill *agua,* they beat. Cry, they beat. Lewis Clark strong. Work hard."

Tears filled Sac's eyes. She jumped up and said, "Those dirty, nasty whores! I hate 'em! Let me go down there and cut their throats right now! Lewis Clark's just a little boy! How can they treat him like that?"

The rage flying from her mouth startled me, but I understood how she felt. I'd wanted to do the same thing to Daddy's murderers. I stood up, wrapped my arms around her, and whispered in her ear. "Listen to me. Listen! We have to think like Rufus told me. He said, 'Ye gotta be cold and cakilatin' . . . ye gotta be thinkin' all the time . . . ye can't let your feelings tell ye what to do.' "

Yellow Boy said, "We go to *hacienda.* Take

193

Lewis Clark before Elias come and trades back Lewis Clark from Comacho. I think now Elias wants Lewis Clark to kill him so I no get."

Billy said, "Yes, sir, I think yer right. Old Elias is damned mean an' ornery." He pointed toward the south side of the *hacienda.* "Yonder is where we oughter go. They's a little *arroyo* that runs right up to the courtyard wall where mosta the womenfolks work. They walk down it to git to th' creek. We'n climb over th' 'dobe wall. Ain't no door or gate on th' east side. Ever since I cut ol' man Comacho, they's lots a guards walkin' around down there, just a-hopin' I'd come back. The women is most likely keepin' ol' Lewis Clark sleepin' where they'n keep a close eye on 'im."

Yellow Boy's eyes were narrow slits. He said, "Creek speaks straight. *Agua* by cliff *es* place to go *en hacienda por* Lewis Clark. We find Lewis Clark *y vamonos pronto. Comacho y vaqueros* no find. Elias goes home. Fights another day."

"When will we do this, Yellow Boy?" I asked.

"Mañana por la noche."

"How?"

Yellow Boy gave one of his sly, Coyote-the-trickster grins, and squinted at us through his cigar smoke. *"Hombres* watch door *por* Billy Creek. Think maybe he come back. If they catch, nut-cuttin' time by *Señor* Comacho *por* Billy Creek. If *vaqueros* see Billy Creek, they ride *pronto."*

He raised his eyebrows and said, "Maybe *vaqueros* see Billy Creek? *Sí?"*

Billy was grinning and nodding through his cloud of cigarette smoke. Yellow Boy took another puff and blew it up into the still night air. *"Vaqueros* go after Billy Creek, no stay *en hacienda.* Yellow Boy *y* Arango go over wall from *arroyo.* Find Lewis Clark. Take *y ellos van.* Hombrecito uses Shoots Today Kills Tomorrow. No let *vaqueros* chase Yellow Boy *y* Arango. *Vaqueros* see fire from Shoots Today Kills Tomorrow *en noche. Vaqueros* know their shots no reach Shoots Today Kills Tomorrow. They stay *en hacienda,* watch *por* Shoots Today Kills Tomorrow shots for long time, no leave *hacienda.* Sac *y* Rafaela hold horses ready to ride. Yellow Boy *y* Arango come *aquí con* Lewis Clark *y vamonos.* Find Billy Creek *y* Hombrecito *en* El Paso Púlpito. All ride to Rojo's camp."

Arango had a little *cigarro* clamped in his teeth and his big *sombrero* tilted back. He grinned and nodded. He snapped his big, nickel-plated Colt out of its holster, gave it

195

a twirl, slapped it back in, and said, "*Sí.*"

Rafaela, who rarely spoke except to Billy or Sac, nodded and smiled.

Sac frowned. "If Lewis Clark makes any noise when you take him, the women will raise the alarm. The men left in the *hacienda* will come running. Then you and Arango will have to shoot it out with them. With all those bullets flying, Lewis Clark might get killed, and you, too. Let me go for him. I can get him out without any noise, and we can disappear before anybody knows the difference. I can get in using the door from the stables. Last night, I saw women visiting the *vaqueros* over at their fire by the bunkhouse and taking cozy walks with them off to the willows by that little creek up against the cliffs. Nobody will pay any attention to me coming back to the fire from those bushes and going back in the house. Please let me do this. I want my brother back safe. He's my blood. He's my responsibility."

Yellow Boy crossed his arms and stared at her, the concentration as he considered the possibilities making his normally smooth brow a map of canyons and dry washes. I smiled with pride at her bravery and brains. Arango and Billy stared at her and then at each other as though she were crazy. Rafaela smiled too, hugging her, saying nothing.

"*Usted muy* brave, *señorita. Sí,* Lewis Clark *es su* blood. *Es su* right to take *su hermano. Muy bien. Mañana por la noche usted* take Lewis Clark. *Compañeros* help."

Sac shook her head. "But why can't we do it tonight? He's being whipped and worked to death. Let me get him tonight. I know I can."

"No, *señorita.* Rufus say, 'Cold and cakilatin'.' Use head. Plan escape. *Vaqueros,* they follow, they chase. Need one day to make horses ready. One day *por* rest. We go fast when *usted* have Lewis Clark. Plan hiding places, maybe fights. *Comprende?*"

She bowed her head and nodded. I could see the tears at the edge of her eyes.

"*Sí, comprendo.*"

I understood how she felt, but Yellow Boy was trying his best to be careful to get the boy out alive and make a clean getaway so none of us were hurt. My experience in trying to kill Jack Stone, who murdered my father, had taught me a hard lesson: the value of planning and patience against a tough enemy. Sac hadn't learned that lesson yet.

Yellow Boy laid out all the things we'd need the next day to make Sac's idea work, and we talked through our ideas about how and what to do. The moon was rising, casting sharply etched shadows in its soft, white light over the mountains when we went to our bedrolls. As usual, Yellow Boy slept up in the rocks to cover us if we were discovered. I took the first watch and told Sac to get all the sleep she could, because there wouldn't be much in the next few days. She was still awake, the moon, high and bright, when Billy took my place and I lay down beside her.

The sound of a shot reverberating off the cliffs, echoing down the canyons, and distant yells and screams at the *hacienda* jerked me out of a sound sleep. I grabbed for Little David. Across the glow from the nearly dead coals in the fire pit, Billy was on his knees. His revolver drawn and cocked, he was sweeping the camp in all directions. He nearly shot Arango, who ran into camp with his Winchester cocked. We would probably have killed each other there in the dark had the moon not been so bright.

"What the hell's goin' on down to the *hacienda,* Arango?" Billy slowly lowered the hammer of his revolver, straining to see anything in the dark shadows through the little clouds our breath formed in the cold air.

Arango shrugged his shoulders as he swept

the perimeter of our little camp with his rifle. *"No sé, señor."*

Seeing nothing to cause alarm, he put his rifle on safety and asked, *"Dónde están las mujeres?"*

I suddenly felt sick, knowing in my gut the cause for the uproar at the *hacienda.* Arango and Billy were quick to cock and point their weapons at a shadow that moved on the women's path. Yellow Boy appeared, his face grim in the stark light and shadow around us. "*Mujeres* go *por* Lewis Clark."

I ran up to the place where we'd watched the *hacienda.* It was lighted like they were holding a big *fiesta.* Every torch in the place was lit, and the dark figures and their shadows against the courtyard walls running about in the flickering light gave the place an appearance of an angry anthill. Yellow Boy stood beside me, surveying the *hacienda* courtyard, *vaquero* bunkhouse, and corrals a foot at a time with his telescope. Arango, chewing on an unlighted cigar, stood on my other side, his rifle in the crook of his right arm, his left hand holding Billy's shoulder. Billy stood beside him, gritting his teeth and stamping his foot as his rage ebbed and flowed. He mumbled under his breath. "Why'd that fool woman do that?

Now we's gonna have to cut us some more nuts."

Yellow Boy handed his telescope to me. As I began trying to find some sign of Sac and Rafaela, he spoke. "No see *mujeres. En hacienda.* We wait. *Sol* comes. See what Comacho do."

I couldn't find the women, either, but I saw men with rifles, watching in all directions, stretched out on the top of the *hacienda* walls. Although I couldn't see them in the dark, I was certain men were climbing up the cliff to the hidden shelf that overlooked the place. The corrals were empty, all the livestock moved into the barns where they could be guarded by a handful of men or let out to graze beyond the barbed wire. Even if we'd had a hundred fighting men, the place was practically impregnable. Yellow Boy was right. We could only wait and be patient. The only ally we had was Comacho's uncertainty about how many we were. If they tortured the women long enough, that ally was gone.

We went back to camp, got our blankets, and came back to watch and wait in the rocks. The hours dripped by, as the moon floated to rest just above the western mountains. The cold black of the hour before dawn covered our eyes and our hearts with worry and despair.

The dark, fuzzy gray in the east began to turn through morning shades of pink, red, purple, orange, and gossamer turquoise. Then we saw movement around the barns. Arango, using the telescope, watched for a few moments before he handed it to Yellow Boy and pointed toward the action. Without the telescope, I was still able to make out dark figures of men moving toward the big bare area in front of the *hacienda*. Some had rifles, some carried long poles, and it looked like some had picks and shovels, maybe even a set of posthole diggers. Yellow Boy stared through the telescope as they moved forward. He grunted as he handed the telescope to me and said, "No good."

When the group was within fifty yards of the front of the *hacienda* gates, the ones with the rifles made a rough semicircle around the men carrying the poles and digging tools. The diggers set to work digging two small deep holes about fifteen feet apart. Billy was gritting his teeth and mumbling again, slowly pounding a fist into an open hand. I handed the telescope to Arango, who sat watching poker-faced.

"What are they making?"

He shrugged his shoulders. *"Una horca?"*

I was incredulous. "A gallows? Sac and Rafaela didn't do anything except try to take back a relative."

Yellow Boy said, "*Sí, una horca. Pero,* no kill women. Torture first. After torture, maybe kill."

Billy was in a state of suspended animation, perfectly still. As he stared at them, his mouth hung open.

The men digging the holes worked fast. Soon two long poles were brought and slid into the holes, stood up straight, and dirt was tamped and packed down around them to hold them in place. They brought a ladder forward and tied a crosspiece across the top. Two nooses were thrown over the crosspiece and tied off, one to each of the support poles. With that done, the men with the rifles formed a circle with their backs to the men who built the gallows. Then the group moved as a unit toward the big gate in the *hacienda*'s front wall.

My instinct was to bring up Little David and begin shooting them all, but reason took hold. I tried to think without any emotion. It was apparent that our options were limited. If we started shooting when the women appeared, the Comacho men would kill them and be done with it.

I turned to Yellow Boy. "Why do they

torture and murder two women they can rape or work to death? That's *dinero* out of their pocket. No *comprendo.*"

Before he answered, Billy, who looked like he was just awakening from a dream, spoke up. "They's bait. The Comachos is after me, that's why. They'd just beat the hell out of Sac an' sell her to a whorehouse madam fer tryin' to steal their property, even if the slave is her little brother. But they done caught her with Rafaela. Rafaela's a slave who run off. She's a-gonna git a hard beatin' cause o' that. They's gonna hang 'em cause I cut ol' man Comacho's nuts off fcr whut he done to Rafaela. But first, they's gonna try an' use 'em to catch me. Bet ol' man Comacho's a sharpenin' a knife now to do a little nut cuttin' of his own 'fore he hangs me on that there *horca.* If'n I don't git down there rat now, them women's gonna suffer bad. I'll take as many of 'em with me as I can, boys, but that ol' bastard ain't gonna cut me while I'm a-breathin'. You boys is gonna hafta snatch 'em while we's a-goin' at it. Be seeing ya'll in hell."

Billy started to leave. Arango grabbed him by the arm and jerked him back. I was so stunned by what was happening, I was paralyzed. Yellow Boy, his eyes flashing, gave a little nod when Arango stopped Billy from

203

leaving. Arango spoke low, with a menace that would bring fear to any man's heart, "Listen, *Señor* Creek. *Usted* no save *las mujeres* by fighting and dying now. The Comachos kill them whether *usted* live or die. The Comachos must show the *peones* they cannot challenge the *patrón*. I know the Comacho kind. They're evil *hacendados*, just like the *hombre* who raped my sister. They torture *las mujeres* slowly so all *peones* learn *hacendado*'s power from their suffering. They know *usted* watch the suffering. They want *usted* to break and come to die. *Las mujeres*, they suffer today. *Es* hard to do *nada* now, *pero mujeres* live. Tonight *Señor* Yellow Boy, *usted*, Hombrecito, *y yo*, we free them. *Usted* seek revenge? Come back another day. *Comprende?*"

Billy's face became hard, unflinching, and his eyes narrowed to slits. He looked at Arango's hand holding his arm. Arango let it go, stepping back a little, calmly watching Billy's every move. Billy spoke through clenched teeth. "Ain't no woman gonna suffer 'cause 'o me, Arango. I'm settlin' with the Comachos now."

Arango's fist was faster than a striking rattlesnake. He hit Billy square on the point of his chin with a solid thud that sounded like a sledgehammer driving a fence post into hard ground. Billy's head snapped back. Staggering, he sagged to his knees, his eyes staring blankly.

Kneeling on one knee, Arango eased Billy down, rolled him over on his back, and studied his face for a moment. He dragged Billy around so his head was a little lower than his feet. Standing up, holding his hands to his waist, he said, "*Por favor, Señor* Hombrecito, find a little rope so we can tie his hands and feet until he thinks with his head again."

I looked toward Yellow Boy, who nodded, and then I ran to find the rope. We tied Billy so he was comfortable but couldn't go anywhere.

Arango squatted by Yellow Boy. "*Señor,* what we do, eh?"

Yellow Boy stared at the gallows. After a while, he said, "Night come. Arango *y* Hombrecito hide in front of *hacienda.*"

He pointed to a large depression in an arroyo, about a hundred yards off the main road, running by the main gate. "Leave *caballos en arroyo.* Hombrecito shoots torches on *horca.* Muchacho Amarillo *y* Billy take *mujeres y* Lewis Clark to *caballos en arroyo.* Bring *aquí pronto.* Eat, drink, rest, make ready to ride. *Vamos a ir a sierras* through El Paso Carretas *en un día,* maybe *dos.*"

Arango nodded. "*Bueno. Es muy* dangerous, *señor. Es uno o dos noches* enough
horas por mujeres rest?"

With the slightest trace of a smile, Yellow
Boy said, "*Sí. Muy* dangerous, *estas mujeres
muy* strong."

My guts were churning. It was one thing
to shoot at men from long range or even
close up with revolvers. It was quite another
to fight them up close with stealth and cun-
ning. If I made a mistake, I'd be killed. I
wasn't sure I was man enough to face
torture if we were caught, but I didn't want
to shame Yellow Boy.

Sitting against a rock after I'd tied his
hands and feet, Billy shook his head, trying
to make his eyes focus, his words slurred
and mumbled through the fog clearing in
his mind. "Arango, you son of a bitch, you
sucker-punched me."

Arango smiled. "*Sí, senor,* a good one?"

Billy rubbed his bruised chin with the
back of his hands. "Like a damn mule kick."

He relaxed against the rock, apparently
trying to let his throbbing head clear.

A bugle sounded, its notes harsh and grat-
ing like some demon screaming in pain. The
front gates of the *hacienda* opened. Men
with rifles stepped out, formed a semicircle
out from the gates, and waited, carefully

scanning the ground in front of them. Four figures in long black dresses, their heads covered with heavy, black lace *rebozos,* two carrying pieces of rope, two holding long sticks, slipped through the gate. Two women in bright white dresses, their hands tied in front, followed the black dresses. Rafaela and Sac always wore pants and shirts when they were with us. It was startling to see them in long dresses. Their heads were uncovered. Sac's brilliant red hair stood out like fire against her white dress. Rafaela usually kept her honey-blond hair rolled up in a twist under her old hat. I didn't realize how long and beautiful it was until I saw it reaching all the way to her waist, a shining cascade flowing over her shoulders and the back of her dress.

There was something peculiar about the black dresses. Yellow Boy stared at them with his telescope, grunted, and handed it to me. They were all taller than Sac or Rafaela, who were not small women. Sac was nearly as tall as I was. Those in black dresses held their sticks with short, powerful fingers. One even wore leather work gloves. I tried to see a face, but they were all hidden by the *rebozos.* I looked at Yellow Boy and frowned.

He smiled and said, "*Hombres!* See feet

and hands?"

I studied the shoes sticking out from under the dresses. *Cowboy boots!* I looked at their hands. They were big, powerful, and a couple of the figures had coarse, black hair on the back of their hands. I figured the whole charade was probably a trap to catch Billy or maybe to keep him from shooting them. I handed the telescope to Arango. He looked a few moments and nodded, smiling as he handed the telescope back to Yellow Boy.

An old fat man dressed in a fine black suit followed them out. He dragged Lewis Clark by his shirt collar with one hand and carried a bucket with the other. Lewis Clark squirmed and wiggled to get away, lunging toward his sister, but his captor held him tight. As soon as Lewis Clark and his captor were through the gate, it closed.

The men with rifles, forming a circle around the group, moved slowly and deliberately toward the gallows. Yellow Boy grunted, and again handed me the Big Eye as he leaned forward, a hunting wolf studying the herd, looking for the weakest member. "What *usted* see, Hombrecito?"

I felt sick and outraged when I saw Sac. Her right eye was nearly swollen shut, her lower lip was split, and there was a long, ugly bruise on the left side of her face. I'd seen that kind of damage before. She'd been pistol-whipped. Her bare shoulders were bruised and scratched like she'd been beaten with a stick. Still she walked with her chin up.

Rafaela's face was a puffy mess. It looked like she had been beaten by fists. Her shoulders showed long, red stripes that disappeared down her back under her dress. She walked like a queen between her captors.

I heard Arango mumble, *"Dios mío!"*

When the group reached the gallows, the fog had cleared from Billy's brain. He stood up, hopped to where we sat, and leaned over the rock's edge to see what was going on. He saw the two battered women in white and growled like a wounded animal. "Those bastards! I knew it! Arango, damn it, cut me loose!"

Arango looked Billy in the eye and shook his head. "No, señor. *Las mujeres* suffer today, we take them back tonight. We need *usted.* Be still and be quiet if *usted* want to save *su mujer.* Remember what I told you?"

Billy glared at Arango. "Yeah, yeah. I'm a-hearin' ya. I ain't goin' nowheres. Now cut me loose."

With his left hand, Arango pulled the long

knife from its sheath and cut Billy's ropes. He appeared ready with his right to draw his revolver and knock Billy unconscious again if need be, but Billy was calm, watching what happened below without flinching.

Two of the black dresses stopped about twenty feet from the gallows and stood unmoving, shoulder to shoulder, as the two others led Sac and Rafaela forward. At the gallows, the nooses were slipped around their necks. The ropes were stretched and tied off. There was just enough tension to take up the slack. Their feet were tied so they couldn't move, and their hands were tied to the rope around their feet so they couldn't raise their hands any higher than their waists. As long as they stood up straight, they wouldn't choke.

Lewis Clark's feet were tied far enough apart so he could take short steps if he wanted to walk, and his hands were tied in front to the rope around his feet so he couldn't raise them above his waist. The rope around his feet was tied to the piece that bound Sac's feet, so Lewis Clark had maybe seven or eight feet of play. They put the water bucket ten feet in front of the women so near, yet so far away. As soon as Lewis Clark saw the bucket, he headed for it, but he stopped with a little jerk when the rope between his and Sac's feet ran out. Sac spoke to him, trying to calm him and keep him from jerking her off her feet so her own weight strangled her. He came back and sat down beside her in the dust, waiting.

I was transfixed, but Yellow Boy shook me to action. "Hombrecito. Be ready. Shoot ropes with Shoots Today Kills Tomorrow if women choke. *Comprende?*"

I was already stretching out to a prone shooting position on our watching rock. Dropping the breech on Little David, I nodded. It was about two hundred yards to the gallows. Ordinarily I would have had to guess where the rope was, but the crosspiece was a good four feet above the women's heads. The sun shining on the white hemp and its four feet of straight length was something I could see and sight on without a telescope. I figured I could cut the ropes in maybe three or four shots, less than ten or fifteen seconds. That was fast enough to keep Sac and Rafaela from choking to death.

The old, fat man stepped up to the water bucket, looked toward the sun, and surveyed the mountains and foothills in front of him, but he never swung his gaze far enough around to look in our direction. He bellowed in a gravelly voice that echoed down the valley and bounced off the cliffs, "*Señor* Creek! We have our slave back and her *amiga*. We have your *mujer, señor.* Come and take your medicine for the evil *grande usted* bring *mi hermano.* Come take your medicine, and this beautiful slave suffers *no más.* Her *amiga* must be taught she cannot take *mi hermano*'s property, *pero, ella es* valuable *tambien* and suffers *no mucho.* We will not let her *hermano* kill her *por el agua. El sol es muy caliente,* and they are very thirsty. Don't fire on us, *señor,* or they die. Come *en una hora, señor, o las mujeres* suffer *mucho.*' He then led the group back toward the gate and disappeared inside the *hacienda,* leaving Sac, Rafaela, and Lewis Clark standing in the sun unable to slake their thirst with water only ten feet away.

13
THE DAY GOD WAS SILENT

When Billy didn't show up as old man Comacho's brother demanded, one of the men
in a black dress stepped through the gate
with one of those thin sticks. It was about
five feet long. Walking up to the gallows, he
stuck the stick in the sand. Stepping behind
Rafaela, he grabbed the back of her dress
and yanked. In one violent jerk, he tore it
all the way to her waist, exposing her back.
She staggered and almost hanged herself
trying to keep her balance. Her back already
showed ugly red welts.

Billy cursed in an insane rage. "Gawd
damn it! They already whupped her! The
sons of bitches! By damn, I'm gonna cut all
their nuts off!"

The man walked around to face her. He
yanked down the piece of dress left in front,
stripping her bare to the waist. Modesty
made her try to cover her breasts with her
upper arms, but the way her hands were

213

tied prevented it. I wanted to kill the man in the dress and even had my hand on the hammer to cock Little David when Yellow Boy put his hand firmly over mine and shook his head.

"Wait, Hombrecito, wait."

I looked at Billy. His face was a hard mask of hate, but he wasn't moving. Arango sat with a *cigarro* dangling from the corner of his mouth, his eyes narrowed and hard. The tormenter ignored Sac. We could just make out the sound of her voice speaking to Rafaela. Lewis Clark sat on the ground in the dirt next to Sac, staring up at what was happening.

Then the man walked behind Rafaela and pulled out a long, shiny skinning knife. Yellow Boy's jaw muscles rippled. He struggled to keep control. "If *hombre* cut Rafaela, *usted* kill. No wait."

The hammer was already pulled back on Little David and the set trigger pulled as I sighted on the middle of the man's chest, my finger cold and steady at the trigger, ready in an instant to cut him in two. He grabbed her beautiful, long, golden hair, jerked her head back, and cut it off at neck length. I felt Yellow Boy's hand on my hand again, telling me not to shoot.

Rafaela stood there, her chin up in defiance, and we heard Sac screaming profanities at him I thought were impossible to come from the mouth of a Mormon woman.

He sheathed his blade, stepped back and, pulling the stick out of the sand, whipped it up and down making it look like a long, wedge-shaped fan in his hand. We were too far away to hear much of anything coming from the gallows except the muted sound of Sac talking to Rafaela, but it didn't take much imagination to hear that limber stick whipping through the air as Rafaela steeled herself for the beating that was coming.

I started forming prayers in mind, "Please, God, don't let her suffer like this. Please, God, help her. Please, God, strike the bastard dead who's going to beat her. Help us, God. Help us save her."

Then the man stopped flexing the stick and waited. The gate cracked open. A gray-haired old man in a frock coat and big Panama hat slid through the opening. Wiggling through the gate, he looked like a snake coming out of its hole. I heard Billy snort as he grinned and said, "You're lookin' real good after yer operation, you ol' son of a bitch."

Old man Comacho bellowed toward the hills, "*Señor,* come forward! This *señorita* will be beaten until you come or she dies. It

215

will be a long, painful death, *señor. Por favor,* do not hurt her like this. It will be a shame to destroy such a tasty morsel of a woman. *Usted* must pay what *usted* owe me. Come now, and I will spare her!"

Billy grabbed for my rifle. "Le' me kill that ol' bastard."

Arango grabbed his arm and pulled him back. "No, *señor. Usted* do this, *usted* murder the *mujeres y muchacho.* Wait. Save both *señoritas y el muchacho. Es muy difícil. Comprende?*"

Billy stared at Arango for the space of two heartbeats, nodded, and relaxed. Arango let him go but kept a close eye on him.

When there was still no sign of Billy, Comacho and the Black Dress retreated behind the gate for a few minutes leaving Rafaela to stand in the bright sunlight exposed to every man staring at her from the gun slits and the top of the *hacienda* walls.

Soon the gate creaked open again, but only a Black Dress returned. He whipped the stick back and forth again, paused, stepped back, and casually swung the stick with one hand. We heard the sickening smack against Rafaela's back, but she stood straight and never made a sound. When Lewis Clark heard the impact of the stick, he looked up at Rafaela and started sobbing. I knew he had seen and heard that stick before. Wailing in terror, he wrapped his arms around Sac's knees, nearly knocking her off balance.

Sac spoke to him. After a few interminable moments, he quieted down, released her, and sat back in the dirt, crying. The stick swung again and again. I realized an expert was using it because there was no pattern to the timing of the blows. The intervals between some were long, making Rafaela stand trembling in the heat, anticipating a strike that didn't come, then being startled when it did. Sometimes, expecting to gather her strength after a blow, she was unable to brace herself because the next strike followed the previous one so quickly.

All through the beating, Sac screamed at the man in the black dress. Drops at first, and then little streamers of blood began appearing on the dress hanging in tatters about Rafaela's waist. Her knees slowly began to buckle, making the rope around her neck tighten. Still, she had not made a sound or cried out in pain.

What was happening seemed only to happen in dreams. It felt so surreal. I kept sighted on the rope, ready to shoot in an instant. I focused all my attention on those ropes, afraid that if I let my attention wander, I'd either kill her tormentor or vomit. As she sagged, the rope tightened, but then the beating stopped.

The man put down the stick, went to the water bucket, and slowly drank a dipperful. He carried the dipper back for Rafaela to drink, but when he offered it to her, she spat on him. He raised his hand to strike her, then slowly lowered his arm, threw the water away, and stalked back to the gate.

Rafaela managed to stand straight and stare off toward the mountains, never looking in our direction. The rope around her neck grew slack. Flies started to darken her back, but she never flinched. I'd never seen such courage and sheer willpower in anyone, man or woman. My heart swelled with great admiration for her. I hoped I'd have her courage when the tests in my life came.

Lewis Clark was thirsty and kept pointing at the water bucket. He even stood up and started walking toward it before Sac talked him back. I kept the rifle sighted on Sac's rope, uncertain how long she'd be able to keep Lewis Clark from bolting for a drink of water. I would have sold my soul to shoot that rope or somehow help them, but I believed Yellow Boy and Arango were right. If we wanted them back alive, we had to wait until dark.

Billy sat beside me staring and mumbling at Rafaela. "Ya got steel girl. Hang on now. We're a-comin'. You'n do it." The afternoon sun crawled across the sky, its arc casting brilliant golden light on the suffering of Sac, Rafaela, and Lewis Clark. Yellow Boy spent most of the afternoon studying the ground around the *hacienda* and gallows with his telescope. He, Billy, and Arango talked, but I heard little of the conversation. After a while, Billy saddled his horse and disappeared back up the trail toward the top of the ridge. Late in the afternoon, Arango began packing supplies, making ready to load the animals. Holding Little David ready to shoot, the muscles in my arms and back knotted and cramped, screaming for relief. The hot rock where I stretched out frying me every time I twitched. Unable to reach out and ease the suffering of the little boy and two women, I felt my hate for the Comachos growing and burning in my gut. I tasted the insane rage I knew Billy felt. Only the discipline I had learned from Yellow Boy and Rufus kept me from spiraling out of control.

When the sun neared the edge of the western mountains and the shadows were growing long in the orange and purple light, Yellow Boy brought me a canteen and some jerky and said, "Rest, Hombrecito. I watch *mujeres.*"

I sat up, placed Little David across my knees, and took what he offered, never taking my eyes off the figures under the gallows. My muscles felt as though they were frozen in place and might never work again. I could imagine how Sac and Rafaela must feel, having stood in one place under the fiery sun all day. I was just thankful it was the middle of the fall and not the middle of summer. If it had been summer, I don't think they'd have made it.

Yellow Boy sat, sighting down his rifle toward the ropes, and told me the plan. "Comachos make fire *grande* by Sac *y* Rafaela for light *en* night. Use fire to see Billy when he comes for Rafaela. Billy ride *en llano* so Comachos see him. Comachos send *vaqueros* after Billy. Billy ride por El Paso Carretas. *Vaqueros* chase Billy. Billy lose *vaqueros,* come back to *hacienda.* Help take back women *y muchacho. Comprende?*"

I nodded as I stretched the stiffness out of my back and arms. "*Sí, comprendo.* There'll still be many *vaqueros* in the *hacienda* after the others leave. The women will still be easy to see from the fire. We can't just walk in there and take them without all us of being under fire."

"*Sí,* Hombrecito. *Es verdad.*" Yellow Boy glanced off the Henry's sights toward me, his eyes narrowed, a hint of a smile at the corners of his mouth. "*Vaqueros en hacienda* no watch women when barn burn."

He pointed. About fifty yards out from the gallows was a tiny grove of four or five large *piñons,* growing close enough together that our horses could be hidden from the *hacienda,* especially in the dark when the only light was that from a distant fire.

"*Usted,* Arango, *y* Billy leave *caballos en piñons.* Crawl close to Sac *y* Rafaela. Stay *en* dark. Barn burns, all *hacienda,* even *muchachos,* fight fire. No watch *horca. Usted,* Arango, *y* Creek take *mujeres y* Lewis Clark. *Usted* cut ropes, cover Arango *y* Billy. Arango *y* Billy carry *mujeres. Usted* carry *muchacho.* Ride here. Give Sac *y* Rafaela *agua,* meat *y frioles, y* medicine Rufus used *por* cuts. Ride *en uno o dos días.*"

"*Bueno.* Then we ride for El Paso Púlpito?"

"No, Hombrecito, El Paso Carretas."

"But that's away from the direction of Rojo's camp, and the direction the *vaqueros* chase Billy. We'll run into them. They'll catch us!"

"No, Hombrecito. *Vaqueros* see barn fire from El Paso Carretas, forget Billy Creek,

221

ride *pronto por hacienda. Mañana,* Comacho send *vaqueros* out again. Comacho *es loco.* Thinks he must find Billy. *Vaqueros* follow Billy's trail. We follow *vaqueros.* Stay behind *vaquero* dust. No see us, no chase. Follow *vaqueros* over El Paso Carretas. *En* El Paso Carretas, hide where we stay before. Rest. Women *y muchacho* grow strong. *Vaqueros* no find Billy, ride back to *hacienda. En dos o tres días* we ride *por* Bavispe, follow trail down río back to Rojo."

He smiled, holding up his right forefinger, tapping his temple. "Apache think like Coyote. Apache trickster against enemies. No do what enemy think."

"Comprendo. Muy bien."

We sat watching as the shadows grew longer and the day began to cool. Suddenly there was a scramble of activity inside the *hacienda.* We saw thirty or forty *vaqueros* running for the barn. Yellow Boy grinned and pointed south toward a small hill beside the El Paso Carretas trail. Off in the distance was a tiny figure on an unmistakable spotted pony. It was Billy, big as you please. In a couple of minutes, a group of *vaqueros* came thundering out of the corral on their horses.

Billy stayed put, teasing them before turning and riding off in the dusk in a hard gallop toward El Paso Carretas. The *vaqueros,* racing toward Billy's hill from the *hacienda,* made a large, low-lying dust plume in the still, cool air. When they reached Billy's hill, the dust from his pinto was about a half-mile in front of them disappearing into the dark.

I slid off the boulder, stretched, and went to relieve myself. I hadn't gone all day, hadn't noticed a need to go. Now I was in pain. When I returned, I spoke with Arango. *"Señor, usted* have *los caballos* ready, *sí?"*

He tilted his hat back and nodded. "*Sí,* Hombrecito."

I noticed he was working on a gallows noose and that there was a finished one on the ground beside him and asked about them. He said, "*Por* Muchacho Amarillo. He asks *por* them."

I couldn't imagine why Yellow Boy wanted two nooses, especially if we were returning later to repay Comacho for the torture of Sac and Rafaela.

Night sounds of crickets and frogs down by the little creek running behind the *hacienda* were filling the evening, and bats fluttered around us, gorging on insects flying toward the creek. I climbed up on the boulder by Yellow Boy and saw the gallows

223

area lit by a large fire built near the women, just as he'd figured it would be.

14
RESCUE

We continued to watch the women for another hour. There was no moon yet, but the stars were out. Yellow Boy studied the *hacienda* walls for a while and then said, *"Vamonos."*

We tightened the cinches on our horses, mounted, and rode down the crevice from our camp to the little stream that ran behind the *hacienda*. Yellow Boy swung down a trail to get behind the *hacienda*. He had a torch ready to light and the nooses Arango had made him. After we crossed the stream, Arango and I headed for the *piñon* grove where we planned to hide the horses.

Within a quarter of a mile of the *piñon* grove, we dismounted and approached it on foot. As we picked our way out of an *arroyo* through cactus and brush, the light from the big bonfire grew brighter, the figures of the women black silhouettes against the fire.

I didn't see Lewis Clark moving around at all.

We were almost to the *piñon* grove when I heard a low, rasping whisper. "Howdy, boys. Whut took y'all so long?" I must have jumped ten inches off the ground, and Arango's revolver filled his hand faster than I could blink.

"Easy there, *compadres*. It's jest ol' Billy back from the chase a-waitin' fer ya."

Arango lowered the hammer on his revolver and holstered it slowly. *"Buenas noches, Señor Creek. Usted aquí pronto."*

Billy whispered out of the darkness. "Yeah, I know. But I's lucky an' found me a good cattle-made sneak-back trail. Them Comachos got 'em some fine-lookin' beef, Arango. We oughter come back an' take a few purdy soon . . . When's the fire at the barn a-comin'?"

Arango replied with some irritation, "Muchacho Amarillo *es en* barn now. Fire comes *pronto.*"

Billy nodded. "Okay, then, let's see if'n we'n get closer 'fore that barn goes up an' puts light all over the place."

We tied the horses and began working our way toward the *horca*. I kept my eye on Sac as we moved forward. The ground was sprinkled with patches of prickly pear cactus and covered with sandburs, so we duck-walked forward slowly.

We came within twenty-five yards of the gallows, stopping just outside the circle of firelight. The walls of the *hacienda* loomed dark and foreboding before us. My thighs were screaming to rest when we stopped and sat down in the darkness. We picked sandburs off our pants while we waited.

Sac's thick red hair, stiff from sweat, dirt, and blood, stuck out in every direction. I thanked God she had not been beaten as badly as Rafaela. Light from the fire occasionally flickered across Rafaela's bruised and battered face. Her breathing sounded raspy and irregular. I heard Billy mumble, "I'm a-gonna kill those bastards."

I was afraid Rafaela might faint before we could reach her and was reaching to cock Little David when Arango put his hand over mine and shook his head when I looked at him. He held up his cocked Colt and nodded toward Rafaela. I understood and relaxed a little. At that range, he could break the rope using his revolver, and he was ready.

A faint yellow glow appeared on the cliffs behind the back corner of the *hacienda*. I heard horses neighing and cattle beginning to bellow. There was yelling from inside the *hacienda* and the sound of doors flying open and slamming against walls. I started to rise and run toward the gallows, but Arango grabbed my arm and shook his head. He held up his forefinger in a sign that said, *Wait a minute.*

The chaos inside the *hacienda* grew. Then Billy was on his feet running for Rafaela. I was right behind him, and Arango was with me. The barn exploded in a roar of flame. Screaming horses and bellowing cattle broke through the corral fence, heading for the little stream behind the *hacienda.*

I passed Billy after we'd run ten yards. Rafaela slowly raised her head and saw me burst into the light. Her first instinct was to bring her forearms forward to try and cover her breasts. She lifted her eyes toward the stars, her mouth forming words I couldn't hear. I slashed her noose in one quick slice. She collapsed into Billy's arms as I kneeled and ran the blade through the rope holding her feet together and cut the piece tying her hands to her feet. Her back was a scabby piece of bloody meat. Billy put her over his shoulders and headed for the horses, swearing revenge with every breath.

The fire in the barn was a loud roar, and its flames looked like they reached halfway up the cliff behind the *hacienda.* Lewis

Clark was on his knees, trying to scream in his fright, but his mouth was so dry, all that came out was a guttural, animal sound. Arango cut the rope tying Lewis Clark to Sac. I was slashing at her noose when I heard her coarse, rasping whisper, "Thank you, dear God. Be still, Lewis Clark. They've come to help us."

I grabbed Lewis Clark with my left arm and held him as he struggled to hold on to Sac while I cut the rope from around her feet and hands.

Arango lifted her gently in his arms and ran for the horses. I had to tear Lewis Clark from her. He struggled against me, making those eerie animal-like sounds. I tried to calm him by holding him close to my chest and whispering comforting words in his ear, but he'd have none of it. He was reaching with both arms for Arango, so I put him down on the ground, held his hand, and let him run as fast as he could after her.

The burning barn was making so much light we were, no doubt, easy to see from the *hacienda,* but no shots were fired in our direction. I looked over my shoulder back toward the gallows just in time to see three figures emerging from the shadows. I thought they were chasing us, and was about to stop and take a shot, when I realized one of them was Yellow Boy. I kept running for the horses.

Billy was already climbing on his horse, Rafaela still over his shoulders. When he was mounted at the back of his saddle, he eased her around in front of him and backwards on his saddle, supporting her back just below where the stripes stopped. She was in shock and practically unconscious as she slumped forward on his chest. He charged down the trail back to camp.

I swung up on Midnight at the back of my saddle, and Arango handed Sac up to me. The cramps in her legs were terrible. She moved as if she were paralyzed from the waist down. Arango, mumbling apologies for appearing to take indecent liberties with her, helped her move her legs so she could straddle the saddle. Lewis Clark was out of breath but reaching his hands up to her. Arango looked at me, and I nodded. He lifted Lewis Clark and put him in the saddle in front of Sac. She wrapped her arms around him, and I slid my arms under hers. Lewis Clark appeared to relax and made no more noise. Arango handed me the reins, and we moved off at a fast trot for the camp trail.

By the time we reached camp, Billy had pants on Rafaela, and she was stretched out on her stomach on a large, flat rock near the water tank, a canteen in her hands, the torn, white dress under her. Billy was gently washing the dried blood off her back, whispering comfort to her. "Ye're gonna be okay, little woman. We're gonna git ya outta here."

Arango took Lewis Clark from the saddle and helped Sac climb off. She staggered, almost collapsing, but she held on to the saddle until she steadied. I slid off to run for a canteen. Arango helped her over to our bedroll, waited until I returned with the canteen, and then took his rifle and headed for the rocks where we'd watched the *hacienda* all day.

Sac knew not to drink too much too soon. She gave Lewis Clark a couple of small swallows, and then took some small sips herself. I couldn't help staring at her. Some bastard had used his fists on her. I swore to myself I'd come back with Billy to do some nut cuttin' of my own. She waited a bit, then took a couple of large swallows, and gave more to Lewis Clark.

She looked up at me with tears streaming down her swollen cheeks. "I knew you'd come for us . . . I was hurtin' so bad . . . my legs feel like they're dead. I can barely tell if they're attached to my body. I'm so sorry I caused so much trouble . . . I just had to get Lewis Clark outta there."

I can imagine the expression that was on my face as she asked, "Do I look that bad, Henry?"

"Yes, ma'am, you do. Those bastards beat the hell out of you. Rest here and drink some more water, but take it slow. I've got to build up the fire and boil some water to make poultices for you and Rafaela. If you've got the strength, try to rub some circulation back into your legs." She nodded, and, gritting her teeth, began to massage her legs.

Lewis Clark crawled up next to her and lay down. She said, "Please get me some hot water so I can wash Lewis Clark and myself."

I put two pots over the fire, one for heating wash water and one for making poultices. I made the poultice out of the same weed and other herbs Rufus had used for the gash on my face after Yellow Boy found me. Though it smelled like fresh cow manure, it was very potent in stopping infection and helping wounds heal fast.

I brought Sac a bucket of hot water. She was out of her dress, sitting in her pantaloons, mashing and rubbing the circulation back into her legs. "Can I help you with your legs? There's a poultice coming *pronto* for that ugly bruise on your jaw."

She managed a smile with her swollen lips that made me glad I was alive. "I think my legs will be okay. They feel like they're being stuck with hundreds of pins and needles. I think that means the blood's starting to flow. The swelling's way down. I'll be able to walk in a little bit. I'll clean us up, and then you can apply the poultice. Thank you, Henry."

"I'm just glad we were able to get you out of there. I'll be with Rafaela or Arango if you need me."

While Billy massaged feeling back into Rafaela's legs, I tore long strips off her dress and wrapped them around the poultice on her back. Billy slipped a shirt over it to keep her warm and protect her modesty, and eased her over to her bedroll so she could sleep.

I joined Arango, who was watching the *hacienda*. The barn was a mass of glowing coals. Black silhouettes moved about, throwing buckets of water here and there, creating short puffs of steam where little flames once sputtered. No horses or cattle were in the corral, probably having escaped through the gaping hole in the fence next to where the barn once stood. I glanced at the gallows and did a double take. Two figures stood under it, just like Sac and Rafaela. I saw in the bonfire's dying light that they both wore white dresses, and the one standing in Rafaela's place was stripped to the waist! Arango looked at the surprise on my face and grinned. "Muchacho Amarillo *es un* trickster *grande, eh,* Hombrecito? *Señor* Comacho *no comprende estas mujeres no son* Sac y Rafaela *hast el sol.*"

I was trying to figure out how he had done it when I felt his hand on my shoulder. As usual, I hadn't heard him coming. "Sac *y* Rafaela? Lewis Clark?" he asked.

"I'm no doctor, but I think they'll be all right. Their legs are swollen and cramping pretty bad, but Sac says she's starting to get some feeling back in hers. I made them poultices. Rafaela's sleeping. I think Sac just needs rest and the blood moving in her legs more than anything else. Of course, Rafaela is a lot worse off than Sac, and Billy won't leave her. Lewis Clark sleeps."

"*Bueno.* Rest until we ride for El Paso Carretas."

The sun was a red ball on the horizon as the morning came to the Comacho *hacienda.* A pall of white smoke hung up against the cliff, shrouding the *hacienda* in patches

234

of gray to white fog. Small, slowly drifting, translucent windows in the cloud showed men, women, and children hurrying between the *hacienda* and outbuildings. Cattle and horses that escaped from the burning barn or adjoining corral wandered in and out of view. Riders came in off the *llano* and then left a short time later. Three *vaqueros* pounded out of the smoky fog, heading down the road toward Janos. They soon disappeared in the distant haze.

Cold air began rolling off the mountains and soon blew away the smoke to reveal the organized chaos below us. The once-beautiful white barn smoldered in ugly, black ashes and a skeleton of partially burnt timbers, but none of the other outbuildings had burned. Cows and horses were being herded into other corrals. A large crew of peons soon appeared and began clearing the remains of the burnt barn. Others emerged from a couple of the large outbuildings with wagonloads of lumber they unloaded close by the smoldering ruins. The efficiency with which the place ran was truly remarkable.

Riders we'd seen leave as the sun rose began drifting back and were followed by five to ten other riders. By nightfall, there were well over a hundred heavily armed *vaqueros* lounging around the *hacienda.* Billy, who had stayed by Rafaela's side all day and helped me change her poultices a couple of times, wandered over to the boulders where Yellow Boy, Arango, and I watched.

"How's Rafaela doing, Billy?"

He nodded and puffed his cheeks with a silent whistle of relief. "She's a whole lot better. Her back's already startin' to heal up, an' it don't bleed no more when she gits up to go down the women's trail. Them laigs of hers held up real good. Her face is kinda yaller an' purple from them bruises where they beat her, but your poultices is a-doin' real good to make her better, even on the sunburn. Says she'n ride tomorry. I believe her, but it ain't gonna be easy. Ye're a good doctor, Hombrecito. How's Sac?"

"She's better. She could ride now if she had to. She just wants to sleep all the time. Probably the best thing they can do until we ride."

A big grin spread over his face as Billy watched what was going on below. "Reckin the ol' bastard thinks I burned th' barn, too. He's a-gonna be outta his mind to catch me now. Looks like he's a-gatherin' his whole bunch to go after me. Muchacho Amarillo, reckin I oughter saddle up an' give 'em a

236

little look down there toward the south to-morry mornin'?" Yellow Boy nodded and smiled.

The next dawn, Billy saddled his horse and was ready to ride out when Yellow Boy told him to wait. Something strange was going on at the *hacienda*. Nothing was happening with the small army of *vaqueros* Comacho called in from his herds. The men appeared to be having breakfast and doing a few chores, but none of them were getting ready to ride. The peons, working on clearing the burned barn and rebuilding it, had already set some poles in the ground where burnt ones once stood. We waited. Every hour we delayed, Sac, Rafaela, and Lewis Clark grew stronger.

15
ESCAPE TO EL PASO CARRETAS

Just before dark, a rider, a soldier on a horse about to drop, rode up to the *hacienda* gates and was let in. Nodding his head, Arango studied him with Yellow Boy's telescope. *"Señor* Comacho sends for the army. They come. *Uno o dos días."*

Yellow Boy and Arango talked for a while before calling Billy and me to join them. Yellow Boy decided it was best to keep the army contingent away from the *vaquero* posse, but to keep them all going in the same direction. If they organized and began searching the mountains north to south, there was no telling how much harm they might do to Apache camps like Rojo's.

Yellow Boy's idea was to have Billy tease the *vaqueros* into starting the chase south before the army arrived. We were taking a risk trying to ride between the two groups, but he thought we'd be safe enough just following in the *vaqueros'* dust through El

238

Paso Carretas and then dropping off to hide where we'd camped earlier in the pass. We'd just wait for the army to pass and then follow them south, staying behind their dust before turning north. That way we'd have some idea of what they were doing so we could warn the Apache camps scattered in the northern Sierra Madre.

Billy left before dawn the next day. We watched and studied the *hacienda* through most of the early morning. The *vaqueros* continued to lounge about, as though resting up for what they knew was going to be a long, hard chase. Billy suddenly appeared from behind a low ridge on the El Paso Carretas road, no more than a mile from the *hacienda*. I was watching the guards on the *hacienda* walls. One pointed toward Billy and yelled at the others. The men up on the *hacienda* walls took three or four shots that fell far short of Billy, who turned and rode out of sight at a fast gallop toward the pass. There was a mad scramble at the *hacienda* as the *vaqueros* found their horses and made ready to ride.

Yellow Boy watched all this with his arms crossed and smiling. Nodding slowly, he said, *"Bueno."*

An old gray-haired man who wore a big pistol and rode a silver-trimmed saddle on

239

a great, golden high-stepping palomino stopped the *vaqueros'* rush and made sure the men had their supplies and their pack animals carried sufficient water. They left, organized and ready for a long chase. With their delay, they weren't gone more than an hour before Billy returned at midday after doubling back from the trail he laid for them toward El Paso Carretas.

We were ready to ride. Rafaela was still too weak to sit on a horse by herself, so Arango and I lifted her to sit in front of Billy again. Sac climbed on her horse with only a little help from me, and Lewis Clark wouldn't ride with anyone but her. Yellow Boy led the way, and Arango brought up the rear.

We followed Billy's sneak-back trail, staying far off the main trail to the pass. We rode at a slow pace, making steady progress. Yellow Boy kept stopping in clear spots in the bushes along the trail, where he had a clear line of sight with his telescope up and down the road running from El Paso Carretas to Janos.

As the *hacienda* disappeared in the lazy, blue haze, I heard Billy mumble under his breath, "Don't ya'll worry none, *muchachos.* I'm a-gonna be back one of these days an' settle up with ya."

Rafaela actually seemed to get stronger as we rode. The poultice had done wonders for her back. She was alert, and she stayed in the saddle without complaining. The poultices on their faces made Sac and Rafaela look like mud-caked specters from a bad dream. Lewis Clark, for the most part, rode sleeping against Sac.

Billy's sneak-back trail paralleled the main road, but it was high up on the ridges, hiding us from the view of anyone on the road. Nearing the entrance to El Paso Carretas, the trail dropped off the last ridge, ending in the junipers and *piñons* close to the road. We made a slow, careful ride off the last ridge down toward the pass, watching the trail for potential ambushes or small groups of *vaqueros* that might have split off the main bunch to search side trails. Along the way, Yellow Boy stopped often to use his telescope. In the distant haze, a dust cloud was growing on the Janos road. Wanting to give the women and Lewis Clark a short rest before the long, hard ride up the pass, we stopped at a grassy spot surrounded by juniper bushes about a hundred yards off the main road.

As the sun dropped toward the ridgeline, the ground started cooling under long mountain shadows. Frowning, Yellow Boy stared at the dust cloud. Collapsing the telescope tube, he stuck his knife in the ground, put his ear against the handle butt, and suddenly jerked his head up. *"Muchos caballos* come, *pronto!"*

We tightened our saddle and pack-frame cinches, readying for a fast ride up through El Paso Carretas. Rafaela, her shoulders hunched over in pain, leaned against Billy's horse, holding on to its mane. Sweat covered her forehead, and her hands were trembling. She whispered in a raspy voice through swollen lips, "Stron' 'nuf. I'n ride okay. Go on. Saddle up fer me. I'n do it."

Billy opened his mouth to argue but, apparently seeing a determined look in her eyes, he turned away to begin saddling her horse.

A quail called from somewhere up on the other side of the trail. Yellow Boy froze, his ear cocked in that direction. Another quail on our side answered the first one. Farther up the trail another one called, and then another still higher up. I'd never heard quail calling to each other like that.

Arango pulled his pistol and cocked it, glaring up the trail disappearing into the pass. Billy left Rafaela standing beside her horse, pulling his carbine from its rifle scabbard. I told Sac and Lewis Clark to be quiet and stay by their horse, ready to ride. I took Little David out of its saddle case. Dropping the breech, I slid a shell into the chamber. Yellow Boy motioned to us as he stared up the trail into the pass and listened.

Billy squinted at Yellow Boy's poker face and asked, "What's goin' on?"

Yellow Boy knocked his fists together. "Many army riders come from Janos. Ride to help *vaqueros*. Quail signal *es* Apache. Elias *y* Juan *hombres* wait in pass. They plan ambush."

We were caught between the army, the Apaches, and, if they returned, perhaps the *vaqueros*. But we had two aces: Yellow Boy's quick mind and knowledge of guerrilla tactics, and the fact that neither the army nor the *vaqueros* knew the Apaches were in the pass. He dropped to one knee, and with his knife, he started sketching a map in the sandy dirt.

"Army come, Janos road. El Paso Carretas, *aquí*. Elias *y* Juan *aquí*. We *aquí*. *Vaqueros en San Miguel o en paso aquí. Vaqueros* look for Billy. First shot, *vaqueros* maybe come."

I said, "It seems the best thing we can do is just backtrack to El Paso Púlpito and leave Elias and Juan to sneak out of the way of the *vaqueros* and army." Arango and Billy

243

nodded.

Yellow Boy shook his head, grinning with his Coyote trickster look. "No. Elias *y* Juan watch *hacienda* from *sierras.* Know we take Lewis Clark, burn barn. Elias plan ambush this night for us, *no sé* army come."

His eyes became narrow slits of anger as he drew his rough brown forefinger across his throat in a slashing motion. "Elias *y* Juan think they ambush Muchacho Amarillo *y compañeros.* Send to land of the grandfathers. Take Lewis Clark *y mujeres.*"

Looking back up toward the pass, he nodded. *"Ahora,* Muchacho Amarillo *y compañeros* pay Elias *por* war against us. Pay *muy bien, sí?"*

We all nodded. He scratched a line in the dust that ran north, parallel to the mountains from the pass trail. "Hombrecito takes women *y* mule to El Paso Púlpito. Hombrecito *no sé* trail through mountains from El Paso Púlpito *a* Rojo camp. Hombrecito goes on across El Paso Púlpito to *Río Bavispe. En* Bavispe Valley *es* trail Muchacho Amarillo followed from Rojo camp to *Río San Bernardino.* Find and use trail back to Rojo camp, Hombrecito?" I nodded, swallowing back disappointment that I was asked to look after the women rather than fight Elias and Juan.

Yellow Boy turned to his map in the dust. "Muchacho Amarillo, Arango, *y* Creek stay *aquí* close by Elias ambush. Shoot at army. Army shoot back *y* charge ambush. Too many *hombres por* Elias *y* Juan *hombres* to fight. They run! Ride *por* Bavispe through El Paso Carretas. Maybe *vaqueros* hear guns, come down pass *pronto.* Maybe Elias *y* Juan caught between *vaqueros y* army.

"Up *en paso uno* place *bueno* to hide — where we camp. *Es* Elias's only chance. Fight *en paso es muy difícil.* Many Elias *hombres* die if find no hiding place *en paso.* After army ride *en paso,* Muchacho Amarillo *y compañeros* follow Hombrecito *a* El Paso Púlpito, take trail across *sierras* to Rojo camp. Make Rojo camp *en dos o tres días.* Hombrecito, Sac, Rafaela, *y muchacho en* Rojos's camp *cinco o seis dias.* Comprende?"

We all nodded. It was a clever strategy. "How will I know El Paso Púlpito?" I asked.

Yellow Boy turned to his map in the dust once more. "Ride *norte.* Stay close to *sierras.* Ride slow. *Hombres* no see, *y* women get stronger. Trail crosses wagon road *grande.* Wagon road goes down wide canyon with cliffs *muy grande.* Deep *en* canyon see notch, El Paso Púlpito *en sierras* to south. No stay on road through canyon.

245

Many *hombres* ride El Paso Púlpito. Many ridges lead off wagon road. Take fourth one. Find trail Apaches *y* Yaquis ride many times. Follow toward notch *en sierras. Río Bavispe en* valley below notch. Follow *Río Bavispe norte a* Colonia Morelos *y Río San Bernardino.* Follow San Bernardino, find trail out of *sierras* we use from Rojo's camp. Ride toward *sol en* east until *usted* cross *Río Bonito. Comprende?*"

"Sí, comprendo." My heart was beating in my throat. I was scared, but I didn't dare show it. It was a big responsibility to get the women and Lewis Clark out of there without being caught or getting us all killed. Yellow Boy, Arango, and Billy could take care of themselves in a close fight. I knew I was still green when it came to that kind of fighting, and I was the best choice to take care of the women and little boy. Still, if I'd had a choice, I'd have taken my chances triggering the army's attack on the ambush rather than the responsibility for the lives of two beat-up women and a child.

"Go now. Army comes *pronto.*"

Yellow Boy looked in my eyes and put his rough hand on my shoulder with an easy comrade's squeeze. *"Buena suerte,* Hombrecito. *No en* Rojo's *camp en cinco días,*

Muchacho Amarillo finds. *Adiós.*"

Billy and Arango came up to shake hands with me and wish me luck. Billy's eyes sparkled with excitement, but he was concerned about Rafaela. "Rafaela's back's in bad shape an' I'm thinkin' she ain't gonna sit a horse by herself fer long. You gonna let her ride with you like she did with me? Can Sac take keer of herself an' the boy, too, if'n you do?"

I nodded. "Don't worry, we're going to be okay. I promise to take good care of her for you."

I could see Billy's teeth gleaming in the low light. "*Muchas gracias,* Hombrecito. I know ya can. I'll owe ya when we get back to Rojo's."

Arango smiled and clasped my shoulder. "*Buena suerte,* Hombrecito. *Adiós.*"

I nodded, knowing Arango and Billy were true friends. "Good luck yourself, *amigo.*"

Rafaela was a little shaky getting in the saddle, but when I asked if she wanted to ride with me, she shook her head. I helped Sac mount and handed Lewis Clark up to her. I swung up on Midnight and took the lead line for Elmer. The last glory of the day was shining on the tall, thin *llano* grass, the mesquites, creosotes, and junipers scattered about in the late afternoon haze, cast-

247

ing long shadows. We waved goodbye to our friends and started the climb back up the ridge covered in the long, cool mountain shadows.

When we got to the top of the ridge trail, there was still enough light to see the road below. The army horsemen were less than half a mile from Yellow Boy, Billy, and Arango, who were hiding in the junipers, dark in shadows stretching off the mountains. We stopped to watch.

When the lead riders were five or six hundred yards from Yellow Boy, there was a bright flash from the junipers and, two or three seconds later the distinctive cracking boom of Yellow Boy's Henry came rolling over us as it swept on up the ridge to come back an echo from the dark cliffs. One of the troopers in the lead pitched off his horse backwards, and the animal, a beautiful roan, reared up, neighing, and ran off into the dusky *llano.*

Almost at the same instant, two more flashes, their thunder rolling up our ridge, came from other spots in the dark juniper bushes, but these shots fell far short of the front of the column. The soldiers, who were well-trained and disciplined, immediately followed their *comandante,* racing their mounts in a broad sweeping circle of retreat out into the *llano* and back toward the road to face the pass. We held our breath, praying we had guessed correctly that they'd charge the pass.

The column leaders wound up a couple of hundred yards back from where the soldier lay in the dust. With a couple more arm-waving signals from the *comandante,* the column formed into four long rows symmetrically straddling the road, stretching into the *llano* in one direction and toward the ridge where we sat in the other. I breathed a sigh of relief. They were preparing to charge.

The *comandante* reined his prancing horse to the east side of the road in front of the first row of troops. He drew his saber and held it vertically, its point resting on his shoulder. They waited! I began to worry that we had guessed wrong about the army charging the pass.

Then the *comandante* barked orders, the sound of his voice indistinct, far away. A stripped-down wagon pulled by four horses plunged down the road, and short sections of the trooper rows broke open to let them pass, closing like a gate behind them when they were through the line. The wagon carried some kind of cannon. It looked as if it were made from a big brass tube that had a series of holes in one end and a hand crank on the other.

Rafaela looked at me, her eyes wide with misgiving, her bruised, swollen lips trembling. "Wa's thet, Homr'ito?"

I shook my head, mystified as she was. The wagon made a loop within a hundred yards of the soldier's body lying in the road and stopped with its tailgate pointed toward the juniper bushes at the beginning of the pass. The driver and another soldier crawled off the seat and onto the wagon bed, where they fiddled with the cannon for a minute, sticking a long, black bar into its top. They turned to salute the *comandante.*

The *comandante* held up his sword as high as he could reach and shouted, *"Disparar, fire!"*

The two soldiers pointed the cannon toward the dark junipers and began turning a crank attached to a mechanism holding the long, black bar in the middle of the brass barrel. The holes in the end of the cannon tube were actually barrels that rotated around the tube's center when the crank turned. One soldier turned the crank, while the other aimed it. It fired at a rate I'd never have believed possible from a single gun if I hadn't seen it. The deafening thunder from the shots rolled up the ridge and stayed there, pounding on us. Long flames spewing from the barrels made it look like a roaring blowtorch from hell. Pieces of juniper bushes went flying, *piñon* trees were cut down, and bullets hitting the ground created a thick dust cloud in the junipers. Lewis Clark started crying. Our horses began jerking around, nervous and uncertain. Old Elmer just stood his ground, nibbling on grass beside the trail. Sac was having a hard time trying to hold her horse and comfort Lewis Clark. Rafaela, shaking her head, had her hands over her ears. I'd never imagined such a weapon and froze in disbelief.

A voice rang in my head. *Yellow Boy! Billy! Arango!* Those soldiers were trying to kill our friends with that gun from hell! I tossed my reins to Rafaela and was off Midnight in an instant with Little David. I ran to a boulder on the edge of the trail where I could steady my shot. The light was low, and it was a very long shot, but I had to do something. The gun crew stopped to reload just as I pulled the set trigger and centered the crosshairs in a large aperture pinhole on the man turning the crank. I didn't hesitate to shoot. The gunner's head disappeared in black spray as the roar from the old thunder stick hit the rows of soldiers and their co-

mandante. The body of the man I'd shot flopped over the gun's barrel. There was a moment of stunned silence.

The second gunner looked at the bloody mess that was once his partner and jumped down under the wagon. I tried to hit the *co-mandante,* but his horse was prancing around and I missed. The *comandante* never left his position. Two more men whipped their horses forward in a race for the gun. One of the soldiers in the third row was shouting to the *comandante,* pointing toward the ridge in our general direction. I knew our cover in the dark mountain shadow and *piñon* trees along the sneak-back trail was a perfect background against which to see the fire from Little David. Some of the soldier's threw up their rifles and took a few shots, but they never came within a hundred yards of us. With the *co-mandante* shouting encouragement, the two new gunners threw the dead soldier's body off the barrel, finished reloading the gun, swung it in our general direction, and began raking the side of the ridge. Again dust and gravel went flying, pieces of juniper and *piñon* cartwheeling through the air. Fortunately, the gun was pointed way too low, raking its line of fire across the ridge far below us.

I sighted on the gunner turning the crank again, but the light was so poor I didn't get a good sight picture. It seemed a lifetime passed in the roar of that terrible weapon while I tried to shoot our attacker. The cannon cartridge clip finally emptied. As the crew scrambled to load a new one, fire came from three different spots in the junipers on the far side of the road, farther out in the *llano,* but it was far short of the awful gun.

A yell of courage and outrage roared out of the junipers. A brown-and-white pinto raced toward the soldiers. Billy rode, leaning alongside the pinto's neck, firing his carbine. He howled like a banshee in its death throes; his targets, the men sitting in neat rows, their horses jerking their heads, prancing about in fear. We saw flashes of fire from his carbine throwing bullets that raised puffs of dust closer and closer to the gun carriage. His shots, stepping closer and closer toward his intended victims, would make any normal man want to run. I took another shot at the gunners to hold their attention; it ricocheted off a steel box in the wagon bed, making all three gunners hide under the wagon.

The *comandante* barked more orders. The troopers' rifles came up, and, with calm precision, their bullets filled the air around

253

Billy. One hit Billy, and he jerked back as his carbine flew out of his hand and spiraled behind him. The pinto went down with Billy still in the saddle. Neither got up.

Rafaela mumbled, sobbing, "No, Billy. No, Billy." She watched, shaking her head, putting her hands to the poultice on her swollen face as the tears flowed over it, and I felt a sadness in my soul I hadn't known since Rufus died.

Sac stared unbelieving at the scene below and, holding Lewis Clark close, tried to comfort him. He clung to her as though she were the last refuge on earth.

The *comandante* threw his sword hand forward and yelled the word I desperately wanted to hear during those moments in the dusk that lasted forever: "*Carga!* Charge!" At last, the soldiers charged toward El Paso Carretas. I spat on the ground, cursing Elias and Juan, hoping the army charge drove them against the *vaqueros* and wiped them out.

16
El Paso Púlpito

Mounting Midnight, I rode to Rafaela and took her hand in mine. "*Señora, por favor,* I'm so sorry about Billy. He was a very brave man and my *amigo.* I wish we could find him and bury him as he deserves, but if we're going to escape the army and the *vaqueros,* we need to ride now. Can you do it?"

She snuffled back her tears and said, "*Sí,* Hombrecito. Don' go a-worryin' none 'bout me. I'n carry my share o' th' load. We'n go on now."

I looked at Sac. She nodded she was ready. I stayed in front leading Elmer. Sac and Lewis Clark rode in the middle, and Rafaela covered the back trail.

Later, it was black as pitch up high on the ridges, making me take it slow and easy. Off in the distance, we heard sporadic gunfire coming from El Paso Carretas. When the moon rose over the northeastern horizon, we eased our way along faster. After two or three hours of steady riding, I stopped to rest the animals at a spring dribbling out of some rocks into a small pool we'd passed earlier in the day. Rafaela was weak but managed to stay in the saddle and wouldn't let me help her. She and Sac disappeared off into some bushes and left me alone with Lewis Clark.

He walked up as I gave the animals water and grain. Pausing to watch me for a moment, he stuck out his hand. "Howdy, mister. I'm Lewis Clark Langeford. Are you a Indian?"

I shook his hand. "No, I'm not an Indian, but my friend is. My name is Henry Grace or, as some folks like to call me, Hombrecito. We're mighty glad to get you back, Lewis Clark. Your sister's been very worried about you. You had a hard time there for a while, didn't you?"

"Yes, sir, I did. Them Indians killed my daddy and run off with me. They didn't like it when I cried. They beat me good when I did an' give me to some Mexicans. I thought maybe they was going to give me back to Sac." He curled his lower lip down as if he were going to cry, but he didn't. "Then some old women in black dresses made me carry water all day to the kitchen, an' they whipped me more than the Indians did. I didn't like the Indians, but them Mexicans was really mean. They's worse than the Indians."

I nodded and laid my hand on his shoulder. "I saw what they were doing to you. We were trying to think of a way to get you away from the Mexicans when your sister and Rafaela tried to steal you away from them. How'd they get caught?"

As he told me in his childlike way every detail of what had happened after Sac and Rafaela were caught, my fury at Comacho grew. I was tempted to ride down to the *hacienda* and settle accounts right then. Only the memory of Rufus's words kept my fury under control.

Sac came back with Rafaela's arm over her shoulders and supporting her with an arm around her waist. Rafaela appeared weaker. I left them to find a spot to do my business. When I returned, they were all greedily eating jerky Sac had found in Elmer's pack. I let them rest for an hour or so, hoping Rafaela's strength might return.

When we were getting ready to leave, I gave her my hand and tried to pull her to her feet. Her forehead broke out in a sweat, and she stood, swaying, almost fainting. Sac jumped up, helping me ease her back down.

I said, "*Señorita,* you're going to ride with Midnight and me."

She nodded. Sac helped me get her to Midnight. She decided she could stand the pain of her back against my front and that she could stay in the saddle with me behind her. Sac and I helped her mount. She bent over the pommel, gritting her teeth and gasping for breath. Midnight stood steady, her ears back, until I swung up behind her. Sac handed me Midnight's reins. Then she mounted her horse and pulled Lewis Clark up in front of her, and we were off again.

When the moon was halfway to the front side of morning, I saw what looked like a piece of long, white hemp rope snaking its way from out across the *llano* and into the shadows of a canyon in the foothills in front of us. Off to the left, I saw what appeared to be the beginnings of a notch in the dark mountain ridgeline. The white rope off in the distance had to be the road to El Paso Púlpito. I knew that by the time we reached the road, it would be nearly daylight.

We needed to rest before riding across the pass and down El Paso Púlpito canyon to the Bavispe River. I figured if we took the road during the day, we'd make good time but pay for it by being exposed for at least an hour or two. If someone saw our little band of double riders and reported it, the *Rurales* or the army were likely to come looking for us, especially after the attack on the Comachos. We had to avoid being seen. If the canyon was as wide as Yellow Boy said it was, I thought I might find a trail through the *piñons* paralleling the main trail.

Dawn came in a rush of soft, orange fire in the east, and the morning light found us still in the saddle. I tried to keep hidden from the road as we came down off the last ridge. We stopped in a thicket of *piñons* that concealed us well from travelers heading for El Paso Púlpito. I told the others to climb down and rest while I scouted up the canyon. We made a place for Rafaela to lie down with Lewis Clark beside her, and Sac said she'd keep watch while I was gone.

Yellow Boy was right. It was a wide canyon bounded by high cliff walls. I scanned the entrance, looking for signs of another trail that paralleled the main one but didn't see any. Looking both ways, to be sure there was no one on the trail, I rode into the canyon and found its bottom covered with scattered junipers on both sides of the road all the way over to the canyon's dark brown cliffs.

Down the main trail about a quarter of a mile, there was a small wash in the southside cliffs running out to the main trail. At that point, it was a good seventy-five yards from the road over to the cliffs. I rode up the wash toward the cliffs, and within twenty yards, I found what I was looking for. A narrow game trail snaked off through the brush running right between the southern side cliffs and the main road. I followed it for several hundred yards and never saw the main trail. What luck! We couldn't have asked for more.

I rode back to Sac and Rafaela. "You ladies and Lewis Clark rest for a while. I'll keep a lookout. We'll head up the pass after the sun passes midday."

Rafaela seemed to be getting stronger. She said, "That's real good, Hombrecito. I'm a-gonna sleep fer a while an' then maybe I'n ride again by myself."

Sac nodded, smiling. She and Lewis Clark yawned and stretched out on a blanket under a juniper. I was concerned that Lewis Clark might be a handful to keep quiet or that he might wander off. But he rarely made any sound at all and didn't leave Sac's side.

About ten yards from where the women and Lewis Clark were napping, there were clear lines of sight in both directions along the main trail. I found a slab of rock I could sit against with Little David across my knees so I could watch the road. I hadn't been there long and was fighting sleep when I spotted a small, white cloud on the road off to the east. It was bigger than several men might make, or, for that matter, even a small herd of cattle. I watched as it grew closer and larger. I couldn't imagine what might be causing it.

The cloud stopped getting nearer and disappeared. The uncertainty of what to do squeezed my gut as I tried to decide whether to run on or to stay where we were. I decided to wait it out so Rafaela had more time to rest.

When the sun's path began arcing toward the west, the dust cloud reappeared closer, its plume moving toward us. I eased down the slope to the women. Sac jerked awake and stared at me wide-eyed when I touched her shoulder. I put a finger to my lips and shook my head. I leaned down and whispered, "It's all right. Something's coming down the road. Just keep still. They'll never see us. I want whatever it is to be in front of us, so we'll wait to move until it passes. Just keep Lewis Clark and Rafaela still, and we'll be fine."

She nodded and lay back, glancing over at Rafaela who slept on her stomach, her head on her arms. She was so still I thought she might be in a coma. Sac mouthed, "I'll tell her when she wakes up." I gave her a shake of my fist in thanks and eased back up to my spot looking down the dirt road snaking off into the blue haze.

A line of uniformed men on horses followed by several wagons and a herd of cattle appeared. Another army patrol! It was a large one. My mouth was so dry it was hard to swallow. If they had scouts out in front of them, we were likely to be found. It wasn't long before I heard the bellowing of thirsty cattle and the creak of the wagons. One wagon was an artillery caisson that carried another one of those guns like the one at El Paso Carretas. Another held what looked like a small-bore cannon with an extra-long barrel. The soldiers rode silently, bent forward, grim, leaning into the dust and heat. I saw no scouts on their wings and relaxed. If Lewis Clark and the women were still and quiet, the army would never know we were there.

As Yellow Boy had taught me, I counted all the troops and tried to remember every detail about the group passing us. There were over three hundred men, ten wagons, and the two artillery pieces. It must have taken nearly half an hour for them to pass out of sight toward the pass. They passed so close, I heard the men on the wagons complaining about how bad the dust was. I saw three *vaqueros* handling about fifty head of cattle. I knew the commander wouldn't camp in the pass and would try to get down to the Bavispe River before they stopped for the night. A dry camp with thirsty cattle in a close mountain pass or canyon was a prescription for attack by roving Apaches or a stampede by the cattle if they smelled the river down the pass trail.

My mind was in a fever trying to decide what to do. I finally realized that our only option was to follow them. Whichever way they went along the Bavispe, we'd go in the opposite direction. If we were lucky, they'd go upriver toward Bavispe, passing the canyon where there had been a battle with the Yaquis. Then we could go on downriver and be home free as we planned. If they went downriver, I figured we ought to go upriver and hide a couple of days so they were far in front of us when we left for Rojo's camp. I didn't want to risk them catching us if we followed them or for them to follow us right into Rojo's camp if they caught on to us being behind them.

When the last *vaquero* was out of sight up the canyon, I crept back to Sac and Rafaela and told them we needed to be going. I hoped Rafaela was strong enough to ride by herself because riding double with her in that old McClellan saddle was putting a strain on my back and backside. She was stronger after her nap and could stand by herself, but she still couldn't ride alone. I fed the horses and Elmer, giving them most of our water in anticipation of the twenty-mile ride over the pass down to the Bavispe.

By the time the sun was lighting the clouds in the west, we had climbed out of the top of the pass, followed a steep trail down into El Paso Púlpito Canyon, and followed a trail back south toward the Bavispe River. We kept in the cliff shadows as we wound our way along parallel to the main canyon trail. We found a small draw off the main trail where we were able to rest in case other travelers came along, but none did. From the top of the pass, I saw the army was about halfway down the canyon to the river. If they went all the way to the river, it'd be late in the night when they got there. That was fine with me. It would give us an opportunity to find a place where we could rest and watch where they went the next day.

17
TRACKS

When it was dark, I led us out of the draw and on to the main trail down El Paso Púlpito Canyon. At the western entrance to the canyon, star-like points of light soon appeared from the soldier's campfires. My jaw dropped. The campfires stretched from the Bavispe all the way east to where the trail began its climb up into El Paso Púlpito. The fires spread out perhaps a half-mile north.

This camp was far larger than one the soldiers that had passed us might make, so I realized they must have joined a division that was already there. A few buildings in the small settlement of Colonia Oaxaca stood out like giant toadstools by the river, and a few lantern lights from its streets flickered in the distance. I studied the locations of the campfires, trying to figure out the safest way to get around the army camp. I finally found a faint trail that passed off to the south behind *piñon* groves and huge column-like boulders and took it, hoping it would carry us well beyond the army camp and lessen the chance of being caught.

We rode south for a couple of miles until the campfires' fires were long out of sight. It was cold on the river, and my little group needed a fire and some hot food. I found a little draw with a trickling stream and rode up it through the brush until I thought light from a fire couldn't be seen from the river. We were all bone-tired weary, but the women and Lewis Clark held their own without complaint. Sac and I got Rafaela off Midnight and helped her onto a blanket. Sac dug a deep fire pit, Lewis Clark scavenged some wood, and I unloaded, watered, and rubbed down the animals. Sac soon had water boiling and made a stew out of potatoes, onions, and the meat Yellow Boy had taken from the Comacho cliff site.

As we ate, Sac asked, "Are we gonna be able to get around that army camp and get back to Rojo's camp?"

"With the shape Rafaela's in and with Lewis Clark along, we'd best wait a few days for the army to leave."

"What're we going to do? This ain't any place to hide that long. We'll get caught for sure."

Something Rufus said one time echoed in

my brain, *Bes' place to hide's right in front o' the feller that's a-lookin' fer ye.* I remembered that canyon upstream we'd passed on the way to Elias's camp, the one where we'd seen the jaguar. Arango had said the army had fought a big battle with Yaquis in that canyon. Yellow Boy had said that was why the smell of death was on the breeze flowing out of it. The army patrols were likely to ignore it, and Yaquis weren't likely to return to it because they'd fear the spirits of the fallen ones might still be there. That's where we had to go, and that's what I told Sac.

"I know we're short on supplies," I said. "If we run out, I'll sneak down to San Miguel or Bavispe and steal some. There's probably food I can steal in Colonia Oaxaca, but there are too many soldiers wandering around and too high a chance I'd get caught if I raided there."

Sac made a soundless whistle. "You're sure you want go into that canyon where we saw that big cat?"

"I doubt he's still around. Besides if he comes after us, Little David'll put an extra eye between his others, and that'll be the end of that."

She nodded. "Okay! You're the man of the outfit. We'll be ready when the sun goes down tomorrow."

"Can you take the first watch? When you start getting sleepy, come get me and I'll watch the rest of the night. Find a place where you can see where this creek runs into the river."

She nodded. "I can do that. I'll call you in a little while." She took her rifle and a blanket, following the little stream down toward the river.

It seemed as if I had just closed my sand-filled eyes when Sac shook me awake. I jerked up and snapped the hammer back on Little David. She shook her head and whispered. "Everything's okay. I just have to sleep."

I looked up at the stars and saw it was well past midnight. I motioned for her to take my bed, but she went over to Lewis Clark and lay beside him. I crept down the draw and found her nest back in the shadows, well hidden, but with a clear view of the wide water on the Bavispe. After that, I didn't have any trouble staying awake because the air was cold and refreshing.

The next morning, I ate some more stew, drank a little coffee, and eased back down the river to watch the soldier camp until midday. They sent patrols up and down the river, and the ones going upriver went far enough to pass our little draw. They practiced loading and unloading their big guns; they marched; they drilled; they took care of their horses; and they did nothing to indicate they planned to break camp any time soon.

As I approached our camp, I saw Sac's fiery hair in the thicket where she was hunkered down keeping watch. Rafaela was asleep on a blanket on the far side of the fire pit; Lewis Clark was playing in the stream's pools. I decided it'd be fun to see how close I could get before Sac caught me.

She jumped when I sat down beside her. "Henry! You scared the life out of me! Where'd you come from?"

I smiled. Yellow Boy had pulled that kind of trick on me for years. At last I had a chance to practice the skills and tricks he'd taught me without being caught. "Can you keep watch a while longer?" I asked. "I'm so worn out, I need to take a nap."

"Get some rest. I'll be fine." She nodded toward a blanket near where we'd unpacked our gear.

"It shouldn't take us more than a little while to get down to the jaguar canyon and make camp," I said. "I'll scout us out a good hiding place come morning."

She waved me off toward the blanket. I

stretched out, not intending to sleep more than an hour. The next thing I knew, Lewis Clark was shaking my shoulder. My eyes cracked open to see the shadows were long, and the clouds were shades of purple with bright gold outlines.

Rafaela sat cross-legged by the fire shoveling stew into her mouth like a starving woman. When she saw me, she grinned and nodded. Her bruised, swollen face was much better.

Sac had the pack frame on Elmer and the saddles on the horses. She was nearly ready to go.

I staggered up and wobbled down to a small pool to clean up. When I got back, I took a plate of stew and sat down on the blanket with Rafaela. Lewis Clark, already fed, came and sat down by us with two handfuls of small pebbles. He spread them out on the blanket between his legs and tossed them, one at a time, with an easy overhand throw, toward a dark, still pool.

Sac finished packing the frame on Elmer and said, "The animals are ready any time you are, Henry." I looked at the sky. One or two stars high off the horizon were barely visible. "*Muchas gracias, señorita.* You're a mighty big help. We'll leave when it's good and dark."

Suddenly, I saw Midnight jerk her head up and look down the draw, her ears standing up. I held up a hand for everyone to be quiet, trying to hear what she heard. There was nothing except for the occasional muted swirl of the river. I glanced back at Midnight. All the animals were now looking down the draw, their ears raised. Elmer snorted and backed up until the line holding him was tight. I waved my hand toward the blanket for Sac and the others to stay put. I pulled Little David's hammer to half-cock and crept down the draw, careful not to loosen any rocks or splash water in the little stream.

I reached the river and, peering out through some high reeds, saw nothing in the fading twilight. I looked downriver and saw weak firelight flickering against tree branches, but it must have been over a mile away. The canyon walls on either side of the river upstream revealed nothing but steadily increasing blackness as the stars grew brighter.

I was about to crawl back up the draw when I noticed a couple of depressions in the soft ground by the river. The light was so weak, and they were so large, I had to stare at them for a minute to figure out that they were tracks, cat tracks, and that they were heading downstream. I spread my fingers over them. They were bigger than the span of my hand, the biggest cat tracks I'd ever seen, bigger than any mountain lion tracks Rufus had ever shown me. I felt the hair prickling up on the back of my neck. I thought they were probably tracks from the jaguar we'd seen earlier.

I considered my options. I tried to think like Rufus had taught me, but thoughts buzzed about in my head like angry bees. Rufus and Yellow Boy always said, if it was the best or right thing to do, to face any danger, no matter what. They also taught me to pick my fights and to maneuver until I had the advantage. I had hoped and foolishly expected that the jaguar was gone, but this was his range. He wasn't going to leave. If we went to the canyon where we'd first seen him, he'd probably go after the horses and mules first and then try to have us for dessert. I doubted I was good enough as a hunter and tracker to kill him before he came after us.

I had the two women and Lewis Clark to protect. If we went north trying to get around and in front of the huge camp in front of us, the odds were we'd be caught and turned over to old man Comacho. He'd sell the women to whorehouse madams, make me a slave in his mines, and put Lewis Clark in his fields — but only after he beat the hell out of us, trying to break our spirits.

Suddenly it became crystal clear what had to be done. Anger and resolve bubbled up in my center like hot lava. I wasn't going to let some animal affect the way I chose to live! I was a man, the son of a strong frontiersman, raised by a warrior who refused to be wronged or insulted, riding the land as he chose, free and unafraid. I was going to look that cat in the eye. I was king of this land! That cat stayed at my good pleasure. If he didn't like it, he could leave or die!

It was full dark by the time I found my way back to Sac and the others. She was frowning with concern when I stepped into the little fire's glow. Taking her by the arm, I pulled her to one side and said, "We have to be extra careful. I found the biggest cat tracks I've ever seen. It must be that spotted thing we saw in front of the canyon."

She shivered and asked, "Henry, what are we going to do?"

"I don't know the country well enough to risk trying to get around the Mexicans camped downriver. If we try to race through them with a little boy and Rafaela all beat up, they'll catch us for sure. Besides, the cat went in that direction, too. Probably figures there's going to be some fresh bodies to chew on if there's Mexicans and Yaquis around. If the Mexicans catch us, old man Comacho'll get us back. You know what that means. The only open gate to Rojo's camp is downriver past that army camp.

"We have to hide until the Mexicans leave, and staying in the canyon where we saw the cat is our best chance to avoid them. We'll find us a cave or an overhang to camp under. It'll give us and the animals some protection, but it's not going to be easy. If we cover each other's backs, we'll be okay until the Mexicans leave. If that cat fools with us, I'm telling you, he won't be around long. Little David here will take care of him."

I knew I was talking mighty big because deep inside I was scared. My heart was thumping, and I felt sweat dripping off my hair and down my collar. Sac squinted at me in the moonlight as though trying to see if there was steel in my spine or water in my knees.

At last, she stuck her chin out and nodded. "I know you're right. If we cover each other's backs, we can get back to Rojo's camp. I know we can. You're a warrior,

Henry. You're my man. I know we'll make it."

"That's right. We'll make it. Is your rifle loaded?"

"Yes, it is."

"Good, keep it handy, but don't shoot at anything unless you have to. You lead out. Be ready to hide in a hurry. We'll follow the same trail Yellow Boy used down by the river. Don't stop until you get to the jaguar's canyon. I'll cover us from the back and make sure the cat or nightriders don't creep up on us."

18
THE HIDING PLACE

We mounted and rode down to the river. Rafaela rode relaxed and easy without any need of help. Lewis Clark understood the seriousness of what we were doing. He stayed right behind Sac, his arms wrapped about her waist, not saying a word.

Sac well remembered the trail that Yellow Boy followed cutting between bends in the Bavispe. We made good time. I told her to keep riding if I stopped once in a while to listen for anything following us.

I heard nothing, saw nothing. The stars were just swinging to the tops of their arcs when we rode up to the black maw of the jaguar's shadow-filled canyon. We found a place to cross the river a couple of hundred yards upstream from the southern wall, rode up to the canyon entrance, dismounted, and let the horses drink. A stream no more than four or five inches deep flowed slowly out of the canyon on a wide slate bed. It felt still as a tomb, and the air flowing out of the canyon was cold.

I mounted Midnight and let her pick her way up the stream into the canyon. We rode for about a mile before the left canyon wall seemed to pull away from us. I stopped the others while I looked it over. There appeared to be a little grove of trees growing right up against the canyon wall. The trees were far enough apart so we could hide the animals in them, and there was enough dead wood to make a fire last all night. The stream had so many twists and turns through the brush and trees up the canyon, I couldn't imagine our fire being visible from the Bavispe. We stopped and made camp.

I spent the rest of that night in the canyon wrapped in a horse blanket and sitting near a pile of boulders downstream of our little camp, shivering, staring into the darkness, and listening for any unexpected splash in the stream or rustle in the bushes. I don't think my pounding heart eased up once all night long. Every time I started to relax, I thought I heard something. What I heard, and I admit I knew it at the time, were just the usual little night animals, nothing to be alarmed about. But their scratching around and my imagination were enough to keep me on high alert. By dawn, I was exhausted.

I was trying to decide when I should leave my boulders and start looking for a better hiding place when I heard some rocks click together and a splash in the middle of the stream. Little David was on full-cock and against my shoulder when I rolled over and stretched out over the top of the boulders. I scanned through the sights toward the sound. Sac, her hair a fireball floating in the ethereal mists, stood barefoot and her pants rolled up in the middle of the stream. She called, "Don't shoot, Henry! I brought you a jug of coffee."

Smiling, she waded over and handed the jug to me. It was plugged with a wooden stopper and hot. I motioned her over to a rock by the boulder pile where I had my blanket spread, and we sat down side-by-side. Birds in the brush began to twitter and call to each other as the sky brightened.

Sac was warm. She smelled of just-up-from-sleep mixed with new woodsmoke. I twisted the stopper out of the jug and took a sip. I felt her trembling in the cold air. It felt natural and good to reach over, put my arm around her shoulders, and draw her closer to me. She snuggled in close and warmed her hands between her knees.

"How're Rafaela and Lewis Clark? Did you get any sleep last night?"

"They were still wrapped in their blankets when I left. It looks like the swelling is about gone in Rafaela's face, and she's resting a lot easier. I didn't hear any moans from her or Lewis Clark last night. She's gonna be okay. Do you want me to watch while you nap?"

"No, I'm okay. Soon as there's enough light I'm going to start looking for a better hiding place farther up the canyon. I want to get us out of the way of any Mexican patrols that might decide to come in here. I'm nervous about that cat prowling around, too, but it's probably already holed up somewhere full of meat off a cow from the army herd. How are we doing for supplies?"

She made a face and looked off downstream. "We've got enough for maybe two or three more meals if we're careful. About the only thing left that will last a while is the sack of coffee beans. I saw some cattails, prickly pear, agaves, and a few other plants we can eat, so we won't go hungry. If you can hunt this evening, I think we'll be okay until we're back on the trail to Rojo's. How long do you reckon the Mexicans are going to hang around?"

"I don't know. They might leave this

morning, or they might be here a month. We'll burrow in and stay as long as we have to. When Yellow Boy and the others get back to Rojo's, they'll wait a couple of days and then come looking for us. I'll put out a marker on the trail, so they'll know to come down the canyon if we're here that long."

She nodded, slid her arm around my waist, and gave me a little hug. "I'm not worried. I know we'll be all right with you looking after us." My chest swelled with pride, and I wasn't sleepy anymore.

By the time I finished off the coffee and handed the jug back to her, the birds were starting to flit up and down the canyon, and the light was filling nooks and crannies along the cliff tops as the edge of the sunlight crept down the mountain ridges at the end of the main canyon.

"I'm going back and make something to eat and let Lewis Clark and Rafaela know I'm still around. Are you coming with me?"

"I'll walk back with you, but I want to explore up the canyon a bit and see if I can't find us a place to roost before I eat."

I kept her close walking back to the fire, my arm around her shoulders, my heart swelling with pride and joy that this beautiful woman felt safe with me. I guessed then that the feeling was like what a full-grown man must feel with his woman. When we were within sight of the trees where we'd made camp, I saw Lewis Clark playing at the edge of the water. There was a smell of sizzling meat drifting toward us. It was evident that Rafaela was up, too. My mouth started watering despite my worry that she was using up supplies we needed to ration. My stomach made an embarrassing growl.

Sac smiled and gave me a squeeze. "I think you'd better eat before you start roaming this canyon."

"Ma'am, you're not gettin' any argument out of me this mornin'!"

Rafaela was humming a Mexican dance tune, busy with the big iron skillet when we sat down by the fire. "Mornin', folks! This here meat's gonna be ready to eat purdy soon."

She handed us cups and poured more of that steaming, coal-black coffee, called to Lewis Clark to come eat, and set out the dented and scratched old pie pans. Lewis Clark came running from the creek. Plopping down beside Sac, he chattered about the fish he saw under a shelf of rock in the stream and how he was going to catch them after we ate.

Rafaela divided the skillet of smoky chilies, beans, and what was left of the meat into portions, scooped them into the pie pans, and passed them around. We wolfed down the food like we hadn't eaten in days. Lewis Clark finished first and headed back to the creek to wash his pan and play.

I said, "I'm going to find us a spot that offers more protection. Sac, keep your rifle within easy reach. I don't think you'll need it, but now's not the time to be caught asleep. At the latest, I'll be back this afternoon."

They looked at me with solemn faces and nodded. I saddled Midnight and led her to drink where Lewis Clark played. I knelt on one knee and put my hand on his shoulder.

"Lewis Clark, I have to find us a better place to camp. I'll be back before dark. While I'm gone, will you look after Sac and Rafaela?"

He bowed his head while I spoke, gave a quick nod, and then he reached over and hugged me. "Come back quick, Hombre-cito. Maybe we can throw some rocks in the creek after we move?"

"That we will, *muchacho.* That we will. *Adiós.*"

As I rode, I searched for signs of a cave or a big overhang to camp under. Upstream, the canyon became wider than where we camped by maybe fifty yards. The walls reached a height of two or three hundred feet in places. The sides were mostly vertical, and the cliff faces had strips of dark red and orange stripes running through them, especially near the top. Within half a mile, the canyon divided. The smaller of the two branches continued west before curving north and rising up toward the mountain ridgeline. The larger branch pointed southwest and widened out before it began narrowing as it snaked back west toward the mountain ridgeline. There were a lot of horse tracks, and even some signs of wagon tracks headed up the southwest branch. I saw signs of wolves and bears, and what might have been the pugmarks of the jaguar in the chewed-up dirt on the trail side of the creek. I pointed Midnight up the northwest branch, which began a slow but steadily rising ascent as it angled toward the ridgeline.

There was a stream in the northwest branch, narrower and with a faster flow than the southwest branch, and there were many more large cottonwoods and bushes in that canyon branch than the other. The trees and brush were so thick that within fifty yards of entering the northwest branch, I couldn't see where I'd started. I had to stay in the middle of the stream to get through without getting off Midnight to pick our way around the big trees and occasional boulders.

In another fifty yards, the trees and brush thinned out, the canyon narrowing to a width of about fifty yards. The stream was five or six yards wide, slowly moving over smooth slate. Upstream a hundred fifty yards was an outcropping fifteen or twenty feet up on the right-hand canyon wall, which was at least a hundred feet high. The outcropping was covered with junipers and looked five or six feet wide. Directly opposite the outcropping were a couple of big cottonwoods and, just beyond them, a large pine tree. Thick bushes and saplings grew around the cottonwoods.

As I stared toward the trees, I couldn't see any sign of the beige limestone color of the canyon walls. The canyon wall behind the bushes looked like it was in dark shadows, but the light wasn't right for shadows to be there. All the shadows from the trees and brush were pointed toward the west. I climbed down from Midnight and led her over to the cottonwoods. Looking through the brush toward the dark spot, I stared for a moment before realizing the dark place wasn't shadows at all but the entrance to a cave. Even as it dawned on me what I was seeing, another part of my brain was saying, *This'll work.*

I tied Midnight to a bush, cocked Little David, and began easing my way along the canyon wall past the bushes in front of the cave. The cave entrance was about twenty feet wide, its floor dry and elevated about knee high off the floor of the canyon. From the small amount of light that penetrated the entrance, it looked to be forty or fifty feet to its back wall. I thought I could hear water dripping toward the back. I stood there a while staring into the darkness, letting my eyes adjust to the dim light, my head cocked to one side, listening. On the right-hand side, I noticed a little stream of water running off the floor in a kind of gutter, then cascading down across the rocks until it disappeared into the roots of the bushes just to my right. There was enough room inside for us and the animals if we took them out every day and kept their "stable" cleaned out.

I picked up a rock the size of my fist and threw it hard against the back wall so it ricocheted a couple of times off the floor and side walls. Loud, angry rattles began even before the rock stopped rolling around.

My perfect hideout was already claimed

as a winter rattlesnake den, but it was perfect for what we needed, and the fact that it was filled with snakes meant bears, wolves, and even that cat refused to call it home. I could handle a few snakes. Besides, we needed fresh meat, and rattlesnake wasn't bad at all when cooked properly, even if Yellow Boy wouldn't eat it.

I found a stick of pine with a knot on one end and some grasses to wrap around it to make a torch. I made a little fire at the entrance where there was plenty of light. There was enough drying sap from the big old pine tree to smear on the grass to make a dandy torch. I found another stick under one of the cottonwoods that made a nice long club, and another one that had a nice fork on the end for pinning the snakes' heads down. I stuck the burning torch up in a crack in the wall so I'd have enough light while I went after those snakes. There was a bunch of them, including a couple of granddaddy-sized ones. I had to be real careful — a bite from one of them, and I'd never make it out of there alive. I killed fourteen. The granddaddies were over eight feet long and the size of my arm. I cut off their heads and laid the bodies aside for cleaning. It took me an hour to clear them all out, turn over all the large stones, and shuffle through leaves blown inside. I wanted to be sure I didn't miss any. I killed a couple of big centipedes that were wintering in there, too. It was halfway to noon by the time I'd cleaned the snakes worth keeping to eat and climbed on Midnight to ride back down the stream.

We packed our stuff, loaded Elmer, saddled the horses, and were just leaving when I thought I heard voices downstream near the canyon entrance. I told Sac and Rafaela how to find the cave, that they couldn't miss it because there'd be rattlesnake carcasses hanging in front of the entrance. Reassuring them that I'd be right along, I told Sac to ride as fast as they could without making a lot of splash or clatter on the rocks in the stream while I covered our back trail.

Soon, a Mexican patrol came up the creek. It wasn't more than five minutes behind us when we left. Fortunately, they weren't in any hurry to get up the canyon and dawdled along. Sac didn't waste any time getting the animals, Rafaela, Lewis Clark, and herself upstream. I think by the time they got to where the canyon forked, they might have gained more than five minutes on the patrol. She didn't hesitate to head straight up the middle of the creek on the canyon's northwest fork. Following Sac, I'd ride a couple of hundred yards before stopping to listen for the approaching patrol. I waited to move until I clearly heard them but stayed well ahead and out of sight.

The patrol rode right past where we'd camped the night before. When I got to the northwest fork upstream, I checked to be sure there weren't any signs of Sac's passing and didn't find any. Breathing a sigh of relief, I continued upstream until I could barely see the spot where soldiers turned to follow the southwest fork.

In a few minutes, the patrol came moseying along. They were smoking and talking. Two or three toward the back of the column were even singing a sad tune about a dead soldier and his grieving lover. Indifference to their surroundings told me they were familiar with the canyon. I figured they must be returning to the Yaqui battle site. If Elias or Juan and their warriors had been where I was, they could have wiped out the patrol, leaving the Mexican government to blame the Yaquis. I shook my head at the stupidity and incompetence of the man leading them. After they were out of sight, I headed on up the canyon.

At the cave, my heart skipped a beat. Sac and the others were nowhere to be seen. At first I thought they might have ridden past it and were still headed upstream. I was about to tear out after them, when I noticed the snake carcasses I'd tied hanging from their rattles on a sycamore sapling were gone. I heard Sac giggle as she stepped from behind the bushes where I'd found my way into the cave entrance. "Where you goin', Henry?"

"I was about to light out upstream after you when I noticed the snake carcasses were gone."

Sac wrinkled her nose and made a face. "Can't say I'm eager to eat rattlesnake or share their former house, but Rafaela says it's pretty good eatin', and home is where you hang your hat. She's already skinning them and washing the meat. This is a perfect place to hide! The horses were a little skittish when we tried to lead them in there, but they calmed down. Climb down. You need to rest. Rafaela and I will take turns on watch tonight while you sleep."

"No need to worry about that. We'll figure out something come dark." I dismounted and led Midnight around the brush to the cave entrance.

Rafaela sat with her legs crossed, humming a snappy peasant song in the dim light over on the far side of the entrance. She'd already skinned and sectioned the meat from the two biggest snakes and was skinning the others. Lewis Clark was pulling sticks and pieces of wood out of the brush to make a big pile of firewood near where I made my fire. As my eyes adjusted to the midafternoon gloom, I saw a rope line strung across the back part of the cave with the animals behind it. Elmer was unloaded and the saddles were off the horses and arranged with the pack frame in a neat stack to one side.

I pulled Midnight into the cave, unsaddled her, and tied her beside Elmer. Sac and I rubbed the animals down with handfuls of dry grama grass we found next to the cave entrance. We had enough oats for two more feedings. I figured I was going to have to go on a little raiding party the next night to restock supplies for the horses as well as ourselves.

We were all busy the rest of the afternoon. I explored the ledge on the other side of the creek from our cave. Sure enough, there was room enough for four or five adults to stretch out behind the junipers. I smiled. It reminded me of Rufus Pike's lookout and the good times I had playing on it. It was a perfect place to hide if we had to evacuate the cave, and it gave a clear shot at anything in front of the cave. My only concern was the women and Lewis Clark being able to climb up the niches in the rocks fast enough to hide from danger. We'd have time to practice climbing the next day, so I assumed there wasn't any question that it was a place we'd all use. I carried a small water cask up to it in case we had to stay up there a while.

I followed the stream up toward the mountain ridge for another mile or so. The floor of the canyon started a brisk rise about a quarter of a mile from our hiding spot, in a series of long benches that looked like giant stair steps. The water flow became faster as the canyon narrowed and rose toward the top of the mountain ridgeline. Waterfalls splashed at the beginning of every new step. I used the first one I came to for a shower. It was ice-cold, but it sure felt good. I was so happy to scrub away the trail dirt that I did a very foolish thing. I put Little David out of instant reach while I enjoyed my shower. I was lucky nothing disturbed me. Later, when I thought about what I'd done, I vowed I wouldn't do it again.

I was quick to backtrack downstream and tell the women and Lewis Clark to go take a shower in the first waterfall. They were gone in a wink. I sat drinking coffee and, as Yellow Boy taught me, studied every nook and cranny around us. The walls of the canyon were high and smooth. Looking upstream, the brush around the trees was thin and easy to see through except for a few small canebrakes, but it was relatively thick where we were. If we kept a careful lookout from the overhang, I thought we'd be safe.

The women and Lewis Clark returned looking scrubbed, their faces glowing red from the cold water. Lewis Clark watched for fish or played with the crawdads he found under rocks near the edge of the stream. Sac sat down on a small boulder to watch him and dry her wet hair, now a dark, almost black auburn color. I watched her in wonder. How could such a beautiful woman just drop into my life without warning? Curiosity and desire for her began filling my mind. I remembered how I felt after our long kiss on watch at the Comacho *hacienda*.

Rafaela built up the fire to start frying the snake meat she'd prepared earlier. A bubbling pot filled with the last of the beans and chilies was already going. Her honey-blond hair, still wet and shiny, was pulled back and tied with a red bandana Billy had given her. With her hair now just shoulder length and the red bandana around her head, she looked like a blond Apache. She moved slowly, apparently still stiff and sore.

Watching day to day how she recovered from the beating, I knew she was strong enough to live any life she was given, even as I had been after Daddy was murdered. It made me feel I had a special bond with her. I admired her strength, her courage, and her loyalty to her friends.

I sat for a little while watching her work. Her brilliant, green eyes were sad, floating on the edge of tears. I knew she must be thinking about Billy, grieving for the hellion who had saved her from slavery and personal degradation.

Rafaela and Sac kept the fire high during the rest of the daylight hours so we'd have plenty of heat from the surviving coals and hot rocks during the cold night but little light to give us away when it got dark. The heat from the big fire made my brain fuzzy. As the afternoon drifted away, I kept jerking myself awake watching Lewis Clark play in the gurgling water. I finally crawled over to my blanket and fell into a deep sleep.

Darkness ran up the canyon, the only light coming from high clouds in brilliant gold outlines, painted in blood reds and dark purples. As if sleepwalking, I came off my blanket to see Sac tasting the beans and chilies and fried rattlesnake. My stomach growled, and even through the haze of just waking up from my afternoon *siesta,* my mouth watered from the delicious smells of our food.

The women smiled at me as I staggered out of the cave to relieve myself and to splash cold water on my face. Lewis Clark was still playing in the water. I sat with him while the fog cleared from my brain, and he told me about the fish he'd been trying to catch in the pool just above our hiding place. The frogs were beginning to croak with the cricket and tree-peeper chorus when Sac and Rafaela called us to a great meal. The snake was tender and had a delicate taste. Rafaela had made golden brown fry bread to go with the beans and chilies.

19
TERROR IN THE NIGHT

I offered to go out that night to find more supplies, but both women assured me that we had enough for another day or two. Where they kept finding the supplies, I never knew, but I've long suspected Sac had packed her own reserve before we left Rojo's camp.

She begged me to let her and Rafaela keep watch that night so I could get some sleep before looking for supplies the next day. Because I was so tired, I didn't turn her down. I figured that after a good night's sleep, traveling by myself during the day gave me a better chance of finding supplies than wandering around in the dark, and less chance of getting caught by the Mexicans.

Sac took the first watch. She didn't want to climb up on the outcropping on the other side of the creek while it was light, so she took a blanket and her rifle and climbed to the top of a boulder about twenty yards downstream from the cave entrance.

The horses snorting and stamping around woke me up. I sat up, eased Little David across my knees, and waited. I sensed more than saw the dark outline of something at the cave entrance. Little David's warning click filled the air as I brought it to full-cock.

"Easy, Henry, it's just me back after Rafaela came to relieve me. Said she couldn't sleep and for me to come on to bed. Everything's all right. Haven't seen or heard a thing all night."

I let the hammer down and puffed a sigh of relief. "Well, climb in here under this blanket and get yourself some rest where it's nice and warm."

"Thank you, sir. That's the best invitation I've had all evening." She giggled as she lifted the blanket, and slid in beside me. She was cold! I was about to lie back so she could put her head on my shoulder when I heard the unmistakable boom of gunfire echoing up the canyon.

I grabbed Little David and was out of the cave in an instant, telling Sac to stay put. I stumbled through the bushes toward the boulder where I thought Rafaela had taken up watch. I busted my tail once, sliding down in the water and making enough noise to awaken Bavispe. I moved slower after that, trying to avoid breaking a leg. I got to the boulder and looked up for her dark outline against the night sky, but she wasn't there.

I shouted in a hoarse whisper, "Rafaela! Rafaela!"

"Over here!"

My thudding heart slowed. She was at the base of the boulder and slightly behind it. The blanket covered her, and the long barrel of Sac's rifle poked out. She was all but invisible. Smart girl. "Where's the shooting coming from?"

She was excited but steady as I eased down beside her. "I ain't fer shore. But I'm a-thinkin' it's in th' other canyon. Maybe it's them army troops you's a-watchin' 'fore you follered us into camp."

I put my finger to my lips and shook my head for her to be quiet. Even the insects and frogs, with another week or two left before the cold air finally silenced them, weren't making any noise. We waited for maybe another minute, then another shot, then two more in quick succession. They were followed by the echoes of several men yelling and one man screaming as the sounds echoed down the canyon past us. I felt prickles on the back of my neck.

We waited. No more shots or yells. Nothing. It was so quiet I heard Rafaela's little anxious puffs as she tried to quiet her nerves. The thudding of my heart sounded in my ears like some kind of big tribal drum. I tried to think of what might be attacking the Mexican Army patrol camped up the other branch of the canyon. The only thing that made any sense was a Yaqui ambush. I wanted to see for myself, but had no idea how far I would have to go or what the canyon terrain was like in the southern branch. Besides, I couldn't risk the women and Lewis Clark being caught by Yaquis who might not understand why we were there. I cursed myself for being so foolish as not to reconnoiter the Mexican camp when I had the chance rather than sleeping. I knew Yellow Boy didn't make mistakes like that, nor had Rufus — most times. They had taught me better, and I knew it. Now there was nothing to do except wait for daylight to learn what had happened.

After breakfast the next morning, I leaned over my saddle and said, "I'm going to scout out where the Mexican patrol's camped and then find some supplies. I'll try to be back by dark, but don't worry if I'm not. Keep the fire going, but keep it small, and take turns on watch until I get back. If anyone you don't know shows up, hide in the cave and wait for me. *Comprende?*" They nodded. "Lewis Clark, how about you looking after Sac and Rafaela for me until I get back?"

He stood up tall and straight and gave a respectful salute with his left hand. "Yes, sir! I will, Hombrecito."

20
PLACES OF SLAUGHTER

Midnight picked her way downstream until I saw where the streams from the north and south branches ran together. I stopped and listened for anything that might tell me humans were nearby. There was only the water gurgling over the rocks. The birds stopped their twitter as I approached. Waiting until they began again, I rode out into the main canyon and up the south branch, following the trail the Mexican troops made through the shallow stream and in the soft sand and gravel along its sides. The early morning was so still, it felt like I was the only human left in the world. There was an ominous feeling in the pit of my stomach, a sense of impending doom I couldn't shake.

Pausing every two or three hundred yards, I looked and listened for anything that might be out of the ordinary. Little David lay across my saddle pommel, loaded and ready to fire. I was trembling inside, my heart beating a tattoo, and my breath coming in long, nervous puffs.

The canyon snaked between high, smooth walls that were a copper-orange color slashed by narrow streaks of black. The little gorge ran almost due south and slightly west toward the mountains, widening as I rode deeper into it. The east side of the canyon steadily pulled away from the little stream that rippled over the rocks by its western wall. Large cottonwoods, their leaves turning dull red, formed a thin line of sentinels watching my progress. Smooth white boulders with lichens on their sides were scattered among the trees all the way from the edge of the stream to the eastern wall. The boulders and trees provided enough cover for an army to ambush anyone foolish enough, like me, to ride exposed down the canyon.

A proverb says God looks after women, children, and fools. It held true that day for me. After about half a mile, the canyon began to swing away from its mostly southern track around a gentle bend to the west. Nerves were squeezing my bladder so bad I had to relieve myself. I slid off Midnight and led her over to a cluster of cottonwoods growing near the north wall where I hid her while I did my business. I was just stepping out of those trees when she turned her head and stared upstream. Her ears went up, and she snorted, staring toward the sound coming around the bend. I heard the unmistakable click of iron horseshoes on the big, flat stones and splashes in shallow pools.

Holding her muzzle and backing into the shadows, I waited. My ears strained to hear every sound above the pulse pounding in my ears. Two soldiers, one leading a pack mule, rounded the bend. There was a roll of canvas about eight feet long lying across the mule's pack frame. It covered a body. I know because I saw a hand, streaked by dark rivulets of dried blood, dangling out one end. The soldiers, hunched over with fatigue, rode by without looking to either side and disappeared downstream through the trees.

I waited a few minutes, rode into the stream, looked and listened, and then rode on round the bend. Looking up, I saw black smoke. It couldn't have been more than a half-mile away. I got off Midnight and, leading her, worked my way around the trees and boulders toward the source of the smoke. A soft breeze drifting toward us brought a strong odor of fetid rot and decay. I had to swallow back bile to keep from gagging. The odor became stronger, almost unbearable, as we worked our way forward.

Through the trees, I saw orange flames from a fire, flashing and sputtering like a guttering lantern running out of fuel. At one time, it had been huge; the ground was black from residual char over at least a twenty-five-foot-diameter circle. Eight men from the Mexican Army detail, their faces covered by bandanas, worked in a long, narrow field littered with rotting corpses. Boulders everywhere showed slashes and gouges from direct or ricocheted bullet impacts. Several big tree stumps looked like the bases of huge weeds that had been torn off by a giant's hand. Body parts lay scattered near large holes, which, I learned later, were made by exploding artillery shells. Buzzards and crows, their gimlet eyes watching every move of the detail, covered the trees that still stood near the southwest wall. I gagged and almost threw up at the stench and horror of it all.

Most of the bodies were Indians. The ones I clearly saw looked like wild animals had chewed on them, and they had been picked over by the buzzards and crows. Some of the swollen corpses were draped over the boulders or dangled from the branches of trees. I saw women and children, some with weapons still in their hands, scattered among them. The Mexicans had formed two teams, each with a litter made by stretching canvas over a pole frame. The teams wandered the field picking up soldiers' bodies and carrying them to the cremation fire. They left the bodies of the Indians where they lay.

I saw military tents a couple of hundred yards upstream from the battle. There had been four, but one was torn down and partially burnt. The detail's horses were on a tie line next to a mess tent with the sides up, where a cook worked by a fire. A soldier, apparently on guard duty, lounged with a rifle near the stream. Neither the cook nor guard paid much attention to the cremation teams, or, for that matter, to any of the surrounding canyon. None of what I saw made any sense. If Yaquis had attacked the camp, wouldn't the soldiers still be on high alert, vigilantly watching out for new attacks? It was as though they knew they weren't going to be attacked.

Puzzled, I turned away and started working my way back downstream. I hadn't gone more than two or three hundred yards when I noticed a small patch of long, green weeds and cattails turning tan and dark brown in the cool, fall air. The middle of the patch looked like it was tromped down. Midnight stared at it, snorted, and bobbed her head a couple of times. Rufus had taught me always to pay attention to how horses and mules react to anything. He said it might save my neck someday and, as usual, he was right.

I tied Midnight back in the trees and duck-walked through the patch of weeds to where the tops of the weeds were missing. Pulling the weeds aside, I looked into the flattened spot and sucked air across my teeth in surprise. Dark, drying blood was splattered everywhere: on the soft ground, on standing weeds, on the weeds pushed down, and on exposed rocks. It looked, at first, like some struggling animal had been slaughtered there, bleeding out in its death throes. I studied the ground where the weeds were pushed over but saw nothing except boot tracks. I figured one or two of the men in the detail must have killed a deer and dressed it there. I was about to turn away when something reflecting sunlight caught my eye. I edged around the spot until I could reach to pick it up: a Mexican coin, a *peso.*

Tossing it back, I was leaving when I noticed a track in the soft ground where it landed. It was the same big cat track I saw earlier down by the Bavispe, except this one was fresh. There was no blood on the ground where it was. My mouth became very dry, and even though the morning air was cool, I felt sweat running down my face and in rivulets off my chest and belly under my shirt. My mind raced with this new information — the shooting and screams from the previous night, the bloody hand hanging out of the rolled-up tarp, the chewed-up corpses — it all fit. The big cat had a definite taste for man.

I looked around in all directions, slowly backed up to Midnight, and got out of there as fast as I could. There was no telling where the jaguar was. I just hoped he was full of his latest victim and was lying up somewhere sleeping off his meal.

Before I reached the northern branch of the canyon, I decided to warn the women to stay close to the fire. Then I'd try to find supplies while the cat was full rather than stay near camp. I didn't waste time trying to be quiet going up the northern branch of the canyon, so it didn't take long to reach the cave. There was no sign of anyone. If I hadn't known they were there, I'd have passed on without noticing anything. I rode Midnight up to the brush covering the entrance, and called into the cave. "Sac?"

She appeared almost immediately, squinting against light. "Henry? Are you all right? We didn't expect you back so soon and were afraid there were Mexican riders looking for us."

"I'm fine. You did the right thing. Where're Lewis Clark and Rafaela?"

"Lewis Clark's inside." She pointed to the far wall. "Rafaela's on the ledge keeping watch. It's my turn this afternoon when you were supposed to come back."

I looked over my shoulder toward the overhang and saw Rafaela's arm poked through the bushes waving at me. I waved back and leaned over the saddle so I could speak to Sac without Lewis Clark hearing me. "I found the Mexicans' camp about a half-mile up the southern branch of the canyon. They're burning Mexican bodies from a battle with the Yaquis, but leaving the Indian bodies for the scavengers. It's bad, real bad.

"Listen close, now. I have reason to believe that the big cat we're worried about has been feeding on those corpses and has a taste for humans. All the commotion we heard last night was probably because he took one of the Mexicans on the cremation detail. You've got to stay close by the fire in case that thing comes around here lookin' for easy pickings. Use the rifle if you have to. If that no-account Mexican burial detail hears the gunfire, they'll stay where they are. They aren't going to get involved in any kind of confrontation if they can help it. Just don't do anything foolish. I'll be back by dark, even if I'm empty-handed."

21
RAIDING THE ARMY

I rode down the canyon toward the river in a damned-if-I-do, damned-if-I-don't box. I needed to be back before dusk when the jaguar would rouse from his afternoon *siesta* and start to hunt. However, the safest places to steal supplies were around the villages up and down the Bavispe, but it might take a day or two of hard riding to find what I wanted and get back.

I could go in the opposite direction, downriver to the soldiers' camp, with time to spare. However, the risk of being caught was high if I sneaked inside their camp circle. It didn't take me long to figure that, given my situation, there was only one option, and that was the soldiers' camp. Getting supplies there would be a real test of all the warrior craft I had learned from Yellow Boy. I believed I was good enough to pull it off.

When I got to the Bavispe River, I tied Midnight behind some bushes back in the trees so that riders along the river trail couldn't see her. Finding three flat stones, one about the size of a plate, one saucer size, and one, teacup size, I stacked them on top of each other in an out-of-the-way place beside the trail. I put a rock about the size of my fist on the ground by the stack on the due west side. It pointed straight into the canyon. If Yellow Boy came looking for us, I was certain he'd see it and come for us. When I returned up the canyon, I would make another stack where the canyon forked to show the branch where we hid.

For a while, I rode downstream beside the Bavispe, and then I headed overland to bypass the river's twists and turns along a hard-to-see path leading up out of the river's canyon toward the army camp. It was rough, barren country covered with creosote bushes, ocotillo, and, occasionally, tall, stately saguaros punctured with woodpecker holes the desert wrens used for houses. I stopped often to listen and scan around me as far as I could see. Even taking the pains I took to avoid being seen, I still got to the soldier camp before midday. I tied Midnight in a shallow *arroyo* and climbed up to its top with Rufus's old brass telescope.

Supply wagons stood near a tent with the sides up. Inside it was a fancy dining table made of dark wood with elegant, carved legs and scrollwork around the sides. I figured that must be where the *comandante* and his officers took their meals. Watched by a couple of drovers, a small herd of cattle grazed down by the river. Most of the horses were gone. There weren't more than ten men moving around in the entire camp, not including the ones walking sentry duty around the main edges of the camp. I recalled the story Daddy told me about capturing and killing the bandit El Tigre, and how that had been his lucky day. He said everything he did that day seemed to go right. Maybe this was going to be my lucky day! All I had to do was get in that camp and steal sacks of beans and oats without ten soldiers and a few guards seeing me.

I waited. A short time after I started watching the camp, the cook served up the noon meal. The men gathered around the cook's wagon and gobbled it down. Even the guards wandered over and ate. When they finished, they lounged around smoking while a private, a kid no older than me, washed their mess kits at the river. When smokes and coffee were done, all but one guard crawled up in the shade under the wagons for an afternoon *siesta*. The lone guard walked over to the far side of the camp nearest the river and kept watch to the north as though he were expecting someone. I stared in that direction with my field glasses, but I didn't see dust rising anywhere.

After a while, the field glasses showed the whole camp was napping. Even the lone guard was dozing off and then jerking awake when his head dipped too far forward. He soon made himself more comfortable and began to snore with his mouth open, his rifle loose, almost falling out of his hands.

It didn't take much skill then to ease into their camp and over to the supply wagons. I might as well have visited a trading post. There were twenty-five-pound sacks of brown beans and flour, fifty-pound sacks of corn, and in one wagon I even found fresh cuts of beef hanging from a pole running down the middle. I made three trips, being careful to wipe out my tracks as I retreated with a haunch of beef over my shoulder on the third. I had to laugh on the way back. I was sure I had more than enough supplies to last us and the animals until we returned to Rojo's camp. I'd be back to our camp by sundown and, if I was really lucky, the Mexicans wouldn't even know they'd been robbed.

22
BLOOD FOR BLOOD

The sky was just turning red to the west, and long shadows were swinging across the mountains as I started up the canyon's northern branch. When I reached the cave, I rode up to the bushes at its front and tossed the sacks of grain and beans off Midnight and called, "Sac?"

"Over here, Henry! I'll be down in a second. Had you in my sights for a while. If you'd been old man Comacho, you'd be dead by now."

Sac was climbing down from the ledge on the south wall as she talked. Lewis Clark ran out of the cave with Rafaela right behind him. He was so excited to see me that he was jumping up and down, shouting, "Hombrecito! Hombrecito!"

Rafaela nodded, smiling. "We's shore glad to see ya back. How'd it go?" Her smile grew as she looked over my pile of loot. "Why we'n live off this here stuff fer a month!" She lifted the big haunch of beef off my shoulder, exclaiming, *"Dios mío!"* With a little help from Lewis Clark, she lugged it into the cave to hang up, and came back for the rest of the supplies. She was strong and hefted a fifty-pound sack of corn without seeming to strain. I got the other one, and Sac and Lewis Clark got the twenty-five-pound sacks of beans and flour. Lewis Clark had to struggle with his, but he made it.

Rafaela made a supper out of some of the leftover fried snake and the rest of the beans and chilies left from our original supplies. Lewis Clark chattered away about the fish, crawdads, lizards, and other critters he'd played with in or around the pool just up the stream from the cave. The women were anxious to learn if the army was close to leaving and how I'd foraged such an unbelievable store of supplies. We had a good laugh at how I'd taken advantage of the camp's *siesta,* but they were disappointed that there was no sign of the army leaving.

I sat by the fire sipping Rafaela's strong, boiled coffee while she straightened up the camp. I was a lot more worried by the cat than I was the Mexicans or even Elias's warriors stumbling onto us. I didn't know anything about the jaguar's habits, except that it was a man-eater. I knew we had to be extra careful and decided we couldn't risk sitting out in the dark with little or no fire during a watch.

Lewis Clark sat beside me, sorting through a handful of creek gravel looking for special pebbles. After a while, he asked, "Hombrecito, when will I be old enough to be a warrior like you?"

"Why?"

"Cause when I am, me an' Sac's gonna get even with Elias for killin' my father and then sellin' me to the Comachos."

I stared at Sac, who was nodding agreement. I was stunned to think they wanted revenge. Hot fire for revenge still burned in my soul, burned to make Oliver Lee pay for what he'd done to my daddy, done to our entire family, and done to me. The death of Rufus was heavy on my heart, and every day I remembered my blind rage as I smashed in the face of Stone when he shot Rufus after our ambush of Stone and his men.

Yet it had never entered my mind that Lewis Clark and Sac wanted revenge for the murder of their father. They were Mormons. Weren't Mormons supposed to forgive their enemies? Revenge didn't seem right for Lewis Clark and Sac.

But Elias had murdered their father. Why wouldn't they want to swear vengeance for their father's murder just as I had for Daddy? If Lewis Clark were my brother-in-law, then according to everything Yellow Boy had taught me, he was family, and I had to help him avenge that murder. That was the warrior's code.

I looked at Sac's glittering eyes across the fire and recalled something I'd read to Rufus, I think maybe from Herodotus. Spartan women expected their men to march off to war, and either to come back victors or be brought back dead on their shields. How did the phrase go? *I tan I epi tas — Return with your shield or on it.* That's what Sac expected from me. That was the idea she was planting in Lewis Clark's mind. That was what I had to do if she truly became my woman. The light began to dawn about family responsibilities and why a man needed to be careful about his commitments.

I looked Lewis Clark in the eye and spoke to him man-to-man. "Well, little man, I'm about ten years older than you are, and I'm about five years younger than I should have been before I tried to take revenge on some of my father's murderers. So I'd guess it's going to be at least ten, maybe fifteen years before you can go after Elias.

"During all those years I waited, I worked hard, and my friends Rufus and Yellow Boy helped me train, so I grew to be strong, a good shot with Little David, and knew how to survive in the desert like an Apache. Are you willing to do that so you can kill Elias? You ought to know that if you kill Elias, you'll have to kill his son, Juan. You can be certain he'll come after you if you kill his daddy."

Lewis Clark's face fell for a moment. He looked down at the stones he was sorting, and then he brightened and looked me in the eye. "Ten years, that's an awful long time, Hombrecito. But I can do it. Elias or Juan ain't gonna git away with killin' my daddy. You're gonna help me, ain't you? You're family now that you and Sac is married, ain't you?"

I looked at Sac. Her eyes danced in the flickering firelight, her smile filled with mischief. She was nodding. I suddenly felt very old. Already married and didn't know it! I saw Rafaela watching all this out of the corner of my eye. She wasn't smiling. I think she knew as well as I that the thing Lewis Clark and Sac wanted would lead to an unending river of blood and death.

"Lewis Clark, I had a lot of help surviving

and taking revenge when I wasn't much older than you. I'll help you find justice for your daddy, even if I'm just your friend and not married to Sac. I'm not so sure Sac thinks we're married. I'm just protecting her right now. Maybe she'll decide she wants me for her husband, maybe not." Sac was giving me quick little oh-yes-I-do nods. I grinned when I saw her and felt my chest swell with pride. I looked back at Lewis Clark and added, "So, my little friend, maybe brother-in-law, you can count on me helping you, and I expect Yellow Boy will help us, too. After all, he's like my grandfather. Remember now, you have to train real hard to be a warrior. If you don't, you'll die in this country."

He looked at me with a solemn face and said, "Yes, sir. I'll train real hard. When can I start practicin' my shootin'?"

"Not for a while. You're a little light in the britches to be shooting a gun."

Lewis Clark frowned and stuck out his lower lip. Sac spoke up. "I showed you how to load and pull the trigger on my rifle yesterday, Lewis Clark. Henry'll show you how to shoot when you're old enough. You can wait."

Lewis Clark nodded, saying nothing.

"Tell you what, pardner, I'll start you out

318

on a warrior's first weapon, a knife. I'll make you one to practice with until we can get you a better one. How about that?"

"Oh boy! Will you, Hombrecito?"

"Sure."

I put the coffee cup down. I found a branch in the firewood pile that was just about the right size to fit his hand. I cut off a piece about twelve inches long below a couple of small branches growing on either side of the main stem, and left about four inches above them for a handle so they made a blade guard.

As we sat by the fire and talked about the kinds of training that went into being a warrior, I whittled him a wooden hunting knife. I noticed the women were listening carefully to what I said. Apparently a warrior's training was something of a mystery to them. The wood I used had seasoned a long time and was very hard. I was able to shape it so it looked almost exactly like a real hunting knife. It turned out to be more of a weapon than I intended for a child so young. I asked Sac if I should blunt it for safety's sake.

She shook her head. "Lewis Clark will be careful with it, won't you?"

His grin reached from one ear to the other as I leaned over and gave it to him. "I sure will! Thanks, Hombrecito! Thanks a lot! Can I start training to be a warrior tomorrow?"

"We'll see. Maybe when I get back."

"Where are you going, Henry?" Concern filled Sac's voice. Rafaela frowned, but didn't say anything.

"In the morning, I'm going back to watch the camp downriver a while. We'll never know they've gone unless we check 'em every day. I'll be back by midday."

Sac appeared relieved. Rafaela didn't look too happy about the plan but crossed her arms and nodded.

The fire was getting low. Rafaela said for the rest of us to get some sleep, that she'd take the first watch. I told her to call me when she got sleepy and handed her Sac's rifle.

There was just enough light filtering into the cave for us to move around without stumbling over the gear. I lay down while Sac tucked Lewis Clark in. He was so proud of the knife I'd whittled for him that she had a hard time making him put it aside so he wouldn't stab himself with it as he slept.

She came to our blanket, sat on the corner, pulled off her boots, and lay down beside me with her head on my shoulder. Her closeness and warmth made my heart pound. She was still for a while, then rolled on her side and whispered in my ear.

"Soon, Henry. Soon, when we get back to Rojo's camp, you'll know me as a man knows a woman. You'll know me as your wife. Goodnight, my warrior." Her kiss was soft and warm on my cheek, and it made my blood race even faster. I didn't care about the price of commitment. I wanted her.

Sac was deep in sleep, but I was still awake when Rafaela tapped my foot with her rifle. I took Little David and stepped out into the chilly night air. Total darkness was kept at bay by the slow coals burning in the fire pit and a fingernail moon back toward the south. I looked at Rafaela, who shook her head. Nothing had happened on her watch. She went back into the cave as I slouched down close to the fire to keep watch.

23
EL TIGRE COMES

Rafaela was up just as the sky started showing gray. She bathed, made coffee, and
drank a cup with me. We watched the sun
put fire on the mountain ridges across the
Bavispe with unforgettable red and purple
streamers in the high clouds. Lewis Clark
and Sac crawled from their blankets still
groggy with sleep, and Sac stumbled off
upstream. Lewis Clark sat down beside me,
rubbing his eyes and shivering in the cold
air. The knife I'd whittled for him was stuck
under his belt.

"You going to practice with that there
sticker today, pardner?"

He yawned and looked up at me. "Yes,
sir, I aim to. Maybe you'll show me how to
throw it when you get back?"

"That's a good idea. I'll do just that."

He grinned and nodded before running
off to the creek. While Sac and Lewis Clark
gathered up a fresh supply of firewood, Ra-

faela cut some steaks off the haunch of beef and heated up the beans from the night before. That breakfast was a mighty nice change from leftover rattlesnake.

After we ate, I saddled Midnight before telling the others to be quiet and stay close to the cave. Lewis Clark pulled the knife out of his belt and waved it back and forth, cutting through the air in long, slashing strokes.

I saluted and rode off down the creek. Stopping where the canyon forked, I watched and listened for riders, saw and heard nothing, and rode on to the river. I took a different trail to the soldiers' camp and found a draw to hide in that was closer than the one I'd used the day before.

Again I looked over the situation using my field glasses. I was dumbfounded by what I saw. The number of tents had more than doubled. There were five or six new artillery pieces lined up next to the wagons, and there were four large squares of soldiers standing at attention in their best uniforms while some peacock of a commander addressed them from the back of a wagon. I had hoped that, with the camp as thinly populated as it was the day before, the soldiers might be packing up soon. It was obvious we were going to be stuck where we were for at least a few more days.

Disgusted, I headed back to our little hideout. Yellow Boy and Rufus had taught me to avoid taking the same trail twice, so I took a different, longer trail back. It was midday before I rode up the canyon from the Bavispe.

At our camp, I didn't see signs of anyone. *Bueno,* I thought. They knew to hide at the first sounds out of the ordinary. I waved toward the ledge, but I didn't see any arm reach through the junipers to wave back. I rode Midnight up to the bushes in front of the cave.

"Sac? Rafaela? I'm back. Lewis Clark? Ready for your knife-throwing lesson?"

There was no answer, no sound anywhere, not even birds twittering. A bad feeling started gnawing at the center of my stomach. I climbed down from Midnight and led her inside. No one was there. The other two horses and Elmer looked at us with raised ears. Sac's rifle was gone, but her pistol was still there. Nothing seemed out of place. Maybe they were just bathing and playing upstream. I rushed to unsaddle Midnight, anxious to join them, but was nagged by a vague sense something wasn't right. I gave Midnight some grain, checked for any signs of danger around the fire pit, didn't find any, and relaxed a little. I crossed the stream and climbed up to the ledge we used for a lookout. Nothing. I saw no sign of them when I rode up from the big canyon. They had to be upstream ahead of me.

I took Little David and started wading up the middle of the creek, looking for some sign of them on either bank. I thought they probably had waded up the stream, playing in the water, and I knew I wasn't likely to see any sign of them until I got to the higher waterfalls. It was quiet and cool wading in the stream.

The creek, which was less than a foot deep in the deepest pools, flowed over a smooth slate bottom, and the current was very slow. The east bank, where trees, bushes, and weeds grew, was ten to twenty yards wide. Big, smooth, multicolored boulders, carried down from the mountains during monsoon flash floods, were scattered about, caught by the big trees that refused to move under their onslaught.

About fifty yards upstream from the pool where Lewis Clark played, I saw footprints on the east bank. The flickering sunlight filtering through a hole in the leafy canopy was like a spotlight highlighting them. I waded over and looked them over. Sac had stood there, her feet spread as though she was watching something. The mix of wet alluvial dirt and sand made a nearly perfect cast of her bare feet. I saw no sign of Rafaela's Apache moccasins or of Lewis Clark's little bare feet.

About thirty feet from the first set, I found another set of standing footprints. Between the two sets of standing prints, the heels of individual steps were pounded into the sand and dirt like she had run a few steps before stopping to look again.

From that set of prints, there was a single print, then another, and another, all of them separated by very long strides. In every footprint, her heel pounded into the dirt as if she was running hard. I felt the ball of dread in the pit of my stomach grow and tasted the bile forcing its way up my throat. The temptation to run headlong as fast as I could upstream, following her running footprints, was overpowering.

I took a few running steps and stopped. I made myself take a few quick, deep breaths, and stood there, willing myself to calm down. I'd find them. They'd be all right.

Moving upstream, I studied both sides of the creek for signs that might tell me something more. My heart thumped in my ears, and a thousand black images fluttered in my brain. Another hundred yards upstream, I saw a big, flat rock on the west bank that glistened in a bit of sunlight, making it look wet. Maybe Lewis Clark had waded out there, running from Sac as they played on the way to the waterfall. My legs didn't want to move as fear of what I might find grew. I felt heartsick and wanted to throw up when I got a good look at the rock's wet spot.

Blood was splattered everywhere, drying from bright crimson to purplish black. In a little depression, where some of it collected, a huge paw print I'd seen before stared back at me. I saw Sac's footprints where she had run through the puddles and tracked it across the rocks for a few strides. The blood trail led upstream. The splatter became less and less, farther and farther apart. I began running along the west bank.

The cat had Lewis Clark and Sac was chasing it. There was no doubt in my mind that Lewis Clark was dead and, if Sac wasn't mighty careful, she was running straight for her own death. I knew she would be like a bloodhound, and she'd chase the cat until it caught her. I knew, too, Rafaela wasn't about to let Sac face that cat alone. I kept praying over and over, *Please God, please.* Images of Lewis Clark playing in the stream, riding long miles bouncing against Sac's chest, and asking me to help him avenge his father drifted through my mind like falling leaves. I clenched my teeth and sucked in air to keep from vomiting. I saw no sign of Rafaela.

I kept running, dodging tree limbs, jumping over boulders in the way, tripping but not falling, a couple of times. The blood trail up the creek was as easy to follow as a highway. I knew my only hope was to save the women, but if that cat dropped Lewis Clark and turned on them, they wouldn't have a chance. I couldn't figure out why they hadn't shot at the jaguar when it first attacked Lewis Clark. My breath burned in my lungs and whistled through my cheeks. I ran harder.

The blood trail passed the waterfall we used for bathing. The blood-splattered rocks led higher and higher, up across the giant slate and sandstone steps where the water flowed faster and faster. With every step, the canyon narrowed and closed in around the stream.

Panting and sweating from the run and fear of what I'd find, I scrambled to the top of a ten-foot waterfall about half a mile from where I'd found the first blood sign. Rafaela sat on a boulder in the middle of the stream, about halfway across the step to the next waterfall. She faced away from me, her shoulders shaking, her head buried in her hands. I saw brown, drying blood all over her shirt. Sac's rifle was across her knees.

The waterfall was so loud, she didn't hear me splashing in the stream. I ran up and put my hand on her shoulder. The touch made her jump up, jerk around, and stumble backwards, a look of horror on her face. She landed in the creek on her back in a splash. I pulled her up and held her, trembling, next to me. Heartfelt tears poured from her in deep moans and sobs. I held her shoulders and shook her. "Rafaela."

She continued to sob as though she were in horrific pain, so I shook her again. "Rafaela! Are you hurt?" Her eyes flew open as if she had just awakened from a trance, and she dumbly stared at me. *"Que paso?* Where's Sac? Are you hurt?" I was still gasping for air, half-blinded by salty sweat running down my forehead and into my eyes.

She lifted her face, still streaked with dark brown splatters of blood. Her eyes were red and swollen. She tried to snuffle back her tears and moaned with her head down against my chest. "No, Hombrecito. I ain't hurt."

I hugged her, my knees sagging in relief.

She looked toward the rocks climbing up by the next waterfall and trembled. I asked her again, holding her close to my chest, patting her back to comfort her. "Please, tell me. *Pronto.* We have to help them."

She nodded, wiping her face with her sleeve. "I . . . I ain't hurt, Hombrecito. Lewis Clark and Sac, *el tigre* took 'em. They's nothin' we'n do." Her eyes grew wide. "*El tigre*'s a witch, *el diablo,* the devil his own self! I tried shootin' it, but this here rifle of hers didn't fire. *Diablo* musta cursed th' rifle, so it jammed up. I coulda killed it fer shore if'n the rifle had fired."

She pointed a trembling finger toward a big, flat, white rock near the waterfall. Scarlet stains and maybe a few small pieces of body parts were turning black in the yellow sunlight shafts filtering through the trees. "After it took her, it run up there."

I stared where Rafaela pointed. The jaguar had carried Sac up to the next step and disappeared. Even from where we stood, nearly thirty yards away, I saw the blood trail splattered on rocks up the side of the waterfall. I hugged Rafaela again and tried to speak brave words. "Wash your face and come on. We'll find her and put an end to that cat."

Rafaela dropped to her knees in the creek and threw water on her face. To wash the blood out of her hair, she dipped her head in the current, the streamers of her hair looking like veins of gold against the black slate bottom.

I waded up the stream and stared at the blood-covered rock. All that was left of Lewis Clark was his right hand and a couple of toes. I felt tears of frustration and despair running down my face, and a cold, furious rage growing in the middle of my chest. I had to find Sac and give what was left of her and Lewis Clark a proper burial before I destroyed the demon that had killed them. I prayed I'd find that cat still with her. It wouldn't live another second if I did.

We worked our way up two more of the stream's giant stair steps. Near the back waterfall of the second step, the cat's tracks, which had stayed along the east bank, swerved toward some big sycamore trees and willows growing up against the canyon wall.

I took a long time to study the ground up and down the bank where the sycamores were, but found no signs, not even any blood drops. Rafaela stayed by my side, keeping a close eye out for the jaguar, while I concentrated on finding any signs of where they might be. We sat down to rest on a boulder by the creek.

"Tell me . . . Tell me what happened."

She sighed a long, sad sigh, trying to hold back more tears. "Lewis Clark wuz playin' in th' creek with that there knife you made him. I's a-watchin' from th' lookout ledge. Sac's a-cookin'. Then I noticed they's no birds a-singin'. Even Sac, she sensed it, too, an' waved up at me to see if I seen anything. I studied the creek up an' down th' canyon an' waved back ever' thing looked okay to me. I's a-thinkin' maybe it's a sign th' *federales* is a-comin' an' watched the creek real close downstream."

Rafaela sniffled and wiped her eyes with her hand. "Las' time I looked upstream, Lewis Clark's a-goin' in th' bushes to make water. I weren't payin' much attention to him, but it seemed like he'd been gone a long time when I looked again fer him an' didn't see him. Then Sac seen that Lewis Clark wuz gone, and she run to where he usually went in the bushes and called him. Then she started a-runnin' up the middle o' creek a-screamin', 'Lewis Clark! Lewis Clark!' "

I could picture the scene as she described it and imagined the pitch of terror Sac's voice must have carried.

Rafaela said, "I thought th' *federales* wuz gonna hear her an' come down on us, so I

332

climbed down to hush her an' help her find him. By th' time I's down an' lookin' up th' creek, I couldn't see her. Then I heard her screamin' farther up the creek. When I seen the blood, I knowed that big cat had Lewis Clark. When I caught up with Sac, she wuz a-standin' in the creek a-facin' *el tigre*."

Again, I could picture the scene. Though she should have run, since there was nothing she could do, I knew Sac would try to get Lewis Clark's body away from the cat. Rafaela continued, "*El tigre* wuz stretched out a-finishin' off Lewis Clark on that there rock by the waterfall! They's blood all over his mouth. They weren't much left o' Lewis Clark, an' that cat's a-lickin' its mouth like it done finished beans an' steak at ol' Comacho's table. Sac, she's a-screamin' an' throwin' ever rock she'n find in the creek at him. She hadn't hit him yet, but she wuz a-gettin' closer an' closer. That there devil's 'bout had enough o' Sac. It stood up, lowered his head, an' roared. He showed them fearsome teeth, an' he layed them ears back. That there cat weren't about to run off an' give Sac what wuz left o' Lewis Clark, an' she weren't about to back up." Again Rafaela paused to wipe tears from her face. I wanted to ask her why she didn't shoot it, but I restrained myself.

She said, "Soon as I saw *el tigre,* I tried to use the rifle. I knowed at that range I'd kill it fer shore. I aimed real keerful an' pulled the trigger, but it didn' fire! I couldn't even lever another bullet into it. I started yellin' fer Sac t' git back, that I's a-comin', but she didn' pay no attention."

I was distracted for a moment, wondering why the rifle didn't fire, trying to figure what could have been wrong with it, since Rafaela certainly knew how to use it.

I was about to ask why, but Rafaela said, "By that time I wuz within about ten feet of her, I wuz throwin' rocks, too. We weren't doin' no damage with them rocks. He weren't even scared. Sac wuz crazy an' outta her mind. I begged her to wait. She didn't stop, jest kep gittin' closer to th' devil. We throwed more rocks, missing nearly ever' time. Then Sac chunked a little un that hit *el tigre* square on his nose bone. That cat's eyes looked like they wuz filled with fire from hell. It come a-runnin' fer us. I screamed, 'Run! Run, Sac!' But she weren't about to run. I grabbed the rifle by the barrel fer a club, but I knowed we wuz dead. Th' devil took Sac right here in th' creek. She wuz a-tryin' to fight him with a rock. I run up a-swingin' th' rifle an' tried to hit him in the head but bashed him on his back instead. He swatted at me, and his big claws whipped across Sac an' throwed her blood all over me while she's still a-fightin'. He pushed her down like she wuz some kinda doll an' clamped down on her head."

Rafaela snapped her fingers. "She's gone jest like that. That there devil stood over her body an' looked at me like he wuz a-askin', 'You gonna be next?' I took a couple of steps back, an' he picked her up in by middle of her back like she didn't weigh nothin' an' took off." The tears came again.

All I knew to do to comfort her was to be quiet and hold her close. After a while, her trembling passed.

24
LONG WALK TO DARKNESS

I looked up through the trees, trying to get the ball of thorns in my throat to go down. Then I saw the arm of Sac's shirt, dirty and torn, in the fork of one of the big sycamore trees up against the canyon wall. Her arm, bloody tears in its fair skin, dangled out of it. I couldn't see the rest of her. That devil had left her there, stashed ten feet off the ground, away from the bears and wolves, to ripen for his next meal while he hid away to sleep the rest of the day.

I told Rafaela where Sac was and asked her to take Little David and keep watch for the cat while I climbed the tree to get Sac down. When I got up to where she lay, a wave of sadness and grief rolled over me. I wanted to sit down and cry, but I knew we had to get out of there fast. I hoped that if there was a God, Sac and Lewis Clark were in a better place than where I'd led them. Her skull was crushed. Black blood matted her beautiful, long red hair, and there were black open slashes across her chest and back where it had grabbed her. I knew *el tigre* was just an amoral animal that looked at humans as meat on the hoof, but I hated it, hated it in the same way I hated the men who had murdered my father. I made a silent vow that only one of us was going to leave that canyon alive.

I took off my shirt and slid it under Sac's back and tied it tight just under her arms. I was strong from all those years of carrying rocks for Rufus, but it was a strain to pick her up, a hundred pounds of dead weight, in the fork of that sycamore. Working hard to gently lower her to Rafaela, I remembered Rafaela saying *el tigre* carried her off like she didn't weigh anything, and I realized what a powerful animal it had to be. Bracing my legs against the tree notch, I eased her down until Rafaela could reach up and take her to help me get her to the ground.

When I got down, I asked Rafaela to carry Little David and hand it to me if we needed it. I picked Sac's body up and balanced her across my shoulders. Starting back, we crossed the stream to the west side so the cat wouldn't have much cover to ambush us. We stopped at the bloodstained rock. Rafaela picked up the little pieces of Lewis

Clark and wrapped them in my shirt.

It was a long, hard hike back to the cave, but we never saw any more signs of the jaguar. The sun was low on the western mountains when I knelt to gently lay Sac on her blanket. I staggered out to the fire pit and sat down by Rafaela. We sat for a while not speaking, hung our heads, and waited for our strength to come back. The muscles in my shoulders felt like I'd never be able to raise my arms again. Rafaela finally spoke from the depths of her broken heart. "If'n you'll find 'em a place, I'll make 'em ready to rest with God."

I stepped into the yellow glow of the late afternoon light, crossed the creek, and looked up and down the sides of the east canyon wall for a burial place. I remembered seeing a deep recessed shelf up the canyon from the ledge we used for a lookout post. It was about four feet up the wall from the canyon floor, maybe a foot and a half high, eight feet long and three or four feet deep. A big willow hid most of it. It was a good spot for Sac and Lewis Clark's final resting spot. I started picking up smooth stones and stacking them next to the shelf to seal it closed.

When I had enough rocks, I returned to

the fire. Rafaela said, "I washed her and wrapped her in her blanket. All that was left of Lewis Clark is in the blanket with her. They're ready."

I picked up the blanket Rafaela had tied around them with several strips of rawhide, and we carried them across the stream to the place I'd found. I slid the bundle as deep into the recess as I could, and we covered it over with the rocks and packed a thick wall of mud over them. By the time we finished, the stars were nearing the top of their circle, and the only light we had to work by was from a little fire we made there.

After a while, I turned to Rafaela and said, "Sac and Lewis Clark were Mormons. I don't know what they believed about their lives after they die. I don't know what to say over them."

"They's strong and brave. They's good *amigos.* Send 'em to God with strong words to comfort our hearts. They's with Him now. We ain't."

The only thing I could remember that seemed appropriate was the Twenty-Third Psalm. I'd read it so much, I had it memorized. At last, I managed to get the words past the sorrow stuck in my throat, speaking them for Sac and Lewis Clark, to Rafaela, to the night sounds and bright moon,

to the gurgling water, to the lonesome
breeze, to myself, and to God.

The Lord is my Shepherd;
I shall not want.
He maketh me to lie down in green
*   pastures:*
He leadeth me beside the still waters.
He restoreth my soul:
He leadeth me in the paths of
*   righteousness for his name's sake.*
Yea, though I walk through the valley of the
*   shadow of death,*
I will fear no evil; for thou art with me;
Thy rod and thy staff they comfort me.
Thou preparest a table for me in the
*   presence of mine enemies:*
Thou anointest my head with oil;
My cup runneth over.
Surely goodness and mercy will follow me
*   all the days of my life: and*
I will dwell in the house of the Lord forever.

I wiped the mucus off the end of my nose
with my sleeve. The tears finally came,
emptying the springs of my heart. I hated to
cry in front of anyone, especially a woman.
I knew Rafaela must think I was a weak and
sorry excuse for a man since I'd let those in
my care get killed and then cried about it.

Whatever was due me in her esteem, I knew I deserved.

I stared into the darkness, thinking I would never forget that year. It seemed all I did was kill my enemies and bury my friends. I wondered if it would ever end. Rafaela, wiping away her tears with the sleeve of her shirt, stood up. She pulled at my arm to stand up with her. "What you spoke over them wuz mighty beautiful, Hombrecito. *Muchas gracias.* Sac, yer woman, and her little brother is gone. Billy, my man, is gone. We's still alive, an' that there is a good thing. *El ligre*'s gonna die *pronto*, by our hands, ain't that right? Then we's goin' on to Rojo's camp, ain't that right?"

That brave, unassuming woman gave me courage. I croaked, "We're gonna get that demon an' get to Rojo's as fast as those horses can carry us."

We doused the fire and covered the ashes with sand and gravel. I took her hand and waded back across the stream to the little fire in front of the cave where she cooked us a meal. We ate in silence, lost in our misery and thoughts of what to do next.

25
FACING DEVILS

I focused on how best to kill the jaguar. I had hunted mountain lions with Rufus in the Organs when they took his calves. I knew those big cats were smart, dangerous adversaries. I figured jaguars probably had habits similar to mountain lions, so I didn't exactly go into the hunt blind; still, I knew it was the little things I didn't know about predatory animals that could get me killed.

Thinking back over all I'd seen that day, I tried to piece together what I knew about this cat. It hunted in the early part of the day; it didn't mind getting wet; it used trees and was probably lying up in one until it came down to hunt; it had a taste for human flesh; and taking its next meal away meant it would be hunting again tomorrow.

We had to be careful, or we'd wind up being left in a tree like Sac. Since the cat wasn't shy about walking right up to camp and taking Lewis Clark, I thought maybe the best way to take it was to wait for it to come to us.

Rafaela cleaned up around the fire, fed the animals, and poured me more coffee while I sat and cogitated on how to trick that killer into walking in front of Little David's sights. She poured herself a cup of coffee and sat down beside me. "You git some sleep. I'll take the watch after I wash up. Is that there all right, Hombrecito?" Her sad green eyes searched mine for approval.

"Yes, ma'am, that's fine. Hand me Sac's rifle, and let me see if I can figure out what's wrong with it while you bathe. Are you worried about *el tigre* right now? I'll keep an eye out for him while you bathe if you want."

"Naw, it ain't around here now. It ain't gonna be ready fer fresh meat till *mañana*."

As I looked over the rifle, trying to figure out why it had jammed, she called over her shoulder, "*El diablo* cursed that rifle. You ain't a-gonna fix it."

The rifle still had the cartridge that had failed to fire jammed in the loading breech. It had somehow caught in the extractor. I managed to back it out with my knife. It had been struck several times by the firing pin and was just an empty shell casing! I wondered how in the world that happened, and then I remembered Sac saying she showed Lewis Clark how to use its sights and pull the trigger the first day I was gone. I'd have bet a fortune she had used an empty shell to show him how to load one at a time, pull the hammer back, and squeeze the trigger. She probably forgot she'd left the empty cartridge in place. I cycled the remaining cartridges out of it, cleaned and checked it, and decided it was okay.

When Rafaela returned from the creek, I handed her the rifle and dropped the battered empty shell casing in her hand. "The cat didn't put a hex on it. It works fine now. I think Sac was teaching Lewis Clark how to use it, left an empty cartridge in the chamber, and it jammed when you tried to lever another one into the chamber. It just wouldn't extract without some extra help."

A big smile spread across her face. "*Gracias,* Hombrecito. It's a comfort knowin' th' rifle's a-gonna shoot, an' th' cat ain't no witch. If'n I get the chance, I'm gonna drill that evil devil an' give a extry eye. Go on an' get some rest. I'll watch. I'll call you when the moon's over yonder." She pointed to where the rapidly rising moon would be in a few hours.

"*Bueno.* I'm going to bathe before I hit the blankets."

She nodded and started loading the rifle. I slipped over to Lewis Clark's pool and eased into the cold water again. It made me want to jump up when I squatted in it and sat down, my teeth chattering. It wasn't more than knee-deep, but the bottom was smooth and sandy. I used handfuls of sand to scrub myself and felt much better when I returned to the fire.

Rafaela sat with the rifle across her knees, running her fingers through her hair to dry it. Now it reached only to her shoulders, but it was still beautiful. I sat by the fire for a little while soaking up the heat with my cold, damp body. Her smile held me when she looked at me with her brilliant green eyes.

She had a strong woman's proportions, trim and muscular, and she moved with a smooth grace that didn't waste any motion. Her lips were red and full, and her breasts, high and firm, still very much those of a young woman. But as much as she had been abused by old man Comacho and then led around the countryside by Billy, she was still very modest. I felt an attraction for her I'd never known for Sac.

After I'd been warmed by the fire, I pointed high toward the eastern sky. "Don't forget to wake me when we agreed."

"Yes, sir, I won't. Rest good, Hombrecito. *Buenas noches.*"

It felt lonely in the cave without Lewis Clark and Sac. I lay down on my blanket and listened for a moment as the horses snorted and stomped around, restless and alert, but it didn't take more than a few breaths before I fell into a deep sleep.

In an instant, or so it seemed, Rafaela shook me awake. In the dark gloom, she made a face and shook her head to say she'd seen and heard nothing. I picked up Little David and staggered to the stream. The moon was brighter than it had been even two days before, and it stood out with startling clarity through the brightly lit branches and leaves. I returned to the fire and found the fresh coffee Rafaela had made me.

"*Buenas noches,* Hombrecito. I'm hittin' the blankets."

I called after her, "Use my blankets. They're still warm."

"*Gracias!*" she said softly from the cave.

After the morning meal, I asked Rafaela to cook several large pieces of meat and a large pot of beans. She looked at me like I'd lost my mind until I explained how we were going to use it. I spent an hour or so getting supplies, including another full water cask, up to the lookout ledge across the creek from the cave entrance. I figured we might need to stay on the ledge two or three days, and we'd need to cover each other when we fed the horses and mules or when we went to relieve ourselves.

When Rafaela finished with the meat and beans, I took a length of rope, threw it over a tree branch, and pulled what was left of the haunch about ten feet off the surface of the water right at the front of the cave. It was an easy fifty-yard shot from the ledge, and high enough that the jaguar had to jump to reach it. I wanted to make sure he couldn't just snatch it and run away. I figured the odor from the meat, and the absence of a fire in front of a cave that didn't hide the smell of the animals or humans, ought to be enough to draw the cat in pretty quick. Then it dawned on me that the meat hanging in the entrance to the cave was probably what drew it to the camp in the first place! I ground my teeth to think that I had been such a fool.

Rafaela and I fed the animals, and with the sun straight overhead, we climbed up to the ledge, hoisting her pot of cooked meat and beans up with us. We made ourselves a comfortable and cozy aerie up on the ledge where one of us could watch the bait and the cave entrance all the time. There was enough room to spread our blankets and to put the supplies at the far end, out of our way. At the end of the ledge, we could sit with our backs to the canyon wall and rest the barrel of Little David in a fork of the juniper. I'd never had a sweeter set-up for an ambush. I put some cartridges in a little cranny that was easy to reach, even in the dark.

As I sat there watching the front of our cave, my yawns became more and more frequent. Rafaela, gathering her hair into a short ponytail, laughed and said, "Go on to sleep. You watched since 'fore dawn. I's a-watchin' now." All I did was nod, hand her the rifle stock, and crawl over to my blanket.

I jerked awake. It was dark and much cooler than when I'd first stretched out on my blanket. I sat up, confused about where I was for a moment until I heard her whisper, "It's all right. Ever'thin's okay."

I saw her outline in the dim moonlight. She was right where I'd left her when I flopped on my blanket. "Thanks for letting me sleep, but you ought to have called me sooner for your rest. You didn't see *el diablo,* eh?"

"Naw, no sign. Come on an' take yer turn. I got to climb down fer a bit."

"No! It's too dangerous. *El tigre* might be out there. Stay here."

She looked at me, gritting her teeth. "I got to climb down now."

I opened my mouth to tell her again, but the pressure on my own bladder reminded me why she had to leave. I looked through the bushes. By moonlight, I could see all the approaches to the bushes where she usually went. I had made a rope with knots spaced every couple of feet for quickly climbing down and pulling ourselves back up to the ledge. I tossed the rope down and said, "Forgive me, *señorita.* I'll go when you come back. Use this rope. Go quick! I'll keep an eye out for *el tigre.*"

"*Gracias,* Hombrecito. Ya don't have to worry none about me being quick."

Chewing my lip, I watched her dash across the stream and disappear into the inky shadows and bushes. I swung Little David up and down the approaches where she went. She seemed to take a long time, and I was trying to decide if I should go after her when she reappeared out of the shadows. Before heading for the rope, she stopped at the stream to drink and throw water on her face.

Then she was up the rope in a flash, her bright, white teeth flashing in a smile as she crawled over the edge. Before I could fuss about her taking so long, she spoke. "The horses is okay, an' I give 'em their corn. They's plenty of water fer 'em, too. Git goin'. I'll cover ya with this here thunder gun." I must have had a flummoxed look because she asked, "What's the matter? *Que pasa?*"

I just shook my head as I started down the rope. The moon, in a quarter phase, still made the canyon floor surprisingly bright, but where the shadows fell it was pitch-black. Expecting to be pounced on at any moment, my heart was going like a trip hammer as I ran to my spot in the bushes. I did my business, forced my fear to quit growling, and took enough time to look for cat signs on the way back but I didn't see any. Naturally, I had to stop, wash, and have a drink out of the stream as Rafaela had, because I wasn't about to let a woman show she had more courage than me. I didn't hesitate to go back up that rope in a hurry, either.

After I settled down to my watch, Rafaela handed me a plate of cold meat and beans, and told me goodnight. It was still as a tomb — no night birds, no frogs, no crickets. After Rafaela crawled in her blankets, I don't think she moved all night either. The moon stayed high in the sky even as the sky started to lighten.

A few birds began their morning calls. Rafaela sat up, glanced through the junipers toward the cave, made a big cat-like yawn, and said, "Mornin'. *Que pasa?*"

"*Nada.*"

"I'm a goin' down the rope again."

I frowned and asked, "Can you wait until the light is better?"

She made a face and nodded, pulling her blanket up around her throat as she leaned against the canyon wall, her legs drawn up under her. The bird chorus grew louder, and a large flock of cawing crows flew over the canyon toward the mountains. Soon we had a bright, morning sky, and I could see up and down the canyon. I waved Rafaela out of her blankets and down the rope. She fed the horses and Elmer and gathered up several armloads of sticks she had me pull up to make a small cooking fire. It wasn't long before we were eating hot beans and meat out of pans that were too hot to hold with bare hands.

After coffee, I climbed down from the ledge, took Little David, and left her with Sac's rifle. I wanted to do a little scouting around after my visit to the bushes. I checked on the stock, then went all the way down the canyon to the fork and back upstream past the cave to the first step waterfall. I didn't see any cat signs until I was on the way back and noticed a rough spot in the sand on the east side of the stream. It was a paw print, and it was fresh. For a moment, I wanted to run for the ledge rope, but then a cold stone of hard fury settled in my gut. I'd rather die there than let that damnable killer get away.

I cocked Little David and followed the tracks. *El tigre*'s tracks were right up next to the canyon wall. I even saw where it was so close to the ground its chest was turning over pebbles and mashing down weeds as it worked its way toward the cave. Within twenty yards of the pool where Lewis Clark played was a stand of cane surrounding a tall boulder that looked like a gigantic egg balanced on its small end. I saw the cat had crawled through the cane and climbed up on the rock, though it had since moved on. It was a good place to watch the area and stay out of sight. I figured the cat must have seen Rafaela and me when we climbed off the ledge. It seemed he was watching us to learn our habits. Sitting on top of the rock, I saw where he had taken a path straight to the stream when he left. I climbed down and went up the creek, looking in every direction, expecting him to be on me at any moment. He must have gone back up the middle of the creek toward higher ground because I found no other tracks.

Climbing up to the ledge, I sat down beside Rafaela and blew a sigh of relief. The sweat was running down my face in small rivers as she asked, "What'd ya find? Any sign of that devil?"

I nodded. "It's bad, mighty bad. It's hunting us. It's like he's learning what we're doing and is playing his own game with us."

Just before the sun dropped behind the western ridgeline, I noticed Rafaela peering intently through the juniper bush, her rifle cocked, pointed downstream. While using her head to motion me over to her side, she put a finger to her lips for me to be quiet. I crawled over to her, and she nodded in the direction her rifle pointed. Two gray wolves were sniffing their way upstream toward the cave. If they got in there after the horses, there'd be hell to pay. It didn't take me long to decide risking the sound of gunfire if they got too close. It might draw the Mexicans or run off the cat, but if the horses got chewed up or run off, we were in real trouble. I was sighted on one of the wolves, ready to shoot, when they stopped. They sniffed at a bush near where I'd kept watch a few of the nights before. They whined, tucked their tails between their legs, turned around a couple of times looking up and down the canyon, and headed back the way they came at a fast trot.

I figured they'd discovered they were trespassing on *el tigre*'s territory and decided they'd better get out of there *pronto.* I sort of wanted to do the same thing as I watched them disappear through the brush and trees, but I wasn't running. There was a score to settle.

I looked in Rafaela's eyes and said, "We'll wait through the night. Then I'm climbing down *mañana* and going after *el tigre.*"

The fire in her brilliant eyes and the iron in the tilt of her chin filled me with pride and courage that I was fighting *el tigre* with this strong woman. She handed me Little David and dipped us out some green chili stew from the pot she had bubbling on the little fire. We sat back against the canyon wall, eating and talking as if we had known each other all our lives and there were no secrets between us.

I asked her if what Billy had told me about her being stolen by the Apaches and sold to the Comachos was true. She sat back next to me and sighed. "I ain't a-knowin' what Billy told ya. I figure it's my business an' nobody else's. I ain't got no need fer folks a-feelin' sorry fer me. I tol' Billy not to tell nobody else whut I tol' him, but I might as well been a-talkin' to the wind. Billy ain't ever listened to nobody. I'll tell ya, Hombrecito, it's just that I'm askin' ya to keep my business jest 'tween us."

I raised my right hand and I promised I wouldn't tell a soul. I didn't either, until now.

She said, "I'n just barely remember bein' taken when we lived up near Pinos Altos, New Mexico. Geronimo murdered my mama an' daddy, burned down th' house, an' stole th' mules, cattle, an' me. He give the stock to his people an' traded me to a Mesican peon family that let 'im and his warriors drink at their well without no fight. He give me to 'em fer two boxes of Winchester cartridges an' a burro, which he and his warriors et right there on th' spot. I ain't ever understood why he didn' just kill that family, too, and take what he wanted, but he didn'. Th' family worked me hard in th' *patrón*'s fields till I's twelve or thirteen, but they worked hard, too, so I didn't think nothin' 'bout bein' different from 'em. They's kind and treated me like one of th' family."

She reached in her pocket and pulled out a piece of blue turquoise, holding it up in the dim light for me to see. It was a little smaller than a silver dollar. It looked like an eagle, wings spread out, talons extended.

"*Papacito,* he give me this here blue eagle when I'd been with 'em a couple a years. After supper in the evenin's, he carved lots o' stuff in blue stone fer his *amigos* who helped him out when he's short o' *pesos.* They's good pieces an' they's like money 'cause they wuz a-sellin' 'em down to the stores in the villages. Carvin' in stone jest seemed to come natural to 'im. He said his carvin's brought ya luck when ya needed it. I watched him carve on this here eagle fer a long time. Ever' time I seen him a-workin' out on the porch in th' evenin's, I'd sit an' watch him grind on it with them ol' files an' grindin' stones o' his'n. When he's through, he give it to me. Said it showed I's his little girl an' fer me to take good keer of it 'cause it'd give me luck in the tomorry days. So I wrapped it in a little piece o' cloth an' kept it with me all th' time."

She handed it to me, and I examined it closely. It was a very fine piece of carving. "How did you manage to keep it after you were captured with Sac at the Comacho compound?" I asked.

Rafaela blushed and said, "I hid it where I knowed they wouldn't look."

I shook my head and handed it back to her and watched her put it back in her pocket.

She said, "One day we all climbed in the ox cart an' went to Janos fer supplies. While *papacito* and *mamacita* bought supplies at a mercantile store, the little 'uns played 'round the cart. Old man Comacho an' his *rancho* foreman saw me a-sittin' on the cart seat keepin' an eye on 'em. Comacho stared at my blond hair and at my blouse where my breasts was jest startin' to fill out fer a long time. I's embarrassed 'cause it felt like he's lookin' at me without my clothes. He come over to the cart and asked where my guardians wuz. I pointed toward the store. He climbed off his big black horse with the silver-trimmed saddle and bridle and disappeared inside." Rafaela looked off across the canyon as if she could still see that scene in the distance.

After a while, she said, "When *mamacita* and *papacito* come out of the store, they's followed by the store owner an' two clerks, their arms all filled up with sacks of supplies. They loaded the cart until it's 'bout to run over. *Papacito* told me to climb up on the horse behind the man with *Señor* Comacho. Said I's to go with 'em and do whutever *Señor* Comacho tol' me. Th' little ones was a-wavin' goodbye and cryin' fer me as th' wagon disappeared in th' dust down th' road. I ain't never seen 'em again. I tried makin' a brave face, a-smilin' an' a wavin' back at 'em, but I's scared, more than I am now by *el tigre.* I's scared right down to my soul by the flat, dead eyes o' Comacho an' his hateful grin when he looked at me."

I didn't know what to say, and just placed my hand over hers.

Rafaela bit her lower lip and said, "At th' *hacienda* they put me to work in th' kitchen. Fer a couple of years, life wuz easier because workin' in th' kitchen is easier than workin' in th' fields. I started believin' God's a-smilin' on me. I filled out purdy good, and th' old women taught me how to keer fer myself as a woman. I thought maybe *Señor* Comacho's gonna marry me off to one of his *vaqueros* so I'd make 'im some more *peones* with yeller hair, but I changed my mind on that there idear when *Señor*

Comacho come to th' kitchen door one day. He's a-smilin' and lookin' me over like I's a piece o' meat an' he's a hungry dog. I felt neked and embarrassed like I had two years before. He motioned fer me to follow 'im." She paused for a moment, and I could tell it was hard for her to continue.

Rafaela said, "He led me to a bedroom back in a far corner o' th' *hacienda.* Then he closed and locked th' door, an' says fer me to take off my dress so's he'n inspect me. Then fer' th' first time in my life I said no to a man's command. I'll never fergit th' hateful, mean smile that filled *Señor* Co-macho's face. He walked over to me and punched me hard below my belly button. Th' pain wuz so bad I near passed out. I doubled over and staggered back against th' bed. Then he ripped off my dress, pulled his belt off, an' start beating me. I screamed fer help, but nobody came. I slapped, punched, and scratched at 'im, tryin' to make 'im go away, but he kept whipping me on my back and legs with his belt. He finally threw down th' belt and gave me a hard punch on my jaw."

Again she paused, and I could sense her anguish over the memory. I was about to tell her I'd heard enough, that I could guess the rest, but she drew in a deep breath and said, "He raped me there on th' big rug by th' bed. He wuz like a madman, frantic an' wild. It felt like he's tearing me to pieces. I screamed and cried, a-beggin' 'im to stop. When he's finished, he relaxed an' lay on top o' me, not movin'. I'n remember his hot, wet breath on my neck an' feelin' like I wuz going to smother under 'im. I decided to play like I'd fainted so's maybe he'd leave me alone. After a while, he got up, poured some water in a bowl, and washed hisself. Then he put his pants on an' combed his hair. When he left, he looked at me and said, "Remember, *señorita,* the *patrón* broke you. He owns you. You do as he says, or he gives you to the *vaqueros* for their pleasures."

We sat there on the ledge not speaking for a long while, and I imagined she'd told as much as she cared to tell, but then Rafaela said, "I stayed on th' rug fer a long time, not sure I could even stand up, and not wantin' to, afraid to look at myself. I wanted to crawl under th' bed an' hide from th' world. Then they's a little knock on th' door. I's ashamed to answer, but one of th' old women from th' kitchen come in. She said *Señor* Comacho had sent her to help me. She brought a bowl of warm water, towels, cream fer th' welts on my back and legs and th' torn, bleeding places and bruises between my legs. After I got cleaned up, she helped me into a new dress *Señor* Comacho told her to bring me. She's gentle an' easy talkin', an' begged me to do 'xactly as th' *patrón* said. She said if I didn' resist, he'd lose interest in me purdy quick."

"How did you survive in that place? I mean, what kept you from losing your mind?" I asked.

She shrugged and said, "I don't know. It was just three days 'fore Comacho summoned me to th' back of th' *hacienda* again. I wanted to kill myself, but I went after th' old woman pleaded with me to go and not fight him. She said he wouldn't take long and I'd wash afterwards. I jest laid there when he's on me, an' washed fer an hour afterwards. Even with all th' washin', I still felt dirty 'cause I didn't have th' courage to kill myself. He called fer me ever' afternoon fer five straight days after that. *Señora* Comacho wuz a-shoppin' in Janos or Casas Grandes, so he used me in their bed. When th' señora returned, he didn' call me no more. Th' day after she come back, *Señora* Comacho come in th' kitchen, held up a strand of long blond hair, slapped me hard across th' face, and says, 'Stay away from my husband, whore.' That very same day, he called me to a different bedroom and wuz quicker an' rougher than th' days before, so I had to git away. I decided it wuz better to die freezin' in th' mountains or to be eaten by a bear than to have that monster a-tearin' at me. That night, I took my blanket, stole some supplies from th' kitchen, an' run."

"I'm amazed you got away," I said. I couldn't imagine the courage it must have taken for a young woman to attempt an escape with all the guards around the compound.

Rafaela nodded and said, "It weren't easy. Then I saw th' tracker comin' fer me a day later. He's like a dog on th' scent. He went down lots o' false trails, but kept gettin' closer an' closer. I had a knife and decided that when he caught up to me I'd kill myself. I warn't about to light no fire with 'im a followin' me. I slept in trees an' nearly froze to death fer two nights. On th' third day, I stumbled into Billy's camp. I reckon you know about how he caught that tracker and hung 'im upside down in a tree."

We both laughed, and it made the tension on both of us drop away.

Rafaela said, "That night, I cooked a meal fer us, and I's glad I's with this strong, brave *Americano*. He never tried to force hisself on me. I's so grateful to be away from *Señor*

Comacho that I'd a-been happy to give myself to 'im then if'n he'd wanted me."

She sighed and said, "We stayed together while he hunted fer venison and wild goat meat to sell fer supplies in Janos. He wuz lookin' to buy supplies fer Rojo, who's a-stealin' cattle fer 'im. I come to 'im on my own one night in th' *sierras.* I come to love 'im, an' I think he come to love me. I wanted 'im fer my man. He made me understand th' true pleasures 'tween a man and a woman. He didn't talk Mesican so good an' my *Americano* warn't much, so he taught me how to talk *Americano,* an' I's talkin' to 'im purdy quick, but I still like to talk Mesican 'cause it's whut I growed up with. I's with 'im fer five moons when I finally told 'im whut *Señor* Comacho done to me."

I shifted my weight and asked, "How did he react?"

She smiled and said, "Billy cursed and swore that *Señor* Comacho wuz a-goin' to pay fer th' evil he done me. Th' next time after that, when we's in Rojo's camp, he asked fer warriors to help 'im avenge his woman. They's a bunch eager to go with 'im. He picked five o' th' best. They's gone 'bout six or seven days, an' I ain't ever seen Billy so happy as when he come back. He handed me a little leather pouch. Inside wuz a blood-soaked handkerchief wrapped around two little pieces o' meat. Billy told me they's old Comacho's nuts. He said, 'Comacho ain't never gonna rape no woman agin.' "

She wrapped her arms around herself and said, "Billy and me were together fer two summers before ya'll come to Rojo's camp. Now Billy's dead, an' it's my fault. I keep wonderin' when this ol' blue eagle is gonna bring me luck. I shore hope it'll drop in fer a visit tomorry."

Even in the low light after the sun had fallen behind the mountains, I saw the tears streaming down her cheeks and said, "No! It's not your fault. Billy let his heart rule his head all the time. He played a fool's game, and it got him killed."

26
HOMBRECITO'S WOMAN

The air was turning black and cold. She shivered, and I wrapped an arm around her shoulders and pulled her next to me. "I'll get *el tigre mañana,* and then we'll go back to Rojo's. Don't worry. I want you to stay with Yellow Boy and me. I'll look after you, and maybe someday, you'll want to come to me, too."

I hadn't planned to say it. I just knew that I had a special feeling for her and didn't want her to ever think she'd be an outcast of some kind with Billy gone. She sniffed and snuggled up close under my arm. "*Gracias,* Hombrecito. Now tell me 'bout yore life."

So I told her what happened to Daddy and me, how Yellow Boy found me, how he and Rufus Pike trained and raised me, and about all the hours I trained to be a marksman with the Sharps. I told her about the ambush of Stone and Tally and Yellow Boy cutting off Tally's head. Then I told her about Rufus dying and how Oliver Lee was the last man I had to face before I called it even for Daddy's murder.

When I finished, we didn't speak for a long time. We just listened to the crickets, tree peepers, and the big frogs down on the creek while moonlight filled the canyon. It felt wonderful to have her there by me. We were quiet again for a long while before I climbed down to take care of the animals in the cave.

Back on the ledge again, I had to ask, "Can you tell me what happened when the Comachos caught you and Sac? If it's too hard to tell now, I understand. I can wait, but someday I want to know."

She bowed her head, and I felt her hand tremble in mine. Even in the dim light, I could see the water in her eyes. She shook her head. "I'll tell ya now. They's no need to wait. Sac, she's a lot like Billy. She let her heart think fer her. She believed Yellow Boy's waitin' till th' next night only meant more sufferin' fer Lewis Clark. She's a-thinkin' that maybe he's 'bout to die and that she had to get 'im *pronto* 'fore th' old women in th' kitchen broke 'im. When we went to th' bushes, she told me she's going down to th' *hacienda.* She thought she could sneak in an' take 'im without gittin' caught, an' she begged me to show her the way inside. I tol' her we'd git caught, but she weren't listenin'. She asked me to help her. I just couldn't say no. It's certain she'd git caught or killed if'n I didn' go, so I went."

"I wish you'd have told Yellow Boy or me what she was up to," I said.

"I would have, but there wasn't time. She'd a-been gone without me. We followed a path down to th' stream 'round behind th' *hacienda.* Th' door in th' wall leadin' to th' barns wuz unlocked. We crossed th' courtyard, a-stayin' in th' shadows. I knowed where th' kitchen servants wuz a-sleepin' an' led her over there. I opened th' door real slow an' keerful. I remembered how much it creaked and groaned when I's there. I opened it just enough fer her to slide in while I watched. She took a long time. I's shakin', I's so scared. Then I heard Lewis Clark yell, 'Sac!' Then lanterns lighted up all over th' *hacienda.*"

As she spoke, I wondered why Sac hadn't anticipated this outcome. She must have expected to take the sleeping boy away quietly.

Rafaela continued, "In less time than it's

taken me to tell ya 'bout it, we's surrounded by them *vaqueros* on guard. They's ever'where. Then *Señor* an' *Señora* Comacho came. When he seen me, he smiled and said, '*Dios mío,* there is justice in the world! Where this whore is, nearby is the *hombre* I wish to hang after I make him sing like a *castrato*! *Pero,* who is this beauty with you, whore? Who is this beauty trying to steal my property?' "

I could picture the scene clearly as Rafaela paused for a moment. She said, "I made Sac promise me not to speak if we's caught, but she didn' listen. She said, 'This is my brother! He's no slave. I want 'im back right now!' Then *Señor* Comacho leaned back an' laughed loud an' hard, an' so did th' crowd. He said, '*Mis vaqueros* bought this worthless slave from the Apaches. You can buy him back by telling me where *Señor* Creek is.' Sac wuz foolish, but brave. She stuck out her chin, an' said, 'I ain't tellin' you nothin'.'

"*Señor* Comacho, he stepped up and slapped her hard. Blood's in her mouth an' on her lips, but she spat it on his robe. He slapped her again on th' other side of her face and nearly knocked her down. Lewis Clark wuz a-screamin' fer 'im to leave her alone and swinging both his fists at *Señor*

368

Comacho's legs as hard as he could. Before Comacho could cuff 'im Sac grabs Lewis Clark in her arms and tries to hush 'im."

"Was she able to quiet him?" I asked, and I looked away so Rafaela wouldn't see my eyes were beginning to well up.

She nodded and said, "Then *Señor* Comacho looked at me and asked, 'Where is he?' When I shook my head, he smiled real big and said, '*Bueno,* whore! You give me the pleasure of making you tell.' They tied us up in chairs near th' kitchen and beat us. Then they left us a while before they come back an' beat us and asked us agin. They weren't beatin' us real hard because *Señor* Comacho told th' men who beat us that he wanted us to last a long time. Th' beatings stopped just 'fore sunup. An old kitchen woman come an' washed th' blood off my face, combed my hair, an' told me to put on th' clean white dress she give me." She paused again and said, "I ain't ever wore such a beautiful dress. I wonder why they give it to me."

I nodded and said, "They wanted us to see the blood clearly when they took you outside to beat you."

Rafaela frowned and said, "I reckon that's right. When they tied us under th' gallows, I wuz thinkin' this weren't so bad, that I could stand here all day and not hang myself. But in a while, I wuz feelin' prickles in my feet an' they wuz a-feelin' numb. My legs, they wuz hurtin' mighty bad. When th' beatings come, I thought I'd pass out, it hurt so bad. I knowed if'n I did, I'd hang myself fer shore. I made myself stand up to it. I knowed we had to wait till it's dark 'fore you could come, and so did Sac. It wuz that hope that kept us alive. You know th' rest."

I nodded and felt my blood get hot. "I promise you, Rafaela, one day I'll make the Comachos pay for what they did to you."

She looked at me in the inky shadows falling on our ledge, and then she hugged me and said, "No, Hombrecito. They's no end to vengeance. I'm alive; it's enough. Satan, he's done took their souls. They's no joy, no peace in their lives now. They's sufferin', not me. I lost my man, and you, yer woman 'cause o' them. They's nothing we'n do to bring 'em back. Now I have you. You'll be my life. Let it be."

My blood was still hot, but I heard the wisdom in her words and the come-to-me invitation in her voice. I nodded I understood. We sat for a while holding hands as the shadows from the moon's soft glow swung to our side of the canyon, leaving us covered in inky darkness. In the coolness, I

370

felt her breath and then her lips as she turned and kissed me. I kissed her back. I felt like I was floating in a dream, lifted beyond the cares of the day, no longer tethered to earth's hard reality. I remember her soft touch, her hand on the back of my neck, the smell of her hair, and the roar of desire filling me. She took my hand and held it to her breast. "Come to me, Hombrecito. We have this night. Maybe there ain't no more."

Most men only dream of nights like we had. Most have no idea what lovemaking is about, and most young men only fantasize about being taught the great secrets of life by an older, experienced woman. Rafaela made love to me. She loved me with her body and showed me how to love her with mine. In a few hours, she gave me a lifetime of lessons. The most important lesson I learned that night was always to make love as if I might never have the opportunity again, for it is always true that perhaps there is no tomorrow, no second chance to enjoy a great gift.

27
FIGHT TO THE FINISH

I sat up with a start. The sun was turning the western sky light blue, and the birds were calling up and down the canyon. All the worry and tension I'd felt the day before was gone, and I was happy to see the day, no matter what challenge it might present. Then I realized Rafaela was not beside me. My heart skipped a beat, but I looked over my shoulder and saw her by the fire. Her hair was wet, and her face had a fresh-scrubbed look. She was making coffee to go with the stew.

"Good morning! You took a mighty big chance going to the creek without me covering you. That demon likes to hunt early."

She smiled, her white teeth startling against her sun-bronzed skin, and my heart groaned with love and desire for her. "Mornin'! Yeah, I had a bath, an' fed the animals. I ain't afraid of that there devil no more. I know you're gonna kill 'im today.

Yer name may be Hombrecito, but you ain't Little Man no more. You're a big man, my man, *mi hombre.*"

She gave me the rest of the stew. I wanted to share it with her, but she refused and, without looking me in the eye, said she'd already eaten. I was starved and gobbled it down, confident that this was the day *el tigre*'s reign of terror ended. She sat down beside me with a hot cup of coffee cradled in her strong hands, its steam rising to meet the coming light. As I ate and watched her, still, serene, and enjoying the coming of the day, all I thought about was crawling back under the blanket with her and feeling her warm body next to mine. But the bright light of day soon brought those fantasies to an end, and I began to concentrate on how best to kill the demon that was after us.

She poured us another cup and said, "I know you're a-wantin' me to stay here an' cover ya, but ya gotta let me come with ya to cover yer back. That devil'll be on top of ya 'fore ya git a chance to use Shoots Today Kills Tomorrow. Please let me come with ya."

I shook my head. I wasn't about to risk her getting torn up by that killer. "No, it's better if you stay here. I got a better chance of drawing him out if it's just me, and I'm not about to risk losing you because of some mistake on my part. I'll be fine with you safe and covering me from here. It's even more important for you to guard the stock. If that cat gets in with the horses and Elmer and kills them, we'll be a long, long time getting back to Rojo's. It's not a trip I'd want to make on foot."

She studied me for a long time with those beautiful, green eyes, finally nodded, and didn't say any more about coming with me. I sipped a last cup of coffee while I made a final check of the Sharps, stuffed some cartridges in my vest pockets, and took a few sharpening swipes against a piece of river stone with my knife.

When I was ready to climb down, Rafaela, her eyes wet, hugged and kissed me. "You come back to me, Hombrecito, *mi hombre.* I'm a-waitin' and a-watchin'."

I climbed down to the stream, washed where Rafaela could cover me, checked on the animals, and, with a wave toward the lookout ledge, started moving upstream. I moved slowly and carefully, walking in the middle of the stream, looking for tracks on the opposite banks, checking above me in the trees and cliff ledges. I checked all the clumps of bushes and stands of bamboo cane where *el tigre* might be waiting in ambush, especially the stand of cane where it had watched us and had taken Lewis Clark. I kept Little David cocked, ready to fire. I climbed the waterfall steps, but I stopped when I reached the one where Sac had been taken. The big rock in the middle of the stream where it had eaten Lewis Clark was licked clean, except down in the cracks that had turned dark reddish brown to make the white stone a map lined with the life of Lewis Clark.

The tree where we found Sac showed claw marks up and down the trunk where the cat reached up high and ripped down the side for several feet to sharpen and clean its claws. When we'd found Sac, those tears weren't there. The air was still as death. No birds singing, no frogs, no insects. Nothing made any sound. I felt the hair prickling on the back of my neck, and my mouth went dry. I felt eyes following me. I looked everywhere, but I saw nothing. The urge to run was overpowering, but somehow I didn't panic. I knew if I did, I'd die before I'd made a hundred yards.

I climbed more of the steps. The waterfalls between them became higher and higher, and the canyon grew into a narrow, water-filled gorge. The brush was thinner and there were no more tall trees. I scanned both sides of the canyon, looking for a cave where the cat might have a den but saw none.

The sun was approaching the top of its arc, and I knew I had to return or be caught in the dark before I reached the ledge's safety and the comfort of Rafaela. I worked my way back down the series of waterfall steps, looking up and down the canyon as I went, listening for the least extraordinary sound. I heard nothing except the splashing of water, my heart thumping, and the short, quick gasps filling my lungs. I was moving slowly, but I was breathing and sweating like I was running hard and fast between the Organs and Tortugas Mountain.

I got all the way back down to the cave and neither saw nor heard anything. I breathed a sigh of relief as I waved at the bushes on the ledge and saw Rafaela wave back. I pointed downstream and kept moving. I wanted to check all the way to the main canyon. Afternoon shadows were filling the canyon, and a shaft of bright sunlight playing on the water ripples hurt my eyes, making me squint to keep from being blinded. I stood there a while, watching, listening. Nothing. No sign of the cat anywhere. *Maybe,* I thought, *it's left for easier pickings.*

I walked back up to the cave in the middle of the stream, much more relaxed than I had been the entire day. The sun was just above the edge of the ridgeline, the light easy in the warm glow of the late afternoon. I waved again at Rafaela before I went toward the cave to take care of the animals. I heard them nervously snorting and stamping around and was instantly on alert.

There was the slightest tremble in the bamboo thicket where the jaguar had waited to take Lewis Clark. I thought I heard something scratching against rock, like a knife chipping on it . . . like big claws digging in and tearing against it! I turned, swinging Little David to my shoulder.

Rafaela screamed, "Hombrecito!"

The jaguar sailed off the top of the boulder and through the bamboo, practically flying over the bushes between the bamboo and the creek. It landed at the edge of the stream with a terrific, angry *Uh! Uh! Uh!* It came snarling up into another huge leap straight for me. I can still remember those huge paws spread straight, their rapier claws out, the cat's mouth wide open, big, curved teeth set to crush my head while it held me and tore my guts out with its hind claws.

My heart stopped thumping in my ears,

my mind forced total concentration, and everything slowed down so fractions of a second became minutes. I clearly saw everything happening. I wasn't nervous, but in those moments slowly pouring out of time's bottle, I couldn't move fast, either. I strained every fiber of my being, as though in some nightmare, to kill the jaguar before it killed me. Little David roared. I don't even remember pulling the trigger.

The cat jerked and twisted a little at the bullet's impact. Its paws started flailing in the air as if it were trying to catch onto something as it fell. I tried to duck under it, but it flew into me, knocking me backwards. The Sharps flew out of my hands. I hit the big, flat, sandstone bottom in the creek's shallows, knocking the wind out of me and cracking my head. I saw a universe of bright, silver stars slowly floating past like leaves in an autumn creek. I was so stunned, I couldn't move. I just lay there trying to make the floating stars go away, trying to suck air back into my lungs and make the darkness vanish.

The cat was furiously biting at the black bullet hole in its chest a few inches below its chin, like it was trying to get rid of some stinging insect. Then it saw me lying in front of him, almost within reach. Snarling and roaring *Uh! Uh! Uh!* so loud, I was sure I was one bite, one second, away from dying, the cat tried to stand and come after me, but it couldn't move its hind legs.

From a long way off, I heard Rafaela screaming, "Move, Hombrecito! Get out of the way! It's a-comin'! *Madre a Dios!* Move!"

The fact was, I couldn't move. I was too stunned and dizzy. I tried to use my hands to push myself up so I could roll over and crawl away, but my hands kept sliding in something slick on the rocks. Through the haze and stars in front of my eyes, I looked at the palm of one of my hands. It was smeared with blood. One of the cat's claws had ripped a gash in the back muscles of my left upper arm, and I was losing blood.

The cat started dragging itself toward me with one huge paw, swinging another through the air in long, slashing strokes to grab me. I was trapped in a nightmare, frozen in an image, unable to move. The paw swiping the air just missed my side and hooked into my vest. I felt myself being dragged toward that big, snarling mouth with teeth that could crush my head as easily as I might bite a ripe tomato. Straining to hold back, I dug in my heels, frantic, searching, trying to wrap my fingers around the handle of my knife. Rafaela suddenly appeared behind the cat, holding a big, round river rock high in the air with both hands.

El tigre never saw it coming. She smashed the rock squarely into his head between his ears and knelt beside me. She was gasping for air, and tears were streaming down her face, as she ran her hands over my shoulders, looking to see where I was cut. She grabbed me under my shoulders and, groaning with the effort, pulled me away from the cat to the edge of the stream, splashed water on my face, and washed the blood off my arm so she could see how bad the rip was. She pulled the rawhide strip holding a little bag from around her neck and used it to tie off my arm.

I coughed and gagged as my wind came back. "Lordy, woman. You saved my life."

"Thank the great God in heaven you're a-livin', Hombrecito, jest thank God," she whispered. She scooped up a palm full of water, spread it over her face, and shook the drops and streamers off as she held my head in her lap.

I looked at the gash in my arm. She was going to have to sew me up.

"There's a little buckskin bag covered with beadwork in my bedroll. If you'll get it, then we can stop the bleeding and sew up this gash."

"I'll be right back. I'll find it."

She left me with a nice smooth rock for a pillow and ran to the cave. I turned my head and looked over my shoulder at the cat. Even with half its skull caved in, its head still looked huge. *What a shame,* I thought, *to kill such a magnificent animal.*

I tilted my head back and looked toward the red sun nearly gone behind the mountains. We needed a fire for her to see by when she started sewing. I managed to get to my feet and wobble toward the fire pit. She came out of the cave with Rufus's possibles bag before I'd taken three steps.

"We're going to need a fire so you can see to doctor me."

"Let me help ya over to th' cave. There's wood. I'll make us a fire."

She got me over to the fire pit and fixed me a comfortable place to sit while she worked. Before she started the fire, she went to the jaguar and cut its throat. It was on a big, tilted, flat rock with its head sloped down, almost in the stream. Its blood seeping toward the water made dark red streams that matched the color of the dying sunlight rushing away in long streamers.

When she returned to the fire pit, I asked

why she'd done that.

"We gotta eat, *mi hombre.*"

By the time a bright little fire crackled in the cool evening air, the night sky was black, and a soft light filled the sky behind the southern mountains as the moon waited to make her grand entrance. Rafaela was a good doctor. She had sewn up cuts before. Her stitches were evenly spaced, neat, and effective. I was lucky Rufus's powder was still an excellent antiseptic and helped stop the bleeding. By the time she finished, my arm throbbed. I still felt woozy from the smack on my head and loss of blood.

Climbing up to the ledge, she got the pots and blankets down, retrieved Little David from where it landed in the bushes, and made coffee. The smell of the brown beans and coffee she put on to boil and her fry bread sizzling in the old black skillet made my mouth water.

It was the sweetest time of my life. When a woman teaches a man the secrets of life, and the woman is his best friend and lover, it's like being thirsty in the desert. He never gets enough of her — whether he's making love with her, talking to her, watching her, smelling her — he just never gets enough. I never got enough of Rafaela.

■ ■ ■ ■

We were at the cave three more days. Rafaela skinned the jaguar. She scraped the hide and on the flesh side smeared it with some kind of mixture she made out of the cat's brains and old oak leaves. She wanted to keep the hide soft and flexible until we returned to Rojo's where the women, who were leather experts, could help her with it. She cut up the meat for us to live on. It wasn't bad either.

Rafaela was able to get its bladder without breaking it, and she used the urine around our campsite to warn other predators off our territory. That was a great trick. We even saw a big grizzly turn and discreetly walk back down the canyon after it got a whiff of those markers. I worked around the camp as best I could, but with my arm in a sling, I wasn't much use. Of course, when the sun was coming up or going down, or high in the sky, we were in each other's arms on the blankets there in the cave.

28
THE BLESSING

On the morning of the fourth day, I was at my morning constitutional when I thought I heard unfamiliar splashing downstream — maybe horses coming up the canyon. Worried that Rafaela might be at her morning toilette, that we'd literally be caught with our pants down, I hurried back to the fire. She looked at me with a questioning frown as I ran up.

"I think there're horses coming up the canyon. Come on! Grab your rifle, and let's get over to the ledge!"

She didn't say anything. Putting down the stew she'd been making, she grabbed her rifle and we ran, splashing across the stream. She went right up the rope, but it was hard for me with my injured arm. She reached down, grabbed Little David's barrel, and pulled me right up over the edge. Gasping for air, my arm throbbing, I sat back against the canyon wall beside her, looking out through the juniper bushes. I brought the hammer back to safety on Little David, dropped the breech, and checked the cartridge. Rafaela levered a cartridge into her rifle's chamber and let its hammer down to safety. We waited.

Looking downstream, I finally saw some motion in the shadows and brush. Two horses, one behind the other, picked their way slowly across the rocks and around big boulders in the stream. I cocked Little David and sighted on a place where they would pass us if they stayed in the stream. I was certain I wouldn't miss if I had to shoot. I heard the hammer come back on Rafaela's rifle as she, too, readied for our visitors.

I whispered, "I'll take the one in the lead, you get the one in back."

The lead horse stopped in the shadows as the riders scanned the bright sunlit area in the middle of the stream in front of us. I brought Little David to my shoulder, and rested the barrel in a fork of the juniper beside me. It was too dark in the shadows downstream to see more than the slightest outline of the horses and their riders. It couldn't have been more than a couple of minutes, but it seemed an eternity, until the riders moved forward.

Yellow Boy and Arango. I turned to Rafaela. Her smile lit up the shadows. She squeezed my shoulder with relief. I put my finger to my lips to sign for silence. *Thank you, merciful God!* was all I could think.

They came up the stream at a slow walk, scanning every bush and every boulder on both sides. When Yellow Boy was nearly even with the cave, he stopped. Taking deep breaths he smelled the air, pointed his rifle directly at the cave, and nodded to Arango, who smiled and nodded back.

I couldn't hold back any longer. "Muchacho Amarillo *y Señor* Arango! *Como estas?*"

The horses pranced in circles, splashing water in bright little sprays, as they wheeled, searching for our hiding place. Yellow Boy turned no more than once before he stopped and faced the ledge, the butt of his rifle resting against the top of his thigh. The smile of relief filling his face warmed my heart.

"Hombrecito, you hide *muy bien,* grandson."

Arango grinned and shook his rifle above his head. *"Buenas días,* Hombrecito! *Como esta?"*

I was ready to call back *muy bien* when the full weight of what had happened to Sac and Lewis Clark fell on me. Rafaela and I had been living and loving like they'd never existed. How could we do that? I guess we just hadn't been able to come to terms with the horror of what had happened. It was as if we were denying anything bad had happened at all. I felt sick when I answered, "Rafaela and I are here. Sac and Lewis Clark are with the grandfathers."

Yellow Boy's and Arango's smiles fled. They waited quietly as Rafaela helped me back down off the ledge and climbed down herself. She nodded at them, but never said a word. I saw Arango study her for a moment before giving his head a little nod as if somehow he'd known Rafaela would be here but not Sac. We walked with our friends to the fire in front of the cave. They led their horses inside, unsaddled them, wiped them down, and came back to the fire.

Rafaela had made fresh coffee while we waited for them to finish with their horses. Yellow Boy, eyeing the bandage and sling holding my arm, sat down by the fire and crossed his legs. Arango sat down on a flat rock with his back against a big log covered with velvety, emerald-green moss.

Yellow Boy squinted at me through the vapor across the top of his cup. "*Es bueno* you hide *bien aquí,* Hombrecito. Soldier camp on *río. Usted* hide from this camp, *sí?*"

"*Sí.* They were at the *río* when we came down from the pass. So many. The camp stretched from the pass road to the river and a long way north and south. I decided it was too risky to try and ride around it. I thought we'd be caught for sure if we tried to outrun 'em with the women hurt, Lewis Clark riding double with Sac, and Elmer to slow us down. I decided to hide and wait 'em out. It was fool's work."

Arango frowned and looked around. He spoke in Spanish. "Why, Hombrecito? You hide very well. You're wise, with the little boy and injured women, to avoid the soldiers. You're a great warrior with Little David. A man with two women, here? This is paradise."

Yellow Boy took my bandaged arm and gently raised it, watching my eyes for some sign of pain. I tried to keep my face a mask of iron, but I know he saw me flinch. "Hombrecito, speak of this wound."

I told him how the jaguar carried off Lewis Clark and how Sac and Rafaela had chased it. His brow furrowed, and his lips formed a silent whistle. He glanced in admiration at Rafaela for her loyalty and bravery. I told him Rafaela's story of how Sac went after the cat with only rocks in her

388

hands and how it slaughtered her, and I described how we found Sac's body in a tree.

By the time I finished the story with how Rafaela finished off *el tigre* by smashing in his head, Arango was staring at us with round eyes, his mouth forming an O, and Yellow Boy, sitting with his rifle across his knees, nodded slowly.

Yellow Boy said, "Hombrecito, you and your woman are great warriors. You showed *mucho* courage fighting a powerful enemy. Maybe the enemy was even a witch. My chest swells in pride for you, my son."

I was dumbfounded. I knew we'd have a lot of explaining to do about how we'd become intimate, and I wanted to ask his blessing for her to be my woman. Yet Yellow Boy hadn't even blinked when he called Rafaela my woman. Arango sat there nodding his agreement with a big smile, mumbling under his breath, *"Muy bueno, muy bueno."*

I glanced at Rafaela. She was still watching the stream drifting down the canyon. Her beautifully bronzed skin was turning red, and there was a smile playing at the corners of her mouth.

Yellow Boy said, "Hombrecito, show us the skin of *el tigre.*"

I pushed myself up and led them behind

389

the bushes at Lewis Clark's pool. I showed them the frame of bamboo cane Rafaela had made to keep the hide stretched tight while it soaked up her tanning mixture. She'd done a fine job with it, even to the point of saving the smashed skull with the intention of making one the same size out of wood and using its canine teeth to make it look realistic.

When Arango saw the hide stretched on the frame, he gave a low whistle. "*Magnífico. El tigre* was beautiful and a killer. *Muy bien,* Hombrecito *y* Rafaela."

Rafaela said nothing, but she nodded her appreciation for the compliments.

Yellow Boy's eyes glittered as he rubbed a hand over the fur and measured the bullet exit hole, a few inches from where the tail joined the body, by filling it with three fingers. He then eyed the much smaller entry hole in the soft white fur that once covered the jaguar's chest.

We stared at the pelt a few minutes before Yellow Boy turned back to the fire and took his seat. Rafaela poured us more coffee. We sat for a while, enjoying the cool breeze floating down the canyon from off the mountains. I was ready to sell my soul to hear Yellow Boy's story, but I knew custom between us dictated we wait until he asked if we were interested in hearing it.

Finally, he asked, "Shall I speak of El Paso Carretas?"

"*Sí, por favor.* We were worried all these days about you, grandfather, and our *amigos,* Arango *y* Billy Creek. We saw Billy go down. Rafaela and I think he's no more."

"*Sí,* Hombrecito *y* Rafaela, Billy Creek *es no más.* Soldiers shoot many times when Billy charges them. The charge the soldiers make for *paso* runs over him. The horse of Billy is there, but no Billy Creek. We look *por* Billy, but he is *no más.* Maybe soldiers take his body. We do not know. He is with the grandfathers."

Rafaela made no sound, but we all saw her wiping her eyes with her shirtsleeve.

"When soldiers charge, they ride hard for *paso* Elias *y* Juan take men, turn *y* ride for San Miguel. Run like rabbits. *Vaqueros* come back across *paso.* Elias *y* Juan hear *vaqueros* come. Hide in same little canyon in El Paso Carretas we use before we come to Comacho *hacienda. Vaqueros y* soldiers no find Elias *y* Juan.

"Elias thinks maybe soldiers ride over us in charge up road. Arango *y* Muchacho Amarillo return to Rojo. Then Elias sends *un hombre* to Rojo. Elias's *hombre* looks over camp, but no see Arango *y* Muchacho

Amarillo. Elias's *hombre* tells Rojo that Arango *y* Muchacho Amarillo killed by soldiers. Rojo no say not true, just nod head. Send *hombre* back with meat to thank Elias for the word."

I rarely saw Yellow Boy laugh, but he did then. I thought it was one of his better tricks, and all the more enjoyable because it was played on Elias and the Comachos.

"We wait. You no come to Rojo with women *y* Lewis Clark. We leave Rojo. Ride to find you. Ride to El Paso Púlpito from east side of *sierras.* No find on trail, no find *en* pass. We ride around soldier camp *y* look for you on *río.* Find sign you leave at canyon where we see *el tigre.* You hide *muy bien,* Hombrecito. You miss soldiers *y* Yaquis. *Mañana* we go to Rojo camp, *sí?*"

"*Sí,* Grandfather. We go."

Rafaela wandered over to sit in the sun on a large boulder near the stream. Arango unrolled his blankets in the shade under a large cottonwood. He tossed off his hat and took off his revolver, but kept it within instant reach and, with a great, lion-like yawn, stretched out and lay down for a midday *siesta.*

It was quiet there at the fire between Yellow Boy and me. The sunlight, filtering down through the fall leaves, sparkled on the ripples in the stream, reflecting dancing patterns on the vertical canyon walls. The place was beautiful and serene. But my heart was heavy. I needed counsel from Yellow Boy on my situation with Rafaela, and I was feeling mighty guilty about not taking a respectable amount of time to grieve for Sac and Lewis Clark before I was under the blankets with her. I said, "Grandfather, I need your wisdom."

He nodded, stood up, and started walking up the stream with the Henry in the crook of his arm. We walked past the pool where Lewis Clark had played and then along the edge of the stream. About a hundred yards up, he found a large boulder and sat down, resting his rifle across his knees. I joined him and waited for him to speak.

"*Que paso,* Hombrecito?"

I sighed and said, "Rafaela and me, we fought for our lives against *el tigre.* Then, within two suns of *el tigre* taking Sac and Lewis Clark, we were under the blankets. We thought then that *mañana,* maybe we would be no more. We used the day we had. She's taught me many things about life. Things I never imagined, very good things. Before this time, I never imagined women brought such pleasure and feelings to an *hombre.*"

He looked at me and smiled.

"*Sí,* Hombrecito. A good woman teaches *un hombre* many things *no hombre* can teach him. Rafaela is a good woman and very brave. You choose well, my son."

I felt my neck turning red and nodded. "*Sí,* but now we are under the blankets and not married. She is no woman of loose virtue. Will the People accept this? What must we do for her to be my woman in the People's eyes? She has no family. Will we live with you as if she were your daughter? We didn't grieve a long time for Sac, Lewis Clark, and Billy. Was this wrong?"

Yellow Boy stared down the stream for a while and then shook his head. "It is good, Hombrecito. Rafaela has *un hombre* before you. She is no more a girl. She is a woman who has known a man. Sac, your woman in the People's eyes, *es no más.* Only you are left. When we go to Rojo, we'll tell the People Rafaela is my daughter and your woman now. I know you never take Sac as your woman. She *es amiga* but not your woman under the blankets. Now *usted y* Rafaela, *usted hombre y mujer en los ojos* of the People."

A wave of relief rolled over me. I had vowed to myself that I'd never leave Rafaela, no matter what anyone else thought or said, but I knew I'd never turn away from Yellow Boy, either. He was all the family I had left and had raised me the past six or seven years. It was important to me that he approve of what I had decided, regardless of the face he put on the matter for the rest of the people.

I sat there for a minute and became a little puzzled. "How did you know Sac and I had not yet been under the blankets?"

He looked at me with a sly grin. "*Sus ojos,* your eyes are now the eyes of a man. They were not so with Sac." It was years before I understood what he was talking about, so I let it end there.

When we wandered back to the fire, Arango was still asleep, snoring with his face under his hat, a hand wrapped around his revolver. I heard the occasional clink of steel cinch rings against the cave's floor and knew Rafaela was working with the pack gear.

Yellow Boy poured himself some more coffee and sat down. I went in the cave. Even in the dim light, I saw that Rafaela's eyes were red and puffy. The horses and mules were a little nervous and stamping around. She was packing the jaguar hide.

"Why do you cry?" I asked.

"I wuz thinkin' on Billy. Billy saved me from them Comachos, maybe even from

395

bein' killed. He filled my heart with the wantin' for a man, and he meant a lot to me. He wuz my *hombre.* Now he's gone forever."

I looked away and felt bitter disappointment settle in my guts. But when she saw my face, she was off her knees and had her arms around me. "Hombrecito, ye're my man now. I'm cryin' only as foolish women cry when they's lost a man close to their heart. I'm cryin' only for yesterday, not tomorrow. Yesterday ain't no more."

I took her in my arms and said, "I understand. Cry for Billy until there're no more tears. I came to tell you that Yellow Boy approves of our union, and if you agree, he'll adopt you, and I'll claim you as my wife when we return to Rojo's camp."

She hugged me, smiled, and nodded. "You know I want ya, Hombrecito. They ain't no question 'bout it." She let her hand pass over my breechcloth and said, "Why, I'n tell ye're ready fer the marriage blanket right now."

29
THE RETURN

We all thought our best chance to pass the Mexican Army camp was to travel at night, but we needed rest, so we slept that night. Breakfast the next day was leftovers of beans and jaguar stew Rafaela had made. We spent most of the morning getting packed and ready to ride. The animals were well rested and eager to get back on the trail. They needed and wanted exercise.

While we were packing, I found Sac's old revolver. She'd been far too small around the hips to cinch the holster tight enough to support her father's old 1873 army revolver, so she'd carried it on her saddle. The revolver was .45 caliber and had a seven-and-a-half-inch barrel like Arango's. It seemed to be in good mechanical condition, but the finish showed a lot of use. I walked out of the cave with the revolver hanging on my hip. Arango was sitting in his favorite place next to the old log, still slurping on his morning coffee. He had his hat pulled down close to his eyebrows. When he heard me approach, he tilted his head back and looked down his nose to see me. He grinned when he saw the revolver on my hip.

"*Señor* Arango, Billy Creek once told me you were one of the best men in this country with a handgun. Sac had this one. Will you teach me how to use it?"

Arango held out his hand and said nothing. I handed him the old Colt. He took it, checked the action a couple of times by half-cocking it and opening the gate where the cartridges were loaded, flexing the extractor against a couple of bullets, and returning them to the cylinder. Then he put it on safety, twirled it about his finger, and brought it to full-cock before easing the hammer back down. He left it on safety and handed it back to me, handle first. "*La pistola es en condición bueno,* but *es* very old. *Sí,* I show you how to use it."

He pushed himself to his feet and strode off toward Lewis Clark's pool, motioning for me to follow. When we got there, he sat down on a boulder and held out his hand. I gave him the revolver again, and he showed me how to load it and extract empty cartridges. Arango fished around in his jacket pocket and found several empty shell casings. He told me to unload the revolver. He took the cartridges and handed me the empty casings with instructions to load them and to leave an empty chamber under the hammer. He laughed when I looked at him like he was crazy. He told me to always dry-fire with empty shells in the cylinder so it wouldn't damage the firing pen, and to get in the habit of leaving an empty chamber under the hammer when I loaded it. Arango said to practice loading and extracting empty cartridge cases so that I became fast and smooth, keeping it loaded and ready to fire.

Arango showed me how to hold the gun with two hands for a long shot, how to stand relaxed for a smooth, effective draw, and how to shoot where my hand pointed once it cleared the holster. I soon realized that learning to use a revolver was going to be much harder than I had imagined.

Showing me how to draw in one smooth motion, he cautioned me about trying to be so fast that I didn't know where my hand was in the draw or where my target was. I remembered Daddy saying years before that it was much more important to be cool and accurate under fire than it was to get the first shot off. It occurred to me that Daddy and Arango must have attended the same school of firearms. I spent the rest of the day practicing loading and unloading and dry-firing using the empty cartridges.

We fed the stock an extra ration of grain at midafternoon and started packing and saddling them as the sun started falling behind the ridgeline. We rode down the canyon with just enough light to avoid the big boulders and trees until we got to the big canyon leading up from the river. Yellow Boy led the way. Arango stayed in the rear, and Rafaela and I stayed in the middle with the pack animals.

Yellow Boy stopped when we reached the river. It was full dark, and the moon's glow was just starting to show behind the mountains off to the northeast. As soon as the sun fell out of the sky, it was cool enough to see vapor from our breath. When he was sure there were no patrols nearby, Yellow Boy led us out of the canyon and down the river. We rode along the east side until we gained the plateau above the river and headed almost due north, using one of the narrow trails through the creosotes and mesquite I'd used when I'd scouted the army camp nearly a week earlier. We made good time and, in a couple of hours, swung east toward El Paso Púlpito and then back west, passing the army camp, and then back along the Bavispe. There seemed to be even more campfires and soldiers in the camp than the last time I'd seen it.

Arango rode up to Yellow Boy, and they had a short palaver before he rode off. He saluted Rafaela and me with a touch to the edge of his *sombrero* as he rode past us and off into the darkness toward the camp. Yellow Boy told me later Arango wanted to spend a little time studying the camp to learn what he could about the way the army organized before big battles. He thought it might be useful information someday.

As the moon started to fall, Arango caught up with us. He said he counted at least ten small-bore cannons and a couple of Gatling guns, and that there must be at least four or five hundred men in the camp. The army wasn't taking any chances in battles to wipe out the last of the Yaqui uprising.

By the time Arango returned, we had already crossed the hard, dry country between the mountains and the river and were heading up toward the pass we came down when we first rode from Rojo's camp over to the Bavispe. It was nearly dawn when we rode up to the cave we had used. Rafaela cooked us some fry bread, beans, and meat and made a pot of coffee. Arango and I unloaded the horses and mules and rubbed them down. Just the smell of that bread was reward enough for a hard night's ride.

Yellow Boy disappeared to scout the surrounding area to make sure the army or Elias's Apaches didn't surprise us. He returned just as the dawn sky was turning from dark gray to delicate pinks and the birds in the bushes and cactus were beginning to chirp. That canyon pass was colder than what we were used to in the jaguar's canyon. As I sat by the fire, trying to warm away the shivers, Rafaela came and sat down beside me and threw a blanket over our shoulders. Yellow Boy gave a little nod and smile of approval as he sipped his coffee.

Riding into Rojo's camp was like the first day I'd entered it. A crowd formed around us. Moon came forward with Redondo, her smile glowing in the soft half-light of the morning as she took the reins from Yellow Boy. Yellow Boy nodded and turned to smile at Moon and Redondo. Rojo stepped through the crowd and said, "You have returned, *amigos*. *Bueno!* Where are Sac and her brother, Lewis Clark?"

Yellow Boy slid from his paint and said, "Sac and Lewis Clark are *no más.* They go to the grandfathers. Now, Rafaela *es* Hombrecito's woman. The lodge Rojo gives to Hombrecito and Sac? Hombrecito still has it, *sí?*"

Rojo's face betrayed no questions. "*Sí.* We talk after the meal."

The crowd drifted back to their fires. Rafaela and I unpacked and unsaddled our animals, but Yellow Boy and Arango gave theirs to some young boys to take down to the corral. I took ours while Rafaela stored the gear inside our lodge and started cooking at Moon's fire.

It felt like we were home. The canyon wrens were in fine voice, and the tart smell of cooking fire smoke was like fine perfume in the chilly air. I was so thankful to be alive and with a good woman.

After eating, Yellow Boy motioned for me to come with him, telling me to bring the jaguar hide. Rafaela went to our lodge, returned with the canvas in which she had wrapped it, and told me she would make our lodge ready and wait for my return. At Rojo's fire, Arango and several of the old men were sipping their coffee and smoking. We sat across from Rojo on a blanket his woman spread for us. Yellow Boy rested his rifle between his knees and accepted the coffee one of Rojo's women offered to pour for him. I shook my head when she offered me some before she disappeared from the council of men.

Rojo nodded at Yellow Boy. "Arango says there is much to tell in the finding of Hombrecito and the woman Rafaela. Give us this story, *amigo*."

Yellow Boy nodded. "*Sí*. There is *mucho* to tell. Hombrecito *y* Rafaela are mighty warriors against a strong enemy. He will tell you. Shall he bring her to speak with us? She also fought the enemy with Hombrecito."

Rojo smiled and nodded. I set the canvas aside and went to fetch Rafaela. She appeared puzzled when I returned from Rojo's fire so quickly and was reluctant to go to the council until I said they asked for her. Then she lifted her chin and walked proudly back to the little group with me.

For Apaches, it was unusual, but not unheard of, for women to ride with the men, and when they did, they were fierce fighters. The men didn't hesitate to accept them, either. If you had the right stuff when it came to war, it didn't make any difference if you were a man or a woman, so it didn't surprise me she was invited to the council.

She sat down beside me on Rojo's blanket, and we told our story while the others sat drinking their coffee and listening, heads tilted toward us to be sure they heard every word. All of them, with a couple of exceptions, wore puzzled looks when we showed them the jaguar's hide. Two of the old men had seen a jaguar while raiding to the south with Geronimo. They were still surprised to see how big this cat was compared to a cougar. They all grunted and nodded in appreciation at the courage Sac and Rafaela showed in trying to save Lewis Clark and Rafaela's bravery in saving me.

Yellow Boy told Rojo he wanted to have a feast to celebrate Rafaela becoming my woman and, since she had no living parents, she was to be part of his family. Rojo and his old men nodded their approval.

After the council, Rojo called the village together. He said Rafaela and I were married and that in three days Yellow Boy was giving a feast to celebrate. He said we were both great warriors, that he was happy to have us, and that the People should be glad we were with them and living with Yellow Boy's family.

Moon gave Rafaela a beautifully tanned buckskin shift that had miles of long narrow fringe and was covered with magnificent beadwork. Rafaela was a vision of beauty and grace wearing it. Moon and Rafaela were soon fast friends and worked together often in the days before the feast.

At the feast we danced, ate, drank, and told our stories. The celebration fires roared high and the People made good the joy of the celebration. Like a giant thumping heart, a big drum kept up a low, rhythmic thunder nearly all night. The young women and men danced for hours. The older women watched them to be sure none of them slipped off into the night. The older men sat back in the edge of the shadows, watching too, telling tales of Power from wars and raids in the old days.

Rafaela left the fire first. Catching my eye as she drifted into the cold night, she held up her forefinger for me to wait a few minutes before I came to her. Rafaela was three or four years older than me. Even though she had been used and abused by old man Comacho, had lived with Billy Creek for a couple of years, and had made love to me the night before we killed *el tigre* and practically every day after that when we had some privacy, she was still very modest with me on the night of our marriage feast.

When I finally slipped from the circle of

firelight and the dancing, my heart hammered and my steps were quick. Reaching the blanket over the lodge's doorway, I paused. I wasn't sure what kind of etiquette a bride expected from her bridegroom. I asked, "May I come in, Rafaela?"

I heard the blankets inside rustle and her low, husky voice. "Come, Hombrecito."

A small oil lamp burned by the blankets. It cast a soft glow that fluttered against the smooth brown- and gray-speckled river rocks forming the walls and the dark rough branches supporting the canvas cover making the ceiling. She lay under a blanket, her honey-blond hair cast up on the sleeping pad like shafts of light from the sun. The smoke from the lamp carried just a hint of sage. I stared at her beauty, feeling my heart thump.

She patted the blanket beside her. "Come, *mi hombre.*"

30
STEALING *HACENDADO* CATTLE

A few days later, I went with Arango, Yellow Boy, and five other warriors to rustle cattle. Many days of watching and scouting the cattle herds out on the *llano* identified those herds from which to pick small groups when raiding time came. The Apaches stole just enough from a herd to make the effort worthwhile, but not so many that angry *hacendados* sent their *vaqueros* into the mountains after them. A few cows — what was the difference? They were not worth the risk of having good *vaqueros* shot to pieces.

Rojo and the leaders of bands scattered throughout the Sierra Madre finally had the balance about right for how many head to steal from a particular herd and not be chased into the *sierras.* In those days, an uneasy truce existed between the Apaches and the Mexicans, even though there were still murders and slaves taken by both sides.

They kept a close eye on each other, ready for the dry tinder of hatreds over two-hundred-fifty years old to flare into a hot and angry blaze, but there were no major attacks by the Indians on the small Mexican villages down in the valleys, and none by the Mexicans on the Indian camps up in the mountains. It didn't seem right to steal cattle, and I said so before I agreed to go. That was when Arango explained the facts of life in Mexico to me.

"Hombrecito," he said, "*el llano* was, as *Americanos* say, open range. Before *este* robber *Díaz,* the *peones* keep their herds together *en* the *llano.* They must protect them only from the wolves and the Apaches. The *bandido,* no take cattle often *en llano.* Work *con* cattle *es* . . . how you say? . . . very hard. *Los bandidos* wait until *peones* sell the cattle and then rob them. Díaz, he sends the surveyors, from the *peones* he steals the lands and the cattle, and then gives them to *hacendado*s like the *familia* Comacho. *No más* free range.

"The *hacendados* pay the *peones* to look after the cattle stolen from them, but the *pesos* are few. *Bandidos* can no longer get their share of the cattle money by robbing the *peones.* The *hacendados* have their *vaqueros* drive the cattle to the trains. The

409

money stays *en los bancos. Es muy* dangerous robbing *los bancos. Bandidos* use *los
cabezos. Los bandidos,* now they steal the
cattle and sell them across the border to
Americanos. We give the *peones* a share of
the *pesos* from the cattle we steal. They
look the other way when the cattle are
taken. Why should they fight *y* die for cattle
theirs *no más?* I ride with my boss, *Pancho
Villa. El* use *cabeza.* Give *peones uno peso
en diez,* Apache *tres pesos en diez,* his *hombres tres pesos, y el* keeps *tres pesos.* Little
work, *pero mucho dinero por el jefe, sí?"*

I had to admit it was a pretty clever arrangement, except I didn't believe it. "How
do the Apaches keep from being cheated?
How do they know they're getting three
pesos out of every ten? What would they do
with the *dinero* even if they had it?"

Arango grinned and nodded. *"Es verdad,*
es true, *el sol es en su cabeza,* Hombrecito.
Rojo knows numbers and sometimes he
watches. When he is not there, Apaches take
one cow *en tres* with the others they keep.
When there is only *dinero,* I buy them guns,
bullets, *mucho* cloth, and perhaps a few pots
and pans. I do not cheat the Apache, *señor.*
They are *mis amigos. Es muy* dangerous to
cheat *un* Apache, *sí?"*

I nodded to him. "*Usted* are wise, *Señor* Arango."

"*Gracias, señor.*"

Arango continued to explain that when the Apaches worked with the bandits or anyone else, like Billy Creek, to steal from the *hacendados'* herds, they always kept half the cattle and got one-third of the rest. To me, that sounded like a burdensome share, but they usually got blamed for the raid, and they provided good protection against the army and *hacendado vaqueros* while helping their partners herd their share of the stock north toward the border. They earned every *centavo*. Besides, if they didn't get their full measure, they felt free to steal what they wanted from the men they helped.

The Apaches usually ran their share of the herd up into their canyon corrals where they slaughtered the cattle, kept the hides, and cured the meat. They'd set aside all the meat they needed for winter and pack the extra north across the border to trade for horses and salt from relatives living at San Carlos or Mescalero.

Any work you do with cattle is hard work. Oh, there's a rush of excitement when they're first stolen, and if the army or *rancho vaqueros* chase you, you run the risk of being killed. Once you have the herd, though,

411

it's tough, dirty work. The dust that's kicked up gets into every cranny of your body. Your eyes get filled with it, and you can even feel the grit on your teeth. The cows will try to kill you if they think you're after their calves, and the bulls will come after you just because they can. The herd spooks easily and runs until it drops. If they don't get water every two or three days, they die. All the work has a high chance of coming to nothing. No wonder in the old days the *bandidos* rarely stole livestock. It was a lot easier to just take the money after the herd was sold.

The cattle we stole on my first raid were driven from the *llano* up into the Sierra Las Espuelas, about thirty miles from the New Mexico border, just south of the bootheel. They followed a long series of connected canyons that had water even in the late fall. Using the canyons offered an easy way to control the herd with only a few men in the front and back.

When we reached the first canyon leading from the *llano* midmorning of the third day after the raid, Yellow Boy, Arango, two of his *compañeros,* and I hid at the canyon mouth to keep anyone away who was following or chasing us until the herd was far enough up the canyon that they didn't dare follow. Once the herd was well into the canyon, there were so many labyrinthine splits, dead ends, and wrong turns, the herd could disappear, never to be tracked except by the very foolish who were open to an ambush around every bend.

It took us two days and nights to get the herd to the canyons leading into the Sierra Las Espuelas. On the afternoon of the second day, we saw dust on the horizon, but the cloud never got near enough for us to know what was making it. Then, as we waited at the mouth of the canyon, we saw it again, and it came steadily in our direction. We didn't want to shoot unless we had to. If we did shoot, we'd have to kill every one of our pursuers and make their bodies and tracks disappear. If word got out that the canyon we used was a gateway into the *sierras* for Apaches stealing stock, it would be blocked to prevent its further use. It wouldn't be long before we'd have to deal with the Mexican Army, sure to come to protect the wealth of the big *ranchos.*

Unless pursuers knew where to look as they approached the mountains from the *llano,* they wouldn't see the canyon we guarded until they were right on top of it. Yellow Boy had his Big Eye out, watching the riders approach. When they were within half a mile of the cliff walls guarding the mountains, they stopped. Yellow Boy described what he saw. "*Cinco hombres. Vaqueros.* Carry Winchesters. Stop. See *sierras con un ojos grandes,* with Big Eyes, turn, ride away."

Smart men. They knew they'd probably ride into an ambush if they tried to follow the cattle into the mountains. I breathed a sigh of relief. I didn't think I could kill anyone over a few cows. We waited until midafternoon and saw no signs of anyone else. Yellow Boy decided it was safe to leave, so we rode on up the canyon following the cattle. It took us five days to drive the cattle to the corrals below Rojo's camp.

The entire village was there to help pen the stock and separate out the animals the Mexicans wanted. My heart took wing as soon as I saw Rafaela there with the other women. As the people celebrated the raid's success, we had another honeymoon night. We couldn't get enough of each other. Yellow Boy teased me about wanting to stay around the women too much. I laughed with him.

"Grandfather, a new husband needs to be near his wife."

He nodded, smiling. "*Sí,* Hombrecito.

These are good days to be alive. You must lie with her many times so your sons come soon."

He gave me pause for thought, though. I wasn't ready for children. I still had a score to settle with Oliver Lee. Rafaela and I had discussed this, and I'd told her that when I went after Lee, she might wind up a widow. I didn't want her to be without a husband when there was a baby at her breast.

She had stared at me as her eyes filled with tears.

"Why do you cry, *mi corazón*?"

"I'm afraid Comacho made it so's I ain't never havin' *niños*. Maybe I'n never give you sons, Hombrecito. None ever come for Billy Creek."

I'd been speechless, then angry, as I remembered what Comacho did to her, did to us. I looked in her eyes, took her hand, and spoke from my heart, knowing what I said might not be true. "There's no need for tears. Our *niños* will come. We won't consider this anymore. *Sí*?"

She nodded, drew the sleeve of her blouse across her eyes, and managed a little smile. I knew a big weight had been taken from her shoulders.

Yellow Boy, two other warriors, and I helped

415

Arango and his men drive his share of the herd through the mountains west to a little mining town in the Sierra El Tigre, near where *Pancho* Villa's *bandidos* hid out. He sold the stock at an inflated price to the miners, bought us some cartridges and a few old rifles as goodwill presents, and remained with his gang while we returned to Rojo's camp.

Arango told me later that the gang's *jefe,* Pancho Villa, had been killed in a bordello fight. The gang decided it would be smart if the name of Villa survived to keep the goodwill of the peons. After a fight or two for the gang's leadership, Arango became Pancho Villa and the gang actually did better than when it was led by the original *jefe.* Pancho Villa was how Arango wanted to be called and no one I knew except Yellow Boy called him Arango in his later life.

By the time we got back, our camp had slaughtered nearly all our share of the herd. Hides were pegged out for tanning on every bare spot around the camp and down by the corrals. The poles on curing racks sagged with fresh meat, and every man, woman, and child was working day and night. Rafaela helped Moon. Between them, over the space of about two weeks, they prepared meat from four steers and had the hides stretched, scraped, and covered with a tanning mixture that made them soft and pliable.

Winter was coming, and it was getting pretty cold high in the mountains. We were still below the snow line, but you could see it dropping lower almost daily as thick gray clouds dropped snow and then sailed on, catching the winds from the west.

Yellow Boy and I helped the women. It was no time for the manly custom of sitting around while the women did all the work. It was hard work. Rafaela and I were so exhausted we were too tired even to think about lovemaking at the end of the day.

About halfway down the canyon trail from the lookout ridge was a small cave where the village kept the food stores it saved for winter, the time they called the Season of the Ghost Face. All during the summer and fall, the women had collected and dried berries, cooked and dried mescal, and saved nuts for this season. Yellow Boy and I worked several days going up and down the side of the canyon carrying meat and hides to store against the cold winter months and the winds of spring, the time the Apaches called the Season of Little Eagles. In another cave, close to the corrals, we stored grain for the horses and mules.

When the Season of the Ghost Face settled down to stay, it was a slow, hard time, but in its way, a time of rest and renewal. The women worked on clothes for their families. The men repaired their weapons or made new ones. We used some of the hides to make new rawhide ropes.

The Season of the Ghost Face was a time of sitting by the fires and telling stories of war, hunts for great bull elk or mountain lions, and the skills of the great leaders. Rafaela and I must have told the jaguar story a hundred times. It was a time when men stayed near their wives and children and enjoyed their domestic life as much as the days of battle. Rafaela and I lay together often. She taught me much in those days about the ways a man can please a woman and how women think about their men and their families.

I listened to stories of battles that seemed long ago, but were, in fact, only about twenty years old. I listened to how revenge was taken using the worst of tortures. I dreamed of the day when I knew how to use tricks of torture that drove men crazy with pain and made them beg to die. I dreamed of using them on the man I was going after in New Mexico for the murder of my daddy. But most of the time, in that first winter, high in the Sierra Madre with the Apaches, Rafaela's sweet body and the wisdom of life kept my mind from the dark places.

31
BILLY CREEK RETURNS

In the Season of Many Leaves, it must have been mid-April, when the westerly winds still swirled across the mountains and whistled fiercely across the tops of the canyons, there came a warm, sunny day when the wind rested. After a long Ghost Face Season, it was wonderful to be alive. Rafaela went with me down to the corrals to care for the horses and mules. We laughed and played on the trail back up to the village.

When we passed through the village, I noticed there were new horses being unloaded near an empty wickiup. Guests had come to call. It was getting close to time for scouting the herds and going to the little towns for more supplies. I recognized one of the horses. I nudged Rafaela, nodded toward the wickiup, and said, "Looks like Apache Kid is back."

She looked in the direction I nodded and

started to agree. Instead, her hands went over her mouth as though she were about to scream. She turned and ran for our lodge. I couldn't imagine what there was about Apache Kid that upset her so. Then I looked back in the direction of the wickiup and stared in disbelief. Billy Creek.

I walked toward him, feeling like I was underwater. The thoughts running through my mind were tearing at each other like two feral tomcats tied inside a feed sack. Billy wore shotgun chaps, a soft buckskin vest, a fresh white shirt, and a black, wide-brimmed hat pulled low over his eyes. His revolver hung in a cross-draw holster, and his boots were tall and shiny black. He was untying his saddlebags when I walked up to him.

"Billy? We thought you were dead."

He spun around, his hand flying to his revolver. When he saw me, he relaxed and grinned, his yellow teeth standing out against a scraggly beard. His face was thin and hollow-cheeked. His feverish eyes seemed to burn like two black coals in his sunken eye-sockets. "Well, howdy, Hombrecito." He stuck out his hand, and I took it, his grip like a blacksmith's as he pumped my arm and said, "Naw, th' stories o' me a-dyin' is jest a bit early's all. How the hell ya doin'? That Mex cavalry sent a slug

421

through my upper laig, an' one stunned me when it grazed my head. Knocked me clean back'ards an' nearly off my horse, but I crawled under some junipers an' got the bleedin' stopped. Lucky fer my nuts, them soljers or ol' man Comacho never foun' me. Day or two later, ol' Kid here come along an' foun' me. Carried me to a doctor over to Casas Grandes. Got there jest in time 'fore th' infection got so bad I mighta lost this here ol' laig an' I'd been a-ridin' 'round with a wooden laig. Laid up all win'r, I was. Still ain't right but gittin' better ever'day.

"Kid says he hear'd you's a keeping Rafaela fer me. I's mighty grateful to ye fer that, Hombrecito. Is she roun' here someplace? Shore would like to see my ol' gal."

I shoved my hands in my pockets and said, "But Billy, we thought you were dead."

He pulled his saddle cinch loose and nodded. "Yes, sir, I thought I was, too, there fer a while. Where'd ya say Rafaela was?"

"Billy, she's not your woman anymore. She thought you were dead. She's my woman now. We're married, Apache style."

He dropped the cinch, but left the saddle on the horse and whirled to look at me, red in the face, those feverish, feral eyes on fire. "Why, you little bastard. You telling me you done stole my woman? Why didn' you keep

422

that'n you's a-livin' with, that there one with her little *hermano* that 'bout got us all kilt? I shore as hell aim to fix yore ass if'n ye're stealin' my woman."

I saw his hand on his revolver, and it was out of the holster and halfway up to my chest when out of nowhere appeared a Winchester rifle barrel crashing down on the hand with the gun.

"Ow! Damn it to hell!" The revolver fell to the ground, and Billy grabbed his smashed hand.

Apache Kid rested the business end of his rifle in the middle of Billy's chest. Billy stared at both of us, the fire in his eyes beginning to dim.

"*Buenas días, Señor* Hombrecito. Do you want to see how good my rifle shoots now?"

I shook my head. "*No, gracias, Señor* Kid. Billy's just not thinking too good right now. He'll be all right after he cools down a little and he knows the whole story. Isn't that true, Billy?"

Billy didn't say anything. He just bent over and picked up his revolver. Kid kept his rifle on full-cock and, covering him with it while he holstered the revolver, turned to take the saddle off the horse, and mumbled, "We'll talk later."

I nodded. "Yes, sir, I expect we will. In

the meantime, you stay away from Rafaela. If she wants to see you, we'll find you. *Comprende?*"

"Yep. *Comprendo* jest fine."

I had enough fire flowing through my veins to light the wilderness. This time, Billy was in my territory, and I wasn't afraid of Billy Creek. For me, he was just another of life's dangers to be handled in the Apache way — walk around it, outsmart it, or kill it.

I headed for Yellow Boy's fire and found him sitting on a blanket, staring down the barrel of his old .45-caliber revolver. The cylinder was out and his gun cleaning supplies were around him. Moon nodded hello when she saw me, pointed at the big, old black pot sitting by the fire, and raised her brows to ask if I wanted coffee. I nodded, so she pulled out an old enamel cup and filled it for me. I took the cup and sat down on a log close by Yellow Boy's blanket, waiting for my elder to speak.

He brought the revolver's barrel down from his eye and looked at me. He cradled the seven-and-a-half-inch barrel revolver frame in his right hand, the cylinder he had yet to clean in his left. He balanced them back and forth a moment as if they were on the scales of justice.

"So Billy Creek returns from the land of the grandfathers. He says Rafaela is his woman. You must give her back. *Sí?*"

My jaw dropped. "How did you know all that?"

"See Billy come. *Usted y* Rafaela *en* corrals. *Comprendo* what he wants. Apache make war since before the grandfathers. Sometimes dead warriors come back. This isn't new. *Hombre* always want back *mujer* he left, but she is other man's *mujer.*"

I frowned and asked, "What's the custom when the warrior returns and wants his woman back?"

Yellow Boy started cleaning the cylinder and said, "*Mujer* belongs to her family. Husband, he lives with *mujer*'s family. Supports woman's *padres*. When first husband comes back from land of grandfathers, woman's *padres* give first husband back gifts he gives for *mujer*. He finds *mujer nueva*. Rafaela now my daughter. *Usted es mijo,* my son. *Señor* Creek gives *yo* no bride gifts. He takes only Comacho's *cajones*. These are *por mi*? *No*. They *por Señor* Creek. *Señor* Creek, he must find *mujer nueva*. Give *padre* bride gift. Rafaela *es su mujer*. She speaks to no *hombre* outside *ésta familia* unless I say this is so. *Comprende?*"

I nodded and felt the thumping of my heart slow down. Billy was going to forget about Rafaela or face Yellow Boy and me. I finished the coffee, thanked Yellow Boy for his words, and went to comfort my woman.

I pulled back the blanket and looked in the lodge's dim light. Rafaela sat on our sleeping blankets with her legs crossed and her face buried in her hands. She looked up with red, swollen eyes, her face bathed in tears. She ran her shirtsleeve over her face and beckoned me inside.

When I sat down beside her, she said, "I'm an evil woman, Hombrecito. I've taken a man while my first one still lives. The *padres* say God will cast me into hell. I'm a whore. I'm so sorry I've wronged and burdened you with this. I must go with Billy. If I don't, he'll kill you."

I sat there, shaking my head. "No. You're not evil. If the *padres* say so, they're wrong. God won't put you in hell for this, and I've never had a whore living with me." I pulled her close and said, "Listen to me. I've spoken with Yellow Boy. He says that you're not to speak with any man outside the family unless he says you can. You're his daughter. Stay away from Billy. Yellow Boy and I will speak with Billy. He'll come to know

426

it's the right thing for you to be with me. You'll see."

I kissed her and rubbed her back to soothe her. Soon she wiped her face with her sleeve and managed a little smile. She gradually relaxed in my arms, and I felt the tension draining from both of us. She kissed me, and I returned the favor. Before long, kissing wasn't all we were doing.

The sun was casting long, streaming rays through the trees around the little village, and the night birds were calling when we finally drew the door blanket back and went to sit at Yellow Boy's fire for the evening meal. After the meal, he told me to be at his fire the next day when the sun made no shadows.

I spent the next morning taking care of our animals and working on a rawhide lariat. When the sun was straight overhead, I walked to Yellow Boy's fire. Kid and Billy were sitting on a log, having a casual conversation with Yellow Boy. Kid kept his Winchester with the stock planted between his feet and the barrel resting against his shoulder. Yellow Boy sat relaxed, his Henry across his knees. Billy didn't appear to have any kind of firearm, just a skinning knife in a scabbard stuffed in the back of his belt. I sat down across from Billy, who, with Kid, nodded and smiled at me.

Kid finished his story of an ambush of some miners near Warm Springs, in the New Mexico Territory, back in the Season of the Ghost Face. Yellow Boy grunted and pulled out one of his black Mexican *cigarros*. Billy stared across the fire at me, a little ambiguous smile on his lips. We all waited for Yellow Boy to speak. He lighted the *cigarro,* got a good coal on the end, and blew smoke in the four directions before passing the *cigarro* for the rest of us to do the same so we all knew this was serious business. The *cigarro* returned to him, his face a mask showing no emotion, Yellow Boy looked at Billy. "*Señor* Creek, you return from the grandfathers. *Bueno.* Now you want Rafaela *por su mujer, verdad*?"

Billy nodded and looked him in the eye. "Yes, sir, that there's what I want. She wuz mine 'fore the Mex Army shot me outta my saddle. Saved her when she wuz a-runnin' from ol' man Comacho's tracker, an' I cut ol' Comacho's nuts off fer the way he 'bused her. She done lived with me fer nearly three Seasons of Many Leaves. That there makes her mine fer all seasons, don't it? Ol' Hombrecito, I heerd he took her in whiles I wuz laid up, an' I wuz mighty grateful. Hell, I don' even mind if'n she rewarded him in a womanly way. Why, he had it comin'. 'Spec she's th' first woman he ever had. She's a good'un under the blankets. Musta teached him a lot 'bout how t' take good keer of a woman. But I'm back, an' I want her back now, or me an' ol' Hombrecito there, we's a-gonna have to have us a manly argument 'bout who her man is."

I felt the blood pound in my temples and the heat rise in my face. He made Rafaela sound like dirt, some horse to be swapped around, something to service a man when he demanded it, but I loved her. He wasn't any better than old man Comacho. At that moment, it would have given me the greatest of pleasures to kill him just to wipe that nasty little grin off his face.

Yellow Boy continued to look Billy straight in the eye. He took another puff and blew it toward the fire. "Hear me, *Señor* Creek, I speak one time and say *no más.* Rafaela *es* my daughter now. She is the daughter of *mi mujer* Moon on the Water. Rafaela stays near my lodge with her husband, Hombrecito. She is one of my family. She helps her mother and cares for her husband. Hombrecito *es mi* grandson. Rafaela es Hombrecito's *mujer.* Rafaela *es* not your *mujer.*

429

Es Apache way when warrior comes back from the grandfathers to give warrior back bride gift when *mujer* goes to other *hombre.* I have no bride gift from you. You no give Muchacho Amarillo *cojones* of Comacho. I no give you back any bride gift *por* Rafaela. *Comprende?* Rafaela no talk with you, ever, unless Muchacho Amarillo or Hombrecito says it will be so. You stay away from Rafaela." He pointed at his eye and then at Billy. "I see this is not so, you go again to the land of the grandfathers *pronto, y* next time, you no come back. *Comprende?* This is all I have to say."

As Yellow Boy spoke, Billy's face went from benign indifference to a hard squinting mask. He nodded. "Yeah. *Comprendo* jest fine. This ain't right, *señor,* an' you know it ain't. Yore's ain't th' las' words in this here talk."

I heard Yellow Boy's rifle click to full-cock and saw his brows go up in a question mark as the Henry pointed straight at Billy's guts. Kid was grinning. He stood up, walked around the fire, and sat down beside me, out of the line of fire. Billy's Adam's apple bobbed up and down, and his jaw muscles flexed. He looked over at me with burning, feverish eyes and back to Yellow Boy. He shook his head, and said so low I had to strain to hear him, "Not today, *señores*. Not today." He set down his cup and stood up. "Thanks fer the hospitality, Muchacho Amarillo. Be seeing ya, Hombrecito."

Stepping over the log where he had sat, he turned his back and walked toward his wickiup. Kid looked at Yellow Boy and then me, smiling. *"Muchas gracias, señores,"* he said as he walked off in the same direction as Billy.

Although I expected trouble, as the Season of Many Leaves passed Billy minded his own business. We all kind of relaxed, believing he'd come to terms with the hand fate had dealt him. He was friendly with Yellow Boy and me, and he acted like Rafaela didn't exist when she was in his vicinity, which wasn't often. However, she believed he was faking his indifference and told me so.

Cooling down after our meeting at Yellow Boy's fire was not something I wanted to do. I was tempted to go after him, but I waited. I knew when I went for him, I'd have to kill him. Besides, Yellow Boy had given him a warning to stay away from Rafaela. To maintain his authority, Yellow Boy warned him only the one time, and then acted as if it never happened. A strong war-

431

rior has to show his word is so powerful that when he warns a man once, it is enough. If the man doesn't listen, then he's due the worst kind of death, and the warrior has to make certain he gets it. It's a hard, brutal way to live, but it kept killings and feuds between clans and tribes to a minimum.

The days slipped through summer. Billy's threats faded into a distant memory. It rained hard one night just at the beginning of the monsoon season. It must have been early August. The heat in the middle of the day was insufferable, even as high in the mountains as we were. As the sun was fading at the end of the day, clouds blowing in from the Pacific formed on the west side of the mountains, starting major thunderstorms slamming north and east toward El Paso right over the top of us. The lightning show was spectacular as big, sizzling bolts flashed back and forth between clouds. It rained hard for a while, and then settled into an easy dribble for a couple of hours. It was wonderful lying in our lodge, listening to the light patter of the rain on the canvas and holding each other.

32
KIDNAPPED

The morning after the storm, Rafaela and I left our lodge in the dim, wet light of a gray dawn. I went down the canyon trail to feed the horses and mules, and she built up the fire to fix the morning meal. The stream was in full flow, once more rushing over the big, smooth boulders on its edges. The normally dry, small natural tank in the back of the corral was full of fresh water, and the horses and mules stood around sipping at it as though it were fine wine. I threw a few armloads of grass over the corral fence. The young boys in the village had cut it for the animals and stacked it nearby under ledges and out of the rain. It was quiet, just bluebirds and a few canyon wrens beginning a soft twitter as they awoke to the light.

In the distance, I heard a clang, the hard rap of iron against iron, a pause for a heartbeat, and more clangs. Then deafening silence. Fear filled my guts. I'd never heard the alarm bell before. The soggy air seared my lungs as I charged up the trail. Soundless, three or four women with babies in their arms and a couple of heavily armed men ran past me toward the corrals. My lungs were on fire when I finally reached the village. Everyone had vanished. I ran to my lodge and found that Rafaela was gone. I puffed a sigh of relief.

Yellow Boy and I had discussed what to do if the bell ever rang. We were to get the women and children and head south up the ridge path to the top edge of the canyon. There was a cave near the top a couple of miles away, hidden among ancient oaks and ash trees that sheltered piles of rocks stacked like ancient crumbling cathedral columns. We had stashed supplies and extra weapons there against this day.

Keeping a close eye out for the attackers, I melted into the brush and worked my way toward our sanctuary. The sun was well up when I got there. I saw no sign of any attackers, or of anyone else, heading for the cave. I took a final look around before I started climbing through the stone pillars and ancient trees. I walked around one of the piles of stones not twenty-five yards from the cave entrance. There were no sounds of any kind. Even the birds were quiet.

Yellow Boy and Apache Kid rose like spirits right out of the ground in front of me. I had to blink a couple of times to be sure I wasn't hallucinating when I saw them. Yellow Boy held up a finger for quiet, cocking his head to one side listening and motioning me toward the cave. Kid stayed where he was.

At the cave, I saw Moon back in its dark gloom. She was holding Redondo, and the other women and children were huddled near her. Yellow Boy looked over my shoulder to the path behind me. "Hombrecito sees enemies come?"

I shook my head.

"*Dónde ésta* Rafaela?"

I felt my mouth get dry and a cold stone of dread start sinking in my guts. "I don't know. I thought she was here. I was feeding the animals when the bell rang. She was going to the fire when I went to the corrals."

Yellow Boy frowned. "Rafaela's not there. I looked when the bell called." He stared out into the rocks and trees. It was as if we were underwater, struggling to get our bearings and air.

He walked out to where Kid stood watching. "*Dónde ésta* Billy Creek?"

435

Kid frowned and shrugged his shoulders. *"No es en* wickiup when bell calls. I don't know. Why? Ah. Rafaela *no es aquí."* He raised his brow and shook his head.

I felt the cold stone sinking in my gut turn to molten lava. I hefted Little David and turned to run for the main camp, but Yellow Boy had my arm in a steel-trap grip. I jerked at it to get free but he held me fast. "Wait, Hombrecito. No sure Billy Creek takes her, *y* we know *nada* of the raiders. Wait. I say when you go."

I stopped struggling against his hold and nodded, deferring to his wisdom. Yellow Boy went to explore the canyon, and I climbed up on a pillar of rocks and found a spot to wait and watch. A thousand questions and a hundred scenarios to answer them filled my brain. Soon, the dead certainty that Billy Creek had stolen Rafaela settled in my mind. I ground my teeth, thinking how I'd make that sorry excuse for a man pay for kidnapping her.

After a while, Yellow Boy returned and said, "No attack. Billy Creek ring bell. He take Rafaela. Hombrecito, we ride *pronto.* Billy Creek must die."

Kid's face was dark with rage, too. *"Señores, por favor,* I ride with you?"

Yellow Boy didn't hesitate. He nodded

and walked into the cave to gather his family and the others there with them. I wanted to saddle up and ride as soon as we got back to camp. Yellow Boy insisted on us taking our time, packing sufficient supplies, and finding out all we could about what happened.

It turned out that Billy had climbed up on the lookout rock well before dawn, cold-cocked the woman keeping watch, and bound and gagged her. He then climbed down and ran a long rawhide string from the bell down to a spot in the bushes that wasn't far from my lodge. He waited for Rafaela and me to start our little morning rituals. He had his big gray stallion, an extra horse, and a pack mule waiting up the trail by the lookout rock. That spot was probably the safest place to hide them in the whole camp with the sentry out of the picture. As soon as he rang the bell, he grabbed Rafaela and headed for the lookout rock.

Their trail led away from the lookout rock down the same trail we used when we first entered the camp. I was sick at heart. Billy had nearly a day's start on us with his big stallion. We didn't know where he was going. Yellow Boy was the best tracker I've ever known, but if they got to the road toward one of the big villages first, it might be months or years, if ever, before we found them. I told Yellow Boy we had to hurry up or we'd never catch Billy.

He frowned. "Where goes Creek, Hombrecito?"

I looked at the ground and shook my head. I didn't have an answer. "I don't know, but we have to do something."

"I know where goes Creek."

"Where?" I was practically shouting. "How do you know this?"

His eyes had that squint that reminded me of a hunting wolf as he tightened the cinch on his old McClellan saddle. I heard Kid chuckle as he saddled his horse on the other side of him.

"Kid tells me. Creek want Rafaela *muy mucho*. Creek *es loco*. Thinks when he kills Comacho, Rafaela wants him. Then she forgets Hombrecito. Creek tells Kid this many times. Creek *y* Rafaela ride *por* Comacho *hacienda*. Only trail to Comacho *hacienda* Billy Creek can take without passing our hiding place this morning *es* to *Río San Bernardino,* down *río,* up *Río Bavispe y* then ride east through El Paso Púlpito o El Paso Carretas. We take short trail. Catch Creek *y* Rafaela before they come to Comacho *hacienda. Es bueno?*"

I felt like an idiot. It never occurred to me

to ask Kid where Billy might be going. "*Sí, muy bueno,* very good."

Kid laughed aloud, looking over his saddle at me and grinning. We rode down the canyon toward the caves where we'd hidden earlier. The canyon walls rose higher and higher in soaring black shadows filled with the coming night. The stream down the middle of the canyon rushed on with higher velocity and volume, sending up bright sprays of shining droplets as it roared around boulders hung in midstream crevices. The sky framed by the canyon walls was starting to take on the deep royal blue that comes an hour or so before sunset. I was beginning to wonder if we had to camp there in the bottom, when Yellow Boy pointed his paint through some big sycamore trees toward the high east wall. There, a narrow trail ran up the canyon side right up to its top. I was astonished. Unless I'd known exactly where to look, I'd never have seen it.

It took close to an hour to get to the top. The sun was nearly gone; its only trace when we topped out on the east wall, a low glow in the west. In the dim light, we looked over some of the roughest, most ridge-covered country I'd ever seen. Yellow Boy followed a series of ridges over to another long canyon that seemed to snake away toward the southeast. It was fully dark when we found a place in some rocks near a trail that led down into the canyon, dug a pit, and built a small fire. Yellow Boy said he often used this trail going to the east gate of El Paso Púlpito, but it was so narrow in spots and tricky to navigate that we had to wait for daylight before we attempted it. I took the first watch. Kid said he didn't think we even needed to post lookouts. Yellow Boy laughed at him. "You will not last a season *en Sierras Azules* (Blue Mountains), *señor.* Sleep too much *y usted* die."

The next day, we rode from one canyon to the next, some deep, others shallow, but they were all connected. There was very little water in the pools left in those stream-beds. The rains we were getting on the west side of the mountains hadn't reached there yet.

At last we came to the intersection of our canyon with another large one running east to west. The new canyon walls were high and vertical, the distance between them in some spots more than a couple of hundred yards. Down the middle of the east-to-west canyon ran a long, winding, rutted road. Looking east, I saw the *llano* shimmering in the distance. The spot looked familiar, and it didn't take me long to realize that we were at the canyon road leading into El Paso Púlpito. I was pleasantly surprised. I'd wondered where the canyon trail we were now on led when I passed it with Sac, Lewis Clark, and Rafaela.

We stopped. Yellow Boy climbed off his paint and held up his hand for us to stay mounted. He studied tracks in the dusty road leading from the pass and some horse apples. Shaking his head, he grabbed the pommel and vaulted back into his saddle. He looked back at Kid and me. "No come this way. *Es bueno.* We come first. Creek *y* Rafaela should come through this *paso* maybe today or maybe *mañana* early. We wait here tonight. Creek no come, we ride for El Paso Carretas."

He led us to a spring in a tall tumble of rocks on the north side of the trail where we made a little camp and settled down to wait. I watered and fed the stock, brushing them down while Kid and Yellow Boy made a fire pit, gathered some brush, and built a hot, smokeless fire to make coals that would keep us warm but make low light when it was dark. Kid crawled up in the shade made by a single large boulder sticking up above the rest. He laid his Winchester lengthwise up his chest with the barrel poking past his ear, crossed his arms over it, and lay back. In four or five breaths, he was snoring.

Yellow Boy crawled up high in the rocks so he had a clear view up the trail coming down from El Paso Púlpito. It was mid-afternoon. The western horizon against the rough, dark line of the mountains was starting to gather little puffs of brilliant white clouds, rolling in from the west and bringing evening showers.

I crawled up in the rocks beside Yellow Boy. We watched the El Paso Púlpito trail all afternoon. It was just about impossible for anyone coming down the trail from the pass to see us, and the trail passed within two hundred yards of us. It would be an easy shot with the Sharps.

Yellow Boy sat with his back resting against a big boulder, shadowed slightly by another boulder just to his right toward the west. Not speaking, we enjoyed the fading day for a little while. He eyed me with an easy watchfulness while he slowly ran his thumb up and down the seam between the barrel and the cartridge tube of his Henry. He asked, "*Que es,* Hombrecito?"

"What will you do when Billy comes?"

"Take him. Go high *en sierras.* Day after

442

day, he dies. No listen to Muchacho Amarillo? He die. Rafaela *es mi hija.* He no take *mi familia y* live. He dies hard." His eyes were narrow slits, and the calm way he spoke told me Billy was a walking dead man.

I nodded. *"Sí, comprendo,* but the woman he takes is mine. I claim a husband's right. I claim his life. Will you give me this honor, *mi padre?"*

He stared at me for a long time. I didn't have any idea what was behind his black marble eyes, and I wondered if I had overreached in asking this from the man who was now my surrogate father. "Billy Creek dies by your hand? How?"

I held up my index finger. "One shot from Little David. One shot from where we sit now."

He looked off toward the dark clouds, shot through with long, straight beams of yellow light. When he looked back, he nodded slowly. *"Sí.* His life, I give you. You miss. I kill. *Comprende?"*

"Comprendo. Muchas gracias, mi padre."

As I had thought about it, I realized my wanting to send Billy to the demon hole with one shot was appropriate. There was no honor in dying without suffering. Billy had once been my friend. He'd saved Rafaela twice and fought, although foolishly, to

443

save her by charging a cavalry column that shot him to pieces. It was a miracle he'd survived, and for that, he deserved honor. For stealing her after she was my wife and Yellow Boy's daughter, the slate was wiped clean. We owed him no honor.

I told myself the reason I needed to kill Billy was to do him and, ultimately, Yellow Boy a favor. If Yellow Boy caught Billy, he'd take him high up in the mountains, invite Rojo and the elders to be witnesses, and spend three days torturing him to death. He'd warned Billy what would happen if he didn't stay away from Rafaela. Since Billy had ignored him, Yellow Boy had no choice but to show his steel. If he didn't, he'd lose respect from the entire band.

I couldn't even imagine the torture Billy would endure if Yellow Boy caught up with him. On the other hand, if I just happened to be in a rage over Billy stealing my wife and killed him before Yellow Boy stopped me, then Yellow Boy was off the hook. My killing Billy meant he'd die quickly. It was something I felt I had to do and something I figured Rafaela expected and wanted me to do.

33
FINDING BILLY

That evening it didn't rain on our side of
the mountains. We took turns watching
through the night, but Billy and Rafaela
didn't come down El Paso Púlpito trail. The
eastern horizon was just turning from light
gray to a line of brilliant white when Yellow
Boy climbed down to join Kid and me at
the fire. He took the coffee I offered him,
and stood drinking it with the Henry cradled in his arm, watching the day being
born. He finished the coffee, handed the
cup back to me, and nodded south.

"We ride. Billy goes through El Paso Carretas."

"Why?"

"*No lo sé,* I don't know. He no come El
Paso Púlpito. We ride. Catch Billy with Rafaela when *sol* there."

Kid nodded his agreement when Yellow
Boy pointed his rifle two-thirds of the way
to noon. I said no more and started break-

ing camp. We were about ten miles from the Comacho *hacienda.* Five miles south beyond the *hacienda* was the beginning of the trail down from El Paso Carretas. Yellow Boy didn't like to travel during the day, but we had no choice if we wanted to catch Billy in time. It wasn't long before we were off down the canyon trail toward the *llano.*

We had to ride fast and stay off the main roads to avoid being seen by other travelers. It wasn't long before we cut the trail I had led Sac, Rafaela, and Lewis Clark along riding away from El Paso Carretas. In about three hours, Yellow Boy stopped to rest the horses.

We were on a ridge directly above the Comacho *hacienda* in the distance. Smoke from the *hacienda*'s kitchen sent a long plume straight up into the still, cool air lying in shadows from the cliffs rising behind the house and barns.

We rode on, anxious to reach the pass before Billy crossed through and had the full spread of the *llano* over which to run and hide before getting himself and Rafaela killed by the Comacho family. In another five miles, the trail led over a ridge and down to the road leading into El Paso Carretas. We were just starting down the ridge when Yellow Boy stopped behind a couple of big juniper bushes. He pointed toward the road as he pulled out his telescope.

We were at least a mile away from the road, but even at that distance, I saw a good-sized group of Apaches. They were riding at an easy trot with what appeared to be a couple of Americans. One of the Americans was obviously a cowboy; the other one looked like he might be a miner. I noticed there was something strange about the way the miner rode. After staring for a couple of minutes, I realized that the miner sat the horse without a saddle. Then I saw honey-blond hair sticking out from under a big, floppy hat. Yellow Boy heard me suck in my wind in surprise.

He handed me the telescope and said something in Apache to Kid I didn't follow, but Kid nodded agreement and, with hawk-like eyes, followed the group. The image in the telescope showed Rafaela and Billy were in good physical shape and weren't showing any obvious bruises or cuts on their faces. They rode with their hands free. However, the three men riding behind them had their Winchesters ready for instant use. Juan and Elias were leading the group. They were in great humor, laughing and joking, turning in their saddles to speak to Billy and Rafaela. Billy laughed with them, but Rafaela's face might have been carved in stone.

I handed the telescope to Kid and dropped the breech on Little David to make sure it was loaded. I started to pull the hammer back when Yellow Boy grabbed my wrist and shook his head. "Wait. Watch a while."

We sat there watching them ride along like they were out for a Sunday visit after church. I was frantically trying to figure out what the Apaches were planning.

We didn't have long to wait for a hint of their intentions. A Comacho *vaquero,* his horse in a trot, rode down the road toward them whistling and sitting tall in the saddle. The Indians stopped in the middle of the road waiting for him. When he saw them he stopped, stared for a moment trying to decide whether to advance or run, his horse wheeling up on two legs as he jerked back on the reins, and then he took off his hat and waved. He obviously knew who they were and was shouting something about *esclavos,* slaves, but we were too far away to make out what he said. He galloped toward them.

The Apaches just sat there until he was about twenty or thirty yards away, and then Juan raised his rifle in one quick motion and shot him. He fell backwards out of his saddle, landing in a puff of dust in the middle of the road. The horse wasn't spooked by the shot or the sudden loss of its rider. It just stopped in the road, waiting for the rider to remount. Two Apaches rode forward; one grabbed the horse's reins, and the other threw a lariat loop over the *vaquero*'s boots and dragged him off through the creosotes and junipers so he couldn't be seen from the road. They stripped his body, leaving it naked under a juniper bush before riding on toward the Comacho *hacienda* to rejoin the main group continuing down the road. We followed them from up on the ridge trail, watching and waiting for an opportunity to steal Rafaela away from them.

The Apaches rode off the road and up to the top of the cliffs, following the same trail we'd used the year before when we rescued Lewis Clark. They camped a couple of hundred feet behind the ridgeline to stay hidden from the *hacienda.* Even from that spot, the *hacienda* was less than half a mile away, and they had a perfect view of the road running past the front of the *hacienda* toward El Paso Carretas from Casas Grande or Janos. They put Rafaela to work digging a fire pit and finding wood. The warriors disappeared into the creosotes and junipers down the ridge. Elias, Juan, and Billy climbed up to the ridgeline with a pair of binoculars to study the *hacienda.*

We came down off the west ridge, crossed the road, and trailed along behind them until we were on top of the cliffs and stopped where we could watch them and the ant-like activity down in the *hacienda.* I dug a deep hole for a fire pit and found some kindling, but I didn't light it. Yellow Boy studied those left in the camp for a long time while Kid and I watched and waited.

Then I joined Yellow Boy, who handed me the telescope and pointed toward the *arroyo* that ran alongside the road in front of the *hacienda.* One of the men with Juan and Elias was already in the creosotes lining the bank, not more than two or three hundred yards from the *hacienda*'s front gate. I heard Kid pull the hammer back to full-cock on his Winchester. Yellow Boy didn't even turn around. "No. Wait. *Es* too many. Night come, we take Rafaela, leave *pronto.*"

I looked over my shoulder at Kid and nearly dropped the telescope. He was four or five feet behind us and had his Winchester pointed at Yellow Boy's head. He said, "Lay your rifle butt at my feet, and take off the belt holding your knife and *pistola, señor. Pronto.* I won't deny our friends their satisfaction much longer."

Yellow Boy, his face an unblinking mask,

slowly laid the Henry at Kid's feet, stood up, and unbuckled the ammunition belt from which he carried his ancient Colt and a long blade.

"Hombrecito, lay Shoots Today Kills Tomorrow beside Yellow Boy's rifle."

I did as Kid told me, furious that he had betrayed us, sick that we had trusted him. A feeling of cold rationality took hold of me. Rufus's advice rang again in my brain, *cold and cakilatin', Henry, cold and cakilatin'.*

"Muchacho Amarillo, lie in the dirt. Put your hands behind your back." Yellow Boy turned and did as he was told. The smirk on Kid's face and the victory in his eyes were unbearable. He looked in my eyes and put the end of the Winchester's barrel against the back of Yellow Boy's head. He pulled a long, rawhide whang out his vest pocket and tossed it to me. "Tie his hands well, Hombrecito, or he will never see the camp of Juan and Elias."

My mind raced furiously trying to figure out how to tie the rawhide so Yellow Boy could get free. I tried three times to tie a knot that wouldn't hold, but Kid made me retie it each time until he was satisfied. Then he had me help Yellow Boy stand. He tossed me a rawhide lariat and told me to make a noose on one end. When I finished, he had me slide it over my neck and pull it tight. I'll never forget the feeling of that rough leather braid digging into the skin around my neck. I wondered if he was he planning to tie me to a horse and drag me to death.

He told me to tie a second loop around Yellow Boy's neck and give him the end of the lariat. He tied the end of the lariat to his saddle horn, dropped the horse's reins, and pulled another rawhide whang out of his vest pocket. If the horse spooked and took off, Yellow Boy and I were dead men. Kid had me make a loop in the rawhide whang, then he took it and tied my hands. When he was finished, he stood back, admired his work, picked up the horses' reins, and took a long swallow from a canteen.

He said to Yellow Boy, "Let's go. I've waited a long time for this. You and your pup shamed me in our shooting match. Now you'll know the anger of true men, and I'll have Shoots Today Kills Tomorrow. No man shames Kid. No man shames Elias before his people and lives. Elias *y* Juan come to meet you, Hombrecito. They plan special rewards for you and Yellow Boy." He picked up our rifles and jabbed me in the back with Little David.

It took us an hour or so to get around the

ridge and over to Elias's camp. As we neared where Elias and Juan sat talking with Billy, I saw Yellow Boy stand a little taller, and I tried to do the same. When we walked in among the camp bedrolls, they stared at us. Old Elias's eyes were sparkling with delight, a wolf's grin spreading across his face. Juan said nothing. He just crossed his arms and stared at us.

Billy made a crooked little smile and, raising his brow, spoke first, as he pulled the makings for a cigarette out of his vest. "Well, now, ain't this here a nice surprise? Glad you fellers dropped in today. Course, I kinda figured you'd come, ya'll a thinkin' ya gonna settle a score with me an' all."

He paused, finished rolling his smoke, poked it in his mouth, and lit a match with his thumbnail, cupping his hands around the wiggling flame while he lit up, eyeing me all the time. I stared back at him and didn't blink. I'd rather have died than show any emotion, whether it was fear or hate. I just kept thinking over and over, *cold and cakilatin', Henry, cold and cakilatin'.*

Billy took a deep draw and blew the smoke skyward. "You fellers a-lookin' fer me? Well, here I am, by God, just happier than a colt pulling on a big ol' full tit. Got me some new, first-class Apache friends that ain't afraid o' nuthin' and got my woman back." He looked over at me and laughed. "Damn! Ain't she a good piece, Hombrecito? Gonna get a little myself soon's I have this here meetin' with ol' man Comacho. If'n ya'll is good boys, I might let ya watch, too."

I would have sold my soul to kill him on the spot and close his vulgar mouth forever, but like Yellow Boy, I managed to keep the anger boiling in my guts under control. Billy looked over at Kid helping himself to the stewpot. He was eating directly out of the pot, stabbing pieces of meat with his knife. Billy asked, "Kid? Where's them famous rifles of these here sharpshooters? We gonna need 'em."

Kid nodded and swallowed. "*Sí*, Billy. They're over yonder in their camp. I go back for them *pronto*. I finish eating, *sí?*"

"Naw, *hombre*. Ya need to go right now. Bring 'em on down here 'cause we gonna need 'em purdy quick."

Kid scowled, tossed the end of the lariat to Billy, and, without a word, started on a fast trot back toward our camp. Billy walked around behind us, grabbed the piece of lariat strung between our necks, and jerked down on it. "Have a seat, fellers."

We staggered backwards, choking, and fell

454

on our backsides. Juan squatted down, eyeing me the whole time, and pulled a skinning knife out of a scabbard stuck in his belt and a whetstone out of a vest pocket. He spat on the stone and began drawing the blade back and forth, making a smooth, even grinding, sound. Elias climbed back up in the rocks on the ridgeline above our old camp, took out an old pair of cavalry binoculars, and began watching the *hacienda.* Billy climbed up and sat down by him. They pointed first to one part of the *hacienda,* then another, talking and nodding their heads.

When Rafaela walked out of the junipers, her arms filled with wood for the fire, she saw Yellow Boy and me. She made no sound, but her face first flashed relief that we were there and then horror that we'd been caught. Billy looked over his shoulder at her, grinning before turning his attention back to the *hacienda.* She stacked her wood next to the fire and disappeared back into the junipers.

Juan never took his eyes off me. After a few strokes of the blade on his whetstone, he'd hold the blade up and feel the edge with his thumb. After a while of stroking the whetstone and testing the blade's edge with his thumb, he called up to Billy. "Ho,

Señor Creek. How sharp you need this blade to make Hombrecito a gelding?"

Billy looked over his shoulder and called, "I ain't a-gonna use no knife. Yer daddy's gonna use Little Man's own thunderstick to snip 'em right off. That there way's quicker'n a blade. I kinda figure I owe ol' Hombrecito a nut cuttin'. But yore daddy's the chief, so he's got first cut — uh, I mean first shot."

The sun became unmercifully hot as it fell toward the west. Billy and Elias took long swallows of water, eyed us, and spat swallows on the ground before recapping the canteens. I hadn't been so thirsty in a long time. Rafaela appeared out of the junipers several more times with armloads of firewood. Her last load, she took a canteen, drank, and then held it for Yellow Boy and me to have a drink. I know Billy saw her, but he didn't interfere. He pointed toward the northwest road and said something to Elias, who stared through his binoculars for a while and then nodded. I looked and saw the faint smudge of a dust cloud in the distance. Yellow Boy squinted at it. I saw the muscles of his arms rippling and straining under his shirtsleeves. I glanced behind him and saw his wrists were raw from straining and working against the rawhide.

34
Comacho Ambush

Kid walked in from the junipers, leading the horses loaded with our rifles and supplies. Billy looked at him and grinned. "Ya cut that 'un a little close, Kid. Yer jest in time. I think ol' man Comacho is a-comin' down the road yonder."

Tying the horses to a rope forming one side of a temporary corral, Kid started unloading the gear. *"Bueno,* Billy. Now we have plenty womans *y mescal, sí?"*

"Yes, sir, I 'spect we gonna have both of 'em purdy soon. Ya ready t' go t' work, *amigo?"*

"Sí, ready." He jerked his head toward Yellow Boy and me. "Where do we hide these *hombres* while we work, eh?"

"Aw, we'll jest leave 'em right where they sit so's they'n watch the show, too. They ain't goin' nowheres tied up like they is. They gonna keep quiet 'cause they don't want no mouthful of rifle butt, either. Ain't that right, Little Man?"

He turned his attention back to the road. Before giving his pony a quick rubdown, Kid stacked the gear over on the other side of the camp from us. Rafaela sat down between the gear and us. I saw her watching where Kid put every piece. The dust cloud on the dirt road to the northeast grew larger.

"Kid, you better git that ol' thunderstick an' find ya a shootin' spot. They gonna be here in a bit."

I gritted my teeth as I watched him pick up Little David and rummage through our gear for a box of cartridges. He walked down the ridge until he came to a pile of boulders about two hundred yards from the road. Three or four of Elias's men were with Juan to Kid's left, and another five or six were scattered in the creosotes running along the top of the arroyo in front of the house.

Billy looked over his shoulder at Rafaela sitting across the fire from us. "Ain't gonna be long now, Sweet Woman. We'll be rid o' Comacho fer good, an' these here boys ain't gonna bother us no more. It'll be like the good ol' days again, 'cept ol' man Comacho's jest gonna be a bad dream. You wait! You'll see."

She shook her head and looked at him

with pleading eyes. "Please, Billy. Don' kill ol' Comacho fer me. Let these here men leave. I'n stay with ya an' keep ya warm when the nights is cold. I'll give ya children. I'll send Hombrecito away. I'll put his things outside the lodge an' leave him. Yer my man. Ya don' have t' do this fer me. I'm a-beggin' ya. Please don' do it."

Billy shook his head, cut his dark, burning eyes over at us, and grinned. "Ain't gonna back down now, woman. Hell, them boys there's a-wantin' to kill me. They ain't gonna git the chance. I warned 'em, by God. I warned 'em, an' now they's gonna pay fer what they was a-plannin'. An' ol' man Comacho? After what he done to you? No, ma'am, I ain't lettin' that 'un off fer nuthin'. His days is gonna end ferever."

Down on the pile of rocks close to the road, I saw Kid practicing loading and unloading a cartridge and then tinkering with the sights on Little David. Rafaela kept glancing over to the pile of gear Kid had brought down from our camp, eyeing Kid's rifle. He'd left it and Yellow Boy's Henry there within easy reach. Yellow Boy had rubbed his wrists so raw trying to get out of the rawhide that he was bleeding, and his hands were getting slick. I knew the blood soaking into the rawhide would make it stretch just a little against his constant push. The dust cloud was close enough for me to see a black carriage and a single horse stepping along in front of it. Billy, the Apaches, and Kid were watching it like cats eyeing a mouse, waiting to pounce.

I saw Yellow Boy's right hand pop free, and so did Rafaela. He reached over with his left hand and pulled at the knot on my hands enough to loosen the cord. I was free in a couple of minutes. We sat like we were still tied, waiting to take advantage of the confusion when the shooting started.

Billy looked over his shoulder at Rafaela, motioning her to him with a jerk of his head. "Come on over here and sit down beside me. You gonna wanta see this." She never looked at me as she stepped over to him, kneeling down so her body was in his line of sight if he happened to look toward us when we made our move.

The buggy drew closer. It carried two people and was pulled by a magnificent, trotting Andalusian gray with a proud arch to its head. The buggy went past us and swung around the bend where Kid waited. When the buggy was in sight of the *hacienda,* one of the men in the buggy waved his hat to someone on the surrounding walls watching them approach.

I watched as Kid tracked the buggy with Little David all the way around the bend. He waited to fire until the buggy was even with Juan and three men crouching in the creosotes lining the top of the arroyo. The thundering boom swept past us up the hillside. The gray's legs stopped moving. It stumbled forward in the traces, dropped to its knees, and then fell over on its side. There weren't even reflex kicks; it was dead when it hit the ground. As it went down, the buggy flipped on its side, throwing the passengers out. The echoes from Little David's roar off the cliffs behind the *hacienda* were still rumbling when the men in the *arroyo* ran up on the road and snatched the two stunned men. They dragged them into the *arroyo,* trussed them up like goats for slaughter, crawled back up the sides of the *arroyo* to their guns, and waited.

Billy raised his fist in the air and shook it. Kid stood up, holding Little David, both arms raised in victory. Elias sat with his arms crossed, nodding and smiling.

The front gate in the *hacienda* compound flew open as men, including a couple in suits, house servants, and armed *vaqueros,* fifteen or twenty in all, ran yelling toward the overturned buggy. I remember watching them in disbelief. Any fool ought to have known what was going to happen. The fire from the *arroyo* was deadly and quick, and they fell like wheat before a scythe.

There was a deafening stillness as the smoke from the gunfire cleared. The men in the *arroyo* ran across the road and into the brush and trees along the creek that ran behind the *hacienda.*

From the back of the *hacienda* and around by the barns came a torrent of rifle fire. The screams of wounded men and terrified women and the bawling of cattle sent echoes ricocheting off the cliff. The herd of horses and cattle in the barn corrals stormed through the fence and an opened gate or two when the gunfire started.

As soon as the shooting began, Yellow Boy and I ran for the rifles. I couldn't wait to get Kid's Winchester and put a bullet in Billy. I grabbed it and threw the lever down to load a fresh cartridge. The receiver came back empty. Yellow Boy was already digging through the gear for his revolver belt loaded with cartridges for the Henry. I looked toward the rocks where Billy and Elias sat. They were gone and Rafaela with them.

I tried not to panic while I looked for some .45 cartridges that would fit the Winchester. I stuffed a box of cartridges for Little David in my shirt and found a box of

Winchester cartridges as Yellow Boy finished sliding the last .44 cartridge down the Henry's tube before swinging the loading gate closed at the end of the barrel. I ran to the rocks where Elias and Billy once sat and saw them running down the hill, zigzagging and dodging junipers as they headed toward the *arroyo* where Juan had the two men from the buggy tied. Billy had Rafaela by the wrist, dragging her along with him. He was shaking his rifle in the air and yelling like a madman. He appeared oblivious to anything except the blood he wanted from old man Comacho. I sighted on him, ready to kill him in mid-stride, but Yellow Boy grabbed my arm and jerked his head toward the horses. We ran for them, snatched their reins off the corral rope, and swung up on them.

"What do you want to do?"

"Take Rafaela and Shoots Today Kills Tomorrow. Ride hard for El Paso Púlpito."

We raced out of the stand of junipers to the little bench where rope lines held the horses. Elias and Billy were about halfway down the hill, still running toward the *arroyo.* Yellow Boy paused at the ridgeline, considering a shot from his horse, but decided he couldn't risk hitting Rafaela. He grabbed the Henry's barrel about a foot from the end and swung it back and forth like a big, heavy war club. I grabbed the Winchester the same way as we plunged down the hill toward Elias and Billy.

Juan and his men calmly walked among the men they had cut down, slitting the throats of any still living and stealing anything worth taking. Juan looked up the hill, saw us coming, yelled something in Apache to Elias and Billy, threw up his rifle, and fired. The bullet sailed high, but it was enough to make Billy and Elias turn as we came riding down on them. Billy pushed Rafaela to one side and lifted up his rifle to fire. Midnight was nearly on top of him when I swung the Winchester stock in a great swooping arc that glanced off his shoulder, sent his rifle flying out of his hands, and slapped the side of his head with a lot less force than I intended. I'm not even sure I knocked him unconscious. If his head had caught the full force I intended, he wouldn't have had any face left. Yellow Boy's Henry slammed into Elias's shoulder, probably breaking it, and sending him tumbling off down the hill into a little stand of junipers. I pulled back on the reins hard, trying to make Midnight stop. She was practically sitting down on her back haunches and had her front legs braced in front of her. Rafaela ran down the ridge toward us.

Juan and his men raced up the hill, firing as they ran. Pieces of juniper branches went flying, cut off as the bullets whizzed by. Midnight's long slide stopped. I got her turned around and headed up the hill toward Rafaela. She grabbed my arm and swung up behind me, her breath coming hard and rasping as she threw her arms around me. We rode across and down the hill toward the road through the whine of bullets and curses. I looked back to see Billy stagger up, holding his head with both hands. All I could think was, *I'll be back to finish the job, Billy.*

Yellow Boy rode straight for Kid after he'd smashed Elias. Kid saw him coming and fumbled around, trying to load Little David. He got it loaded and pointed in the general direction of Yellow Boy, who was yelling like a demon straight out of hell as he swung the Henry back and forth. Kid panicked as the paint pounded toward him. He managed to throw a shot that went far wide, raising a puff of dust on the side of the hill. Yellow Boy was within twenty yards of him when he looked up as he dropped the breech to reload. He threw the rifle down and jumped behind the rocks he'd

466

used in the ambush. Yellow Boy thundered past, swinging from the paint's side, holding on with a leg across its back and, using the Henry as an extension of his arm around the paint's neck, he reached down and grabbed Little David in the smoothest display of horsemanship I've ever seen.

Midnight swept by less than a hundred yards behind Yellow Boy, and I saw the top of Kid's head as he peeped out from behind the pile of rocks he'd run for. Bullets still flew, but more and more, they hit the ground behind us. I yelled, *"Hey! Hah!"* in proud victory. We were too clever, too strong for those miscreants.

Midnight shuddered and faltered a step before finding her rhythm again and ran on. I figured she'd probably stepped in a shallow depression and nearly lost her balance. She ran on for another mile. Then I saw blood in her lather, and she started slowing down. I pulled her to stop. Rafaela and I slid off her back just as she collapsed, her wind coming in pants and grunts, getting weaker by the minute. That's when I saw the bullet hole in the space between where our knees were. Yellow Boy turned back to us. I looked at Yellow Boy, who shook his head. The light, a fading candle, went out of Midnight's eyes.

I bit the inside of my lip so Yellow Boy and Rafaela wouldn't see me cry over a horse. I didn't want either of them thinking I wasn't a man. But Rafaela's eyes were wet, and Yellow Boy was deferential as he helped me pull the blanket, saddle, and bridle off of her.

35
RETRIBUTION

We didn't see any sign of Billy or the Apaches when Midnight went down. We were maybe three miles from the entrance to El Paso Púlpito. We were certain they'd try to catch us before we got back to Rojo's camp. I expected at any moment to see them racing down the road after us. But we didn't even see any dust clouds on the road, except perhaps one far in the distance toward El Paso Carretas. Yellow Boy and I could run all day, even to the point of running a horse into the ground, so he put Rafaela on his paint and gave her the extra rifle to carry.

He said, "You ride, Rafaela. Follow Hombrecito *y* Muchacho Amarillo." I started to run toward El Paso Púlpito, but he stood where he was. "No, Hombrecito. This way."

He pointed toward the high trail across the ridges we had used earlier. I shook my rifle in satisfaction. We weren't running

469

from Billy and Elias after all. I looked at Rafaela. She nodded, and, setting her jaw and gritting her teeth, turned the paint toward the trail.

When we had our first clear view of the *hacienda,* it was about a mile away. Yellow Boy pulled out his telescope and studied the place. He grunted in surprise and handed it to me.

It looked like Elias and his men were still at the *hacienda.* The gate to the compound walls stood wide open, and the barn corrals were empty. The dust cloud we thought might be on the road toward El Paso Carretas was clearly visible.

Someone in a bloody white shirt hung from a post stuck in the ground near the front of the gate about where the *horca* had been erected to torture the women. His torso was tied to the post so his feet dangled free about a foot off the ground. His arms and legs were tied so they were free to move, but he couldn't raise them high enough to touch his head or reach across his body to touch the other arm.

A man stood back from the post several yards. He pulled a revolver, pointed it at the man in the bloody white shirt, didn't fire, holstered the revolver, and then did a kind of jerky dance in a big circle all the way around the post, twirling his body and waving his arms. Once around the post, he stopped in front of the tied figure and did the little ritual all over again.

Elias's men, paying no attention to either man, led a long string of mules, maybe seven or eight, through the gate and disappeared into the *hacienda.* Elias and Juan were nowhere to be seen, but I saw their horses tied to the corral fence. I wasn't sure who was tied on the post but guessed that it was old man Comacho and the dancing figure was Billy.

I handed the telescope to Rafaela. I heard her gasp and saw her flinch as if she'd been slapped. "What's Billy a-doin'? Where's th' *hacienda* servants?"

Yellow Boy took back the telescope. "Billy tortures Comacho. Pulls *pistola,* shoots. Has one bullet loaded, *no más.* Billy spin cylinder every time before he pull trigger. Maybe *pistola* shoot, maybe not. Billy shoots ears first, then elbows, shoulders, and knees. One shot each when gun shoot. One ear gone already."

He turned the telescope toward the far dust cloud. "*Hacienda* people run for El Paso Carretas."

Rafaela looked up the ridge toward the mountaintops, shaking her head. She said,

"Why don't Billy just shoot him? I think he's gone *loco.*"

We worked our way down a draw toward the *hacienda,* stopping several times for Yellow Boy to use his telescope. When we were about a quarter of a mile away, but still well hidden by the junipers and creosotes, we saw Elias's men lead the mules, loaded down with loot, out of the *hacienda.* They tied them at the barn corral with Elias and Juan's horses. They went to their horses, looking like they were getting ready to ride. A revolver fired in the distance, and a man screamed in agony. Yellow Boy nodded as he looked through his telescope.

"Comacho. No ears."

The brush in the draw became thicker the closer we got to the road. We were a couple of hundred yards away when we heard the revolver again, this time much louder. The screams became a ghastly wail with intermittent sobs. We heard Comacho begging Billy for mercy. *"Por favor, señor, por favor! Muerte,* death, *por favor, muerte."*

We stopped. Yellow Boy looked through his telescope just as there was another revolver shot, followed by a hoarse, gut-wrenching scream and an eerie, cackling laugh. Yellow Boy studied the old man for a moment before collapsing the telescope, not letting Rafaela or me see. "Comacho, no elbows."

We moved slower and with greater care. Creeping down that draw with old Comacho screaming and begging for death was like a descent into hell. We stopped in a juniper thicket about a hundred yards from where Billy had the old man tied, and maybe twenty yards from the road. Rafaela kept wiping her eyes with the sleeve of her shirt. Billy, filled with blood lust, was acting crazier by the minute. I was sure he'd completely lost his mind.

The old man wailed, *"Madre de Dios, por favor, señor, muerte, no más, no más."*

Billy cackled and yelled, "Not till I got both o' yore knees, ya ol' son of a bitch! Suffer, damn ya! Suffer!" Then he went back into his quick draw crouch and did the whole routine over again.

Yellow Boy shook his head as he spoke. "Hombrecito, shoot Comacho. He suffers *no más.* Comacho suffering *es* no honor. Billy die now. Billy *loco.* No torture for Billy. Shoot both, same time. Elias *y* Juan takes *mucho* from *hacienda;* run when Billy dies. They no run, shoot Elias or Juan, then all *hombres* go. *Comprende?"*

I nodded. Then Rafaela took hold of my arm, but she looked in Yellow Boy's face as

473

she spoke. "*Por favor,* Muchacho Amarillo, don' kill Comacho. Men gotta pay th' full price o' their life — he ain't gotta right to git outta this life 'fore he's drunk the whole cup. Jest don' let Billy do this to 'im." Yellow Boy and I stared at her, the power of her words sinking in.

Yellow Boy looked at me, his jaw muscles rippling. He nodded toward the south, down the road toward El Paso Carretas. The dust cloud from the *hacienda* staff escaping to Bavispe through El Paso Carretas had got much larger and much closer. A large group of riders was coming down the road toward us, and they weren't moving slowly. Elias appeared out of the *hacienda,* ran up to Billy, and pointed toward the dust cloud.

We heard Billy yell, "No! Damn it! I tol' ya, no! I ain't a-goin' till this ol' bastard runs out his strang." He started his jig around Comacho again. The rest of the Apaches swung on their horses, each with a loaded mule or horse in tow, rode across the road just south of us, and headed toward El Paso Carretas up the trail against the mountains from which we had just come.

Juan rode up to Elias and handed him his pony's reins. Elias, one arm stuck inside his shirt, swung up on his little gray, gave Billy a little hand salute, and rode hard with Juan to join his men. Far down the road, we began to see individual figures against the red and brown swirling dust cloud. Yellow Boy whipped out his telescope and looked a few seconds before he handed it to me.

"Comacho *vaqueros.* Stay here. I go, settle with Billy. *Usted* no shoot Comacho."

I took a quick look through the telescope. Ten or twelve *vaqueros* were pushing their horses hard as they came down the road. The one in the front wore a bright red shirt, and he was on a big black that looked like a paint horse, it was so lathered up.

Yellow Boy stood up and started trotting down the draw toward Billy. Rafaela and I stayed where we were. We watched the confrontation untold, our hearts pounding. As Yellow Boy worked his way toward the road, Billy did his jig around Comacho and drew his revolver. Billy snapped the trigger, but the revolver didn't fire. He seemed oblivious to everything except torturing Comacho.

Bursting from the draw, Yellow Boy yelled, "Billy! *Hombre!*"

Billy stopped and looked toward Yellow Boy, a big grin filling his face, and yelled, "Damn, if this ain't my lucky day! Come to git yore dose, too, Muchacho Amarillo?"

Yellow Boy kept jogging toward him: fifty yards, forty, thirty. Billy kept his right hand on his revolver, motioning Yellow Boy closer and closer with his left, all the while grinning and yelling, "Come on! Come on an' git it, damn you!"

My heart was beating in my throat. Why didn't Yellow Boy just shoot him? If he got too close without shooting first, Billy was likely to kill him. Twenty yards. Yellow Boy stopped, holding the Henry across his chest, not even putting it to his shoulder. Billy appeared ecstatic.

I thought Yellow Boy had lost his mind. It was clear I had to shoot Billy before he killed Yellow Boy, but, with the scene unfolding before my eyes, I was slow, almost unable to bring Little David to my shoulder.

Then I heard Billy yell, "See you in hell, Muchacho Amarillo!" I froze when he pulled the trigger. The hammer fell, a loud click from an empty chamber! Billy looked like he had been slapped. Yellow Boy's rifle came to his shoulder in a smooth motion, pointing at Billy's head. Billy snapped the revolver's hammer back, still holding his arm straight, aiming directly at Yellow Boy's heart, in time to get off one more shot. The Henry roared. Billy's head snapped back and then nodded forward. Time's pendulum paused, and he started collapsing slowly to his knees. I saw no sign of a bullet entering Billy's head. Then I realized his left eye socket was black. Yellow Boy's rifle never left his shoulder as he smoothly levered another round into the receiver almost faster than my eye could follow. In less than a heartbeat, he fired again. Billy jerked back again, his right eye socket black. He collapsed on his back, his empty eye sockets staring at the dark blue bordering the infinite space above him.

Yellow Boy said something and, turning away, ran for the draw. He told me later he'd said: "You no see in the land of the grandfathers, Billy. You no see me *o su padre.* This I promise."

36
THE BLUE EAGLE

The riders were maybe a mile away, so we didn't dawdle. Yellow Boy and I ran up the draw, leaving Rafaela to swing up on the paint and pass us. We hadn't run more than a hundred yards before I heard her moan, "*Dios mío!* Billy, ya took my blue eagle."

She charged back down the draw before we could stop her. We turned and ran after her as she dodged junipers and other brush all the way to the road. She swung off the paint, leaving it at the end of the draw, and ran across the road to Billy.

Seeing her, the red-shirt *vaquero* threw up an arm, and the *vaqueros'* horses slid to a stop in a cloud of dust. Red Shirt and two others jumped off their mounts, pulling rifles from their saddles. They knelt to steady their aims and fired. The first shots weren't even close. Hurrying, they adjusted their sights. Rafaela was on her knees, digging around in Billy's pockets. Yellow Boy and I reached the paint. I started to charge across the road for her when he grabbed me by the vest from behind and jerked me back into cover, shaking his head.

"Wait, Hombrecito. No see us. *Más* better wait. Ambush *vaqueros* when they follow! Shooters miss Rafaela. I cover when she come."

The *vaqueros* fired another volley, the rounds spitting in the ground around Rafaela or whining past. She found the blue eagle and, holding it in her palm, stared at it, smiling, oblivious to the wings of death flying around her. I bellowed at her from the edge of the junipers. "Run! Run!"

As if from a dream, she seemed to jerk awake and realize where she was. She slipped the blue eagle into her pants pocket, bent over, and ran toward us. Some *vaqueros* stood up to shoot; some tried to mount their rearing horses, but Red Shirt stayed on a knee, calmly taking careful aim, tracking her with that smoking rifle barrel. I yelled at her again. "Run, Rafaela, run!"

Yellow Boy saw him, too, and threw up the Henry, snapping off a shot without even aiming. It flew over Red Shirt's head, dropping a horse behind him. Then Red Shirt fired when she was only about ten feet from me. The bullet hit her in the back on the right side. The front of her shirt just below her breast exploded with blood, the bullet passing through her. She stumbled forward, falling to her knees. I ran up and scooped her up into my arms. Yellow Boy levered quick fire toward the *vaqueros,* instantly dropping two of them. The others quit shooting to get behind their horses, even Red Shirt. We ran to Yellow Boy's paint. He handed her up to me, and nodded toward the north. "El Paso Púlpito. I stay *aquí. Vaqueros* follow, I shoot. I come tonight. *Vamonos.* "

I made the paint pound up the draw and down the trail toward El Paso Púlpito. Rafaela was conscious but fading. I could hear the same bubbling sound in her breath I heard in Daddy when he was dying. I felt my shirt wet from her blood. At first, I wanted to cry and scream in rage, and then a cold calm settled over me. I slowed down and wrapped the reins around the saddle horn, letting the paint trot along the trail through the tall junipers.

I cut a long piece off her shirt to make a couple of pads for covering the entry and exit wounds and tied them in place with our bandanas.

She started choking on the blood seeping into her lung, but she still had enough strength to clear her windpipe. Her head fell back against my shoulder, blood seeping from her mouth. I urged the paint back into a hard run.

By the time we reached our old camp near the entrance to El Paso Púlpito, she was nearly gone. I carried her high up in the rocks, settled her on the paint's blanket next to a small spring, bathed her face, and washed around the wound. I had nothing to use for saving her except hope. Her eyes fluttered open. She gagged and coughed, and, summoning her last bit of strength, she smiled and said, "Hombrecito, *mi hombre.* We're mighty sorry to go . . . *mi amor . . .*"

There was an awful gurgling sound deep in her chest as she gasped for breath. I held her in my arms, crying and praying she'd stay with me just a little longer.

"Th' blue eagle . . . in my pocket . . . it's fer you. Don' ferget us, Hombrecito. *Adiós, mi corazón.*"

She reached up and touched my cheek. Her hand paused there before sliding to my shoulder. The gurgling wheeze stopped. All I heard was the little spring dribbling slowly on the rocks, the breeze shaking the leaves in the scrub oak, and the beating of my heart. I sat for a long time holding her, feeling her grow cold, staring at the sun as it fell below the ridgeline, bringing darkness to fill my soul.

In the cool of the evening, I undressed her, washed her body, and combed her golden hair. It was beautiful, smooth, and comforting to touch. I dressed her in my shirt after I'd washed it and dried it. I was about to slide her pants back on when I felt something in the right front pocket and realized this was what she had died for and wanted me to have. I took her eagle out, squinting at it in the soft late light: a piece of blue turquoise, maybe half an inch thick, and exquisitely carved by a master. Her *papacito* had told her it would bring her luck. I shook my head when I remembered that, slid it into my vest pocket, and finished dressing her.

I felt a hand on my shoulder, and it didn't surprise me. Somehow, I knew he was there. Yellow Boy knelt beside me and looked at her. "Rafaela is in the land of the grandfathers, Hombrecito. She is welcome there. She was good woman, brave, strong, a great warrior. Ussen smiles on you so you have her for a time."

I showed him the turquoise. There was water in my eyes, and I didn't care if he saw it. "She wanted me to have this. She died for this? Why? Why would she leave me and die for this?"

He stood up, squeezed my shoulder, but said nothing. We waited for moonrise to find a place for her cairn. The golden moon showed us a little shelf in the cliff a couple of hundred feet above the spring, and that's where we laid her.

Yellow Boy took a little yellow pollen from a small leather bag around his neck and sprinkled her with it, making a chant to the four directions, calling on Ussen, the supreme deity for Apaches, to give her a warrior's place in the land of the grandfathers. He chanted some things in Apache that meant she was an honor to her husband and her people. I spoke to the grandfathers as her husband and asked them to guide and protect her. I put Sac's rifle with her because a warrior ought to have a weapon in the land of the grandfathers. It took us most of the night to put the rocks over her.

When we finished, we washed at the spring, built a small fire back in the rocks, and rested. The moon was still high and bright, but the sky was turning gray in the east. Without a word, Yellow Boy climbed down to where I had hidden the paint. He soon returned with the bag of supplies we had brought with us when we left to catch Billy.

"Where . . . how did you get that? I thought it was in the Apache camp."

He nodded. "*Sí, es verdad.* Elias Apaches ride *por* El Paso Carretas. No look back. Leave *mucho en camp. Vaqueros* hunt *por yo* from sun there to there." He pointed over a two- or three-hour span of sky. "They no find. Go to *hacienda.* I go to Elias and Billy camp, find supplies *y* Elmer. Take all. *En llano* find *dos caballos.* Run from *hacienda* corral when Apaches open gate. Elias's Apaches no catch. Yellow Boy catch. Ride here *pronto.* We eat now, rest. Ride when *sol es no más mañana. Es bueno?*"

I saw the food supplies in the sack and realized I was ravenous. I hadn't eaten in nearly two days, and I nearly fainted I was so weak, worn out, and hungry. *"Sí, es muy bueno."*

We each ate two or three acorn cakes while pieces of grilling meat dripped fat in the fire. There was even a bottle of mescal in the sack. Arango's men had made it in Rojo's camp when they had time on their hands. Yellow Boy uncorked it and gave it to me. He said its fire would ease the pain in my soul.

I'd never drunk any kind of liquor before, so I took a couple of long swallows. It was like swallowing the sun. It burned all the way to the bottom of my belly, but then the warmth slowly spread all over my insides. Yellow Boy was right; it did make me feel better. It blunted the edge of the sharp knife cutting at my heart. I wondered if everyone close to me had to die before his or her time. I took another long swallow. Soon, I didn't even feel the knife against my heart. I took another swallow, wanting it to carry me into the blackness in front of my eyes and leave me with no pain. Yellow Boy snatched the bottle out of my hand.

"No más! No más, Hombrecito. You no find Rafaela with *mescal."*

I didn't think I'd swallowed enough mescal to make me drunk; maybe a quarter of a bottle, if that much. But alcohol was new to me, and it didn't take much to do me in. The world started spinning. I sat down and held on tight to a small *piñon* tree so I didn't fly off. Yellow Boy took some half-done meat off the fire and gave me a canteen and another acorn cake. "Eat. Drink. Sleep. I watch."

That meat, even if it was nearly raw, was mighty fine. I ate a large piece of it, ate the acorn cake, drank half the canteen, and

485

slumped back in the rocks. I must have passed out.

I woke up in the middle of the afternoon, confused and disoriented. I didn't remember Yellow Boy moving me to a place in the rocks where I was sheltered from the sun. My head throbbed, my hair hurt, and I was so thirsty I felt like I had been wandering in the desert.

I sat up to get some water, gagged, and rolled up on my hands and knees to heave and vomit like a sick dog. It was embarrassing, and I hoped Yellow Boy didn't see. Of course, he did, but he never said anything. There was just a thin, knowing smile when he climbed down from his perch up in the rocks and handed me a canteen. I drank, went to the spring, washed, and sat down by the fire pit with my head in hands, trying to hide my eyes from the bright light. I thought if I never even heard the word *mescal* again, it would be too soon.

Yellow Boy sat down beside me. "Mescal no like you, Hombrecito? Kick you in your head, maybe? You learn *pronto* mescal *es* mean mule. *Es* Mexican revenge on Apaches. Apache think mescal *y tizwin* brothers. Mescal muy strong. Kick like mule. *Tizwin* weak, kick like child.

"You make fire. Make coffee. I rest, you watch. Moon comes. We eat and go."

"Did the *vaqueros* or Apaches come?" I felt terrible that I was sleeping off a drunk while he watched over me.

"*Sí*. Elias has *hombres en* El Paso Púlpito, *y en* this canyon. Come out when sun high. Meet there." He pointed toward the pass entrance with his rifle.

"Why were they here?"

"To guard trail. Shoot us if Elias *y* Billy no kill. I no kill 'em. Make Elias think maybe Comacho *vaqueros* kill us."

I frowned and said, "I want satisfaction from those *vaqueros* for killing Rafaela. Can we go back tonight?"

He stared at me, looking square into my center, perhaps deciding if revenge might quench my thirst for killing or if I was going to develop a thirst for blood that lasted until I was killed. He held up his right index finger and nodded. "*Sí*. Tonight go. Take only one for Rafaela. *El vaquero* of the red shirt. *Sí?*" He raised his brow to emphasize the question.

"*Sí*, only one, *el vaquero del camisa roja.*"

We waited until the moon sailed past midnight, and the *llano* was bright with its light. I fed the horses an extra ration and packed

487

the supplies and loading rack so that, if we had time, we'd load Elmer and be gone before any pursuers reached our spot.

Yellow Boy led the way back through the junipers and prickly pears toward the Co-macho *hacienda*. The *hacienda* looked strange from the ridge where we planned to watch it. It took me a minute to understand why. Every time I'd seen the *hacienda* at night, torches lighted it. That night, there were no lights anywhere. We rode down into the stand of juniper from where we'd watched Billy.

We loosened cinches. I pulled Little David's case off my horse before sitting down against a boulder crowded between two junipers. Yellow Boy sat on the boulder with crossed arms, studying every detail and shadow around the *hacienda*. He looked for an ambush. It was too quiet, too dark. We waited for the coming light.

37
SATANUS

As the birds started twittering, the long shadow cast toward the mountains from the cliffs behind the *hacienda* began to lighten. Nothing stirred around the *hacienda*. I didn't see any smoke from kitchen fires. Yellow Boy frowned and pulled out his telescope. He took a long time to study the *hacienda*, corrals, and barns in the dull gray of the early morning light.

At last, he took the telescope from his eye and collapsed the tube. "All go. No man, no woman, no child." Yellow Boy and I led the horses down the draw past big junipers and thickets of prickly pear. We crossed the road and approached the *hacienda*. Our rifles were cocked and ready, and we kept the horses between us and the *hacienda* to shield us from gunfire.

Billy lay where Yellow Boy had left him, on his back, staring at the morning sky with two bullet holes where his eyes had been.

Ants and flies were already making a feast of his body. The blood-splattered post where Billy had tied old man Comacho stood alone; even the ropes were gone. The compound gate was closed. It wouldn't open, and a couple of hard pushes showed it was barred from the inside. In order to get in, we'd have to break down a door or climb over the wall. Elias's men had taken everything of value. We didn't need anything on the inside and left the *hacienda* alone.

We walked around the corner of the compound and headed for the barns. The corral, horse paddock, and pens were empty. The door to the horse barn was closed. We pulled it open and looked inside. Shutters over the window holes on the sides of the barn had been dropped, and shafts of light poured into the gloom. Every stall gate stood open down the wide aisle in the middle of the barn, mute sentinels to the chaos that occurred when everyone left. It was quieter than midnight in the middle of a deep canyon.

I blinked and shook my head, not believing what I saw. Sitting on a wooden sawhorse at the far end of the barn was a new saddle trimmed in silver. It reflected the incoming light into dozens of small beams that sprayed against the barn walls and hayloft ceiling. Across the saddle lay a bridle with the same style silver trim. The sight of that rig took my breath away. When Yellow Boy saw it, a big grin spread across his face. We walked down the aisle to get a closer look.

All the stalls were empty except for the one just before the saddle. Inside the stall, even though the gate stood open, was a magnificent black stallion. He stood his ground like he owned it. When he saw us, he backed his hindquarters up against the barn wall, laid his ears back, and thrust his muzzle forward, teeth bared, snorting, tense, ready for a fight.

Yellow Boy quietly closed the stall gate as he studied him, watching his every move. "Open corral door y stay back, Hombrecito."

I pulled the corral doors open at the far end of the barn and, looking back into the dark open doorway, climbed up on the fence outside. Yellow Boy took a saddle blanket and a lariat off a sawhorse, swung the stall gate open, and stepped inside with the stallion. I heard hooves stamping and teeth snapping, but, in a little while, Yellow Boy led the stallion into the sunlit corral, the blanket across his back and a loop of the lariat around his neck up close to his head and around his nose to form a halter. I was dumbfounded. In the barn, the stallion looked mean and unmanageable. I doubted anyone could ever get near him; yet there was Yellow Boy, leading him into the corral.

Yellow Boy first led him to a water trough and let him drink, slow so he didn't founder. He must have been very thirsty, sipping and drinking a long time before he was satisfied. Yellow Boy told me to go in the barn and get a bale of hay. It was the best-looking hay I'd ever seen. It was green-colored and sweet-smelling. I learned later it was alfalfa shipped there just for the stallion. One of old man Comacho's favorites, that stallion was better fed, pound for pound, than most of the peons.

Yellow Boy turned to me. "Midnight *es no más. Usted* need *un caballo nuevo.* Hombrecito, you take *caballo negro,* black horse. *Señor* Comacho rides *no más.* I save life of Comacho; kill Billy. Comacho owes *yo. El caballo negro es* yours."

I was stunned. I looked at the stallion's perfectly formed head, its arched neck, wide chest, and long legs. I'd never dreamed of owning such a horse.

"*El caballo negro es magnífico.* But I don't have enough skill to train or ride such a horse. It's only right that you have him."

He shook his head. "I show you. You ride. Get saddle and bridle with silver."

I scrambled off the fence and headed to the sawhorse. I laid the bridle over my shoulder, pulled the saddle off, and walked out to the corral where Yellow Boy waited.

"Now you ride like a chief, Hombrecito. Ha. *Muy bien.*"

The stallion saw me throw the saddle up on the corral fence, lifted his head, and snorted. But he didn't try to run as he kept his nose in the hay and eyed us while he nibbled. Yellow Boy let him eat for a while, gave him another drink, and then took him off the lariat loop, made him walk for a while, and then trot around the corral fence. Yellow Boy had me come down from the fence and stand in the center of the corral, facing the horse as he trotted round and round. Coaching me in every move I made, Yellow Boy climbed up on the fence and watched us. Every time the stallion started slowing down, Yellow Boy had me flick a little length of the lariat toward the stallion. I never struck him. I used just enough for him to know it was there to keep him stepping along.

The sun climbed high and we kept the stallion trotting, on and on, round and round. In a while, I remember it was getting on close to midday, the stallion's tongue started showing. He was licking his lips, and his head, once held high, started dropping. He was slowing down. Yellow Boy told me to stop driving him, and when he stopped, to walk up to him face-on and rub him with a firm, steady hand. After a while, I slid a lariat loop over the stallion's head, breathed in his breath and gave him mine, and then walked with him around the corral with my hand on his back. Following Yellow Boy's directions, I worked with the stallion most of the day.

It was late afternoon, and I think both of us were worn out from this gentle lesson of who was master. Yellow Boy, who had not left his perch on the fence the entire time, called me over and told me to slip the bridle on him. The stallion offered no resistance. Yellow Boy helped me put the saddle on him. The stallion stood calm and easy. Yellow Boy told me to mount and that, if he wanted to run, let him stretch it out, run hard until he tried to slow down on his own, and then make him run a little longer before I let him rest. Yellow Boy said he'd meet me at our camp in El Paso Púlpito if the stallion ran.

I climbed aboard. The horse took off like a bullet out through the open corral gate and down the road toward El Paso Púlpito, and I heard Yellow Boy yell in triumph, "Hi Ya! Hi Ya!" My heels pounded the stallion's glossy sides to make him run hard and fast. He strained forward, his head reaching ahead in pride, nostrils flaring in the mellow, late, afternoon light. His long, floating stride made a dust cloud behind us, and the wind made my eyes water and my hair stand out straight behind me. I felt like a hawk swooping into the night.

Midnight had been a wonderful little horse, but she'd never dreamed of running like this. I reckoned there were few horses within two hundred miles of either side of the border that might beat him in a race. He ran flat out for a couple of miles and then started slowing down. I put my heels against his sides again, exulting in the glorious freedom of his flight. I made him run another half-mile before I reined him in to an easy walk, turning off the main road and heading for the back trail we'd used from El Paso Púlpito. The building cloud-banks against the western mountains were painted with oranges and purples, the daylight nearly gone.

Yellow Boy galloped up to us, leading the horse I'd used. He nodded for me to follow him down the trail. "Go to spring *en* El

Paso Púlpito. Rest horses. Move on to Rojo camp. Caballo Negro *es grande, sí?*"

I couldn't get the grin off my face as I nodded. I was very proud to have the great black horse, very grateful to Yellow Boy for giving it to me. I remembered Rafaela telling me about Comacho's great black stallion, the one he called Espíritu Negro, Black Spirit. Now the stallion was mine and it would never carry the name a man like Comacho gave him. I remembered the name *Satanas,* an old medieval word for the prince of darkness I'd read in one of Rufus's books. My stallion was royalty in the horse world and he was black as sin. My name for him would be Satanas.

We watered the horses and rested at the spring. I was tired and felt low when I looked up the dark cliffs to the spot where we'd laid Rafaela. Yellow Boy told me to get a little sleep, that he'd keep watch.

That night, I had a very vivid dream. Rafaela had the blue eagle in her hand. She was reaching for my hand across a big, black crack in the earth, and the *vaquero* in the red shirt was aiming for her, slowly, deliberately, making sure he didn't miss. He sent the bullet flying. It flew slow and true. I saw it coming toward her. I tried to yell for her to get out of the way. No matter how hard I tried, no sound came out of my mouth. I couldn't warn her. I couldn't save her.

I jerked awake just as the bullet struck her. I was covered in sweat, filled with the thick, sour syrup of dread. I reached for a canteen, but my hand bumped against the mescal bottle. I took a couple of long pulls from it instead. The warm glow spreading down the middle of my chest and into my belly felt good. I had another two or three long swallow shots, and then fell into a dreamless sleep. The moon was high when Yellow Boy shook me awake. I had a little hangover, but I was relieved. I hadn't dreamed any more after I drank the mescal. I knew I didn't want to spend the rest of my life with dreams like that.

We saddled the horses, loaded the supplies, and trekked for Rojo's on the long canyon trail we took to beat Billy to the *llano* road. The ride was filled with dark shadows and dazzling white moonlight jumping from cliff to tree to bushes and back again. I thought of Rafaela as I watched Yellow Boy's back floating along in front of me. I thought of the life we might have had together; all the good times we'd had since our return from the jaguar's canyon; all the good times we'd never have because that damned *vaquero* in the red shirt deliberately killed her.

I decided then that before the snow came again to the mountains, I'd return and kill him.

Dawn came, making the morning sweet and fresh with dew sprinkled like stars in the big spiderwebs on the weeds and brush. In a while, we found the place where we'd stayed on the ride down to El Paso Púlpito. We off-loaded, rubbed down, fed and watered the horses, and ate some dried beef, pine nuts, and baked hearts of agave. I took the first watch while Yellow Boy slept for the first time in nearly two days. I marveled at his stamina. He was stronger than most Apache men half his age.

38
A TIME OF DEMONS

The morning passed. I let Yellow Boy sleep into the afternoon until I was so tired my head kept jerking up from little naps I couldn't prevent. When he sat up and saw the sun's position, he waved his hand at me, palm out and down from his chest, in appreciation for the extra rest. He climbed up to my watching spot and surveyed the trail for his own satisfaction. I went to the blanket, ready to fall into a coma, but I started thinking about the awful dream I'd had the night before. I decided I'd try a couple of swallows of mescal to see if, in fact, it kept me from dreaming. The warm glow in my belly again made me sweat in the high, warm air. I saw Yellow Boy watching me with a frown as I pulled the bottle down.

I held it up toward him. "It helps me sleep. I don't have bad dreams about Rafaela's murder when I drink it."

"Be careful of the evil spirits in the *mescal*, Hombrecito. Too much takes you to the dark places."

I smiled and nodded. "*Sí*, I'll drink only a little, and they will not take me."

He tapped his temple and nodded. "Use your head."

The mescal worked again. No dreams, good or bad, of Rafaela or of anything else. That was all I needed to know. The moon was up and the horses saddled and loaded when Yellow Boy tapped my moccasin with the barrel of his rifle. I jerked awake, my mouth numb and prickly inside, and I felt like I'd taken a bite of peyote. I had a raging thirst as I stumbled to the spring, drank, and threw water on my face. I tried to shake the cobwebs out of my brain. The mescal was potent stuff. It came back to bite you when you left the fog with which it surrounded your brain. Yellow Boy offered me some beef jerky to eat while we rode. It was going to be a long night if we were going to make it to Rojo's by morning. The stallion snorted and stamped, anxious to be moving. I swung into that beautiful, silver-trimmed saddle, loving its smell and creaking leather, and we were off. The high moon, bright and nearly full, filled the canyons, its soft light filling the dark places.

We made good time.

Dawn wasn't even beginning to show when we rode off the last ridge and down into the canyon where Rojo's camp and main corrals were. We rode up the dark stream toward the stock pens and corral. When we were within a couple of hundred yards of the horse corral, Yellow Boy stopped and called like a nighthawk. The answering call was immediate. Kicking the paint's sides, he rode forward. We never saw the guards, but I'm certain they had us sighted long before Yellow Boy called to them. The stallion was fidgety and hard to control. Smelling the mares and other stallions, he seemed anxious to find the local *jefe* to show him who was boss. Yellow Boy told me to put him in one of the small pens where there wasn't any other stock until we had a chance to introduce him to the rest of the herd.

We unloaded the horses, stacked most of the trail gear by the fence for the young boys to carry up to the camp in the daylight, and, taking our saddles and rifles, we walked up the trail to the camp. Yellow Boy told me to sleep as long as I needed. I stepped inside the little stone-walled lodge Rafaela and I had used, threw the saddle, bridle, and rifle to one side of our sleeping blanket, and collapsed, dog-tired. I thought, *At least I won't need any mescal for this sleep.*

But I did dream. This one was worse than before. Rafaela was running toward me holding out the blue eagle for me to take. I saw the bullet arching toward her back and tried to scream for her to get out of the way, but no sound came from my mouth. I reached for her, trying to snatch her out of its path. Just as she touched my hand, the bullet struck her back and the middle of her chest exploded, showering me with her blood. I jerked awake; it was barely gray morning outside. I lay back, covered in sweat.

I decided I'd keep a bottle of mescal close by to keep the night demons away. I knew the Mexicans who visited the camp always had mescal; I always had hides or meat from deer or mountain sheep that I shot with Little David, and I knew the Mexicans would swap the mescal for the hides and meat.

At first, it was just a swallow or two of their firewater before I went to sleep. After a while, I had to drink more and then more, and I wanted to drink it, had to have it. I started missing easy long shots with Little David because in the mornings I had little tremors in my arms and shoulders from the liquid fire I'd drunk the night before.

I started a drifting spiral into darkness. I knew what was happening. It was like I stood outside myself, watching what was happening with no desire to stop it. I wanted the dark, where I couldn't see, couldn't hear, couldn't smell, couldn't feel anything. After a while, when I got up in the morning, it was too much trouble or my head hurt too much, to walk down in the canyon to the creek and bathe like everybody else. After a while, I didn't want to do anything except drink and sleep. Eating was too much trouble; taking care of myself was too much trouble; living was too much trouble. The people in Rojo's camp knew the mescal demons had taken me, and they avoided me. It was like I was already dead. It didn't help that my unwashed body stank, my hair was matted and greasy, and that I was in such a haze I could rarely recall a name beyond those of Yellow Boy, Moon, or Redondo.

Yellow Boy watched my descent into darkness with sad eyes. He tried more than once to counsel me, but he didn't push it because one man doesn't tell another man what to do. I wouldn't have listened anyway. I didn't care what the mescal did to me, just so the pain from the dreams and memories of Rafaela didn't squeeze the life out of me.

My climb out of darkness began the day I awoke from a mescal stupor and found the only thing in my lodge good enough to barter for more mescal was Little David. I took it, stumbling along past Yellow Boy's fire, heading for the Mexican wickiups. Later, I learned that Moon saw me, and she knew instantly what I was planning and stepped into her lodge to awaken Yellow Boy from a rare afternoon *siesta*.

The Mexicans were lounging around their fire pit as I stumbled over to their leader, his huge *sombrero* pushed back on the crown of his head. I remember thinking how the rowels of his spurs looked big and mean. He eyed me for a moment before understanding that I meant no harm. His beady black eyes studied my disheveled body before he said, *"Buenas días, señor! Como esta? Un cigarro? Es muy bueno."*

I wasn't sure I was able to speak coherently. I just shook my head, lifted Little David toward him, and pointed to a couple of unopened bottles of mescal between his boots. He nodded and was reaching for Little David when a hand flashed out of nowhere and snatched it away.

"No, Hombrecito." Yellow Boy's eyes were

narrow slits as he looked first at the Mexican, then at me. The Mexican showed anger and disappointment on his face, but I knew he wasn't about to cross Yellow Boy. I stood there, swaying back and forth a little, trying to make my fevered brain function.

Yellow Boy spoke in a coarse, angry whisper, "Muchacho Amarillo no pull Hombrecito back from the grandfathers, teach, help many times, so mescal demons take. You come. Now."

Holding on to the rifle, he hooked the fingers of his right hand around the belt used to hold up my breechcloth and virtually dragged me back to his fire.

He handed Little David to Moon on the Water. Still holding onto my belt, he said through clenched teeth, "We go corrals now! Hombrecito wash! You and skunk are brothers." Moon covered her mouth and nose with her hand and nodded.

When we returned to Moon's fire, the sun was on the western mountains. I was sober enough to understand where I'd been. I smelled a lot better, and I was starving. Yellow Boy and Moon considered that a good sign. She feed me an acorn cake and a big bowl of hot beef stew made with chilies and wild herbs. Redondo sat on Yellow Boy's knee while I ate. Moon waited patiently until I wiped out the stew bowl with a piece of acorn bread before offering me some pine nuts and fresh berries. Almost too full to move, I held up my hand and waved her off. Smiling, she lifted the soot-covered coffee pot off the fire, poured two cups of coffee, hiked Redondo off Yellow Boy's knee, bade us *buenas noches,* and stepped into their lodge.

Yellow Boy handed me one of the cups of hot, bitter coffee and sat down beside me on the ground. He leaned against the log on which he normally sat, pulled one of his black Mexican cigars out of a vest pocket, and, lighting it, blew smoke to the four directions before passing it to me to do the same before handing it back to him. I sipped my coffee, filled with shame at what I'd tried to do, and waited for a much-deserved lecture on my sorry condition. It never came. Instead, I heard wisdom and understanding. It was the beginning of my life as a grown man.

He took a few long puffs, blowing the smoke toward the star-filled sky, the cigarro's orange coal glowing brightly in the evening dusk. He offered the cigar back to me. I took a couple of puffs, blowing the smoke toward heaven, and handed it back to him. He took a long slurp of coffee before clamping the cigar in his teeth.

"I speak to *usted* as *niño* today, Hombrecito. I have regret. The demons had you in their power. They make you use your *cabeza* like *niño*. You bargain your treasures *por nada*. Shoots Today Kills Tomorrow *es* your weapon. Rufus gives you it. You no lose. You no give away. Keep until you go to grandfathers. *Comprende?*"

I hung my head in shame and nodded. "*Comprendo. Muchas gracias* for helping me today. I'm weary of living and want to go to the grandfathers. My Power has not found me. It lets me drown in the demon's pit, drowning in the sorrow I feel for Rafaela, drowning in misery for the curse I bring those who are close to me."

Yellow Boy looked at me and frowned. "Curse? What curse? You lie with a witch?"

"No, nothing like that. It's just that Daddy was killed trying to protect me. Rufus was killed helping me avenge Daddy. A jaguar took Sac and Lewis Clark. And Rafaela was killed trying to give me a blue stone. She was killed for nothing, killed for a rock, because I'm cursed."

Yellow Boy stared at me and shook his head. "My son, you have eyes, but your heart does not see." He turned toward their lodge and called, "Moon, come to the fire. Tell Hombrecito of Rafaela and the blue eagle."

Moon came out and studied my face for a moment. I have no idea what she was trying to find in my eyes. She said, "Hombrecito, I thought you knew about Rafaela *y el águila azul.* I'm sorry I didn't speak of this to you when *mi hombre* told me she was in the land of the grandfathers."

I shook my head. I couldn't imagine what she was talking about. "*Por favor,* Moon on the Water, tell me this thing I do not know. My heart is heavy."

"*Sí,* Hombrecito. Forgive me. *El águila azul,* the blue eagle, Rafaela, she says she gives it to you the day she tells you she will have your first child. She is very happy when she tells me, on the day before Billy steals her, how she will give it to you the next day."

I couldn't see as I swallowed the grief and rage around the ball of thorns wedged in my throat. I was ashamed for Yellow Boy and Moon to see water on my face and looked away. I stood up, nodded toward them in thanks, and staggered off into the night. I climbed up the trail to the corrals above the camp on the edge of the canyon. I found a clearing in the brush and slumped down, staring at the dark outline of Animas

Peak far away on the northern horizon, standing proud in the light of the big yellow moon.

I tried to get my mind around what the stone meant and what it was I needed to do. My heart roared for revenge. The man who killed her had to die. I'd watched him murder her. What I really wanted to do was crawl up in a hole somewhere and just hide from the world, hide from my grief.

I felt, rather than heard, Yellow Boy sit down beside me. He studied the far mountains and the dark canyon below us slashed with beams of moonlight. After a while he said, *"Es muy* hard to lose a wife *y niño,* Hombrecito, even one you no see. The wound heals, but the scar stays until you are *no más."*

I nodded. "Yes, it is. I think maybe it's as hard as when Daddy was murdered. I have to kill the man who did this. Will you help me?"

Instead of the quick *sí* I expected, Yellow Boy was quiet for a long time, staring out across the distance. He crossed his arms before he turned and looked at me. "You tell me who kill Rafaela. Tell me why they do this?"

I was surprised at the questions. "Why, the *vaquero* in the red shirt killed her. She was just someone in his sights, and he pulled the trigger. He wanted blood, and he took it, never asking or thinking if it was the right thing to do. She wasn't attacking him; she was running away. He murdered her, and he deserves to die."

Yellow Boy shook his head. "Rafaela wears *hombre* pants *y camisa.* She works and shoots like *un hombre.* She with *hombres* attacking Comacho *hacienda. Los hombres* attacking *hacienda* torture *el patrón,* raid *y* steal from the *hacienda.* Rafaela *es hombre* to eyes of Red Shirt. *Camisa Roja* he fights *por patrón.* He no murder Rafaela. No, Hombrecito, *tres hombres* murder *Rafaela.* Billy Creek *es no más.* Apache Kid, he help Billy steal Rafaela. Kid speaks many lies. He hides. He must die. Elias, he helps Billy more than Kid. He must die. You avenge Rafaela *y* I help. We kill Kid *y* Elias, no kill *Camisa Roja.* I help you when your blood *es caliente no más, y usted* no prisoner of the demons *en* mescal *no más.* Elias *y* Kid, they watch for us now. Wait until they think they sleep safe. Then we come *y* speak *por* Rafaela." He drew his index finger across his throat in a slashing motion and nodded.

It didn't take me long to decide he was right. "*Sí,* I'll wait until you say it's time. Elias and Kid must die."

■ ■ ■ ■

I dried out. There was no more mescal. I had no thirst, no need to drink anymore. I took care of myself. I no longer missed long shots. The dreams that drove me to the mescal demons, for the most part, were gone.

39
RETURN FROM MEXICO

One morning, as autumn drew near, Yellow Boy told me he was moving Moon and Redondo to Mescalero to live with her sister, Juanita, his first wife. He said Moon had told him she was no longer afraid to live on the reservation, and she wanted to be near her sister so they could raise their children together. This arrangement would make things much easier on Yellow Boy, who returned to his first wife many times over the years. He had ridden many miles to keep two households and the sisters happy. He said he probably wouldn't come back to Mexico much anymore and asked me what I wanted to do. I was welcome to stay with his people there, but his opinion was that I needed to return to my own land, and I agreed.

I crossed back to the east of the Rio Grande near El Paso in the fall of 1906. I wanted to settle accounts with Oliver Lee, tell my mother I was still alive, and find something worthwhile to do with the rest of my life. I wasn't a kid anymore. Living with Yellow Boy's people had hardened me into an adult who thought coldly and logically about killing enemies and protecting loved ones. I left a woman I'd loved and her murderers buried in Mexico, and I guess, if the truth were known, a piece of me was buried there, too.

On the ride out of the Sierra Madre with Yellow Boy and his wife and little son, I tried to think of all the angles I needed to consider in settling accounts with Oliver Lee. I knew he was so good with a long gun that I'd better get him with my first shot or he'd kill me. However, I desperately wanted to talk to him to find out why he'd had my father murdered. That meant I had to figure out how to catch and disarm him. I knew from my days growing up with Rufus that Lee often traveled across the Tularosa Basin by himself at night and that I would have to be mighty lucky to cross trails with him, or I could watch his every move from a distance and set up an ambush the night he traveled. In either case, I had to get the drop on him first.

I blamed Lee for everything: killing my father, getting Rufus killed, the pain and misery I knew my mother had suffered, and all the evil that had been visited on me. I swore he'd pay every hundredweight and penny-pound's worth of the debt he owed me, and that he'd suffer doing it.

When we got to the Rio Grande, I parted company with Yellow Boy and his little family as I set out across the desert, heading for Rufus's place. I promised to visit Yellow Boy on the reservation after I'd dealt with Lee.

Approaching the Organs, I rode behind Tortugas Mountain and followed a familiar trail toward Rufus's place. It was getting late in the day and the sun was casting its gauzy light of reds, purples, and oranges everywhere against the mountains and the dark crack of the canyon slashed in the side of the Organs where Rufus's place was. I wished to my soul that he would be there to meet me.

It was a relief to see his shack still standing in the dusty half-light as the sun disappeared. I dismounted and walked around it first. From the general state of repair, it was obvious someone had been living there in the not-too-distant past. The windows had been replaced and bullet holes in the walls plugged. There was no wind-blown brush on the porch. Even so, when I pushed the creaking door open, I could see a thick layer of dust over everything. I figured Buck must have used it for a line shack or maybe even rented it to some drifter. Buck was Rufus's friend and foreman at the Van Patten Dripping Springs Ranch. Rufus had asked Buck to look after the place and his dog, Cody, while Rufus said he was in Mexico to find cattle in the bosque. That was a lie, and Rufus hated to lie to his friend. But Rufus wasn't going to tell Buck he was off to ambush a rancher they both knew. Whatever Buck had done, the shack had been kept in good shape all the years I'd been in Mexico, and I was grateful. It didn't surprise me that the livestock were gone. No doubt Buck had sold them and was saving the money for Rufus. I unsaddled Satanas and stowed most of the gear in the house before I led him to water and then up the trail, deep into the canyon where Rufus had taught me to shoot. It was pitch-black going up there, but I still knew every twist and bump on the trail. I could barely make out the pile of rocks heaped against the canyon wall where Yellow Boy and I had buried Rufus in the little mine he'd started. In the dim light of the stars, the grave looked untouched.

After I rubbed Satanas down and fed him,

I dug a hole and made a little fire in it near the rock pile. I could have dug up the coins Rufus had told me about and paid to stay at a hotel in town, but I couldn't make myself leave the canyon.

I kept seeing ghosts of times past such as Daddy and his death, Rufus and Yellow Boy helping me kill Stone and his riders, and the satisfaction I'd felt when Yellow Boy brought me Red Tally's head. Just one more payback, and I'd be done with the business that had changed my life forever. After a long while, I went to sleep, and when I woke up, I knew what I had to do.

I decided that if I wanted to live a long life, and if I wanted to settle with Oliver Lee, no one could associate me with him. I had to catch him on some long night ride or just shoot him from ambush at a long distance. I wanted to hear him admit he was responsible for those men killing Daddy before I covered my hands with his blood. That told me I had to catch him. If he was as good a shot with a rifle and as quick with a pistol as the backcountry stories said, I knew I had to be real careful when I took him on. The only option for me then was to watch Mr. Lee, learn his every move, and spring a trap on him when he least expected it. It might take a long time for the opportunity to get him, but I didn't care.

I had a little breakfast, saddled Satanas, and rode down trails I hadn't seen in four or five years — around the west side of the Organs, up over Baylor Pass, down across the basin to the northern edge of the Jarillas.

40
OLIVER LEE

In the Jarillas I camped in the little canyon where Rufus had died and I'd buried Tally's head. For a time I rode out toward Lee's place early every morning, hopeful of finding a spot off the eastern edge of the Jarillas where I might keep an eye on Lee's place and learn his habits without being seen. I found a spot about a half-mile from his ranch house where I could stay in the shade of a big mesquite and watch the place with an old pair of army binoculars Rufus had used in his scouting days. My eyes grew to feel as though they had half the desert poured in them from keeping the eyepieces up close for hours at a time while watching the comings and goings at Lee's ranch house. I knew spying made for dangerous business. I risked getting caught if one of Lee's cowboys came ambling by or if someone saw the glint from my long glasses. But I had a clear view in all directions, and I knew no horse in the basin could catch me on Satanas, so I felt fairly safe.

Every morning, Lee was up working like a young buck by first light. He always wore a pistol, and he worked his men right into the ground until the women in the house rang the dinner bell. If a man didn't do a job the way he wanted, he fired him right then. After lunch, he took a little *siesta* out on the porch swing, and the men sat or reclined in the shade of the big barn near the house.

One day I saw a couple of cowhands ride up to the ranch house for the noon meal and tie their horses to the corral fence. The horses were lathered up and looked pretty wore down, but the fools didn't even give them water or loosen their cinches before they went into eat. I sat there gritting my teeth because just watching those animals mistreated like that made me wish I could give those men a rough lesson in how to treat horses.

Lee had headed toward the ranch house with some of the other hands when he noticed the two horses. He pulled his hat down over his eyes, turned from his path to the house, looked them over up close, and ran his hands over both of them. Next, he pulled off their saddles and led them to water. The men with him just stood in a little group with their arms crossed over their chests, waiting. After the horses finished drinking, Lee led them back and tied them to the corral fence.

He faced the house with both hands on his hips and yelled something. I was too far away to understand anything distinct except the angry bellow of his voice. Those cowhands were out the door and running toward Lee in nothing flat. I could tell he was yelling at them and pointing at the horses. He hauled off and swung a fist right into the middle of the face of one of the hands, knocking him flat. The other one started to reach for his pistol, but old Lee grabbed his gun hand and smashed him in the head with his revolver. He yelled something else at them, reached in his pocket, and threw some money on the ground as they started to get up, then walked past them toward the ranch house as if nothing had happened. The hands crawled to their knees, pulled themselves up by the corral fence, and staggered over to saddle their horses. They managed to get mounted and trailed off toward Alamogordo slumped in their saddles.

Later that day, a wagon pulled up to Lee's porch carrying a man and woman and four or five tow-topped young'uns who were playing and fighting like a litter of puppies. Lee came out of the house with a big smile on his face and yelled something that included the word *neighbor.* He motioned for them to get down and come inside while he walked around behind the wagon and took the kids out of its bed by the double handful. They obviously loved him. The little girls hugged his neck, and the boys jumped up and down, apparently begging for something, while Lee tilted his head back and laughed loud enough for me to hear. Lee called for one of the hands to come take care of the wagon while he and the family went inside. Several hours later, Lee and the family came out and stood there talking while the wagon was brought around. When they were gone, he sat down on the porch step and leaned back on his elbows in the cool of the evening.

I reflected that Lee was a very hard worker, smart, kind to women and children and good to horses, and he didn't tolerate anybody on his payroll who didn't live up to his standards. I was beginning to understand why most of the other ranchers looked to him for leadership. He had charisma, and it was easy to see how he might even get others to kill for him.

The next evening rain clouds had been

forming to the west, and it was getting dark fast. I was about to put the binoculars away and get some rest when I saw Lee step out on the porch. He was wearing a business suit, and he was holding a gun holster. He slid the gun out of the holster and into his pants pocket. My heart started pounding because I thought he must be getting ready for one of his night rides into town.

A cowhand brought his horse from the barn. I could just see the outlines of a rifle scabbard on the saddle rig. Lee hugged his wife, gave her a little kiss, then mounted his big roan and rode off toward the setting sun. He might have been going to Alamogordo, Tularosa, or Las Cruces. I had to know, so I risked being seen as I saddled Satanas to find and follow his trail.

I knew that if he went to Las Cruces, he'd ride north and just skirt the edge of the Jarillas, then ride near the same road Daddy and I took the day Stone and Tally killed Daddy. I gambled he was going to Las Cruces and that I could somehow find him if I watched for him from the northern edge of the Jarillas. I rode Satanas hard through the creosotes and mesquite to find a spot where I could watch Lee pass.

I found a place, and I wasn't there more than ten or fifteen minutes before Lee came weaving through the creosotes at a trot, following no particular trail and keeping a close eye on everything around him. After he passed, I mounted Satanas and tried to follow him at a safe distance. It was harder than I imagined. On the way, he stopped at a couple of cowboy campfires and had coffee while he talked to them about their cattle. He never did ride a clearly marked trail or road until he hit the road over San Agustin Pass. When he got past Organ Village on the other side, he wandered off into the creosotes again, just generally following the road a quarter mile or so off to one side. At daybreak, he rode up to the Amador Hotel in Las Cruces and watered his horse before going in the restaurant door for breakfast. I didn't want to be seen, so I decided I'd ride back out to the road to Organ to watch for him when he came back.

I waited and watched for several days, but never saw him. After a week, I gave up and rode back to watch for him at his ranch. When I returned to my hiding place, I discovered he was already there. I felt like a fool. I was mystified at first as to how he got around me without being seen. Then I realized he must have gone to El Paso first, returning home by way of the other side of the mountains. It began to dawn on me that catching and killing Oliver Lee was going to be a lot harder than I thought.

I watched Lee for over two months. It became clear that I would never catch him down there in the basin. The place would have to be some spot where he had to pass, a place where the chances of my catching him were high.

41
TAKING LEE

I rode over to find Yellow Boy in Mescalero
and ask for his help. He was sitting by the
doorway of his tipi having an after-dinner
smoke when I found him. He seemed glad
to see me, but the first words out of his
mouth were, "Have you killed Lee?" I just
looked at the ground and shook my head.
He motioned me inside and said, "There is
still meat in the pot. Eat. Fill your belly.
Come and smoke with me, and then we
talk."

When I stuck my head inside the tipi
doorway, Moon smiled and introduced me
to Yellow Boy's first wife, her older sister,
Juanita, who was already dipping stew into
a pan and loading it with a side of fry bread
for me. My mouth watered because I hadn't
eaten much except a little bacon and beans
over the past three months.

It was dark when I sat with Yellow Boy,
who had built up the fire. It was getting into

early November, and the nights were cold. He motioned me over to sit on his blanket beside him and handed me a cigar. We smoked to the four directions and then sat in silence for a while, enjoying the night and each other's company.

Finally, he said, "So, Hombrecito, Oliver Lee still lives?"

I nodded my head and stared out into the darkness surrounding the tall pines. "No, I haven't killed him. I've tried to watch and understand his tracks to Las Cruces, El Paso, and Alamogordo now for many days. He's smart. He only takes trips to these towns during the day in the company of many or travels at night by himself. He's a strong leader. His cowboys and neighbors respect him."

"Why do you not use Shoots Today Kills Tomorrow and end it?"

"I will if there's no other way. But, I want to take him alive and make him tell me why he had Daddy killed and tried to kill me. I don't understand this man. He's a hard man, but he's fair. He'll beat a man who doesn't care for his horse, and he's warm with *niños.* He's not afraid to fight an enemy with his hands or his guns. The murder of my father was the act of a ruthless coward, one who even murders small children. This man, this Lee, is no coward. I don't understand why he caused such harm to my family. I want to know why. To find out, I must catch him, but he's a very dangerous bear to catch. I need your help and wisdom to catch him."

Yellow Boy was silent for a long while after I spoke. The end of his cigar glowed brightly as he thought. I got up to put more wood on the fire. When I sat down again, he said, "I'll help you catch this bear, Hombrecito, but you must kill him. It's your duty to do this in a feud of blood."

I nodded. It was what I wanted.

"You have hunted and watched him for two moons. How can this bear be taken?"

"I think the only way to take him is when he's alone at night on a trail he has to follow. Otherwise, we wait many months at another place, and he may never pass that way. We must watch his *hacienda* until we see he leaves one night and heads for Las Cruces. He always uses San Agustin Pass over the Organs to Las Cruces, and he goes once or twice in a moon. When we see him leave for Las Cruces, we'll ride like the wind and get to the pass ahead of him. There's a set of big boulders to one side nearly at the top. The trail goes right by them. If you can rope him off his horse from the boulder tops, I'll stay on the ground to get him as soon as he hits the dirt."

Yellow Boy said, "Ummmph. You have thought about this *mucho*. Where you take him after you have him?"

"I'll tie him on his horse and take him to the canyon where Rufus lies. I'll get the truth from him. He'll die slowly and suffer much, and I'll burn his body and scatter the ashes to the winds."

"You were taught well, Hombrecito. We'll ride at first light. I want to see this place in San Agustin Pass at night and test how this plan of yours will work. Soon you have your enemy at your fire."

We talked late into the night about his trip home and happenings on the reservation. When we finally lay down, I don't think I took more than two breaths before I was snoring. It was still dark when Yellow Boy shook my boot.

The women were already cooking a meal, and the aroma was mouth-watering. I staggered outside to relieve myself and wash at the creek. I saddled Satanas and tied my gear on tight. Yellow Boy had his pony and a packhorse ready. It was just turning gray in the eastern sky when he told his wives and children goodbye. He swung on to his pony as easily as a much younger man and waited while Juanita stepped forward proudly and handed him the Yellow Boy rifle and wished him good hunting. Of course, he hadn't told his family what we hunted because, if they spoke out of turn to others on the reservation and word got back to the agent, tribal police would come for him.

We rode toward Tularosa, swung wide of the town, and passed Alamogordo on the White Sands side before we swung south toward the Jarillas. Yellow Boy knew a spot on the northeastern side of the Jarillas where we could camp unseen and watch for passersby. That night we rode to the mesquite where I'd hidden to watch Lee. Yellow Boy studied it, the lights from the ranch, and nodded his approval. He pointed with his nose back toward the Jarillas. "Let us ride back to camp now, Hombrecito, as fast and with as little sound as we can. How long will it take us? Let us learn."

We sat off at a good fast trot, weaving through the creosotes and mesquites. I guessed it must have taken us about an hour, for the night sky had not changed much. Yellow Boy asked, "Was that faster than Lee rides in this direction?" I nodded. "*Bueno.* Now we ride to your spot in San Agustin Pass."

That ride took us nearly four hours,

including a couple of stops to rest the horses at water tanks. We rode for the most part on the main road. I knew that way we would make much better time than Lee, who stayed off the main road and rode close by in the brush, occasionally stopping for coffee and talk with cowboys at their fires.

It must have been just a little after midnight when we got to the spot I wanted to use in San Agustin Pass. We first found a place to hide the horses. Yellow Boy went through every movement and event he thought might happen, from climbing up on the boulders to having me ride by so he could practice throwing loops over me. He never missed with that rope. He was as good with the lariat as any cowboy I ever saw, and I never heard it coming, even though I was listening for it. On the last throw, he actually jerked me off Satanas to see how much pull it took, how much it stunned me, and what the horse did. I was so surprised, I didn't have a clue what happened. By the time I had shaken the stars out of my head, Yellow Boy was standing there with the rifle pointed at my head. Satanas had trotted forward a few paces, stopped, and looked back.

I got up and brushed myself off. "Why'd you do that?" I asked, a little angry. "I coulda broke my neck."

Yellow Boy shrugged and laughed as he pulled the rope off me. "Try everything at least one time, Hombrecito. There must be no surprises. This is a good plan so far. Now let's see if we can get to the canyon where you will kill him before the sun comes. *Vamonos.*"

It was nearly dawn when we rode past Rufus's shack. When we got to Rufus's burial spot, we unsaddled and rubbed the horses down, then watered and hobbled them so they could graze while we slept through the day on the ledge overlooking the house. The next night, as we rode back to the little camp in the Jarillas, Yellow Boy said the plan was good and should work, but that we needed to work out alternatives in case something went wrong. We talked about that for a long time and agreed that, if all else failed, I would kill Lee at the first opportunity and head for Mexico.

From the little camp in the Jarillas, we got into a routine where one of us would leave well before first light to watch Lee's place from my mesquite bush. We'd watch all day and into the evening until we were sure he wasn't traveling in our direction. About two weeks later, I was having a cup of coffee when Yellow Boy's paint popped through the large creosotes we camped behind. Yellow Boy's usually mellow expression was stern, and his eyes were hard and narrowed in concentration. He said, "He comes."

I took a final swallow of the hot bitter brew and then threw dirt on the fire. Excitement coursed through my body like an electric current, and my hands trembled. Checking Little David and my pistol load, I saddled Satanas and swung into the saddle, heading off into the coming darkness for the main road at a gallop. I figured we had at least half an hour on Lee, maybe more.

The only light came from a half-moon shining as a smudge through thick clouds following gusting winds. Once we reached the road, we settled into a steady lope that ate up the miles. We stopped twice to water and rest the horses, knowing that we were now far ahead of Lee. We didn't see a soul for the entire ride or even distant fires from cowboys bedding down with their cattle for the night.

It must have been close to midnight when we topped San Agustin Pass. It was cold and windy in the cut, just as I remembered it being ten years before when Daddy and I had camped there. Without a word, Yellow Boy took his rifle and lariat and walked back down the trail to disappear in the darkness and climb up the boulder we had chosen earlier.

I led the horses a couple of hundred yards off the trail so they'd be downwind and out of sound range of Lee's horse. I watered them, loosened their cinches, and hobbled them so they could graze. Returning to Yellow Boy's boulder, I tossed a pebble up into the darkness where I thought he was. Within seconds, one from the top landed between my feet. He was ready.

Crossing to the opposite side of the road, I drew my revolver and stretched out on the dirt close to a big mescal plant. Time crawled. My patience was shorter than it should have been, and every itch on my body begged for attention, but I dared not move. The man on the boulder had trained me too well for that. My eyes strained without success to find Yellow Boy at the top of the boulder. I pressed further down in the dirt, trying to make myself as hard to see as he was. Getting cold and stiff as the minutes ticked by, I kept flexing my muscles, hoping I wouldn't be too slow when the time came.

I was getting drowsy and fighting sleep as I lay there in the dirt when I heard the crunch and clink of iron horseshoes against rocks on the trail. Instantly I felt the rush of excitement filling my body. Slowly I turned my head and looked down the trail. It was too dark to see anything, although I could tell from the horse's pacing that Lee was coming closer. A dark shadow of man and horse passed within five feet of where I lay. I could have spat on Lee's boots, he was so close. Another fifteen or twenty feet up the trail and Yellow Boy would have him. I dug my toes into the dirt to get a good start, tense and ready to spring.

The horse stopped. It couldn't have been more than seven or eight feet from me. I knew Lee had probably seen me. I clenched my teeth in frustration, swallowed hard, and primed myself to jump behind a small boulder when the shooting started.

With a deep sigh, Lee creakily swung out of the saddle, stretched and yawned, adjusted his holster belt, and, in two steps, moved to the roadside near where I lay. He turned his back to me looking at the stars and fumbled with the buttons on his fly.

His horse snorted nervously and tossed his head. Lee jerked the reins with his free hand and spoke in a calm, croaking voice, "Easy, boy, easy. The old man's just gotta pee." Lee finally got his fly open and took another half step forward to do his business.

I used every bit of Yellow Boy's training to rise soundlessly, and stuck the business end of my revolver hard just behind his ear as his flow started making a noisy splash against a rock. He jumped, the splashing noise instantly stopping. "Wa! What the devil!"

"Don't let me interrupt you, Mr. Lee. You just keep your hand off that revolver in your pocket, or this'll be the last pee you ever take."

Lee snorted in disgust and nodded as the splashing sound resumed. Finally there was no more water in him.

"Put your hands up and keep 'em there until I tell you otherwise."

He nodded as his hands slowly went toward the stars. His horse was nervously jerking his head, pulling on the reins held tightly in Lee's raised hand. He calmed quickly when Yellow Boy's hand reached out of the darkness and took the reins from Lee's hand while he rubbed around the horse's ears and spoke gently to him.

"All right. What now? Stand here and freeze my pod off?" Lee asked.

"Mr. Lee, there's a forty-five cocked behind your ear. Just stay still a minute while I collect your hardware, and you can button up."

I took his revolver out of its holster and stuck it in my belt. I felt his pants pocket for his other revolver, a .45 caliber Schofield with a four-inch barrel.

"Be careful with those pistols, mister. There are full loads in both of 'em. A man never knows when he might need all his shots."

"Don't worry, Mr. Lee. I'm real careful and real accurate when I handle guns. I wouldn't want any gun to kill you but mine. Button up with one hand, then keep 'em both up."

He fumbled with his fly for a few moments before slowly raising that hand up even with the other one. Yellow Boy stepped from the other side of the horse. He cocked his rifle and stuck the business end hard into Lee's back.

"There's a big bore rifle stuck in your back by a man who knows how to use it. You make the first wrong move, and it'll splatter your guts all over this pass. Got it, Mr. Lee?"

"Yeah, I got it plain. You sound like a kid. What'd you want with me, kid? I ain't carrying much dough. It's yours if you want to ride off now and leave me alone. Otherwise, you'll have to kill me. Ain't anybody ever stole or drew down on me and lived. I'll find you, and when I do — "

"Oh, shut up! Put your hands behind your back." I shouted. "You already tried to kill me once, you son of a bitch! I ain't afraid of you or anybody you own."

He put his hands behind his back but showed no fear. I tied him off good and tight and Yellow Boy lowered his rifle. I was so relieved I could feel the muscles in my legs trembling. We'd got Lee without a shot being fired. Finally, I was going to settle the last item of business for my father's murder.

I kicked his legs out from under him and made him sit on the ground with Yellow Boy pointing the rifle at the center of his head. I walked down and got our horses where I'd hobbled them. Then we set Lee on his mount and headed down the pass toward Organ.

42
CONFRONTATION

We saw no one on the ride to Rufus's place, and I believe no one saw us. Lee rode the entire distance without saying a word. It was close to dawn and pitch-black far back in Rufus's canyon when we pulled Lee off his horse.

I sat him down and tied his hands to a stake behind him, then tied his feet together with his legs straight out in front of him. We made a fire in the pit I had dug and put coffee on to boil. I was chilled to the core. The fire's warmth bringing life back to our numb bodies felt good. Yellow Boy and I stood shoulder-to-shoulder, warming our hands and staring across the fire at Lee as we waited on the coffee. Lee stared right back at us, unblinking. Yellow Boy's eyes were narrow slits and his mouth a taut, straight line as he studied Lee.

After a few minutes, Lee asked, "Where'd you get the pup, Yellow Boy? He don't look like any of your kin."

Yellow Boy asked, "You know me, Lee?"

"I know just about ever'body in this here country, chief. We ain't been formally introduced, but I've heard enough tales about the marksmanship of a Mescalero cavalry scout with a Yellow Boy Henry to know who you are. Hope to shoot against you sometime so I can see just how good you are for myself."

"*Señor,* that will never be," Yellow Boy said slowly, shaking his head.

Lee nodded. "Maybe so, maybe not. You still ain't said who the pup is." I couldn't speak, amazed and outraged at Lee's brass and lack of fear. I reached for a stick in our woodpile, but Yellow Boy put his hand on my shoulder.

"*Señor,* I found *este hombre. Sí, señor, este hombre,* I found under a mesquite bush many winters ago." Yellow Boy's voice was warm and soothing, as though he were telling his children a story. "That night, he almost left us for the grandfathers, *pero* Rufus Pike help me keep him here. *Señor,* the day is now here for you to pay for putting him under that mesquite. The day is now here for you to pay for killing his *padre, Señor* Lee."

Lee's eyes narrowed. His lips puckered as

539

though he was about to whistle but couldn't quite find the tone. Still, he showed no signs of fear. "What's your name boy?" he demanded.

I stared at him, hate making my blood hot and my lips slow to form words. "Now I'm called Henry Grace. When Yellow Boy found me, my name was Fountain."

Lee's sunburned brows lifted high, forming large, leathery wrinkles as his eyes grew wide. "Good God Almighty! Everybody thinks you're dead."

"Well, I'm not. I've waited ten years to settle accounts with you, Lee. Today I'm gonna have my satisfaction."

Lee nodded but looked puzzled, even a little confused. "Well, son, if you wanted to settle accounts with me, since you've already made up your mind I did it, why didn't you just have your friend there pick me off at a distance? You seem to know my whereabouts purdy good."

"I don't need Yellow Boy to put a bullet in you at any distance, Lee. I could do that with the old Sharps over there in my gear. I could have done it a thousand times in the last three months. I could have put a bullet in your heart while you had your afternoon *siesta* on your front porch. I don't miss, either. When you get to hell ask your friend, Stone."

Lee's eyes narrowed as he began to study me closely.

I took a step closer and said, "We went to a lot of trouble to take you still breathing. I want to know the truth about my father's murder. I want to know why you'd murder a man over a few cows. I want to know how you set it up and how much you paid Stone and Tally to do it. I want to know how much you paid Tally after the murder. How much money were my life and my father's worth, you son of a bitch?" My voice was getting louder and louder. I was practically screaming at him when Yellow Boy gently squeezed my shoulder.

He spoke under his breath, "Remember, Hombrecito. Remember what Rufus tells you about nut-cutting time. Cold and cakilatin'."

I nodded, lowered my voice to a hoarse whisper, and said without emotion, "This is how it's going to be, Lee. You tell the truth, and I'll just cut your throat. If I think you're lying, I'll tie your head over that fire, but I'll make damned sure you don't die for a day or two. Yellow Boy's people have taught me all sorts of good tricks when it comes to cooking heads. *Comprende?*"

541

Lee stared at my eyes, and I could tell he knew I wasn't bluffing. He believed he was going to die. He slowly nodded and said, "All right, son. I don't lie, and I ain't never backed up for nobody. I'll tell you the truth. You deserve it, but you ain't gonna like it. Now does a condemned man get a cup of that coffee boiling on that there fire?"

I went over to Lee's saddlebags and dug around until I found his cup. Yellow Boy cut Lee's hands free of the stake and pushed him over on his side so he could drag his arms down under his legs and back to the front to hold the coffee cup. I came back and tossed Lee the cup. He caught it easily even with his hands tied. Yellow Boy found our cups, and I lifted the steaming pot to pour a round as the predawn blackness slipped away.

Yellow Boy and I slowly sipped the steaming hot coffee. Lee drank his in long swallows that must have burned all the way down.

"That there ain't bad coffee, boys. How's about another cup?"

I poured, and he slowly slurped the next cup. When he finished, he smacked his lips, set the cup beside him, and looked in my eyes as I squatted on the other side of the fire. Yellow Boy sat about halfway between us and kept the Henry pointed at Lee's chest.

"So, Henry Fountain. This here is one for the books. You want the truth?"

"Yeah, I really want the truth. I just hope for your sake you give it to me. If you do, your death will be quick. If you don't, the last thing you'll hear is yourself screaming and begging me to kill you."

"I got the message. Don't write me no book. Don't do me no favors either. Do what you gotta do. Only take my body back to the ranch for decent burial and so my family will know I ain't coming back. Will you do that?"

"Nope. Your family's gonna suffer like mine did. I'll bury you here so no animals will get your bones, and I'll send your horse home if you tell me the truth. But you, you ain't going home. My Daddy never went home and neither have I. There is no home for the likes of you." I spat some coffee grounds to the side in disgust.

Lee shrugged his shoulders, licked his lips, and stared at the narrow slits that were Yellow Boy's eyes, then back at mine. "I reckon that'll have to do then, won't it?"

I nodded and said, "I reckon it will."

"Truth is, Henry Fountain, I didn't have a thing to do with what happened to you and your daddy."

"Damned liar! Stop lying and tell me the truth. Stop or you're gonna die a bad death."

"I ain't lying. Don't get me wrong. I didn't like your daddy, and he shore didn't like me. I was glad to hear the news somebody had finally given him what he'd been asking for all those years we'd been fightin', until I heard you were involved. Then I got kinda sick. I don't kill little kids. Your mama was right. I'd never have called him out if you'd been there." Lee stared at the ground and shook his head. Then he looked straight back into my eyes, rock steady, never blinking or looking away.

"Your daddy and me had our differences of opinion and were political enemies almost from the get-go. He was always sticking up for Mexicans and Indians. He used them and your mother's family connections to win just about any election he wanted to win around here. It just wasn't fair the way he used those people who didn't have any land or cattle. They had nothing and contributed nothing to the range, but they had the same vote as any rancher who had ten thousand acres to work and twenty or thirty ranch hands to support. It just wasn't fair.

"I had no use for him because of the way

he used the law for his own political advancement. So ranchers, large and small, sometimes we had to play hard and rough. I admit that. I thought about calling him out and killing him several times. But, hell, he had a family. How many brothers and sisters do you have? Ten? Twelve? I just couldn't do it if he wasn't trying to kill me first. If I'd tried to kill him, I'd have taken him on face-to-face, not bushwhack him when a little kid was with him."

Lee stopped for a moment and stuck his chin out. Then he said, "You ask anybody that knows me. I'm of a mind that little ones need a chance to grow. They're the only folks around who're simple and to the point. They're the future. I ain't never hurt a kid for any reason."

I sat and eyed him, scratching my chin as I thought back over the past three months, when I'd watched neighbors visit his ranch. I remembered how delighted he was to lift their children up in his arms for a hug, two or three at a time.

"Is that why you got Stone to do it? You didn't want to be accused of murdering a kid?"

"Listen to me. I already told you I had nothing to do with it. I didn't know it'd happened until Tally showed up at the ranch and wanted to know if I'd give him a thousand dollars for killing Albert Fountain. I asked him why. He said he'd just done it for Jack Stone. He figured since me and Fountain were enemies, it might be extra satisfying for me to sweeten the pot with a little extry."

I eyed Lee warily and asked, "So what did you do?"

"I got mad. I got damn mad." Lee's eyes narrowed, and he said through clenched teeth, "I knew everybody and his sister was going to think I'd done it. That killer had put me in a bad fix. I jerked Tally off his horse and beat the hell out of him. I punched him in the face and guts until my knuckles were bloody and my hands were hurtin' too bad to punch him anymore. Both his eyes were swollen nearly shut, and there was blood all over his face and the front of his coat. I let him crawl over to the water tank and wash himself off. I told him I'd better not see him on any of my range again, and if somebody tried to bushwhack me, he was the first one I'd come looking for. A couple of the hands helped him up on his horse, tied him on so he wouldn't fall off, and sent him on a fast trot toward Tularosa.

"Tally avoided me like the plague for the

next few years. I heard he was going up into Colorado and Wyoming during the summers and coming back to the basin when it got cold. Nobody ever asked me about Tally shooting your Daddy, and I never volunteered any information. It wasn't my business to tell the law anything. I figured they'd find it out for themselves, but they never even come close to thinking Stone and Tally did it."

Lee paused for a moment, as if puzzling over something. Then he said, "I lost track of Tally four or five years ago. He just seemed to disappear. I don't have any idea what happened to him, but I'd tell you if I knew 'cause he shore as hell owes you some satisfaction."

I nodded and took a slurp of coffee. "Not surprising you haven't seen him. Yellow Boy cut off his head. It's buried over in the Jarillas. Rest of him is in the sand somewhere between Dog Canyon and El Paso."

Lee grimaced on one side of his face at the picture it must have made in his mind and nodded. "Good riddance. Too bad that good-for-nothing Stone didn't lose his head, too. What happened to him?"

"My Sharps put a hole through him big enough to drive a buggy through. What bones the wolves and coyotes haven't eaten are scattered at the bottom of the canyon below the Eyebrow Trail," I said in a menacing monotone.

Lee grimaced and nodded.

I said, "Tell me what happened after Tally left. Did Stone come to meet with you and collect his money? How much did you promise him?"

Lee held up his head and stuck his chin out. His eyes got hard. "I'll tell you again, since it ain't sinking in, and you've already been judge and jury for me. I had nothing to do with Stone and Tally killing your daddy. After I sent Tally packing, I rode over to Wildy Well. I told the men over there what had happened. I wanted to let them know I had nothing to do with it and tell them if they ever saw Tally on the ranch to kill him. They believed me and promised they would stand up for me if the law came. I was in deep trouble, and I knew it. I knew I had to lay low for a while and figure out what to do. I knew the law would be pointing its finger at me sooner or later. When the men from the posse trying to track your killers came by Wildy Well and asked for help, I refused. I wasn't about to be accused of leading them on a roadrunner-after-a-snake chase or trying to hide details from the trackers. I thought some more about what to do and finally saddled up and rode into Las Cruces to face my accusers."

I spat in disbelief. "You're telling me Stone did it all on his own?"

"Naw, I ain't telling you that, kid. There were others. Had to be. I'd bet even some of the members of that association your daddy worked for might have been involved. He might have had information that would make 'em look bad or cause 'em to be arrested. Whoever put Stone up to it had a good pile of money to defend and spend. Stone sure as hell didn't. But you can bet he was paid off cheap. He had his own tail to cover, because your daddy was about to put him in prison. He probably had paper on me, too, but I didn't care. My lawyer is old Albert Fall, and I knew he could beat any charge your daddy had. Stone wanted to do the killin', but he was afraid of your daddy. He knew your old man was better and smarter than he was any day of the week. He needed a first-class, experienced killer to help him. Tally was the best around. He just couldn't afford him. So the only one that made any real money off your daddy's murder was Tally."

My mind was in turmoil. Lee's story, which fit every detail I knew, begged to be believed. Either Lee was the best liar in the country, or he was telling the truth. I needed to think. I motioned to Yellow Boy to follow me down the path, out of Lee's hearing. Then I turned to Yellow Boy and asked, "Do you think he's lying?"

Yellow Boy shrugged his shoulders, still watching Lee. "Maybe so, maybe not. My Power is silent about this. You must decide, Hombrecito. What does your Power say?"

I, too, knew I was the one to decide. "I'll go and listen in a place of wisdom. Stay with him. Give him water when he asks for it. Kill him if he tries to run. I'll be back when I have peace with his words."

"*Bueno,* Hombrecito. I watch. You listen. You come when you hear wisdom. I'll be here with Oliver Lee." I knew he'd be there, too. It didn't make any difference if it took an hour or a month; they'd be there when I returned.

43
WISDOM

The Apaches believe there are places that have wisdom. If you go there, sit quietly, watch and listen, wisdom comes to you. The porch on Rufus's shack had always been such a place for me. I sat down on the dust-covered step, leaned against a post, and tried to focus on the bright sunlit valley below.

For a long time my mind was blank. The sun felt warm and gracious on my face as I stared off into that big, hard country that stretched forever into the distance below me. I remembered the story Rufus had told Daddy, Mrs. Darcy, and me on a Sunday afternoon as we ate hot apple pie in Lincoln. He said he'd been careless and two Apaches, Fast Hand and Caballo Negro, caught him asleep. Fast Hand had wanted to teach Caballo Negro how to torture Rufus by cutting him so he'd suffer as he slowly bled to death, but Caballo Negro had refused, explaining that he wanted strong enemies and that Rufus should come back later so they could have a respectable go at killing each other.

Rufus had told me that story several times. He'd always said the only reason he wasn't skinned alive or killed was because Caballo Negro wanted to be honored as a great warrior among the Apaches. He knew he had to have worthy opponents, men who provided him great victories, if stories were to be told about him around the fires at night. Rufus lived because Caballo Negro chose to let him live. Growing up, I'd thought that was an honorable thing to do. The fact that Rufus had lived through a run across twenty miles of desert, near naked and barefooted, to the Morales Place after the Apaches freed him made him, ex post facto, a signatory to Caballo Negro's contract.

The longer I thought about that story, the more I began to see that my situation with Lee was a lot like Caballo Negro's with Rufus. Lee's living or dying was up to me. Revenge was mine for the taking. I could make him suffer all I wanted. It was a debt I'd dreamed of paying for over ten years. But it wasn't just a strong enemy I needed for stories around the fire. I needed satisfaction for my father's murder.

Now I wasn't so sure I'd get the kind of satisfaction I wanted. What if Lee was telling the truth, and I killed him anyway? I knew he probably deserved it. He'd said he'd wanted Daddy dead more than once. I needed a strong enemy, one who gave me satisfaction, not one who was weak, not one who made me doubt my honor if I killed him. There wasn't any satisfaction in that. There wouldn't be any rest at night in killing an innocent man, no peace at all in my dreams.

However, if I let him live, his life was mine to take any time I wanted. If he were lying, he'd always be wondering if somehow I'd discover the truth and come back for him. The longer I waited, the older and weaker he'd get. If he had lied, even if I never touched him again, he'd live a life in hell waiting for me to come again, like a grim reaper out of the dark to snatch him and make him suffer as a weak old man.

Those thoughts fixed in my mind, and I felt better about where I knew my intuition wanted to take me. The day was long. The shadows swung slowly toward the east. I was thirsty and got up from the porch and walked over to the cattle tank where the spring continued to leave fresh water. I pushed my head down in its cold darkness and felt the fog in my brain start to disappear. I stayed buried there until my lungs began to burn. I jerked up, gasping for air, slung the water off my head, and drank from cupped hands several times before I wandered back to my seat on the porch.

It occurred to me that my recent life in Mexico had been like a whirlwind in thorn trees. I had spilled a lot of blood down in Mexico. Blood for a cup of revenge. Blood for satisfaction. I still awoke at times thinking about all the blood I made flow down in Mexico, all the men I killed, all the grief I caused, all the rage I still felt.

Sitting on that porch, I had the first realization of what I'd done and how much blood was on my hands. I had to stop spilling blood. I had to get my life under control rather than being driven from one promise of revenge to the next. I knew there had to be more to life than making my enemies bleed. The longer I thought about it, the clearer it became that I couldn't kill Lee unless I knew for a fact he was responsible for what had happened to Daddy and me. His word that he didn't and some gut instinct that said he wasn't lying were all I had to make me believe that maybe he was innocent.

I sat there on the porch watching the valley and feeling its wisdom until the sun started burning a hole in the backside of the Floridas. Then I got up, dusted myself off, and started walking back up the path to where we'd camped.

The fire had started to cast shadows on the canyon walls in the dying sunlight. Yellow Boy still sat where he'd been when I had left, the rifle still on full-cock. Lee was stretched out with his hat over his face and his hands tied to the stake behind his head. I nodded at Yellow Boy and cut Lee's hands free of the stake. I said, "Wake up, Mr. Lee. We're us gonna have a little talk."

He sat up as though jerked forward by a rope tied to a lunging pony, obviously not asleep as I'd thought. He looked at my face in the fading light and nodded. He must have seen something in my eyes that told him what was on my mind because he asked, "Decided not to kill me, son?"

"Not today, I won't, Mr. Lee. I'm tired of killing. I killed Stone and Tally. I know for a fact what they did. I don't know for a fact what you did. I was sitting down there on that shack porch all day, listening to the valley talk to me and remembering what Rufus and Yellow Boy have taught me. See, Rufus told me a story about how Yellow Boy's father and uncle could have skinned him alive after they'd caught him sleeping. Yellow Boy's father was Caballo Negro, and the Mescalero still tell tales about his bravery with strong enemies. They didn't kill Rufus because there was no honor, no Power, in killing a weak enemy. They told him his life was theirs. They'd take it any time they wanted and be done with him. He was theirs until they chose differently. Rufus was so relieved to be spared when he thought for sure he was going to die, he always believed he was living on borrowed time. It was a matter of honor for Rufus. Caballo Negro always knew where Rufus lived, and he knew Rufus would put up a good fight if he came for him."

Lee nodded. "Rufus always was kinda crazy, wasn't he, son?"

"He wasn't crazy. He just had his code. He was a man of honor. Every man has his code, doesn't he? I know you have yours. I reckon we all look a little crazy with our codes, you know, doing what we think is right. Caballo Negro wanted a strong enemy, and he gave Rufus the chance to be one. Rufus could have left the country and never come back. He'd have been safe. But he wasn't afraid to live right where those Indians could come get him. He wasn't afraid of a fight to the death, and neither were they. Respect for former enemies was what kept him alive."

Lee shifted his weight and asked, "Whatever happened to old Rufus anyway? Buck Greer told me Rufus went down to Mexico to find some cattle and settle some business, and he ain't been seen since."

I looked over his shoulder and nodded toward the canyon wall where a clump of mesquite hid the rocked-over entrance to the little mine where we'd buried Rufus. "He's buried right over there. He got a little careless as Stone was dying. Stone managed to shoot him in the liver. There wasn't anything I could do except watch him die."

Lee nodded. "All it takes in this country is one mistake, kid. Looks to me like ol' Rufus got by with a passel of them before they finally caught up with him. He was a good man. I liked him."

"Yeah. He raised me. I owe him a lot, and I'll never forget him."

Lee studied my face from across the fire and waited.

"This is the way it's going to be, Mr. Lee. There's only your word that you didn't pay Stone and Tally to kill my daddy. Right now, all I have for a fact is your word you didn't do it. Killing you when maybe you did or maybe you didn't do it isn't going to bring me any satisfaction. Like Caballo Negro, I need a strong enemy to find some satisfaction. I'm letting you go, but remember, sir: Your life is mine. Live where I know to come for you if I ever find you had even a whisper in the death of my daddy. Don't run when I come. Face me like a true warrior, a strong enemy. If anybody ever tries to murder Yellow Boy or me from long range, you'll be the first one I come looking for. If any one of those reservation bureaucrats comes after Yellow Boy, I'll come after you. If I can't get close to you, one day you'll find a big hole in your chest, and you'll never hear the gun that fired it.

"As for me, nobody else knows I'm Henry Fountain. I want to keep it that way. My mother has suffered a long time. I don't know if she's ever gotten over it. I'll tell her I'm alive in my own good time. Don't start no tales about me and what went on here. I ain't threatening you, Mr. Lee. I'm telling you for a fact the way it is and the way it's gonna be. Pray I never learn for certain you were involved, and keep your mouth shut about what went on here today, and this ghost of Henry Fountain will fade away like a shadow, never to return. Do you understand me?"

Lee sat and stared with a challenging

squint. I could tell he was angry, but he kept his emotions under control. I was offering him a chance to get out of all the suffering I'd planned for him, but he'd always met danger and threats head-on. Now he had to walk away and trust what I was telling him was true and not just some way to tease him before I killed him. We stared at each other for a long time.

At last, Lee sighed. Hunching his shoulders, he looked down at his hands, slowly shaking his head. When he looked at me again, the challenge in his squint was gone. "All right, Fountain. There ain't many men who've put the clamps on me and gotten away with it. You are your daddy's son, that's for damn sure. Turn me loose, and I'll keep my mouth shut. I'll not leave this country. Even if I left, I wouldn't leave to run from you or anybody else. This here land is my home. If you want me, you'll know where to find me. But you ain't gonna come looking for me, 'cause there's nothing else for you to know. You done killed the men that killed your daddy and I don't have any idee who paid 'em off. If I did, I'd get them myself for all the misery they brought on me. I ain't gonna shoot you or that Apache from long range neither. You're taking a chance, and I'm givin' you my word it ain't the wrong gamble."

I studied his eyes, and then I took my knife and cut him free. I found his pocket revolver, flipped it open, dropped the shells out of it, and tossed it to him. He caught it with one hand, closed it, then flipped it open and spun the empty cylinder. When he looked up at me, I said to Yellow Boy, "Let the hammer down on your rifle." He eased the hammer down as I tossed Lee a couple of cartridges.

"Load 'em up, Lee. If you're as good as I've heard, you might be able to kill both of us. It's your last chance to try, your last chance to prove my wisdom wrong."

Lee shook his head. "No, son. I don't blame you for feeling the way you do. I'm innocent of every charge. I ain't got no quarrel with you or your friend for what happened here today. Do I get my horse and gear back, or do I have to walk and hitch a ride into Las Cruces?"

"We're not thieves. Take your horse and gear and get outta here. Don't ever come back unless you're ready to die."

He nodded and, without a word, turned to get his horse. He found him and brought him up to the fire pit, saddled him, tied his gear on board, and slowly mounted. He put two fingers to his hat in a little salute, then rode slowly down the trail toward the shack. I didn't have any regrets about letting him go.

44
THE RETURN HOME

During the year after I let Lee go, I stayed several months with Yellow Boy on the reservation. Then I rambled all over the basin and spent a lot of time around Rufus's shack. I read most of his dust-covered books again as I tried to decide what to do with my life. I spent hours sitting in front of the little mine where Rufus was buried and on the shack's porch steps waiting to hear some wisdom again. It didn't come.

Early one afternoon in late spring, I was sitting on the porch watching a dust storm from Arizona come over the horizon. I could tell, even though it must have been fifty or sixty miles away, that it was going to be a hard blow. I remember I'd been thinking maybe I ought to go to college and study law. Then it came to me, just like somebody speaking directly in my ear. *When this blow is over, go see your mother.*

Three days later, the dust and wind were

gone. The sky was crystal blue, and the air had that crisp, springtime snap that makes you thank God you're alive. I saddled Satanas and rode down to Las Cruces. The people in the valley and around town must have thought I was an Indian. The man who owned the livery stable insisted I pay him up-front, and the Amador Hotel clerk gave me a close going-over before he said he had a room and asked me to sign the register. I ordered a tub bath with hot water to clean up.

Then I took a walk down Main Street until I found a two-chair barbershop. There was only one barber there, and he was sitting in one of the chairs reading the paper. The kind old gentleman with snow-white hair welcomed me inside. He just grinned and nodded when I told him I wanted the works and to trim my hair short. My hair then was nearly shoulder length, and there was a wave in it where I'd worn a bandana, Apache-style, for years. The barber cut, trimmed, and shaved on my hair for the better part of an hour while keeping up a constant stream of chatter about several new contraptions for riding on that I'd seen around town. He called them velocipedes. I'd seen several of them up close earlier in the day. I couldn't imagine why anyone would prefer some ugly, noisy, and smelly contraption to a beautiful, quiet horse.

I was shocked to see myself when the barber turned the chair around for me to look in his big mirror. It wasn't an Indian's face that stared back at me. Rather, a dark-skinned young man, who would be acceptable in just about any company, peered back at me. "It's fine," I mumbled.

He took his little whisk broom and stroked the stray hairs from around my collar, slapped a little lavender toilet water on the back of my neck where he'd used a straight razor, and whipped the cover apron off me with a flourish and a snap. I gave him a dollar, which was about seventy-five cents more than he charged for a haircut and a shave. His grin made his blue eyes twinkle even more as I walked out.

He called after me, "Don't let them veloc-ipedes run you over, son. Come back any time."

Rufus had often told me about his trips to Las Cruces to buy supplies. He'd said a fellow could buy just about anything he ever needed in Lohman's store, so I wandered around until I found it and bought myself a white shirt and studs, a simple black suit and tie, and a pair of good dress boots. The clerk who sold them to me said I looked fit to kill when I tried them on. I just hoped they would help me get a chance to talk to my mama.

I had it in mind that I'd try to visit Mama after dinner, when she was most likely without the company of my brothers and sisters. I went back to the hotel and tried to nap, but sleep didn't come the whole after-noon. I lay there in the dark gloom of the room, playing different scenarios of our meeting over and over in my mind. Finally, about five o'clock, I gave up trying to nap, planted my feet on the floor with a thud, and dressed in my new suit and shiny black boots.

I walked over to the livery stable to get Satanas. The owner, who had made me pay up-front, flashed me a big grin and said, "Damn, kid. You clean up real nice. Going to see yore girl?"

I said, "No, sir, just business. Is the Fountain place still over on Water Street?"

The livery agent nodded and spat a stream of tobacco juice that would have done Rufus proud. He said, "Shore is. 'Cept I think the only one living there now is Mrs. Fountain and her Mex housekeeper. Pore thang. She's a widder lady, you know. Husband and youngest child wuz kilt by Oliver Lee's crowd, and the rest of her brood has their own places here 'bouts. Want me to saddle that swift black stud o' yorn?"

"Yes, sir. I'd appreciate it," I said, handing him a couple of dollars. "I'll be back later this evening. Will that cover him through tomorrow for a good ration of grain and a rubdown when I get back?"

"Oh, it shore will, son," he said, his head bobbing so fast he almost choked on the wad in his cheek.

I rode down Main Street to the Rancher's Restaurant and had myself a nice leisurely steak dinner. It was late twilight when I finally rode over to the house on Water Street. I stopped at the front gate, and, through the fading light, I heard the voices and saw the outlines of two women sitting in wicker chairs on the front porch. I called out, "*Señora* Fountain?" There was a long pause. I could hear the two of them whispering back and forth.

Finally my mother answered in a voice old and silvered with culture. "*Sí?* What is it you wish, *señor?*"

My heart pounded and my mouth was so dry, I could hardly make my tongue move. I managed to stammer, "*Señora* Fountain, I must speak with you on a matter of great personal importance. May I come through your gate?"

"You are alone, *señor?*"

"*Sí, Señora* Fountain. I'm alone, and I must speak with you alone." Again there were whispers back and forth, one woman anxious, the other curious.

At last, Mother said, "I will receive you in my parlor, *señor.* Marta will make us tea. The night air is a little too cool, I think, for visiting outside. Please, come and be welcomed." I saw their dark outlines arise and disappear inside the house.

I was trembling inside as I walked down the brick walkway to the porch. Lamps were being lighted in the front parlor and in the foyer. I knocked on the door and waited. Within two of my rushing breaths, Marta opened it. She was in her fifties with a thin face, hawk-like eyes, and an arrogant tilt to her chin. She wasn't the friend I remembered handing the basket supper up to Daddy on the wagon all those years ago, and she scrutinized every detail of me from head to toe before she swung her arm toward the parlor and said, "*Aquí, señor. Por favor,* sit down. *Señora* Fountain will come in a little while."

I could feel the blood pounding in my temples as I found a straight-backed chair facing the door. It sat near the chair Mother had often used when I was small. I remem-

567

bered this room well. It still had traces of her perfume. It was overwhelming to be in this house, in this room again, after so many years, so much living and dying between that moment and the last time I was there. Gradually, I relaxed, crossed my legs, and began to study each object in the room, trying to recall some memory I had of it. In a little while, I heard a teakettle whistle in the back of the house and the rustle of skirts in the long hallway to the parlor.

I turned to look at the doorway just as she appeared, my heart hammering in my chest. She was more petite than I remembered, but moved with the same grace and poise I had known years before. I was shocked to see how gray she had become and how sad her eyes looked. She was dressed in black and wore a large pink shell cameo my father had given her.

I stood and faced her. Not quite sure of the proper thing to do, I made a little bow.

Her eyes studied my every detail as she smiled and said with a little twinkle in her eye, "We're not quite so formal as to require bows in this *hacienda, señor.*" She held out her hand for me to escort her to a chair. When she was seated, I stepped back to my chair and sat down. She studied my face, and I thought I saw a momentary flicker of recognition in her eyes, and that made my heart thump even harder.

Marta brought us a tray containing Prince Albert Rose cups, slices of pound cake on small plates, forks, and a teapot. She placed the tray on a table within easy reach of my mother. Eyeing me all the while, she asked, "Will that be all, *señora*?"

"*Sí. Muy bien,* Marta. Close the doors behind you as you leave, *por favor.*"

Marta gave a little nod and, making a presumptuous grand sweep out of the room, closed the double doors together behind her. I had the uncomfortable feeling she waited right outside the crack between the two doors, listening, ready to pounce to defend her mistress.

My mother said, "*Señor,* you are very young to have important personal business with an old widow lady. How can I help you? I have no land or cattle to sell. I have no jobs around this place. I have no unmarried daughters."

I swallowed a couple of times, then murmured as I struggled to hold back tears, "*Señora,* you do have something of great interest to me. You have my blood."

She covered her mouth with a trembling hand and her big brown eyes grew wet as she stared at me. I knew she understood

569

what I meant. She whispered, "*Dios mío!* No. Can it be?"

I was out of the chair and kneeling on one knee in front of her as I took her hand. Tears were rolling down my cheeks. "It's me, Mama. It's Henry. Oh, Mama, I'm so sorry I let Daddy die. I couldn't help it, Mama. I couldn't help it. Can you forgive me? Please say you can forgive me for all the hurt I've caused you."

She squeezed my hand and raised me off my knee as she stood and threw her arms around me, burying her face on my chest, her shoulders shaking as the tears flowed, making a big wet spot on my shirt. I hugged her back. We stood that way for a long time, not saying a word.

At last she said, "Oh, Henry, it was never, ever, your fault. I should never have sent a little boy out in that desert when I knew there was a chance his father would be attacked. It truly is my fault that I lost you both for so many years. I'm so sorry. Please, please forgive me, for I've shed many tears of regret over it. Now I just thank God that He has allowed me to see you again before I die. Tell me everything, my son. You make an old woman's heart sing again with joy."

She wanted to know everything about the

trip with Daddy and every detail about my life with Rufus and Yellow Boy. She made another pot of tea as we talked, and we ate nearly all the pound cake. We talked until after ten. Hearing the rustle of Marta's skirts outside the door, I finally told her I needed to take my leave, take care of my horse, and let her get her rest. I felt emotionally drained and ready to collapse. She was still very excited, but it was obvious she was exhausted, too. She begged me to stay at the house there with her, but I told her I had a room at the hotel and didn't want to get folks too curious about who I was. I knew that if Marta started talking about uninvited guests staying overnight with them, there would be all kinds of rumors and speculation.

Mama wasn't happy with me staying in a hotel rather than her house, but she decided discretion was the better way at that point. I made her promise not to tell my brothers and sisters about me, because I knew one of them or one of their spouses would let the cat out of the bag if they found out. Then there would be hell to pay with newspaper reporters, rumors, and gossip.

Mama said she had to see the place where Rufus had raised me and made me promise I would come back early the next morning to take her up there for a visit. I was reluctant to do that because she was not a young woman anymore. It was an all-day trip to Rufus's place and back, and there was a good chance we might see a nosy neighbor or one of our relatives. Nevertheless, I promised to be there at six, and she promised to have a picnic basket ready to go. She hugged me for a long time, and I could tell my shirt was getting wet again. Then she kissed me on the cheek and let me out the door.

It was hard to sleep at all that night. My heart couldn't stop racing at the joy I felt in finding my mother again and her acceptance of me. I got up with the first glimmer of dawn. I dressed and walked down the street to a restaurant and had a big breakfast. Then I rented a nice one-horse buggy rig at the livery and drove over to the house on Water Street and tapped gently at the front door. In a few moments, Marta's scowling face appeared behind the opened door. Mama had led her to believe that I was trying to sell her some land and was taking her out to show it to her.

Mama appeared and said, "*Buenas días, señor.* How good of you to come this morning so early. Marta, bring the gentleman our lunch basket while I get my hat and parasol."

Without a word, and with a deepening scowl, Marta padded off down the hallway toward the kitchen. She returned with the basket and a cold jug of water. Opening the door wide enough to place them in my hands, she mumbled something I didn't understand just as my mother appeared. Mama frowned at what she'd heard and, looking at Marta, shook her head as she walked through the doorway to take my arm.

"We should be back sometime late this afternoon. Don't worry my children about my whereabouts unless we're late."

"If you're late, *señora,* where shall I say you have gone?" Marta whined.

"Behind Tortugas Mountain," Mama laughed.

It was a beautiful, bright morning, the air cool, and the sweep of the sky ever changing from dark to light blue. I swung south of town, then back toward the east on a dusty road that wound around Tortugas Mountain and out through the yucca and creosote bushes. The road wiggled in and out of sight through the bushes like a long piece of manila rope stretching toward

Rufus's canyon. It was the same area I'd used to run when Yellow Boy had taught me how to survive in the desert. I told Mama about those days. She could hardly believe that I could run miles over this desert holding water in my mouth without swallowing it, much less run such long distances when I was only ten.

We talked about her life since Daddy's murder and how she had worried her other sons would die trying to take revenge on Oliver Lee. She said she still grieved for Daddy and would until she died. However, she said that what almost drove her over the edge of sanity had been my disappearance after she'd pushed Daddy to take me with him. Though the years had been hard for her, she said she'd learned to deal with what had happened and was still a firm believer in God's mercy.

The sun was halfway to being straight overhead when I stopped the rig in front of Rufus's shack. I helped Mama down from the buggy as she stared without speaking at the patched porch once riddled with bullets shot by Stone and Tally when they came for us that night so many years ago. I gave the horse some oats and water, and then tied him and the buggy in the shade behind the shack. When I came back around to the porch, she was on the porch step, looking out across the valley toward the Floridas.

"It's beautiful, isn't it, Mama?"

"Yes, my son, it is. How long were you here? Six years, I think you said last night?" I nodded, and she took my elbow for support and asked, "May I see inside?"

"Of course, Mama. Just remember this is just a place where an old man and boy lived. Our housekeeping standards were nowhere near yours or Marta's." I pulled the latch and pushed the creaking door open. She stepped inside and paused, I suppose, waiting for her eyes to adjust to the shadowy light from the dust-covered windows. Then, stepping over to the old cooking stove, she ran her fingers softly over the smooth surface where Rufus had cooked many a pot of beans and tortillas. She looked over the walls at the places where pots and clothes once hung from nails and at the cots where we'd slept. Then the tall stack of books in the corner caught her eye, and she went over to them and squinted in the dim light to read their titles.

"Have you read any of these books, my son?"

"Yes, ma'am. I've read all of them at least once, and some, two or three times."

She straightened up and smiled. "Rufus

and your Indian friend taught you well. Your father would have liked these books and admired the physical strength your friends gave you. I have no regrets that you grew up here. No regrets at all, except that I thought you were dead. Now, let's see the rest of the place. Where did Rufus teach you to shoot the big gun you talked about last night? Where are all the rocks you and Rufus moved to build a new house? Where is Rufus buried? Show it all to me."

She took my arm and I led her outside. The bright sunlight was dazzling. As we waited for our eyes to adjust to the new light, I asked, "Do you want to walk, or shall I get the buggy?"

"Oh, no. I much prefer to walk."

She opened up her parasol to provide a little shade for us as we started up the canyon. I pointed out the big piles of rocks Rufus and I had gathered but never used, and the ledge where we'd hidden when Stone and his riders came looking for us. When we came to the cairn in front of the little mine where Rufus was buried, she stopped, bowed her head, and crossed herself, her lips moving in silent prayer. As we walked away, I asked what she had said.

"Oh, I just thanked him for being so kind and generous to my son and for thinking of our welfare. I promised to light a candle for him when I attend mass, and I thanked God for all he has done for you through Rufus Pike. He was a good man, my son, a very good man, and I owe him much, perhaps more than you do."

We finally reached the place where Rufus taught me to shoot the Sharps. I pointed out the target locations for the distances we shot over and told her how difficult it was to find lines of sight in the canyon that were more than a few hundred yards long. She studied the places where targets had been and marveled that any gun could be used to consistently shoot at and hit a target at those distances.

A little later, we strolled back down to the shack. I got the picnic basket and water jug from the buggy, and we sat on the steps and spread the lunch between us in the shade of the porch. A cool breeze blew down the canyon, making us very comfortable, and the view was spectacular. The water was cool and refreshing, and the burritos and fruit she had brought easily filled my growling belly. We ate in silence as she gazed out across the valley.

Finally, she said, "Ah me, Henry. I'm so old and have seen so little. You're so young and have seen so much. What will you do with the rest of your life?"

"I don't know. I've thought about going to college and perhaps studying the law to be an attorney like Daddy."

"Yes, I too think you should go to college. I will give you the money you need if you will go. But you can do better than the law, my son. You can learn to heal others and to make lives better. In my mind, you should study medicine. It is the right thing for you to do, for you have spilled much blood to make right your father's murder. God calls us all to atone for the guilt in our lives. Many of your blood sins will be forgiven if you are a physician, my son."

Her words were an epiphany. I had often wished I'd had a physician's skills. The faces of those I might have saved had I been a physician flowed before my eyes. There were many, and Rufus and Rafaela were at the top of the list. I had spent many hours wondering and agonizing over how I might have saved them. I resolved right then that as long as I drew breath, no one would suffer or die if I could help it. I just looked at her and said, "I think that's a mighty fine idea." She didn't say a word; she just smiled and nodded.

It was past noon when we packed up the basket and started back to Las Cruces. It was hot, so I didn't make the horse trot fast. Mother suggested I go East for my education. She thought the best schools were there and told me she would pay for any university I chose to attend. I told her I thought I had enough money from what Rufus had left me.

Mama insisted I move out of the hotel and come live with her until I left for college, so I stayed in my brother Jack's old bedroom. I heard her arguing with all my brothers and sisters about why she'd suddenly decided to take in a boarder since she certainly didn't need the money. It didn't help any when Marta told one of them that I had tried to sell her some land. The next day, Albert banged on my door. When I opened the door, he began telling me in whispered threats up close to my face that if I tried to swindle money out of his mother, he would come looking for me with a loaded pistol. I had to bite the inside of my lip to keep from laughing at him. I assured him my intentions were honorable. I told him I just wanted to get some higher education before I left New Mexico, that his mother and I had become friends, and that she insisted I take a spare room she offered me.

Albert frowned and stomped away, muttering, "Just remember what I said, Mr. Grace, or you'll be a dead man."

EPILOGUE

I learned how to use the library at New Mexico A&M and decided the best college and medical school for me to attend was Stanford in Palo Alto, California. It was just getting back on its feet from the San Francisco earthquake and had joined forces with Cooper Medical School. I wrote the registrar there a letter and asked for admission requirements. It turned out getting into medical school was a lot harder than I had expected. It helped if you had a college degree and had somebody say you were smart and a right fine fellow. So I decided I'd better go to college first, then to medical school. I wrote and asked when I could start in their college. They wrote back and asked to see my academic records and references to see if I was qualified to associate with other fine young men at Stanford. I wrote and said I was a bush baby and didn't have any formal schooling. They wrote back and said there was no chance of my succeeding at their fine school.

Actually, I was better educated than most of the fine young men who were being admitted to Stanford. Rufus had made me read through that stack of classic books he had before I was twelve years old. We talked about what they had to say nearly every night before I tried to shoot Stone and kicked over the anthill of trouble that got Rufus killed. After I let Oliver Lee go, I'd read them again and thought about what we'd discussed. Rufus had also taught me enough arithmetic, algebra, geometry, and trigonometry to do surveying and to locate and track stars for navigating across the desert. Except for composition skills, I was more than ready for college. I knew more than most of the seniors about to graduate.

When it was clear Stanford didn't want me, my mother talked to some territorial politicians, old friends of my father, who knew Leland and Mrs. Stanford personally. She told them she wanted them to pull some strings for a bright young man she thought deserved to go to college. The next thing I knew I was on a train to San Francisco for a meeting with David Starr Jordan, the Stanford chancellor.

I met Dr. Jordan in his office on the

campus where they were still rebuilding from the earthquake. We had a casual chat. He wanted to know how I came by my education. I told him I'd lived with an old desert rat who taught me the classics and the basics of surveying. We talked for a while, discussing philosophy and characters in *The Iliad.* He asked my opinion about some of the classic ideas about ethics, politics, and leadership, right and wrong; the kinds of things I had discussed for hours with Rufus. To me, it was just a casual conversation, merely a couple of men relaxing and shooting the bull. The interview was fun and easy, and I kept waiting for the hard part. It never occurred to me that this talk was any kind of test. I must have spent an hour with Dr. Jordan when he turned to his desk and pulled out a sheet of stationery. With the fanciest fountain pen I'd ever seen, he wrote a note, folded the paper, and smiled as he handed it to me.

"It's been a pleasure chatting with you. Take this note down to the registrar and let me be the first to welcome you to Stanford, Mr. Grace. Your knowledge will represent our fine institution well, and I'm sure you'll be successful. I expect to see you in convocation this Friday. Good luck."

I graduated from medical school in 1915

and returned to Las Cruces. Five months later, Doroteo Arango, who had come to be known as Pancho Villa, sent the *vaquero* in the red shirt who shot and killed Rafaela to summon me to a meeting for help in his Mexican civil war with Venustiano Carranza. That meeting was the beginning of a long journey into darkness.

ADDITIONAL READING

Ball, Eve, Lynda A. Sánchez, and Nora Henn, *Indeh, an Apache Odyssey,* University of Oklahoma Press, Norman, OK, 1988.

Ball, Eve, *In the Days of Victorio: Recollections of a Warm Springs Apache,* University of Arizona Press, Tucson, AZ, 1970.

Blazer, Almer N., *Santana: War Chief of the Mescalero Apache,* Dog Soldier Press, Taos, NM, 2000.

Cremony, John C., *Life Among the Apaches,* University of Nebraska Press, Lincoln, NE, 1983.

Goodwin, Grenville, and Neil Goodwin, *The Apache Diaries, A Father-Son Journey,* University of Nebraska Press, Lincoln, NE, 2002

Goodwin, Neil, *Like a Brother, Grenville Goodwin's Apache Years, 1928–1929,* University of Arizona Press, Tucson, AZ, 2004

585

Haley, James L., *Apaches: A History and Culture Portrait,* University of Oklahoma Press, Norman, OK, 1981.

Opler, Morris, E., *Apache Odyssey: A Journey Between Two Worlds,* University of Nebraska Press, Lincoln, NE, 2002.

Opler, Morris Edward, *An Apache Life-Way: The Economic, Social, & Religious Institutions of the Chiricahua Indians,* University of Nebraska Press, Lincoln, NE, 1996.

Sánchez, Lynda A., *Apache Legends and Lore of Southern New Mexico,* History Press, Charleston, SC, 2014.

Sánchez, Lynda A., "A Brilliant but Doomed Mission," *True West Magazine,* November 2015.

Sánchez, Lynda A., "The Lost Apaches of the Sierra Madre," *Arizona Highways,* September 1986.

Sonnichsen, C.L., *Tularosa, Last of the Frontier West,* University of New Mexico Press, Albuquerque, NM, 1980.

ABOUT THE AUTHOR

W. Michael Farmer combines in-depth research into nineteenth-century history and culture with southwest experience to fill his stories with a genuine sense of time and place. His first novel, *Hombrecito's War,* won a Western Writers of America Spur Finalist Award for Best First Novel in 2006 and was a New Mexico Book Award Finalist for Historical Fiction in 2007. His other novels include: *Hombrecito's Search; Tiger, Tiger, Burning Bright: The Betrayals of Pancho Villa; Conspiracy: The Trial of Oliver Lee and James Gililland; Killer of Witches: The Life and Times of Yellow Boy; Mescalero Apache, Book 1,* 2016 finalist Will Rogers Medallion Award and New Mexico-Arizona Book Awards; *Blood of the Devil: The Life and Times of Yellow Boy, Mescalero Apache, Book 2;* and *Mariana's Knight: The Revenge* *of Henry Fountain, Book 1 of Legends of the Desert.*

The employees of Thorndike Press hope you have enjoyed this Large Print book. All our Thorndike, Wheeler, and Kennebec Large Print titles are designed for easy reading, and all our books are made to last. Other Thorndike Press Large Print books are available at your library, through selected bookstores, or directly from us.

For information about titles, please call:
(800) 223-1244

or visit our Web site at:
http://gale.com/thorndike

To share your comments, please write:
Publisher
Thorndike Press
10 Water St., Suite 310
Waterville, ME 04901